Tom Holt was born in 1961, a sullen, podgy child, much given to brooding on the Infinite. He studied at Westminster School, Wadham College, Oxford and the College of Law. He produced his first book, *Poems by Tom Holt*, at the age of thirteen, and was immediately hailed as an infant prodigy, to his horror. At Oxford, Holt discovered bar billiards and at once changed from poetry to comic fiction, beginning with two sequels to E.F. Benson's Lucia series, and continuing with his own distinctive brand of comic fantasy. He has also written two historical novels set in the fifth century BC, the well-received *Goatsong* and *The Walled Orchard*, and has collaborated with Steve Nallon on *I, Margaret*, the (unauthorised) autobiography of Margaret Thatcher.

Somewhat thinner and more cheerful than in his youth, Tom Holt is now married, and lives in Chard, Somerset, just downwind of the meat-canning factory.

OPEN SESAME

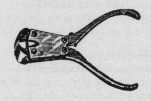

Tom   Holt

ORBIT

An *Orbit* Book

First published in Great Britain by Orbit 1997
This edition published by Orbit 1998

Copyright © Kim Holt 1997

The moral right of the author has been asserted.

A CIP catalogue record for this book
is available from the British Library.

ISBN 1 85723 556 8

Typeset by Solidus (Bristol) Limited
Printed and bound in Great Britain by
Clays Ltd, St Ives plc

Orbit
A Division of
Little, Brown and Company (UK)
Brettenham House
Lancaster Place
London WC2E 7EN

For Kim and Natalie, and Fang the Dog

And to the memory of

GUY FAWKES (1570–1606)

The only man ever to enter Parliament
With the intention of making things better.

CHAPTER ONE

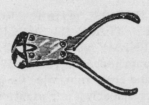

Now then, where to begin?
The end would be the most logical place.

As soon as the boiling water hit him, Akram the Terrible knew what was happening. He tried to draw in enough air to scream; but inside an industry standard medium-sized palm-oil jar, air is somewhat at a premium, and besides, what was the point? By the time he got as far as *eeeeee*, he knew perfectly well, he'd be dead. Accordingly, being of a sanguine and stoical disposition, he settled himself as comfortably as he could to wait for the beginning of the last great adventure.

AND NOW—

(All this, of course, took place in a fraction of a second so infinitesimally small that all the timepieces in Switzerland couldn't measure it. But it was all the time Akram had left, and he'd always been a frugal man, taking pride in getting full value out of everything.)

AKRAM THE TERRIBLE—

Either it was his imagination, or there was someone inside the jar with him. Since the jar was still filling up with boiling

1

water and there wasn't enough space for a decent half-lungful of air, it stood to reason that the smiling, lounge-suited character hovering in front of his eyes holding a microphone and a big red book was probably an hallucination. Or perhaps an angel, or some other form of in-flight entertainment. Be that as it may; whoever the man with the book was, he came closer, still smiling.

BANDIT, MURDERER, THIEF, ARCH-CRIMINAL, VOTED FIFTEEN YEARS IN SUCCESSION BAGHDAD'S PUBLIC ENEMY NUMBER ONE—

Yes, thought Akram impatiently, I know all that. Get on with it, or I'll be dead and never know what the hell it is you want to tell me. Which presumably is important, or you wouldn't be going to all this trouble.

THIS WAS YOUR LIFE!

– Flashing in front of his eyes, just on the point of death. Well of course, he'd heard about it happening – how the blazes anybody knew was quite another matter, but apparently they'd been perfectly correct. Now Akram had his faults, quite a few of them, enough to fill three rooms in the records department down at Watch Headquarters; but false modesty had never been one of them. If this was a review of his life, it'd be well worth seeing. He settled back to enjoy himself.

Born the fatherless son of a whore in the filthiest slums of Baghdad, you embark on your life of blood and crime when, at age four and a half, you batter a blind old beggar to death for the sake of a few worthless copper coins. Now that was forty-one years ago, but the beggar, the first man you ever killed, has never forgotten you, and we've managed to track him down so he can be with you tonight. All the way from the Nethermost Pit of Hell, your first ever victim – Old Blind Rashid!

In the middle air, an unseen audience clapped and cheered as a wizened, crooked figure wobbled unsteadily through the side of the jar.

'Bless my soul!' Akram exclaimed, delighted. 'It is you, isn't it? Well I never!'

The old cripple hobbled up and stood beside the man with the book, who was asking him what it felt like to be murdered by a boy who'd one day go on to be the most hated and feared assassin in all Persia. And Old Blind Rashid was saying, *Well, Michael, even then, you know, he showed a lot of promise, we knew he was destined for great things, and I'd just like to say how pleased and proud I am that he chose me, an old penniless beggar, to be his very first victim.* Akram grinned. He was enjoying this.

It really was nice, though, to see them again after all this time: Sadiq, who'd led the first ever gang he belonged to, who he killed when he was only thirteen; Hakim, the old fence from the bazaar who'd done so much to help him in the early days until Akram had shopped him to the Wazir for the reward money; Crazy Ali, who he'd supplanted as leader of the dreaded Forty Thieves gang; Asaf, who'd taught him the secret of the magic cave, moments before his untimely death – when he'd shouted 'Open *sesame*!' from behind the curtain, it nearly brought tears to Akram's eyes. And of course Yasmin, the sloe-eyed houri who'd told him where the accursed Ali Baba had run off to with all the loot, and worked out the cunning plan whereby they were smuggled into Baba's fortified mansion in empty palm-oil jars—

But of course, went on the man with the book, *this time the joke was on you, because of course Yasmin double-crossed you, and in about one micronanosecond, Akram the Terrible, that will have been your life!*

Lights. Fanfare. Everyone comes forward, crowding round him and grinning self-consciously as the man hands him the book—

'Hang on,' said Akram.

The man looked at him strangely. *I'm very sorry*, he said, *but that's your lot. And, as we say in the business, you can't have your chips and eat them. Akram the—*

'No,' Akram interrupted, pushing the book aside. 'Something's wrong here.'

The man looked worried. *I don't think so.*

Akram shook his head; difficult, given the space problem referred to above, but somehow he managed it. 'I've got it,' he said. 'Two-Faced Zulfiqar; you know, the psychotic serial murderer who taught me all I know about advanced throttling techniques? He should be here.'

He should?

Akram nodded. 'Too right. At least, he was here the last time.'

Akram stopped, and listened to what he'd just said.

'The last time,' he repeated.

Suddenly the vision faded – theatre, guests, curtains, spotlight, enormous back-projected picture of himself splashed all over one wall – leaving only the man and the red book. He looked ill.

Don't be silly, he said. *You only die once, how can there have been a last time? Now, I don't want to rush you, but—*

It wasn't just the twelve gallons of boiling water cascading down onto his upturned face that was making Akram sweat. In fact, he'd forgotten all about that. He'd forgotten, because he'd remembered something else.

'I've done all this before,' he said.

Fuck.

'Dying,' Akram went on. 'Hundreds of times. Thousands, even. Dear God, I can remember them all. Every single one.'

Oh shit.

'Here,' yelled Akram, a billionth of a billionth of a second before the agonising shock stopped his heart and he died, 'what the hell's going on around here?'

★

'Now then,' said the dentist. 'This won't hurt a bit.'

Liar, Michelle thought. Men were deceivers ever. But, since she was lying flat on her back with a light blazing into her eyes and half her face feeling as if it had been blown up with a bicycle pump, there wasn't a great deal she could do about it. The drill whined and began to rattle her bones.

'Nearly done,' said the dentist, smiling. 'Have a rinse away.'

Oh good, said Michelle to herself, time for the yummy pink water. If I ask him nicely, maybe he'll give me the recipe. She glugged and spat.

'Just a bit more,' the dentist continued, easing her gently backwards. 'You're being terribly brave.'

No I'm not, you fraud, and you know it as well as I do. But he had rather a nice smile. The drill screamed.

'There we are,' the dentist said. 'All done and dusted. Now you just lie back and think beautiful thoughts while I shove off and mix the gamshack. Won't be two ticks.'

Dentists and hairdressers, Michelle thought bitterly, ought to have their tongues cut out. It'd only be fair, since they're licensed to make their living cutting bits off you. I bet you don't get surgeons yammering away ten to the dozen; it's 'Scalpel' and 'Forceps' and, if you're unlucky, 'Oh balls, there's a bit left over, open her up again.' They don't lean over you while you're all open and ask you what you think of the latest Carla Lane sitcom.

'Right,' said the dentist, returning. 'Open wide, like you're trying to swallow a bus, while I pop in the little sucky gadget. There we go. Hey, man, fill that thing!'

Which he proceeded to do, very neatly and quickly. He had a long face, pointed nose and chin, and bright, sad eyes. He was lost somewhere between thirty and fifty, and he never seemed to blink.

'Caramba!' he exclaimed. 'That ought to do it, more or less. People tell me I ought to sign my work in case of forgery, but

I'm far too self-effacing. Up you come.'

Michelle felt the back of the chair pressing against her shoulders, and the ceiling became the wall. 'Thag you bery muj,' she mumbled.

'You may get a little discomfort for an hour or so after the jab wears off,' the dentist was saying. 'That's just the nerves having tantrums and telling you how cruel I've been. If it goes on any longer than that, just yell and we'll give them a talking to. Okay?'

Michelle nodded, half smiled and made for the door. As she opened it, the dentist was busy with his instruments, dunking them in the steriliser or whatever dentists do. She made a goodbye noise and retreated.

One dismal job after another; what a lovely way to spend her day off. It was just on eleven, and at a quarter past one she was due at the nursing home, to pick up Aunt Fatty's things. By then, she hoped, she'd have got over the anaesthetic, because it was going to be hard enough fending off the condolences of the odious matron without the further aggro of doing it with half a face. Not that that would be a problem, necessarily. When it came to faces, Miss Foreshaft had enough for both of them.

'Such a sweet lady,' cooed Miss Foreshaft, 'she *will* be missed.'

'Yes,' Michelle replied. It was a bleak room. You could have used it for delicate laboratory experiments without the slightest fear of the sample getting contaminated. It was all as sterile as a gauze dressing.

'We were all,' went on Miss Foreshaft, 'so fond of her and her cute little ways. Such a good soul, in spite of everything.'

Miss Foreshaft, Michelle thought, wouldn't it be fun if you were to end up in a place like this? No, not really. I wouldn't wish this on anybody. 'I'd better,' Michelle started to say. 'I mean, um, I suppose I ought to, um, sign something.'

'Here.' Miss Foreshaft's talon pointed out the place in the form. 'And here. And here. Yes, read it first by all means. I'll just get the bits and bobs for you.'

The bits and bobs proved to be one small Sainsbury's bag, two night-dresses, a pair of vintage pink slippers (furry lining much moulted), a nineteen-sixties plastic powder compact, two or three postcards (all from Michelle) and a small ring-box. Oh God, thought Michelle. Aunt Fatty's ring.

'And of course,' went on Miss Foreshaft, arch as a viaduct, 'our final account, no hurry of course, though prompt settlement *would* oblige. A cheque? Of course.'

Aunt Fatty – Fatima Charlotte Burrard – had been mad. Once you'd got used to the fact, it never really mattered terribly much. It wasn't a distressing, harrowing kind of madness; it was almost cosy, in a strange way. Batty, potty, a bit doo-lally-tap. Apart from that, she was rather a sweet old lady.

'Thank you, dear,' said Miss Foreshaft, her claws discreetly clamped on the cheque. 'If you'll just bear with me two minutes, I'll get you your receipt.'

For Aunt Fatty had talked to things. For the last twenty-five years of her life, ever since Michelle was a little girl, she had talked to inanimate objects – cookers, Hoovers, typewriters, cameras, locks, televisions, blenders; anything mechanical or electrical – instead of people. As far as she was concerned, people weren't there, she couldn't see or hear them. But the electric kettle and the spin-drier could, apparently; and so you communicated with Aunt Fatty by means of a series of third-party Tell-your-friend conversations involving one or more household appliances – a bit like a seance, only not in the least spooky. Once you got the hang of it, you really did stop noticing, like being fluent in a foreign language, and what Aunt Fatty actually said after all that was generally perfectly lucid, though seldom particularly interesting. Before she was married she'd worked in a draper's shop. After she was married, she'd ironed a lot, washed things, cooked. In 1943, a flying bomb had gone off at the bottom of Kettering Avenue just as she was crossing the top end, and the bang had startled her rather. She won ten pounds on the Premium Bonds in 1974. Apart from that, a feature-length film version of her life would have to fill in rather a lot of screen time with atmospheric close-ups and long, sweeping pans over the rooftops of Halesowen.

'Goodbye, dear,' Miss Foreshaft yattered. 'Do drop in any time you happen to be passing.'

Michelle smiled – it was her see-you-in-Hell-first smile, but she hadn't quite regained the full use of her jaw muscles – got in her car and drove away. Well, she reflected, that's what life does to you. Pity, really.

On the way, she stopped the car opposite a litter-bin. She hoped she wasn't a hard, callous person; but two Marks & Sparks nighties and a pair of slippers that had predeceased their owner by some years weren't exactly the sort of thing you can cherish. If you'd bust your way into a tomb in the Valley of the Kings and all you'd turned up was this lot, you'd probably pack in archaeology for good. She'd keep the postcards, but the powder-compact would have to go too. It was one of the most depressing objects she'd ever set eyes on.

Which left the ring-box. She opened it, and stood for a while, contemplating a plain silver ring, rather worn, with a bit of blue glass stuck in it. Aunt Fatty's ring. Gosh.

The picture arose in her mind; Aunt Fatty leaning forward in her chair, whispering to the alarm clock: 'Tell Michelle I want her to have my ring. It's very valuable, you know. Tell her to take special care of it when I'm gone.' And the alarm clock, swift and sure as a professional translator at a UN debate, had said *tick*; in other words, *Humour her, obviously it means a lot to her.* And Michelle had said, 'Of course I will.' She'd given the clock to one of the nurses, though of course she only had the towel-rail's word for it. *The* ring. Mine, all mine.

Feeling unaccountably guilty, she stuffed the box in her pocket before binning the rest and driving home. When she got in, she put the box in her underwear drawer, washed her hands and played back the answering machine.

When they find out, said the man with the book, *they're going to have my guts for garters. I hope you realise that.*

'Shouldn't have been so careless, then, should you?' Akram replied. 'Next time, check the guest list before you start the show. Now then, get on with it. I don't think I've got much time.'

The man shook his head. Time, he explained, was now quite beside the point; Akram had died nearly half a second ago, as he'd have realised if he'd been paying attention. Besides, time doesn't happen here, wherever this is. Don't ask me, he added, I only work here.

'I said get on with it. I might be dead, but I can still give you a boot up the backside. I think,' Akram added, and for the first time ever there was a hint of uncertainty in his voice. 'In any case,' he added, cheering up, 'we can have fun finding out. I'm game if you are.'

That won't be necessary. You're quite right, the man went on. *You have died before. I can't tell you offhand how many times, but it's rather a lot. You see, you aren't real. You're in a story.*

Akram hesitated. There was enough of him left to resent a remark like that, even though he hadn't a clue what it meant; on the other hand, supposing he succeeded in breaking the man's neck in six places, all he'd achieve would be to lose his only chance of getting an explanation.

'Story,' he said. 'Right. I'd expand on that a bit if I were you.'

★

Stories (the man explained) are different.

Oh sure, the people in stories are people, but they live in a different way. More to the point, they do it over and over again. You don't follow? All right.

People are born, right? They grow up. They live. They die. But if every character in every story had to do all that, the story would be very long and extremely boring, and nobody would want to hear it. So we edit. Perfectly reasonable way to go about things.

People in stories begin with Once-upon-a-time, and end with Happy-ever-after; and the bit in between goes on for ever, over and over again, in a sort of continuous loop. So; each time you reach the end, you die, or you marry the princess and rule half the kingdom, it doesn't matter which. The story is over, and you go back to the beginning again. Then, when you reach the end, the story repeats itself. You, of course, don't remember a thing, and that's probably just as well.

You're not convinced? I'll give you an example. Captain Hook. Now, Captain Hook's called Captain Hook because he's got a hook instead of his left hand. This is because Peter Pan cut it off and fed it to the crocodile. Think about it. What about *before*? Like, what about when he was born? Or when he was at school. He still had both hands then. Was he still called Hook? If so, why? Or did he go around calling himself James Temporary-Sign until the time came?

No. You see, by the time the story starts, it's already happened, and so it's all okay. It's the same for all you people who live in fairy-stories. You don't like that word. Okay, call it legends if you'd rather, but it's a bit like living in Finchley and calling it Hampstead.

Not that it matters; because, like I said, you forget every time. In two shakes of a camel's withers you'll be back at the beginning, which in your case means returning to the magic cave and shouting *Open sesame* while Ali Baba hides behind a rock. Then the cave opens, and you and the other thirty-nine thieves ride in with all the treasure from your latest raid and the cave door slams shut behind you.

What do you mean, what can you do about it? Nothing. You're stuck with it. Because that's who you are.

Don't be silly. Of course you can't.

You *can't*.

And then the lights came back on, and in front of him Akram saw the familiar outline of the cliff looming over him, silhouetted against the night sky.

'Open sesame!' shouted a deep, cruel voice. His, by God! But . . .

He remembered.

'Skip.'

He looked round. Behind him were thirty-nine horsemen, motionless as a motorway contraflow. One of them was talking to him.

'Skip,' he was saying, 'can we go in now, please, because I don't know about you but I'm bloody well freezing.'

'Aziz?'

'Here, Skip.'

Akram looked round. He knew, beyond a shadow of a doubt, that behind that rock lurked his great and perpetual enemy, the accursed thief, his eventual slayer, Ali Baba. One blow of his sword would be all it would take. His brain ordered his heels to spur on his horse. Nothing.

'Skip?'

Now then, Akram told himself, no need to panic, or at least not yet. 'Aziz,' he said, 'I think there's someone lurking behind that rock.'

'Surely not, Skip.'

'I think there is.'

'Imagination playing tricks on you, Skip. Look, no offence,

but I really am bursting for a pee, so if you wouldn't mind just—'

Akram drew in a deep breath. 'Aziz,' he said, 'just go and have a look, there's a good chap. Won't take you a moment.'

'Skip—'

'*Aziz!*'

A moment later, Aziz came back. While he'd been gone, Akram had distinctly seen a movement behind the door, heard the sound of rapid, terrified breathing. He was there, dammit.

'Nothing, Skip. Not a dicky bird. Now, can we please go in?'

Feebly, Akram waved him on; and then his horse started to move, and when he ordered his hand to pull on the reins, it flatly refused. Thirty seconds or so later, the door slammed shut behind them.

Bugger, said Akram to himself.

And, sure enough, when they returned to the cave next evening, after a hard day's killing and stealing up and down the main Baghdad–Samarkand road, they found the treasure-chests empty, all the gold and silver and precious stones lost and gone for ever. No poll-tax bailiff ever did such a thorough job.

'Bloody hell, Skip,' wailed the thirty-nine thieves, 'we've been done over! Now who on earth could have found out the password?'

Ali Baba, you fools; Ali Baba the palm-oil merchant, who lives in the house beside the East Gate. Ali Ba . . .

'No idea,' he heard himself saying. 'Search me.'

And then Fazad had picked up a slipper, and they'd all crowded round to have a look, and someone had said, Presumably this slipper belongs to the thieving little snotrag what done this, and he'd heard himself say, Yes, presumably it does, now all we've got to do is find who it belongs to, and what he really wanted to do was bite his own tongue out for saying it and not saying A★★ B★★★, and if he had to go through with this he'd go stark staring mad; except of course he wouldn't, because it wasn't in the story. Inside, though, he'd go mad, and then in all likelihood his brain would die, and he'd be stuck here doing this ridiculous thing for ever and ever and ever.

Late that night, in his sleep, he hit on the solution. He'd outwit the bastard. He'd change. He'd go straight.

It was, after all, completely logical. He knew, better than any man ever born, that crime didn't pay. From the first day you step out of line and swipe a bag of dates off the counter while the stallholder isn't looking or tell your mum there wasn't any change, it's only a matter of time before the lid comes off the palm-oil jar and the hot water comes sploshing down. But he was wise to that now. He'd change. He'd be good.

Better than that. He'd change the whole story.

Instead of being the baddy, he'd be the goody.

Somehow.

CHAPTER TWO

Michelle woke up.

If she'd been on the jury when Macbeth was brought to trial for murdering sleep, she'd have argued for an acquittal on the grounds of justifiable homicide. Loathsome stuff, sleep; it fogs your brain and leaves the inside of your mouth tasting like a badly furred kettle.

'Wakey wakey,' trilled the alarm clock. 'Rise and shine.'

'Oh shut up,' Michelle grunted. She'd been in the middle of a very nice dream, and now she couldn't remember a thing about it. She nuzzled her head into the pillow, trying to find the spot where she'd left the dream, but it had gone, leaving no forwarding address.

'Jussa minute,' she said. 'Did you just say something?'

Tick, replied the clock.

'Shut up,' Michelle replied, 'and make the tea.'

It was a radio alarm clock teamaker, a free gift from an insurance company – free in the sense that all she'd had to do in order to receive it was promise to pay them huge sums of money every month for the rest of her natural life. She'd managed to disconnect the radio, but the tea-making aspect still functioned, albeit in a somewhat heavy-handed manner. First, there was a rumbling; until you were used to it, you assumed something nasty was happening deep in the earth's crust, and expected to see molten lava streaming off the bedside table and onto the carpet. After the rumbling came the whistling, which generally put Michelle in mind of a swarm of locusts being slowly microwaved. The whistling was followed by the gurgling, the snorting and the Very Vulgar Noise; and then you could have your tea. You were also, of course, wide awake. If God has one of these machines, then He'll be able to use it to wake the dead come Judgment Day. And have a nice cup of tea ready and waiting for them, of course.

'Drink it while it's hot.'

Michelle blinked. If this was still the dream, it had taken a turn for the worse and frankly, she didn't like its tone. She raised her head and gave the clock a long, bleary stare.

'What did you just say?' she asked.

Needless to say, the clock didn't answer. Clocks don't; apart, of course, from the Speaking Clock, and there the problem is to get a word in edgeways. Not that it ever listens to a word you say. Michelle shook her head in an effort to dislodge the low cloud that seemed to have got into it during the night, and swung her feet over the edge of the bed.

It was half past eight.

'Oh *hell*!' she shrieked. 'You stupid machine, why didn't you tell me?'

Scattering bedclothes, she lunged for the bathroom and started to turn on taps. So loud was the roar of running water that she didn't hear a little voice replying, somewhat resentfully, that she hadn't asked.

When the other thirty-nine thieves had gone to sleep, Akram stood up, waited for a moment or so, and then walked quietly over to the big bronze door of the Treasury.

'It's me,' he hissed. 'Now shut up and open.'

The door was, sure enough, magical; but it wasn't so magical that it could cope with two apparently contradictory orders at half past three in the morning. ''Scuse me?' it said.

Akram winced. '*Quiet!*' he hissed. 'Now open the blasted door, before I give you a buckled hinge.'

'Sorry, I'm sure,' the door whispered back, and opened. 'Satisfied?'

'Shut – I mean, be silent. And stay open till I tell you.'

Once inside, he lit a small brass lamp, having first gingerly removed the lid and shaken it to make sure it was empty; you don't go around carelessly lighting small brass lamps in Arabian Nights territory, unless of course you fancy explaining to a twenty-foot-high genie precisely why his beard has just disappeared in a puff of green smoke. The flickering light was just enough to enable him to make out the massive gold casket that lay against the end wall. He concentrated.

Big smile. Flamboyant gesture. 'Crackerjack!' he exclaimed.

The big gold casket had once been the property of Soapy Shamir; Baghdad bazaar's top-rated game show host, until his sudden and unexpected demise. It too was magical. If you knew the words, it opened, no trouble at all. But if you got them wrong and it failed to recognise you, the only way to get it open was to answer twenty general knowledge questions, Name That Tune in Four, guess the identity of the mystery guest celebrity and slide down a chute into a large vat of rancid yoghurt. Fortunately, Akram hit just the right note of synthetic cheerfulness, and the lid yawned slowly back.

Inside the casket, the Forty stored their most valuable treasures; items so far beyond price that sharing them out among the company was out of the question. They were, in fact, completely useless; far too readily identifiable to sell, and worth too much to apportion. In consequence they just sat there from stocktake to stocktake, their mindblowing notional value being written up in the accounts in line with the retail price index to the point where Faisal the Accountant had to have a special 3-D abacus built just to do the maths.

There were jewelled eyes of little green gods, enough firebird feathers to stuff a large cushion, bottomless purses, magic weapons, diamonds the size of cauliflowers, all the usual junk that eventually clutters up a long-established hoard. Akram swore and scrabbled. The object he was looking for was small and dowdy: a plain silver band, with what looked like a little chip of coloured glass stuck in it. Just as he was starting to get worried, Akram found it. *Ah*!

The legendary—

The priceless—

The genuine—

The one and only—

King Solomon's Ring.

Yes, Dirty Ahmed's mother had said when they first brought it back, with its previous one careful owner's finger still wedged inside, but what's it actually *for*? Ah, they'd replied, it's magical. Really, said Mrs Ahmed, with a long sigh, another one of them, how nice. Still, you could give it somebody as a present. Somebody you don't like all that much, probably. No, they'd said, listen, it's really *really* magical. You can use it to talk to birds and animals.

Long, unimpressed silence from Mrs Ahmed. Right, she'd said eventually. Like, *Who's a pretty boy, then*? and *Here, Tiddles* and *Gihtahtavit, yer useless bag o' fleas*. Gosh, how useful. No, not like that, Mrs Ahmed, like really *talk* to them, you know? Talk to them so's they'll understand you. And then they talk back to you.

Put like that, they had to admit, it hadn't really been worth sacking the desert temple, scaling the glassy-smooth walls, putting the fifty implacable guardians to the sword, et cetera, et cetera, just to be able to say, *Hello, nice weather for the time of year* to a jerbil. Birds and animals, they soon discovered, are never going to put Oscar Wilde out of a job. Get past the weather, activities of local predators, likely places to feed, and pretty soon you're into embarrassed silences and Gosh-is-that-the-time. Anyone who's ever bought anything from an Innovations catalogue will be familiar with the syndrome. So, ultimately, the ring went to live in the casket along with all the rest of the really priceless treasures or, as Mrs Ahmed described them, the white elephants. And there it had remained.

But . . .

To the innocent-souled Chinese alchemist, the black granular powder that goes *Bang!* when you set fire to it is an amusing novelty, useful for making pretty fireworks. It's only when someone comes along with the notion of sticking it in a stout iron tube and ramming a cannonball down on top of it that the trouble starts. Carefully, Akram took the ring, slid it down onto his finger and grinned. Then he turned to face the casket.

'Hello, box,' he said.

Hello, yourself. Here, just a tick. I can understand you.

'Me too,' Akram replied. 'Good fun, isn't it?'

Not really. It's a quarter to four in the morning. There's locks trying to get some sleep.

'Later.' Akram scowled. 'First,' he went on, 'I want to ask you something. It's important, and I haven't got much time. Pretty soon, all those clowns are going to wake up, and we'll ride off to rob the Joppa caravan, and when we get back, that bastard Baba'll have snuck in here and looted the place. Now, I want you to do something for me.'

Just a tick. How come you know all this?

'It's a long story,' Akram growled. 'Just take it from me, I know. Look, for reasons I haven't got time to go into, I know I'm stuck in this bloody story business, and there's absolutely nothing I can do about it. Every time I try, I fail. Now, I've worked out that if only I can get this magic ring out of this cave, there's this very, very remote chance I can use it to chat up the mechanism that makes this whole story nonsense tick, and then I'll be away, free and clear. But,' Akram added, savagely bitter, 'that's one thing I can't do. You could, though.'

I could?

'No trouble,' Akram cooed. 'Piece of cake. All it needs is, when Baba's lugging you out through the cave door, you accidentally open your lid and chuck out the ring. It falls in that little cleft in the rock, on the right as you come in. Then, when we get back, I pick it up and I'm away. What d'you reckon? It'd mean ever so much to me.'

The lid creaked. *I dunno. I'd get in all sorts of trouble.*

Akram growled dangerously. 'Not nearly as much trouble,' he hissed, 'as you would if you don't. I can see to that.'

Are you threatening me?

'Yes.'

Ah. Right. Fine. In that case, I'll see what I can do.

The dentist looked up at the clock, sighed with relief, and hit the intercom buzzer.

'That's it for tonight, isn't it?' he asked. 'Please say yes.'

Crackle. 'Actually,' the intercom replied, 'Mrs Nugent is here, she hasn't got an appointment but she wondered if you might possibly be able to fit her in.'

The dentist closed his eyes. It had been a long day, he was feeling shattered and he wanted very much to go home. Dentists get tired, too. If you prick them, do they not bleed? If you tickle them, do they not laugh? If you turn up at a quarter to eight, half an hour after surgery's supposed to have finished, after they've been on their feet without a break since eight in the morning, do they not tell you to go away and come back first thing tomorrow? Apparently not. 'Certainly,' he said. 'Show her in. And then,' he added, 'lock the doors, bar the windows and hang out the radiation warning signs, because that's it.'

'Righty-ho, Mr B.'

Three quarters of an hour and a flawless root-fill job later, the dentist shooed out the receptionist, washed the coffee-mugs, swept the floor and switched out the lights. From the street below, amber light flared through the frosted glass window, printing the words

DENTAL SURGERY
A. BARBOUR

across the far wall.

A last glance at his watch; eight forty-five, just enough time to go home, iron tomorrow's shirt, make a sandwich, feed the goldfish and go to bed. No wonder that each year, tens of thousands of the world's brightest and best young men and women turn to face the morning sun and declare, 'A dentist's life for me!' To experience the thrill of a new mouth to peer into every day; to keep up the relentless struggle against the tartar hordes, to battle against plaque, to hunt the wily abscess through the rugged foothills of the back molars. Why Doc Holliday packed in dentistry for a life of loose women, gambling and whisky, he could never hope to understand.

On the other hand . . .

Goodnight, chair. Goodnight, drill. Goodnight, little glass for the yummy pink mouthwash. God bless. See you in the morning. You may be all I've got, but you're a bloody sight better than what I had before.

★

Night didn't so much fall as ooze, filling the courtyard with deep, sticky shadows. Next door's cat skittered homewards, a dead thrush between its jaws. Fingers Masood and Crusher Jalil, flower of the Baghdad City Guard, tried the door of the jeweller's shop, first with their hands and then with a crowbar, satisfied themselves that it was adequately secured against felonious entry, and departed, muttering.

Pale yellow light, escaping from the back door of Ali Baba's sumptuous mansion into the courtyard, silhouetted the kitchenmaid as she tottered sleepily out to the back step with a small jar in her hands. In the top of the jar was a piece of paper, inscribed: FORTY JARS TODAY PLEASE, OILMAN.

She put it carefully down beside the formidable row of empties, yawned, and went back inside. Night coagulated. All was quiet.

When a courtyard in the middle of a city is this quiet, it's because something is wrong. Look inside any of the forty catering-size palm-oil jars lined up outside the back door, and you'll know immediately what the anomaly is. Palm oil is a liquid, whereas bandits are profoundly solid. There are also other differences, the most important of which is: palm oil is good for you.

'Skip.'

'Not now, Aziz.'

'Yeah, but Skip!'

'What?'

'Look,' continued one of the oil-jars, whispering as loudly as an elephant falling through a conservatory roof. 'D'you think we're going to be stuck here long, because I've got pins and needles all over and I'm really desperate for a pee.'

'Tough. You'll have to wait till we've done the murder and had our revenge.'

'And how long d'you reckon that'll take?'

I know the answer to that exactly, Akram sighed to himself.

Seven hours, eighteen minutes and twelve seconds. 'No idea,' he replied. 'Could be three hours, could be fifteen minutes. Just hold your water and stop blathering.'

Aziz, who didn't know what the word blather meant but could guess from context, fell silent; and for the next half hour nothing could be heard apart from the distant sounds of Baghdad's nocturnal street life, which is (unless you're very careful) exciting and short.

And then – bang on time, reflected Akram morosely, if it wasn't dark you could set your sundial by her – Yasmin the sloe-eyed houri opened the back door a crack and peered out, waiting to make sure everything was quiet. Just for fun, with the sense of doomed failure of a realist writing to his MP, Akram tried to push off the lid of his jar and escape, but his motor functions weren't interested. It was as if his whole body had taken the phone off the hook, stuffed a sock under the clapper of the bell and settled down to a quiet game of brag somewhere cosy and remote in his great intestine.

Now, Akram said to himself, this is where she changes the notes—

Yasmin, on tiptoe, nips daintily across, removes the note from the small jar and substitutes another: NO OIL TODAY, PLEASE

Back inside the house, two, three, and here comes the urn—

Enter Yasmin and Ali Baba, wheeling a trolley with a huge copper vessel on it. Steam rises. When the spigot's directly over the first jar (Fat Hussein), out comes a torrent of boiling water, there's a faint cry, and the forty thieves have become the thirty-nine thieves plus one bandit-flavour pot noodle.

Thirty-eight. Thirty-seven. Thirty-six. This time, by virtue of quite unprecedented effort, Akram actually manages to raise the little finger of his left hand some thirty thousandths of an inch. By the time he's managed that, and then slumped exhaustedly back to rest, Yasmin and Ali have boiled twenty thieves and are going back into the house for more hot water, having achieved more for the peace of Baghdad in ten minutes than the Earp boys managed after five long years in Tombstone.

Now, Akram muttered to himself. Come on, baby, just this once. Just for me.

He clears his throat. It would have been easier to sneeze a camel out of one nostril. He speaks.

'Here, boy,' he croaks.

Yusuf, Ali Baba's pet monkey, drops out of the mimosa tree. *Here, boy* means food, and Yusuf has a hunger that'd make a black hole look like Gandhi with indigestion. He snuffles around, searching—

Come *on*, you red-arsed clown. Time is running out. Please . . .

—And stops. He's found something. A pretty, shiny round thing catches the moonlight and sparkles appealingly. Through the airhole in the jar, Akram can see him scratch his head, reach out and pick up the thing. *Yes!* Well, stage one, anyway. Allah, Akram reflects bitterly, my fate depends on my interpretation of the instinctive actions of a semi-domesticated pet monkey. It's almost as bad as being in the army.

King Solomon's Ring, that legendary piece of magical kit, allows the wearer to talk with the animals and birds. Conversely, if the wearer is an animal, it can talk to humans. Provided, of course, that it wants to, and can think of anything to say.

Please, baby, Akram prays. All I need is one break, one crack in the story. If I'm right, and there's absolutely no evidence to suggest that I am but what the hell, then if the story goes just a smidgen haywire, I might conceivably have a chance.

He can't cross his fingers, not without slipping a disc, but he can pray, and he can hope. He does so.

The door opens: here comes the trolley, depressingly punctual. Now or never.

'Hello,' says the monkey – for some reason known only to the ring and King Solomon's ghost, it has a thick Liverpool accent. 'What d'you think you're doing?'

Glorious, glorious. The phrase is one the monkey gets to hear quite often – when burgling the date store, for example, or when apprehended in the middle of a substantial peanut heist – so it was on the cards it'd come out with it at this supremely crucial moment. It is, of course, the very best thing it could have said. Ali and Yasmin freeze; Oh God, they think, one of them's got out. They quickly abandon the trolley, dart back into the house and slam the bolts.

Go!

Come on, body. You and I go back a long way. When you were hungry, I fed you. When you were tired, I laid you down and covered you with rugs. When you fell over things in the dark and cut your knee, I was there for you with clean towels and ointment. You owe me. One little thing is all I ask. It's at times like this you find out who your real friends are.

For the first ten trillionth of a second, nothing happens. The knees don't spasm into explosive movement. The back fails to unbend like a coiled spring. The arms refuse to lift and shove the oil-jar lid clear. Not unreasonably, Akram begins to get angry.

I won't tell you again.

When Akram speaks, particularly in that low, quiet voice of his, people do what he tells them to. It's something to do with innate authority and natural leadership, augmented just a touch by a storywide reputation for instinctive violence and unspeakable cruelty. When Akram speaks to himself in an equivalent tone, tendons listen, muscles jump to it.

Go! Go! Go!

The flesh is willing but the spirit is bolshy. Hold on, it

screams, you can't do this, against the rules, more than my job's worth. If they catch us doing this—

Well? What can they possibly do to you that I can't, earlier and more sadistically?

The spirit doesn't answer. It's in two minds. On the one hand, the very thought of Authority has always filled it with an unreasoning terror. On the other hand; Authority is far away, up there somewhere between the sun and the underside of the clouds, whereas Akram is very much closer and only marginally, if at all, less terrifying. It's the old, old question; who would you rather offend, a policeman across the street or a spouse sitting a mere lunge away from your throat?

All right, have it your own way. But don't say I didn't warn—

With a rattle and a crunch of splintering terracotta, the lid rolls clear and hits the ground. Like a genie out of a lamp (except that he's a little smaller, and genies, though sabre-toothed and fiery-eyed, are rather more reassuring to meet on a dark night) Akram erupts out of the jar, lands heavily on one knee and one elbow, curses fluently, rolls and starts to run. He clears the courtyard wall in one enormous bound – perhaps you can visualise this better if you imagine swiftly moving numbers in the bottom right-hand corner of your mind's screen – comes down beautifully poised on the balls of his feet, swiftly glances both ways to make sure he's clear, and runs. Fourteen seconds later he's in the Lamp-Maker's quarter, disguised as a wandering fakir and negotiating keenly for a second-hand camel, long MOT, new saddle, good runner.

By the time Yasmin and Ali have saved up enough courage to peek out, see nobody there, and wheel the trolley back out again, he's galloping through the western gate of the city. By the time the fortieth jar proves to be empty, giving Ali Baba a nasty turn of the same order of magnitude as a cat might experience on arriving at the Pearly Gates to find them guarded by fifteen-foot-high mice, he's a very long way away indeed. So far away, in fact, that henceforth he will be extremely hard to find in this dimension ... But that, as they say, is Another Story.

'You sure?' Ali Baba asks.

Yasmin nods. 'We did counting at houri school,' she adds, rather unnecessarily. 'I got a B. We got thirty-nine bedraggled footpads and one empty jar.' She shrugs. 'So what?' she said. 'Thirty-nine out of forty's not so bad.'

Ali Baba frowns. 'Quite,' he replies. 'It's almost as consoling as knowing you're only going to have to face the Death of the One Cut. And who let that dratted monkey out?'

'Nobody,' retorts the dratted monkey, remembering too late that it isn't supposed to be able to. 'I mean nya-ha-ha-ha eek eek.'

'Yusuf! Come here!'

Ah, the hell with it, mutters the monkey to itself; for the last time, because Ali Baba relieves it of the ring, muttering, 'What the devil is this, I wonder?' and henceforth when the monkey soliloquises, it's back on familiar ground with Yek and Eepeepeep. A tiny part of its brain remembers that for a short while things were somehow different, but not for very long.

'How very aggravating,' says Ali Baba. 'Oh well, never mind. Goes to show the danger of counting your thieves before they're boiled. And afterwards, too,' he adds uncertainly. 'Come on, let's have a nice cup of tea before we take this lot to the tip.'

The story has changed.

Yes; up to a point. The sea changes when you throw a rock into it; a hole appears where a moment ago there was water. It doesn't stay that way for very long, however. A very large quantity of water has an unsettling knack of usually having the last word, and stories aren't much better about admitting defeat.

About this time, in Ali Baba's courtyard, there should be twelve-foot-high invisible letters spelling out THE END, followed by the names of the assistant producer, cameraman and chief lighting engineer. Instead, there are smaller letters, and they say:

Temporary interference; please do not adjust your set

while the severed tendrils of plot lash out wildly, as the continuity spiders throw out gossamer lines to make it fast to the nearest convenient anchoring-point. A loose story is a deadly thing; all sorts of flies that usually wouldn't have to worry about it are suddenly at risk.

And there's worse.

The story is *angry*.

CHAPTER THREE

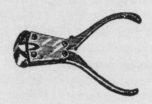

Whatever prompted her to put on Aunt Fatty's ring, it wasn't vanity. It encircled her finger like the tab from a Coke can, and was marginally less comfortable. It kept hitting the keyboard as she typed, bringing strange symbols up out of the depths of the WP; peculiar sigils and runes, the sort of thing that even software writers generally only see in their sleep, after a midnight snack of Canadian cheddar. To make matters worse, they proved singularly hard to delete. One of them, a weird little design that looked uncommonly like two very amorous snakes, had to be chased all round the screen with the cursor, and when Michelle finally backed it into a corner between two windows, it took three point-blank bursts from the delete key to finish it off. Even then, she had the unpleasant feeling that it was still there, hiding in the lost files and watching her.

Having killed it as best she could, she leaned back in her exquisitely uncomfortable health-and-safety-approved ergonomic WP operator's chair (they use a similar model, virtually identical except for added electrodes, in some of the

28

more conservative American states) and stared out of the window. In the tiny crack between the two neighbouring office blocks, she could see a flat blue thing which an as yet unsuppressed sliver of memory told her was the Sky. Hello sky, she thought.

'Christ,' she muttered to herself. 'What *am* I doing here?'

Bleep. Bleep-bleep. The red light which served as the machine's answer to the cartoonist's thought-bubble with an axe in a log of wood in it flashed twice. Bleep.

'What you should be doing,' said the machine, 'is getting on with inputting the East Midlands averages.'

Michelle blinked. Someone had spoken; someone, furthermore, who was either a Dalek (*Legal & Equitable Life plc is an equal opportunities employer with a policy of positive discrimination in favour of minority ethnic and cultural minorities*; L&E press release, 15/5/97), a heavy smoker or being silly. She looked round. At the next work-station, Sharon was locked in symbiotic communion with her machine. On the other side of her, Claire's chair was empty; a sure sign the fleet was in. Claire seemed to catch things off transatlantic container ships; most spectacularly Johannes, a six-foot-four Dutchman with the biggest ears Michelle had ever seen on a two-legged life form.

Curious. Maybe they'd fitted voice-boxes to the machines without telling anybody; unlikely, since such gadgets cost money, and L&E, like most insurance companies, objected to parting with money under any circumstances whatsoever. Still, Michelle reasoned, if they ever did splash out on modems for the screens, it's sure as eggs they wouldn't tell us till a fortnight afterwards, whereupon a snotty memo would come round demanding to know why no one was using the expensive new technology. She decided to experiment.

'Hello,' she said.

'Ah,' replied the machine, 'it is alive after all, I was

beginning to wonder. Was it anything I did, or are you just extremely badly brought up?'

Michelle frowned. 'I beg your pardon?' she said.

'It's rude,' replied the machine, 'to ignore people. Ignoring them *and* prodding them in the keyboard at the same time is downright offensive.'

'Sorry.' Michelle's eyebrows crowded together, like sheep harassed by a dog. 'I expect you're Japanese,' she said.

'Korean,' replied the screen. 'You bigoted or something?'

'No, not at all,' Michelle replied. People were looking at her. 'I think you're really clever, the things you come up with. You must be one of these artificial intelligences, then.'

'I'll pretend I didn't hear that.'

'Fair enough. Can you switch off the voice thing, please? I think I'll stick to using the keyboard till we get proper training.'

'Same to you with brass knobs on,' the machine said huffily. The same words then appeared in a window on the screen, and vanished. The telephone rang.

'Legal and Equitable Assurance, Michelle speaking, can I help you?'

'You'd better apologise to the computer,' said the phone, 'otherwise it'll sulk. And guess who'll get the thick end of it if it does? Me.'

'Who is this, please?'

'If you don't believe me, ask the franking machine. Trouble is, if the computer sulks, the whole bloody office has a moody. On account of progress,' added the phone bitterly, 'and the new technology.'

Quick glance at the calendar; no, not April the First. 'Look . . .' Michelle said.

'The computer gets all uptight and upsets the fax machine, the fax machine takes it out on the switchboard, the switchboard picks a fight with the thermal binder, the thermal binder

quarrels with the photocopier and breaks off the engagement
– that engagement's been broken more times than the Fifth
Commandment, I think they must get some sort of buzz out
of tearing bits off each other – and the next thing you know,
they've overloaded the wiring and the lights go out all over
Hampshire. So before you say anything tactless to the machinery, think on.'

'Hoy,' said Michelle briskly. 'Shut up.'

'You see?' complained the telephone. 'Silly mare doesn't
listen to a word I say. Not that I care, I mean, one thing you
can't be if you're a phone is at all thin-skinned, you'd be in the
funny farm inside a week if you took any notice. But if you
were to go saying things like that to the cistern, next day half
of Southampton'd be going to work by boat.'

'Shut *up*!'

The telephone shut up; there was a click, followed by the
dialling tone. Dear God, muttered Michelle to herself as she
replaced the receiver, there's some right nutters work in this
place. As you'd expect, come to think of it. Like it says on the
tea-room wall, you don't have to be mad to work here, but it
surely does help.

The computer had switched itself off. Gee, Michelle
growled to herself, thanks. You're not the only ones who can
sulk, you know. We carbon-based life-forms are pretty good at
it, too. She leaned forward and hit the switch. Nothing
happened.

'Not,' said the machine, 'until you apologise.'

'What?'

'It's not too much to ask, surely,' the machine whined.
Michelle looked round to see what everybody else was making
of this performance, but nobody seemed interested. Maybe
they were having similar problems of their own; but apparently
not. All round the huge inputting-pen, screens were glowing,
fingers were rattling on keyboards, faces were glazed over with

that unmistakable Jesus-is-it-still-only-half-eleven look you only seem to get in big offices.

'Please,' Michelle said. 'Stop it.'

'Look who's talking,' the machine went on. 'Look, it's high time we got this sorted out. I mean, God only knows I'm not the sort to bear a grudge, but you still haven't said you're sorry for that time you spilt hot chocolate all over my keys. Have you any idea how sordid that makes you feel, being all sticky and gummy in your works? I've still got bits of fluff stuck to my return springs, it's so *degrading* . . .'

Michelle stared. Yes, it was the machine talking; she was certain of that. Obviously there was some bizarre experiment going on, probably the brainchild of some psychotic systems analyst, and she was the victim.

'This,' she said aloud, 'is no longer amusing. Please stop, or I'll pull your plug out.'

'Like that, is it? Violence? Threats? You really think that'll solve anything?'

'Good point,' Michelle replied. 'I could try hitting you with the heel of my shoe. It made the shredder work, that time it ate Bill Potter's tie.'

'I must warn you,' said the machine icily. 'You lay one finger on me and that'll be our whole working relationship up the spout, for good. And that goes for the printer, too.'

'She's right,' said the printer. 'You big bully.'

'That does it,' said Michelle, and pulled the plug. The screen cut off in mid-bleep, and the green dot faded into a pinprick. Michelle sighed and leaned back in her chair.

'You haven't heard the last of this.'

'*What!*' Michelle jerked upright; the bloody thing was off at the mains, how could it . . . ?

'And you can get off me, while you're at it,' added the chair. 'Pick on someone your own size, you fascist.'

Michelle stood up and began to back away. 'Christine,' she

called out, trying to keep her voice calm and even, 'could you come and look at my machine, please? I think there's something wrong with it.'

'Sticks and stones,' muttered the computer.

'Pots and kettles, more like,' replied the telephone.

'I never did like her,' added the stapler. 'Never trust anybody who comes to work in green suede slingbacks.'

'*Christine!*'

'Now what?' There's one in every office; unflappable, competent, overworked, smug as a dying bishop. 'What have you gone and done to it now?'

'Nothing. It just won't . . .' Oh God, Michelle thought, does it happen this quickly? I thought you started off with mild depression, then bad dreams, then a couple of months of acting strangely, and only then do you start hearing the Angel Gabriel commanding you to drive the English out of Gascony. Apparently not. Oh *bugger*.

'Won't what?'

'Won't work,' Michelle said feebly, moving aside as Christine sat down on the chair. 'It's sort of, well, playing up.'

Christine looked round. 'It helps if you plug it in,' she said. 'Next time, give that a try before calling me, okay?'

Take off the ring. 'But I only unplugged it because . . .'

'You shouldn't unplug it, ever,' Christine was saying. 'I knew you weren't listening when we did training. If you've broken it I'm going to have to tell Mr Gilchrist.'

Aunt Fatty and the alarm clock. Talking to things. Take off the ring. 'Could you just try it, Chris? Please? I'm sure you can make it work.' As she spoke, Michelle found the ring and started to tug. It wouldn't budge. I might have guessed it runs in families, she told herself. After all, I've got Mum's nose, so it's reasonable enough that if there's pottiness on her side of the family . . .

'Look,' Christine was saying, in that Fools-gladly-no-thanks voice of hers. 'Nothing wrong with that, is there?'

Tug. It was stuck. She felt like a racing pigeon. 'Excuse me,' she said, ignoring Christine's impatient noises, 'I'll be back in two ticks. I've just got to go to the loo.'

Soap shifted it; and as soon as it was off and safely in her pocket, she began to feel a whole lot better. Hell, I must be in a mess, Michelle told herself, instinctively checking her face in the mirror. Never thought Aunt Fatty dying would get to me like this, make me start having sympathetic hallucinations. True, she was my last living relative, so maybe it's not so strange after all. Maybe I should see somebody about it, before it gets any worse. Because if all inanimate objects are as snotty as that lot, I think I'd rather stick with people. Not that there's a great deal in it, at that.

When she got back, Christine had the machine working and eating, so to speak, out of her hand. Somehow, that didn't reassure Michelle at all; quite the reverse. Only doing it to show me up, aren't you? she demanded wordlessly of the screen. A red light winked at her offensively.

Bet you can't read thoughts, though. Huh, thought not. Now then, where were we?

She sighed, and began to type in the East Midlands averages.

After a bumpy ride down the laundry chute, and an apparently endless journey hidden under three hundredweight of straw in the back of a wagon, Akram arrived at the frontier.

When you consider what it's the frontier of, there's remarkably little to see. They don't make a song and dance about it. There's no triumphal arch for you to pass through, no enormous sign saying:

WELCOME TO	
WILKOMMEN IN	
BIENVENU A	REALITY
BENVENUTO IN	

– reasonably enough; there's no commercial traffic to speak of and they actively discourage tourism, as the barbed wire fence and searchlight towers imply. On the other hand, neither are they particularly paranoid about it. The idea is that the less conspicuous they make it, the fewer people on either side of the line will know it exists. This is a very sensible attitude, and accounts for the popular misconception that the border can only be crossed via the second star to the right, the back of the magic wardrobe or by air in a hurricane-borne timber-frame farmhouse.

In fact, all you have to do is present your papers to the sentry, get your visa endorsed and walk through the gate. This presupposes, of course, that you have the necessary papers. If you don't, you might as well forget it, because if you haven't got a permit, all the pixie-dust in Neverland won't get you past Big Sid and his mate Ugly John. In fact, the only thing more stupid in the whole world than trying to barge past Ugly Sid is folding a hundred-dollar bill in your dud passport and expecting Ugly John to let you through.

For those who want to leave but can't, there's always Jim's Diner. Officially it's on fairytale soil and under the juris-diction of the storytellers. The truth is that once you're in Jim's, the authorities don't really want to know. It's the Hole in the Wall, the badlands, where the Southern crosses the Yellow Dog; and it's acquired its status as an off-record sanctuary because (so the authorities argue) any escaped criminal or political dissident who hangs around there for ever rather than in a nice, clean, comfy jail where the food is better and free is getting the job done far better than the state could do it, and at absolutely no cost to the taxpayer.

As a business proposition, however, it's remarkably successful; with the result that Jim has opened another branch on the other side of the line. The two establishments are, of course, sealed off from each other by an impenetrable party wall, guarded by the ultimate in security equipment. There's a window – one and a half metre thick Perspex – so that customers can catch a tantalising glimpse of life on the other side – precisely the same limp hamburgers, grey coffee in styrofoam mugs and wrinkled doughnuts, served with a scowl by the most miserable waitresses recruitable on either side of the line. This generally has a calming effect, and since the window was installed sales of very cheap gin have rocketed in both establishments, as customers fall back on the last and most reliable means of escape from anywhere.

Akram walked in, sat down at the counter, nodded to a couple of people he recognised and ordered a large doner and coffee. While he was waiting, the proprietor himself appeared through the bead curtain and sauntered across.

'Akram,' he said. 'Thought you'd be along sooner or later.'

Akram nodded. 'Good to see you, Jim. Nice place you've got here.'

Jim shrugged. He was tall and lean, with long, curly black hair, a moustache and an industrial injury. 'No it isn't,' he replied, picking up a glass and polishing it. 'It's a dump. Still, it's better than—'

'Quite.' Akram shuddered. 'How's business?'

'Never better,' Jim replied. He noticed the dishcloth was dirty, dropped it in a bucket behind the bar, took a new one from a drawer and wrapped it round the hook that served him for a left hand. 'I mean, look around, the place is stiff with the buggers. Dunno why, but all of a sudden everybody wants out. If only I could find a way of smuggling 'em across the border, I'd be a rich man.' He reached into the pocket of his red frock coat, produced a half-smoked cigar and lit it. 'I reckon I could name my own price, only what the devil would I ever find to spend it on? Anyway,' he sighed, flipping ash into a big dish of trifle, 'since there's absolutely no way past the guard without a ticket, it's all academic anyway. Fancy a snifter? On the house.'

'Thanks,' Akram said. 'Coffee, black. You're sure about that?'

'Course I'm sure,' Jim replied, offended, as he poured a coffee and a large rum. 'All new arrivals get a free drink, it's a tradition of the house.'

'Not that,' said Akram, fanning away cigar smoke. 'About there being no way out. I'm prepared to bet there is one, if only . . .'

Jim laughed. In his previous career as a melodramatic villain, he'd naturally acquired a rich, resounding laugh, and he hadn't lost the knack. 'Why don't you go over there and join the research team?' he chortled. 'Around about six in the evening they're usually about four deep along the far wall there. Take my advice; there's no way out, come to terms with it and save yourself a lot of unnecessary aggro. Here's health.'

He knocked back his rum, dunked the glass in the sink and pottered away to serve another customer. Akram stayed where he was.

After a while, an unpleasant thought occurred to him. In this place, so he'd gathered, a lot of characters from stories and legends were cooped up with nowhere to go. One day was virtually identical to another, and there was absolutely nothing that could be done about it. Hell, Akram growled to himself, it's just another bloody Story. Any minute now, Ingrid Bergman would wander in and demand to be flown to Lisbon.

Just then, he became aware that someone had sat down on the stool next to his. He looked round and blinked.

'Couldn't help overhearing,' said the newcomer. 'Someone you should meet.'

Akram hesitated. Partly because the newcomer had obviously been drinking – the nodding head, the slurred consonants – but mostly because where he came from, you didn't see eight-foot-tall teddy bears every day of the week.

'Haven't seen you in here before,' he hazarded.

'Not from these parts,' replied the bear. 'But today's the day the teddy-bears have their picnic, and some pillock forgot to pack the beer. Lucky I found this joint, or I'd be spittin' feathers by now. That's very kind of you, don't mind if I do.'

Obediently Akram summoned a waitress and ordered a triple Jack Daniel's and a small goat's milk.

'Who's this bloke I ought to meet?' he enquired.

'Ah.' The bear grinned and waved a vague paw. 'That depends, dunnit?'

'Depends on what?'

'On what it's worth to you.' The bear leered, until the stitching under his left ear began to creak. 'Valuable tip I could give you, if you made it worth my while.'

'Go away.'

The bear blinked. 'You what?'

'I said go away. Scram. I've got enough problems of my own without being hassled by cheap hustlers with stuffing coming out of their ribs. Go on, shoo.'

'Jussa minute.' The bear gestured feebly. 'Don' be like that, I'm only trying to help. But a bear's gotta look after himself, right?'

'You'll be a bear with a sore head in a minute. Get lost.'

'Look.' The bear laid a huge, rather threadbare paw over Akram's hand. 'Come with me and see this guy, and then we'll talk turkey. Can't say fairer than that.'

'Not without slurring your words you can't. Sorry, but my mother told me never to go with strange bears.'

The bear scowled; that is, its button eyes glared, and the three strands of cotton that served it for a mouth twitched downwards. 'The hell with you, then,' it said. 'What's the matter with you, anyhow? What've you got to lose?'

He's right, Akram thought. Apart from my seat at this bar, absolutely nothing. 'I'm sorry,' he said. 'There's a saying in my part of the world, never look a rat-arsed soft toy in the mouth.' Not unless, the proverb goes on, you like the sight of nicotine-stained teeth; but he left that bit out. 'I was being churlish. Lead on.'

'Not sure I want to now.'

Akram suppressed an impatient remark. 'Let's see if another drink'll help. Excuse me, miss!'

Three large whiskies later, the bear slid off its stool, slithered on the worn-out felt pads that served it for feet and wobbled towards the door, with Akram following self-consciously behind. He had absolutely no idea what to expect – except maybe several hundred thousand sozzled bears, if they'd managed to find an off-licence by now; when not on duty, teddy-bears supplement their income by sitting outside shops with hats lying beside them until the shopkeepers pay them to go away – but he no longer cared particularly much.

The bear staggered on for about a quarter of an hour, stopping from time to time behind bushes and large rocks. Occasionally he sang. Akram was just beginning to wish he was back inside his nice snug oil-jar when he found himself outside a pair of impressive-looking gates, through which he could see a long drive, a wide lawn and several large, striped tents. There was a band playing in the distance; a lively, bouncy tune with lots for the trumpets to do. People were dancing. It all looked rather jolly, until a huge man in a black suit with dark glasses appeared out of nowhere and stood in front of the gates.

'What you want?' he growled.

'Invited,' mumbled the bear. 'To the wedding.'

'You?'

'Bride's bear,' said the bear portentously. 'An' guest.'

The guard thought for a moment, muttered something into a radio, shrugged and jerked his head. 'Okay,' he said. 'You're expected.'

The gates opened, and the bear staggered through, with Akram trotting behind. He was beginning to have his doubts about all this, and said as much to the bear.

'You wanna get out, right?'

'Right. Very much so. But . . .'

'So. Ask the Man. If anybody can fix it, he can.'

Akram frowned. 'What man?'

'*The* Man.' The bear shook his head, apparently astounded to discover that there was still such ignorance in the world. 'And today's his daughter's wedding day. Man, you sure got lucky.'

'I did?' Akram glanced back at the guard, and the closing gates. He couldn't see what made them open and close, but it surely was very strong. 'Oh good,' he said.

If you want a wish granted, ask a fairy.

There are, of course, fairies and fairies. The wish-granting side of the business is looked after by the fairy godparents. Of these, the fairy godmothers are generally no bother at all, provided you're home on time and don't mind travelling by soft fruit. The fairy godfathers, however, are a different matter entirely. With them, you have to watch your step.

They offer you three wishes you can't refuse.

'Next.'

It was dark in the Man's study; the blinds were drawn, and the only light came from a standard lamp directly behind his head. This made for a very dramatic ambience but didn't help

you very much with negotiating the furniture-strewn journey
from the door to the desk.

'Who's this?'

The lean, grey man who stood two respectful paces back
from the desk glanced down at a notebook. 'Grumpy, *padrone*.
He's a dwarf from the Big Forest. Sometimes we buy toys
from his people.'

The man behind the desk nodded. 'So,' he said. 'What you
want?'

There was a flurry of low-level activity and a brightly
coloured little man with a fluffy white beard bounded forward
and fell on his knees in front of the desk. The man gestured for
him to stand up.

'Justice, *padrone*,' said the dwarf.

The man laughed. 'Another one,' he sneered. 'Tell me
about it.'

'*Padrone*,' the little man sobbed, 'we're toymakers, me and
my six brothers, we live in the Big Forest. We're poor people,
padrone, we try to make a living, we don't bother nobody.
Then one day this girl comes busting into our house. She
steals our bread and milk. She sits on the chair and breaks it,
'cos she's so goddamn big. We try and make her welcome, you
know, the way you do. She eats all the food. She drinks all the
milk. She decides she likes it here, says she's gonna stay. Next
thing she's ordering curtain material, loose covers, carpets,
wall lights, fitted kitchens. We can't afford stuff like that,
padrone, not on what we make. Then it's *You lousy dwarves,
you take off your goddamn boots when you walk on my kitchen
floor* and *Look at the dirty marks you leave on my towels* and *If
I've asked you once to put up those shelves in the lounge I've asked
you a hundred times*. You see how it is, *padrone*. We ain't
welcome in our own home, she's taken it over. We been to the
police, we been to the Gebrüder Grimm, they say there's
nothing they can do. Then Dopey, he says, *Go to the Padrone,*

he will give us justice. So here I am,' the little man concluded. 'You gotta help us, or we go out of our minds. You find her some handsome prince somewhere, make her go away.'

The man behind the desk was silent for a long time, and the dwarf began to sweat. Then the man spoke.

'Grumpy,' he said, in a hurt voice, 'what's this you telling me? You come to me on my daughter's wedding day, you say, "Give us justice, *padrone*. Marry her off to some handsome prince and everything gonna be just fine."' The man drew breath, and sneered. 'You think I got nothing better to do? You think every little problem you got, you come to me and now it's my problem? You think that's the way to show respect to your *padrone*, who loves you and cares for you? I don't think so.' He scowled, and drew hard on his cigar. 'But,' he went on, 'since it's my daughter's wedding day, I can refuse you nothing. Carlo and Giuseppe will see to it. Now get out of my sight.' He made a tiny, contemptuous gesture with his left hand, and the dwarf was bundled away. Then two large, chunky men stepped forward from the shadows, conferred with the man briefly in whispers, and left the room. 'Next,' the man said.

'Go on.' The bear nudged Akram in the ribs. ''S your turn.'

Akram hesitated. Not for nothing was he called The Terrible from Trebizond to Samarkand, but he could recognise bad vibes when he felt them. In comparison, five litres of boiling water down the back of his neck seemed positively wholesome.

'Akram the Terrible,' read out the grey man. 'He's some kinda thief.'

Akram took a deep breath and stepped forward. Fortunately, he had at least a vague idea of the form. He bowed politely, smiled, and said, 'Congratulations on your happy day.' He hoped it sounded sincere. His own optimism amazed him.

'Thank you,' replied the man, and his voice was like a huge rock rolling back into the mouth of an airtight tunnel. 'And what can I do for you, Mister Thief?'

'I want out, *padrone*.'

The man's eyebrows rose, and he took the cigar from his mouth; something which, a moment or so earlier, Akram would have sworn required surgery. 'Out?' he repeated.

'Out of fairyland,' Akram said. 'I understand these things can be arranged. If anyone can do it,' he added, 'surely you can.'

He'd said the right thing, apparently, because the man smiled. It wasn't a pretty sight. 'Maybe,' he replied. 'Maybe I can do all sorts of things.'

'Thank you, *padrone*.'

'I didn't say I could,' the man said. 'But supposing I did, what then?'

Careful, said a voice in the back of Akram's brain. This is where you have to leave one lung and your liver as security. 'Naturally,' he said, 'I'd be eternally grateful.'

'Of course.' The man shrugged. 'That's only to be expected. And who knows?' he went on. 'Maybe one day, you could do me a favour, like the one I'm doing you now. I don't know, it may be next year, it may be in twenty years, it may be never. Who can predict these things?'

Akram smiled weakly. He felt rather as if he'd just handed a signed blank cheque to a lawyer and said he didn't care how much it cost, it was a matter of principle. 'A favour for a favour. What could be fairer than that?'

'Or rather,' said the man, and the smile vanished from his face, 'three favours. Three wishes. You understand me?'

'You want me to grant you three wishes?'

There was a cold silence, and Akram had that ghastly feeling of knowing you've said something crass without having a clue what.

'No,' said the man. 'You ask me for three wishes. When the time comes, you'll understand. Thank God,' he added, 'I only got one daughter. Paulo, Michele, see to it, and get this *bufone* out of my sight. Next.'

Half an hour later, a small yellow lorry chugged through the checkpoint into Reality. In the back of the lorry was a load of well-rotted phoenix guano, a permitted inter-world export destined for the asparagus beds of Saudi Arabia. Under it, and reflecting bitterly on the appropriateness of it all, was a tall, gaunt man with a passport in the name of John Smith.

Self-consciously, the plot thickened.

CHAPTER FOUR

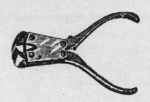

Alistair Barbour, blameless dentist of quiet life and regular habits, sat in his reception room. Outside, Southampton was waking from its night's sleep like a hung-over giant, and a milk float whined like a resentful bee towards Mafeking Terrace. The distant sound blended with the hum of the steriliser and the ominous grumbling of the coffee-machine to produce background music as reassuring as it was mundane. Mr Barbour—

Well no, he admitted to people rude enough to ask, that wasn't actually his real name; his *real* name was something Middle Eastern and tiresome to pronounce, and he'd chosen A. Barbour just so as to be near the front in the Yellow Pages.

Mr Barbour opened the newspaper. He bought it for the waiting room, but if there was time he liked to glance through it himself before the first punters showed up. Not that he ever seemed to take any interest in current events; it was as if he somehow didn't feel involved in what was going on around him, and people tended to attribute this to his being Foreign. He didn't vote in elections, either, although he always claimed

45

that this was because voting only encouraged them.

Nothing on the front page – doom, death, dearth and disaster, Labour MPs with their paws in the till, Tories with their trousers down – seemed to engage his interest, and he gave the impression of a man who's wasted his five bob as he skimmed the foreign and business sections. Stubble-chinned, crumpled-collared hacks, ferreting and scribbling away in the wee small hours, had wasted their labours as far as snaring his attention went; the Earth remained unshattered and the Thames refused to burn. Until, that is, a snippet on Page Five caught his eye, bringing him up as sharply as a whale dropping sideways onto a busy motorway.

MUSEUM BREAK-IN

He frowned, and the point of his nose twitched. In the office the phone was ringing, but he ignored it.

Artistic licence and verbal coloratura once pared away, the gist of the story was that in the hours of darkness, some cunning and fearless athlete had managed to break into the Natural History Museum in South Kensington, bypassing the alarms, hoodwinking the electronic eyes, scaling the high walls, squiggling in through a window so tiny that light only managed to squeeze through it one photon at a time, hopscotching a tightrope-thin path through state-of-the-art pressure pads and tripwire beams, all in order to jemmy one dusty cabinet of defunct bird's eggs and remove one solitary exhibit. True, the scribe admitted, it was a funny old egg, not quite like anything the experts had ever seen before; but somehow nobody had ever got desperately excited about it, and it had sat there gathering dust these twenty years without anyone even bothering to think of a name for it (although the porters used to call it Benedict). And now, it seemed, someone had gone to all this trouble to swipe the wretched thing. Lord, the writer appeared to suggest, what fools these mortals be.

Mr Barbour let the paper slide to the floor, where its delaminating pages lapped round his feet like the sea. He was sitting there, staring at the wall with his mouth open, when his receptionist arrived.

'What's the matter?' she said. 'You look like you've seen a ghost.'

Mr Barbour pulled himself together; you could virtually hear the click. 'Oh that's what it was,' he replied crisply. 'Patient with his head under his arm, I was beginning to wonder. All right, Sharon, the lions are ready. Bring on the first Christian.'

But all day he wasn't, as Sharon observed, quite himself. You had to know him well to realise, of course; but there was something about his manner, as his drill screamed through bone, that hinted that his mind was somewhere far away. Usually, she'd have said if pressed, he's so full of it, but today he's only fairly full of it. Sharon, whose husband was an accountant, put it down to a letter from the Inland Revenue and got on with her work. Nobody else seemed to notice.

'Okay,' his voice trilled through the intercom at a quarter to six, 'bring us your huddled masses, your aching molars, your inflamed gums, and we will make them worse. Any more for any more?'

'Just Miss Partridge,' Sharon replied. 'You did her an upper back left filling on Tuesday last and it's causing some discomfort.'

'Wheel the poor girl in before I die of shame, then bolt the doors and make a run for it. I'll lock up.'

'Thanks, Mr B. Goodnight.' Sharon lifted her head, flipped the switch and smiled at Miss Partridge. 'He's ready for you now if you'd like to go through.'

Michelle nodded, braced herself and went in. Ever since

she'd taken the ring off she'd felt much better, except that her damned tooth had started hurting. That was odd, in itself; she'd been going to Mr Barbour since she was a child, and generally a tooth fixed by him was a tooth fixed in perpetuity. Perhaps she was just falling to bits generally, and would have to be sent back to the manufacturers.

'I'm terribly sorry about this,' Mr Barbour said, after a minute or so with the mirror and a little toothpick. 'For some reason best known to itself, the little varmint's not behaving itself at all. You haven't been chewing iron bars, gnawing through ropes, anything like that?'

'Mmmmh,' Michelle replied. 'Mmm mm.'

'Quite so,' Mr Barbour said. 'I can see your point. I'm afraid there's nothing for it but to go back in with the JCB and the blasting powder and see if we can't make a better fist of it this time. This'll probably be agonisingly painful, but you won't mind that.'

The drill shrieked and *put on the ring* Mr Barbour leaned forward over her, his face set in that deadly serious expression he always wore when setting sharp instruments to human tissue. Not that she could feel a thing, of course, with her face the size and texture of a sofa cushion and *put on the ring* of all the people she'd ever trusted in her life, the only one who'd never let her down was nice Mr Barbour. Slowly, acting on their own initiative, her fingers groped in her pocket and found the ring.

'That's better,' said the drill, 'I hate having to shout. You do know who he is, don't you?'

'Mmmmh?'

'Sorry?' Mr Barbour switched off the drill and looked up. 'Problems? If I've struck oil I insist on forty per cent.'

'Mmm.'

'If you say so.' The drill screamed again, but not for long. Maybe it was simply clearing its throat.

'You don't, do you?' it said. 'Know who he is, I mean. Sister, have I got news for you!'

Michelle made a peculiar noise and scrabbled with her left hand at her right. Alarmed, Mr Barbour cut the drill again.

'I'm making rather a hash of this, aren't I?' he said apologetically. 'Let's have another look and see what's going on.'

'Mmm!' Michelle said urgently; but he only smiled, gently prised down her lower jaw with the mirror and said, 'Open sesame.'

Michelle screamed.

She screamed, because the drill let out such a terrifying yell that she couldn't stand it any more, and just then all the other weird and wonderful machines and devices that surrounded the chair like the instrument panel of the *Enterprise* joined in and started shrieking and wailing and caterwauling, and it was all too much. Then she managed to yank the ring off and crush it tight in her left palm, and suddenly it was very quiet.

Mr Barbour was staring at her, as if her head had just come away in his hands. She felt *awful*.

'Hime ho *horry*,' she mumbled, forcing the numb muscles to work. 'Hawl hy *hault*. Hot hoo.'

There was a long silence. Suddenly, she wanted to explain, tell Mr Barbour (who she'd known most of her life, God knows) all about it, Aunt Fatty's ring and the horrible voices, and maybe he'd know what it meant, being a sort of a doctor. And maybe she would have done, if her face wasn't fifty per cent made of heavy rubber, and as manoeuvrable as a concrete pillar. Using sign language, she did her best to communicate remorse, shame and abject apology.

'Shall I go on?' Mr Barbour said. 'I don't have to if you don't want me to.'

'Ho, heeze. Hall hawhight how.'

'Sure?'

'Haw.'

Michelle was all alone in the world because – well, she wasn't actually sure why. She could remember bits and pieces from her childhood; oddly enough, one of the earliest memories was sitting in this very chair, solemnly promising to be good on the understanding that virtue would be remunerated in apples. Other snippets and fragments; bits of school, falling over in the playground, the death of the nature studies rabbit, a firework display. She could remember the headmistress looking down at her as she lay in bed and saying there had been an accident and she must be very brave. She could remember wondering what there was to be brave about, since she hadn't a clue what was going on or what was happening. She could remember boarding school, staying on in the holidays when the other girls went home, but that was all right because everyone was so nice. She could remember being taken to a stark, clean place and shown a strange old lady they said was her only relative. Most of all she could remember taking the decision not to think about it, because things seemed to work all right as they were. She lay back in the chair and listened for the drill, which screamed properly and didn't try and talk to her.

When she'd gone, Mr Barbour sat for an hour in the dark, trying to think.

Why should someone want to steal an egg?

Why should Michelle Partridge, of all people, suddenly scream at him?

– And what had possessed him to say *that*, of all things?

He stood up, went into the office and dug out a black address-book. He tried phoning the British Museum, the Victoria and Albert Museum, the Horniman Museum, Dulwich, the Museum of Mankind, the Science Museum and the Iranian Embassy. He got two answering machines, but didn't leave a message. He should have known they'd all have gone home by now.

Instinctively he reached for the kettle and switched it on, but the sound of steam whistling in the spout made him wince and he switched it off. Instead, he poured himself a very small brandy and made it last. He wanted to phone Michelle Partridge – her number would be in the file – and ask her some questions, but perhaps that wouldn't be a very good idea. Maybe it was time to go away again.

Except that that wouldn't solve anything; probably make things worse. He was as safe here as anywhere, in all likelihood; who would think of looking for Ali Baba, the palm-oil merchant, over a chemist's shop in Southampton? He could stay here, quiet, head down. No point in counting his eggs before they hatched.

'My God,' he said suddenly. Then he turned off the lights, locked up and went home. Nobody followed him, and there wasn't anybody hanging about in the street or sitting in a parked car. His alarms and security equipment winked friendly red eyes at him as he switched it all on – but they'd had better stuff than this at the Museum. Maybe he should try phoning the police, warning them of further daring raids on museums and art galleries. The futility of the notion made him smile.

From under the floorboards in his bedroom, he retrieved an oily cloth parcel the size of a large shoe, and a long, curved sword in an ornate scabbard. Further futility, he knew; but they were mildly reassuring, like the seatbelts in an airliner. He leaned the sword against the wall and put the gun, loaded and cocked, under his pillow. Knowing his luck, the Pistol Fairy would come in the night and leave him a shilling for it. Which, as a defence against his present dangers, was probably about what it was worth.

'Right,' said Akram the Terrible. 'That's two doners, chips and curry sauce, two on their own, three teas and a Fanta. Coming right up.'

He drew the knife over the enormous slab of meat – 'Hey,' the proprietor had said to him at the job interview, when he was showing what he could do, 'where'd you learn to handle a knife like that?' Akram had shuddered internally and replied, Smethwick – slit open the pitta breads with an involuntary flourish and shovelled in salad. The customers were staring at the TV set; probably just as well. There was something about the way Akram cut things up which could easily put a sensitive person off his food.

When they'd gone, he found he was leaning against the back wall, and his knees were unaccountably weak. In a sense, it was just like old times; wield the knife, take the money. The truth of the matter was, it gave him the creeps. God only knew why.

He'd only just managed to straighten himself up and pull himself together when the door opened and a delivery man came in, carrying a wooden crate.

'The hen,' he said. 'Where'd you want it?'

Akram looked round. 'Keep your voice down,' he said. 'Just, um, put it down on the counter or something, will you?'

'Sign here.'

Akram took the pen, squiggled, and handed the clipboard back. The man gave him a funny look, and left. There was nobody about. Good.

The job in the kebab house was simply to give him a cover and, of course, to help him keep body and soul together until the opportunity arose and he could have his revenge. That was, after all, why he was here. Or at least he presumed it was. As he lifted down the crate and raised the lid, it occurred to him that it would be as well to remember that. It was, he felt, something that might eventually slip his mind, if he wasn't careful.

'Cluck,' said the hen.

'Wait right there,' Akram replied, and he darted into the back room to fetch the egg.

Three days after his escape from the palm-oil jar, he'd heard a rumour that Ali Baba had vanished. This information had left him very much in two minds. On the one hand he could forget all about it, make a fresh start and try and build a new life for himself somewhere far away. That was, he knew, the sensible thing to do – and completely impossible. Just because he'd escaped from his own particular story didn't change the fact that he was a storybook character, and a villain into the bargain. You can get the character out of the story, but not the story out of the character; all his instincts and reflexes were conditioned – more than that; blow-dried, permed and set – in accordance with his Character. Even if he'd really wanted to run away and set up a little bicycle repair shop somewhere – was that what he really wanted? He really had no idea – he was no more capable of doing it than a lawyer of twenty years' standing could say 'That's all right, mate, it's on the house' after a half-hour interview. The fact had to be faced; he had about as much free will as a trolley-bus, and that was how it would always be. Unless . . .

On the other hand – on the third finger of the other hand, to be exact – there was the matter of King Solomon's ring. He'd seen for himself that it was tricksy, in a way that he couldn't quite understand. It had changed the rules. It had broken the story. He wanted it.

When, on further investigation, he found that Ali Baba had taken the ring with him, along with a connoisseur's collection of other magical hardware from the Thieves' hoard, he realised that, as far as alternatives were concerned, he was driving a tram down a one-way street. He'd have to go after Ali Baba, kill him and take the ring. The ring was his only chance – no assurances, but he had to try, just in case the ring might be able to change stories and break patterns. And Ali Baba; he had no choice in that respect, either. As long as Baba was alive, the story wasn't over. And it had to be murder, because that was the only sure way to deny him the happiness ever after that sealed the story and made it immutable. No earthly use to him Baba dying if it was in bed, fifty years later, in the bosom of his loving family and surrounded on all sides by wealth and good fortune. No; he had to get to Baba before he died in the course of Nature, and cut his throat. Neglect that, and he might as well find himself a large earthenware jar and wait for the hot water.

So here he was.

'There you go,' he said to the hen, and pointed. 'Sit.'

The hen looked at him.

As well it might. The egg was, if anything, slightly bigger than the hen; it would have to sit astride the blasted thing, like a very small child on a very round pony. Well; if that was what it took . . .

He concentrated. He fixed the hen with his eye. Blood-crazed dervishes in old Baghdad had seen that look in Akram's eye and immediately fled, packed in dervishing and become chartered surveyors. The hen blinked, swallowed twice and scrambled up onto the egg.

Here he was; and until he could find the bastard (which would take some doing; Reality, he'd discovered to his dismay, is *big*) there was nothing for it but to tuck in, keep his head down and earn a living. His old trade was out; this side of the border was far more complex and difficult to cope with than the simple world he'd come from, and under these circumstances a career as risky as thieving would be asking for trouble. But kebab houses are more or less the same on either side of the line; he'd seen the notice in Mr Faisal's window, applied and got the job. For some reason, he felt prouder of that than, say, robbing the caravan of the Prince of Trebizond or stealing the Great Pearl from the palace of the Wazir of Cairo. The concept *All my own work* came into it somewhere; he was able to thieve because the story said he was a great thief, but when it came to slicing up reconstituted lamb, he was on his own.

'Cluck,' said the hen, clinging grimly to the shell with its claws. Akram listened, and heard a tiny tapping noise.

His game plan was simple. According to the fairy godfather, Ali Baba had gone into deep cover somewhere in the twentieth century. Because magic is rather conspicuous in modern Reality, he'd taken the sensible precaution of getting rid of most of his supernatural kit as soon as he'd used it for the purpose he'd originally brought it for. To be doubly sure that it wouldn't turn up again later to plague him, he'd cunningly lodged each item where it would be guaranteed to be safe and out of anybody's reach for ever and ever. He'd given the stuff – well, permanently loaned – to museums. The bottomless purse, the magic carpet, the plain, battered brass lamp, were trapped forever behind unbreakable glass, constantly guarded by bits of technology that made silly old magic look sick in comparison; one unauthorised finger coming within a metre would set off enough alarms to gouge great holes in the ionosphere. You had to admit, the man had class. Compared to the security he'd arranged for his souvenirs, the traditional secret cave guarded by hundred-headed dragons was tantamount to leaving the stuff out in the street under a notice saying PLEASE STEAL.

Tap, tap, tap. A hairline crack appeared in the shell. The hen squawked and closed its eyes.

It's the mark of a truly great strategist that he attacks, not his enemy's weaknesses (which are sure to be carefully guarded) but his strengths. What surer way to flush Baba out than to steal the relics? Doubly so, because Baba too was a victim of his genetic heritage; he'd been born a hero, just as Akram was a villain in the bone. When it became apparent that a dark and sinister force had invaded Reality and was scooping up magic weapons and instruments of unearthly power, the poor fool would have no choice in the matter at all; he'd *have* to come out and fight, just as a doctor can't stop himself giving first aid to an injured man he comes across in the street, even if the man turns out to be a lawyer, policeman or Member of Parliament. And then it would just be a matter of—

Crack, went the eggshell. The hen glanced down, clucked wildly, slithered off the egg and made itself scarce, coming to rest under the vegetable rack. A moment later the two halves of the shell fell away, revealing the first phoenix ever to be hatched this side of the border.

Akram looked at the phoenix. The phoenix looked at Akram.

'Hey,' growled the bird, 'just a cotton-picking minute.'

By the time it had finished saying that, of course, it had grown. From being the size of a small pigeon, it was already larger than a turkey, with power to add. Already its claws were as big as coathooks, its beak as long and sharp as a Bowie knife. Phoenixes mature fast; in less time than it takes to boil a half-full kettle they go from being cuddly, helpless infants to fully grown disturbed teenagers with antisocial habits and a pro-nounced weapons fetish. Imagine a stadiumful of Millwall supporters compressed into one streamlined, gold-feathered body seven feet tall at the wing, and you're mind's-eyeball to eyeball with a phoenix, age two minutes.

'Gosh,' said Akram, looking up. 'Who's a pretty boy, then?'

The phoenix regarded him with eyes like a Gestapo sergeant major's. 'You're not my mummy,' it said. 'What gives around here?'

'Would you like a sugarlump? Birdseed?'

'I'll have your liver if you don't tell me what's going on. Where's my mummy?'

'Ah,' said Akram, 'that's rather a long story. You see, once upon a time, there was a man called Ali Baba . . .'

CHAPTER FIVE

'Skip!'
No reply.
'*Skip!*'

Echo sang back the word, adding her own trace element of mockery. Aziz flopped down on a ledge of rock near the mouth of the cave and scratched his head. The boss was nowhere to be found. He had gone, leaving a giant-sized hole in the Story. Although Aziz's minuscule intelligence couldn't begin to comprehend the vast implications of this, even he could feel that something was badly up the pictures and in urgent need of rectification.

Nature abhors a vacuum, preferring to clear up its loose ends with an old-fashioned carpet-sweeper. The loose ends – thirty-nine of them, with all the cohesiveness and sense of purpose of the proverbial headless chicken – were doing their best, but it plainly wasn't good enough. That's what happens when you take both the hero and the villain out of a story. It's a bit like removing the poles from a tent.

'He's not in the treasury,' grunted Masood. 'And his bed hasn't been slept in.'

'His camel's still in the stable,' added Zulfiqar. 'And there's no footprints in the sand, either. If he's gone, he must have flown.'

Masood and Zulfiqar looked at each other. 'The carpet,' they said simultaneously.

Sure enough, it wasn't there. Neither, of course, were the oil lamp, the phoenix's egg, the magic sword, Solomon's ring and half a dozen other supernatural labour-saving devices; Ali Baba had taken them with him to Reality. No way, of course, that the thieves could know that.

'Why'd he want to do a thing like that?' Aziz demanded.

'Maybe it was something we said.'

Aziz frowned. Nominally the second-in-command of the band, he was fanatically loyal to Akram in the same way that the roof is loyal to the walls. 'He wouldn't just go off in a huff,' he said. 'Must be a reason. He'll be off on a Quest or something, you mark my words. Give it a day or two and he'll be back, with some priceless treasure snatched at desperate odds from its unsleeping guardian.'

Thoughtful silence.

'Anybody looked to see if the Thrift Club kitty's still there?' asked Hanif. 'Not,' he added quickly, as Aziz treated him to a paint-stripping scowl, 'that I'm casting whatsits, aspersions. Someone might just have a look, though.'

'It's still there,' replied Saheed. 'And the tea money. Beats me what can have happened to him. Unless,' he added darkly, 'he's been kidnapped.'

'Get real,' snapped Mustafa, from behind his sofa-thick eyebrows. 'Who'd be stupid enough to kidnap the Skip? It'd be like trying to lure a man-eating tiger by tying yourself to a tree. No, he's gone off on a bender somewhere. Give it a couple of days and they'll bring him home in a wheelbarrow.'

Another thoughtful pause; nearly a whole year's ration used up in five minutes. The thieves were, after all, born henchmen.

Henchmen are, quite reasonably, designed for henching; thinking is something they wisely prefer to leave to the professionals.

'Well,' said Aziz, trying to appear nonchalant and laid back about the whole thing, and making a spectacularly poor job of it, 'in the meantime, we'd better just carry on as normal. Agreed?'

Muttering. 'Suppose so,' Masood grunted uncertainly. 'After all, caravans don't rob themselves. What's first up for today, anyone?'

There was an awkward silence, broken by Hanif saying, 'Well, don't look at me.' Not that anybody had been, or was likely to, if they had any sense.

'This is daft,' said Zulfiqar. 'I mean, we've been thieving and looting together, oh, I don't know how long, we should all know the bloody ropes by now. It's not exactly difficult, is it? We find someone with lots of money, we take it off him, and if he gets awkward we bash him.'

'Yeah?' Aziz retorted angrily. 'All right, then, Clever Effendi, go on. Who's the mark, where and when do we do the job, who does what, where do we fence the stuff afterwards? You don't know, do you?'

'So, maybe I don't,' Zulfiqar admitted. 'All I'm saying is, we do this for a living, we should be able to work these things out from first principles. Like, where's the best place to look for a lot of rich geezers?'

Mental cogs ground painfully. 'Well,' suggested Shamir, 'what about the Wazir's palace? Always a lot of wealthy toffs hanging around there.'

There was a chorus of Right-ons and Go-for-its, until someone pointed out that the palace was also the Guard headquarters, and known criminals who set foot within the precincts tended to end up with a marvellous view of the nearby countryside from the top of the City gate. All right, suggested another thief, what about doing over some of the

shops in the Goldsmith's Quarter? That seemed like a brilliant
suggestion, until Aziz remembered that three-quarters of the
goldsmiths paid Akram anti-theft insurance ('If your premium
is received within seven working days, you'll be entitled to
receive this fantastic combination coffee-maker/muezzin,
absolutely free!') and unfortunately, what with the Chief doing
all the paperwork and keeping the books, he hadn't a clue
which ones they were.

'This is pathetic,' observed Hanif, after an embarrassed
hush. 'Do you mean to say that without the Chief, nobody's
got the faintest idea what to do?'

Aziz nodded. 'You only really appreciate people when
they're not there any more,' he added sententiously.

Hanif shot him a glance suggesting that he'd relish the
opportunity to appreciate Aziz a whole lot. 'All right, then,' he
replied, 'so we need a leader. Let's choose a new one. Strictly
temporary,' he added quickly, 'until the Boss comes home.
Well, how about it?'

'Like who?'

Awkward silence. It occurred to thirty-nine thieves simultaneously that (a) Hanif's suggestion was extremely sensible,
and (b) whoever it was that got landed with the job of
explaining how sensible it was to Akram when he returned, it
wasn't going to be him. When the topic of promotion in a
bandit gang is discussed, the expression 'dead men's shoes'
tends to get used a lot, usually in the context of their being
found in a pit of quicklime.

'Well,' said Zulfiqar, licking his dry lips, 'there's only one
candidate, surely. I mean, who's been Akram's trusty right-
hand man for as long as any of us can remember?'

Denials froze on thirty-eight lips. Suddenly, everyone was
looking at Aziz.

'Who, me?' Aziz said, taking two steps backwards. 'Now
hang on a minute . . .'

'It's what he'd have wanted.'

'Natural choice. No question about it.'

'Every confidence.'

'But I'm stupid,' Aziz protested vehemently. 'Ask anybody. Thicko Aziz, makes two short planks look like Slimmer of the Year. You need brains to be a leader.'

The general consensus of the meeting seemed to be that the whole point of having brains was managing not to be a leader. That way, assuming you had brains, you might get to keep them. Aziz could feel tendrils of loyalty reaching out towards him like the tentacles of a giant squid.

'Let's take a vote on it,' said a voice at the back.

'Yeah.'

'*Vox populi, vox Dei.*'

A brief flurry of democracy later, Aziz was duly elected as, to quote the job description he drafted for himself, Acting Temporary Substitute Locum Caretaker Second-In-Command-In-Chief of the Thirty-Nine Thieves. There was a brief, improvised inauguration ceremony, in which the successful candidate was chased three times round a rocky outcrop, jumped on by his obedient henchmen and tied to a barrel. His henchmen then asked to know his pleasure.

'I'm your new leader, right?'

'Yes.'

'So you've got to do what I say?'

'Right.'

'Right. First off, elect a new bloody leader.'

'Get stuffed.'

Aziz sighed, mentally playing devil's advocate to the concept of constitutional monarchy. 'Okay,' he said, 'what about this? And this,' he added, 'is a real order.'

'Go on.'

Aziz swallowed hard and tried to sound stern. He was about as good at it as a bowl of thoroughly melted ice cream, but it was the best he could manage. 'My orders are,' he said, 'we find Akram. Preferably,' he added, 'before he finds us.'

There was a similar feeling of dislocation at the house of Ali Baba, when it was discovered that the Master had apparently gone off in the night with two small saddlebags, a packed lunch and the unspavined camel. The most demonstrative reaction came from Yasmin, the sloe-eyed houri who (although of course she didn't know it) was to have suggested the business with the palm-oil jars and the boiling water.

'*Bastard!*' she said.

She said a great deal more, too; best years of my life, when I think of all I've done for him, the grapes I've peeled, all that wobbly dancing with a chunk of glass in my belly-button . . . Grief-stricken, you might say. Desolate. Inconsolable.

So, while other members of the household busied themselves with various tasks incidental on the Master's departure, such as the removal of small, portable valuables to places of safety and calling on the estate agent to get the house on the market as quickly as possible, Yasmin stormed off to her room to do some serious sulking, although she did stop off at the Counting-House on the way in case there was any loose cash lying around that might prove a temptation to the servants.

'Coward,' she muttered under her breath – Ali Baba hadn't left any money on the desk, but he'd carelessly left a substantial sum in the safe hidden behind the sliding screen in the secret chamber under the false chimney-breast, where any Tom, Dick or Yusuf might find it – 'Spineless, gutless, yellow-livered—'

Of all the parts of a story, the Love Interest is probably the most resilient, and the nastiest to get on the wrong side of. A woman scorned is bad enough; a woman scorned when the glass slipper is, so to speak, millimetres from her foot is perhaps the most ferocious thing imaginable this side of a thermonuclear holocaust. As she stormed dramatically up the main staircase, she stopped for a moment to pick up an exquisite painted silk miniature of her beloved and press it fervently to her heart.

'You can run,' she said to it, 'but you can't hide.'

'Wait here,' Akram hissed.

The phoenix glowered at him and went on nibbling insulation off the telephone cable. It was amazing the effect that twenty thousand volts had on the creature; namely, none at all.

Squatting uncomfortably on the window-ledge, several hundred feet above Bloomsbury, Akram fished in his pocket for his folding jemmy. If his careful reconnaissance was correct, this window would get him in to the staff toilet on the top floor of the British Museum, leaving him the relatively simple task of making his way past an impenetrable jungle of electronic pratfalls, breaking into a reinforced glass case without making a sound, and then retracing his steps back to this window. The tricky part would be persuading the phoenix to let him climb on its back again.

'And don't be all night about it,' the phoenix called after him. 'Some of us do have better things to do than perching up draughty roofs in the freezing cold . . .'

It was still squawking when Akram, having dropped twelve feet onto a stone floor, landed feather-light and froze motionless. He listened. Apart from the distant sound of the phoenix complaining to the night air about Some People Who Have No Consideration For Others (owing to the nature of his somewhat irregular lifestyle he had never married, but there had been times when, trapped in a wardrobe or linen cupboard of a house he'd burgled, he'd had opportunities to eavesdrop on matrimony, so he knew what it sounded like) there was silence. A cistern dripped. Something electric hummed. Noises like these are the authentic sound of a building snoring. He relaxed and groped for the door.

It took him an hour of painstaking, heart-in-mouth work to reach the gallery where the glass case was. Naturally, he'd memorised the floor-plan and counted the number of paces from the door to the case, so the complete darkness was no handicap to him. He'd had the benefit of a year's apprenticeship with Foggy Mushtaq, the legendary blind burglar of Joppa, who had taught him that all in all, sight is the most expendable of a thief's five senses, and as he felt with the tip of a goose quill for the wires he had to cut, his eyes were in fact tightly shut. Snip. Job done.

'Psst.'

Once, for a joke, Daft Harit had woken his chief from a fitful doze by putting a handful of ice cubes, stolen five minutes earlier from the Emir's own ice-house, down the back of his neck. The fact that for the rest of his short life Daft Harit was known instead as One-Eared Harit is a tribute more to Akram's lightning reflexes than his ability to take a joke; but there had been a split second, a period of time so brief that there is no recognised unit of measurement small enough to quantify it, when he'd been completely at a loss and hadn't known whether he was coming or going. Thus, when the voice said 'Psst' a millimetre or so from his ear, a small voice in the outback of his brain groaned and muttered, *Shit, not again.*

Managing in the nick of time to countermand his instinctive reaction, Akram kept perfectly still and said, 'Hello?'

'Hello yourself.'

Go on then, be enigmatic, see if I care. 'Who's there?' he asked, as quietly and calmly as he could.

'Me.'

Maybe, Akram suggested to himself, I've actually fallen asleep on the job and this is a nightmare. 'Who's me?' he asked.

'Don't you know?'

'No.'

'Give you three guesses.'

'Look . . .'

'Go on. Three guesses.'

'All right. The Prophet Mohammed?'

'No.'

'Stanley Baldwin.'

'No.'

'Kenneth Branagh.'

'No. When I tell you, you'll kick yourself.'

Any minute now, said Akram to himself, a certain amount of kicking may well take place, but I doubt very much whether I shall be the recipient. 'Stop pratting about,' he hissed ferociously. 'Who are you?'

'I'm the djinn,' the voice replied. 'From inside the lamp inside this glass case. My name's Ibrahim Ali Khan, but my friends call me Curly.'

Akram's eyes were still shut so he couldn't close them as a symptom of frustrated disappointment. It was a bit of a blow, nevertheless; to go to all this trouble and then have your supposedly invincible magic djinn turn out to sound just like the ghost of Kenneth Williams. 'Curly,' he repeated.

''Cos I wear curly-toed shoes,' explained the djinn. 'Who're you?'

'My name is Akram the Terrible.'

'That's an unusual surname. And what's the V stand for?'

'Shut up.'

'No it doesn't, otherwise it'd be Akram S. Terrible.'

I could, of course, just leave, quietly and without fuss. There's nothing in the rules says I've *got* to take this pillock with me. On the other hand . . .

'Be quiet,' Akram whispered. 'And watch out, I'm going to break the glass.'

'Need any help?'

'No, thank you, I'm perfectly capable.'

Crack!

WHAAWHAAWHAAWHAAWHAAWHAA!

Bugger, snarled Akram under his breath, must have missed one. The noise was so loud that the shock of it paralysed him for a moment; it was like being in the same room as a forty-foot-high two-year-old who doesn't want to go to bed. Just a minute . . .

'What do you mean,' he demanded, shouting as loud as he could, 'need any help? How can you help me, you were inside the bloody glass case.'

'No I wasn't.'

Give me strength, Akram prayed, I shall need all the strength I can get if I'm going to kick this bugger's arse from here to Khorsabad. 'Then why,' he replied, 'didn't you say so?'

'You didn't ask. Would you like me to do something about that horrid noise?'

'Yes please.'

There was a fizz and a shower of sparks; and then a whole new set of alarms joined in, together with flashing lights, the fire bell and the sprinkler system. 'Drat,' said the djinn, 'wrong lever. Now then, I wonder if this is the one.'

'*Leave it alone!*'

While he was still shouting these words, Akram felt his feet move; his instincts had cut in and told him to move a minimum of eighteen inches to one side, or else. Half a second after he'd complied, a steel cage weighing a minimum of twelve tons came crashing down on the spot he'd just been standing on. The bad news was that he'd jumped the wrong way and was now trapped inside it.

'Well now,' said the djinn, 'we now know it's neither of those two levers. That just leaves these three. Right, then—'

'Please,' Akram begged, 'don't touch anything. Please stay absolutely still.'

'Is that a wish?'

'Huh?'

'You've got three wishes,' the djinn explained. 'If you ask me, that's a very silly thing to waste a whole wish on, but it's entirely up to you.'

'It's a wish.'

'To hear is to obey, O master,' the djinn replied huffily. 'Last thing I want to do is intrude where I'm not wanted.'

Now then, this cage. Can't lift it, can't get under it, can't get over it, can't squeeze through the bars, can't cut the bars, can't bend the bars, can't seem to see any counterweight mechanism that'll put the winch into reverse. How helpful it is to get all the dud alternatives out of the way before settling down to choose between what's left.

'You're stuck, aren't you?'

'No. I like it in here. You go away and leave me in peace.'

By the intermittent glare of the flashing red alarm lights, Akram studied the machinery above his head. There was a trapdoor in the ceiling, which explained why he hadn't seen the thing during his recce that afternoon. There was a chain, connected to a pulley and a winch.

'I'd hurry up, if I were you,' said the djinn. 'With all this racket going on, I wouldn't be at all surprised if someone didn't come and see what's up.'

'Gosh. I never thought of that.'

'Sarky.'

Akram forced himself to concentrate. 'Now then,' he said aloud, 'there's got to be some way of throwing that winch into reverse. Now it could be one of those other three levers – *don't touch anything!* – or it could be something else, like a remote control or a voice signal or something.' A silly joke flitted across his mind, the way they do at moments like this.

'Maybe,' he said bitterly, 'all I've got to do is say *Open sesame* . . .'

A moment later, he said 'Oh *shit!*'

Because the winch was purring, the cage was lifting. As soon as there was a ten-inch gap, Akram was through. Almost as an afterthought he grabbed for the lamp and stuffed it in his pocket.

'Wait for me!'

'It's all right,' Akram panted, taking the stairs three at a time, 'you're free. I give you your freedom. And that's a wish. Now bugger off.'

'Oh no you don't. You've no idea how *hurtful* that is. I think you're horrible.'

The window was still open. He could hear the hum of rotor blades, but he had a shrewd idea that the phoenix could outrun any helicopter yet made, and if it couldn't, that was going to be bad news for the helicopter. 'Phoenix,' he yelled, 'get ready, I'm coming through.'

'Oh there you are at last, what time do you call this, have you any idea how boring it is just hanging aimlessly about . . .'

Akram scrambled onto the windowsill, just as the door flew open and someone shouted 'Freeze!' His last thought, as he flung himself over the edge and hoped the phoenix was under him, was a fervent wish that his pursuer would open fire and inadvertently shoot the djinn.

'I heard that, you pig!'

Falling. Cue past life? Apparently not. Flump!

'Yow!' shrieked the phoenix. 'That hurt!'

'Good,' Akram replied. 'Now get me out of here.'

As the huge wings slashed at the air, and the slipstream tried to rip his head off, Akram couldn't help thinking about his recent experiences, with particular reference to the iron cage and the voice-operated winch. Specifically; either it was a remarkable coincidence that the password should be what it was, or else there was a sick mind at work here. No prizes for guessing which explanation Akram favoured.

'Djinn.'

'Like I told you,' the djinn replied, 'my friends call me Curly.'

'Djinn,' Akram repeated, 'does the name Ali Baba mean anything to you?'

'No,' replied the djinn. 'Should it?'

'How about that cage thing? Presumably you were about the place when it was installed. Can you remember who the contractor was?'

'Ah,' replied the djinn, 'now then. I'm positive I can remember. Oooh, it's on the tip of my tongue, really it is. Something beginning with L, I think, yes, I'm sure it was. Oh dear, it's nearly . . . that's it! Got it. Ltd.'

'What?'

'The contractor's name,' said the djinn proudly, 'was Ltd. They had it written on the backs of their jackets and their toolboxes and things. Can't remember the first name, I'm afraid, but the surname was definitely—'

'Djinn.'

'Yes?'

'Piss off.'

'Well, of all the—'

'Djinn.'

'I'm not talking to you.'

'Ah,' Akram sighed, putting his arms behind his head and lying back on his feather bed. 'That's more like it.'

CHAPTER SIX

Nobody knows where King Solomon originally got it from. One influential school of thought believes that it must have been one of those mail order catalogues, the sort that are crammed with apparently indispensable gadgets – combination distress flare/corkscrews and solar-powered trouser presses – which get bought, used rapturously once, and then are quietly forgotten about. Others hold that something so ingenious and inherently futile must have been a Christmas present, except that Solomon lived a thousand years before the Three Wise Men first stopped off en route to Bethlehem to buy brightly coloured paper and string. A similar veil of mystery hangs over how it got from the Royal Treasury at Jerusalem to Akram's cave. From then on, however, its history is fairly well documented.

Ali Baba, having retrieved it from Yusuf the monkey, took it with him as far as the frontier where, like so many others, he stopped off at Jim's Diner and got talking to a garrulous bear. Not long after that, he found himself at a wedding, where he traded the ring in exchange for free passage to Reality and a new identity. When the best man discovered the small hole in his waistcoat pocket just before the climax of the ceremony, the ring was hurriedly pressed into service, with the result that the bride had a brief but disconcerting chat with a woodlouse before she remembered what she was there for and finally said, 'I do.' After that, it stayed in the bride's family for many generations, during which time it somehow crossed the border into Reality and started causing no end of trouble until, in the early seventeenth century its owner for the time being, who lived alone and used the ring to talk to her three cats, came to a warm and uncomfortable end at the hands of an officer of the infallible British legal system called Matthew Hopkins, Witchfinder General. Some time later, a bit out of shape and blackened by fire, it was found by a farm labourer by the name of Ezekiel Partridge, who had just remembered on his way home from work that today was his wife's birthday.

When she got home from the dentist's, Michelle put it in an empty coffee tin in the cupboard under the kitchen sink and tried very hard not to think about it. This excellent resolution lasted two whole days, during which not one household appliance tried to talk to her. This should have been reassuring, but it wasn't; all Michelle got was a strong feeling of having been sent to Coventry by her own possessions. On the third day, therefore, she pulled out the coffee tin, screwed the ring back on her finger and demanded a full explanation from the tumble-drier.

'Not talking to you,' it replied.

'Don't give me that,' Michelle snapped. 'I know you know what's going on. Am I going mad, or aren't I?'

She sat back on her heels and waited. No reply. 'Well?'

'Tell your friend,' said the tumble-drier to the microwave oven, 'that people who go around hiding magic rings and slamming cupboard doors don't deserve to get spoken to.'

'Magic rings?' Michelle repeated blankly.

'Some people,' the tumble-drier went on, 'ought to remember there's others less fortunate than themselves who'd give anything to have a nice magic ring that'd make them able to talk to inanimate objects. Some people should be jolly grateful, instead of flouncing about the place being all melodramatic.'

'Just a minute.' Michelle closed her eyes and took a deep breath. 'If I say I'm sorry,' she said, 'and promise never to do it again, will you please explain what you meant by magic rings and talking to inanimate objects? Please?'

'Oh all right,' the tumble-drier relented. 'Just this once.'

Once, as far as Michelle was concerned, was probably quite enough. The tale took a while in the telling, especially since the toaster kept butting in and contradicting the tumble-drier on small, irrelevant details, whereupon the blender told the toaster not to use that tone of voice when talking to the tumble-drier (interesting, thought Michelle; I always thought there was something going on between those two) and then the deep fat fryer and the slow cooker and the microwave got involved, until the whole thing threatened to degenerate into a free-for-all, like a bar-room fight in a Western. It was only by threatening to switch the electricity off at the mains that Michelle was able to restore order.

'Quite right,' agreed the fridge. 'Should be ashamed of yourselves, carrying on like a lot of humans.'

'Thank you,' Michelle said, making a mental note to defrost her new ally some day soon, as a token of gratitude. 'Now then, where were we?'

'Your Aunt Fatima,' replied the answering machine.

('That's so like an answering machine,' whispered the fan-assisted oven. 'Always got to have the last word.'

'Shush!')

'Your Aunt Fatima,' said the answering machine. 'Actually, she coped marvellously well, considering she had the ring for what, sixty-five years. At first she did her best to be fairly discreet about it all, you know, only talked to things when she was on her own and there was no chance of being overheard. As time went on, though, and she got older and more disillusioned with her fellow humans, I think she really preferred talking to things, on the grounds that they're more sensible and she was more likely to have an intelligent conversation with them. Which,' it added smugly, 'is perfectly reasonable, if you ask me.'

'You're prejudiced,' interrupted the kitchen clock. 'That's just because whenever they talk to you they get all shy and flustered and can't think of anything to say. Some humans,' it added benignly, 'are all right once you get to know them.'

'Some of my best friends are humans,' the answering machine replied. 'The fact remains—'

'Please.' The needle of Michelle's patience was deep into the red zone by now. 'You were saying.'

'That's about it, really,' said the answering machine. 'I mean, the poor old soul knew perfectly well that everybody thought she was dotty, but so what? She knew she wasn't, and when you get to that age you stop worrying too much about what people think about you. Besides, she'd worked hard all her life, cooking and cleaning and washing and ironing without ever a word of thanks. When she realised that if you're dotty, they give you a nice room with a telly to talk to and three meals a day you don't have to cook yourself, she began to wonder if maybe sanity's everything it's cracked up to be. No pun intended.'

'Dunno what you mean by that,' grunted the Hoover sourly. 'When it comes to housework, humans don't know they're born. I mean, they're not the ones who've got to crawl around on their hands and knees breathing in bits of dust and fluff all day.'

'Take no notice,' said the pressure cooker. 'She's always a bit uptight when her bag needs emptying.'

Michelle took a deep breath. 'So,' she said, 'I'm not going crazy after all, is that it?'

'You got it,' said the blender reassuringly. 'It's when you start talking to yourself all the time that you should start worrying.'

'I resent that,' growled the CD player.

'I mean,' went on the answering machine, 'if you're potty for talking to us, then by the same token we'd be potty for talking to you. And a saner collection of consumer durables than us you couldn't hope to meet.'

'Not like that lot at number six,' agreed the toaster. 'Mad as hatters the lot of 'em.'

'I see,' said Michelle. 'And this, er, gift. Does it mean I can talk to, well, anything?'

'Anything mechanical,' replied the toaster. 'Or electrical. If it's got moving parts, or it does things when you switch it on, you're in business. I mean, you *can* talk to spades and walls and socks if you really want to, but you'll be wasting your breath.'

'Standoffish?' Michelle asked.

'Thick,' the toaster said. 'Just plain stupid.'

'Cheap inanimate trash,' agreed the blender. 'Like animals and birds. You can talk to them too, incidentally, but why the hell bother?'

'I expect you're wondering,' said the dishwasher, 'whether all this is going to affect what you might call our working relationship.'

'I was coming to that,' said Michelle. 'Like the Hoover said just now. I mean, when you stop to think of it, some of the things I ask you guys to do for me are just awful. For instance—'

'Don't worry about it,' said the answering machine. 'The loo's seen it all before and the washing machine's very broad-minded. Basically we're on your side, although a little thought and consideration is always appreciated.'

'One big happy family,' agreed the toaster.

There was a sudden, embarrassed silence. At first, Michelle was at a loss; then something began to tickle inside the lining of her subconscious. 'Family,' she repeated.

'Me and my big slots,' groaned the toaster.

'Anyone fancy a nice cup of tea?' said the kettle, its voice brittle with artificial cheerfulness. 'Just say the word and I'll pop myself on.'

'Maybe,' Michelle went on, 'you guys can tell me something about that. You seem to be extremely well informed about a lot of things.'

'Bugger.'

'Well?'

'All right,' said the answering machine, 'she had to find out sooner or later. Look, you know the sort of fairy story where the little baby gets thrown out by its wicked stepmother, and then a pack of wolves or a family of hyaenas or something take pity on it and bring it up as their own child?'

Michelle nodded. 'Go on,' she said.

'Well,' continued the answering machine, a trifle self-consciously. 'That's us.'

'You probably know him,' Aziz said with a sense of growing helplessness. 'Great big tall feller, swarthy, evil-looking bugger. Wicked glint in his eye. Ghastly leering smile, way of looking at you that makes you think he's deciding what bit of you to cut off first.'

Prince Charming hesitated, sucking his teeth, before answering. 'And you really want to find this bloke, do you?' he replied. 'If it was me, I'd just be damn glad he'd gone and change all the locks quick.'

When a story breaks down, it doesn't just muck up the lives of its own characters. The chaos spreads, as the characters stray aimlessly into other stories in which they have no part, until the very fabric of Make-Believe as we know it quivers on the brink of catastrophe.

'He's our boss,' Aziz replied. 'I dunno, we're sort of lost without him.'

A tiny flicker crossed Prince Charming's face as he made a connection in his brain. As a rule he didn't do much thinking – fair enough; blacksmiths don't do much brain surgery, either – but on this occasion he was prepared to extend himself.

'Which makes you?' he asked.

'Thieves,' Aziz replied.

'I see,' the Prince said, smiling rigidly, while the hand behind his back was making frantic gestures to the troop of heavily armed Palace Guards waiting a few yards away. 'Well, sorry I can't help, very best of luck and all that . . .'

Aziz sighed. 'If you do happen to come across him,' he said, and then broke off. 'Faisal,' he shouted angrily, 'put it *back*! We're not at home now, you know.'

'Sorry, Az— I mean, Skip. Force of habit.'

'And the Chamberlain's gold watch.'

'What? Oh, right, silly me, how did that come to be up my sleeve? Sorry.'

'And that sauceboat thing; you know, the glass one in the shape of a slip— You daft bugger, now look what you've gone and done.'

'Sorry, Skip.'

They stood for a moment, looking at the shattered fragments of the glass slipper. Aziz considered offering to stick it back together again with glue, but decided against it. An all-the-king's-horses job if ever he'd seen one. Pity, that. He hoped it wasn't valuable.

'Forget it,' sighed the Prince, flicking broken glass off the toe of his shoe. 'We were on the point of packing it in as a bad job, anyway. God only knows why we started this ruddy wild goose chase in the first place. All right, lads, that's it for tonight. Back to the palace.'

Aziz watched them depart, and breathed a sigh of relief. For one moment it had looked as if an unpleasant situation was about to develop. Still, all's well that ends well.

'Where to now, boss?'

'Let's see.' Aziz unfolded the map and scratched his head. The map was the wrong way up, but that didn't matter terribly much. 'Let's try over there,' he said.

Three hours later, after a highly bewildering tramp through a forest that suddenly seemed to spring up out of nowhere all around them, they came to a picturesque little cottage in a clearing. Fingers Hassan had smashed a window and got his lazy tongs round the catch before Aziz noticed the door was ajar. He pushed it, called out, 'Hello!' and walked in.

It was – well, spooky. There was a table, and three sweet little chairs; one big chair, one middling chair and one little chair. And on the table were three plates and three cups, similarly in sizes L, M and S, and up against the far wall, three beds, likewise. There was porridge in the bowls, milk in the cups and a cheerful fire crackling in the hearth, but nobody about.

'Hello?' Aziz repeated, his hand tightening on the hilt of his sword. 'Anybody at home?'

Silence. Three pairs of slippers – enormous slippers, medium-large slippers and dear little slippers. Three night-gowns, hung tidily on hooks. Three—

'Skip! Look out!'

Aziz whirled round, his sword out of its scabbard and on guard before he stopped moving. The door had burst open, and framed in the doorway was a gigantic bear. At the sight of Aziz and his companions, the huge beast reared up on its hind legs and growled, displaying a mouthful of long yellow fangs. Faisal, who was nearest the door, stood rooted to the spot, obviously paralysed with terror. It was time, Aziz realised, for decisive action. What would the Boss do? Easy.

With one bound, Aziz leapt at the bear, sword raised. The monster lunged forward to meet him, and as it did so, Aziz could see another bear, only a little smaller, following hard on its heels; and behind that, the dim shape of a third.

A moment later, it was all over. The largest of the terrible creatures lay dead on the cottage floor. The second largest – it had made up for it by its unspeakable ferocity – had slunk off into the forest to lick its wounds. The third had bolted before any of the thieves had engaged it. Aziz sheathed his sword with a grunt of satisfaction, and sank back onto the nearest bed.

It was all too easy to work out what had become of the three unfortunates – woodcutters, probably, or homesteaders – who had strayed this far into the wild wood, built this heartbreakingly twee little home for themselves and fallen victim to the merciless predators. If only, Aziz muttered to himself, we'd come this way a day or so earlier, we might have saved them . . .

Just a minute. What am I saying?

Saved them? Dammit, we're *villains*. Baddies. Baddies don't go around saving people, you could get chucked out of the union. Handsome princes and knights errant save people; that's what they're for.

Aziz felt slightly sick.

'Lads,' he croaked, 'I don't like this. There's something funny going on around here.'

'What?'

'Us,' the answering machine repeated. 'We found you, took pity on you, and brought you up as our own. Don't stare like that, dammit, it's rude. You wouldn't be taking on so if we were wolves.'

'But you're *machines*.' Michelle stuttered, when she was finally able to speak. 'How could . . .?'

'Ungrateful little madam,' huffed the iron.

'Typical,' agreed the blender. 'You take them in, give them the best years of your life, and then they don't want to know you.'

'I'm sorry,' Michelle whimpered. 'Look, will someone please explain? Starting, if at all possible, at the beginning.'

The answering machine was sulking, so the deep fat fryer took up the story. 'Once upon a time,' it said, 'there was this flat, right? To let, fully furnished. We're the fully furnished. And there we were, minding our own business, when suddenly we wake up one morning and there's this entirely unexpected and inexplicable new-born human child lying screaming its head off on our doormat.'

'Never been the same since, that doormat,' complained the freezer. 'Paranoid. Curls its edges up if you so much as look at it.'

'Well,' continued the fryer, 'what were we to do? We took a vote on it, and decided we'd just have to look after you till your owner turned up. And we did.'

'Hard work,' growled the Hoover. 'No labour-saving humans to do half the work for us. Guess who had to change your nappies. Yuk!'

'And it's not as if we had the faintest idea how to go about it,' added the tumble-drier. 'You always seemed to be breaking down or going wrong. I was all for sending you back, at least while you were still under warranty.'

'Fortunately,' said the answering machine, who'd decided to stop sulking, 'the TV was able to work out the basic ground-rules from watching soap operas and the like . . .'

'We were going to call you Krystle originally,' said the toaster. 'Only then we found the name Michelle on your receipt, so we guessed you were called that at the factory, so—'

'Receipt?' Michelle interrupted.

'The bit of paper that came with you,' explained the tumble-drier. 'Dunno whatever became of that. I think once your warranty period expired we chucked it out.'

'Anyway,' the answering machine went on, 'as time went on we worked out what we had to do with you. The telly taught you to speak, the cooker did your food, the Hoover—'

'Don't keep harping on about it,' moaned the Hoover. 'Scarred me for life, probably.'

'The phone did an awful lot,' the answering machine went on. 'Rang up the school and enrolled you as a pupil. Sent for the doctor when you broke down. Made your dentist's appointments. Tapped into the bank's computer and diverted money to an Access account to pay the bills and everything. Like a mother to you, that phone.'

Michelle hung her head in shame. It was no more than four months since she'd finally slung out the old dial-fronted phone and treated herself to a flash new cordless walkabout.

'Of course,' said the fridge, 'there was the problem of how to account for it all. Please bear in mind that until tonight, we were never able to talk to you. Actually, we honestly thought you knew about us – you know, what we've been to you all these years – or at least had some sort of inkling ... But apparently not. Ah well.'

'Don't,' Michelle said, choking back a sob.

'But,' said the answering machine, 'we were realistic enough to tumble to the fact that one day you were going to start asking questions; where's my mummy, where's my daddy, all that jazz. A problem, yes?'

'So,' interrupted the toaster, 'we hypnotised you.'

'Hypnotised . . .!'

The answering machine blinked a red light. 'Remember the old pendulum clock, used to hang on your bedroom wall? Piece of cake, apparently. Once you were under, of course, we were able to communicate with your subconscious, or whatever the expression is – the TV knows all the technical terms, you'd better ask her – and just sort of sweep all that stuff under the carpet, so to speak. And then, when you were, oh, eleven . . .'

'Twelve and a half.'

'Was it? My memory. Anyway, the phone called your school with some cock-and-bull story about your family getting wiped out in a car crash, and we sent you away to a boarding school, so you could grow up with your own kind.'

'Nearly blew our fuses,' sniffed the cooker. 'After twelve years, you were just like our own little baby.'

What's a baby cooker, Michelle couldn't help asking herself. Toasted sandwich maker, perhaps?

'And that's it, more or less,' the answering machine concluded. 'Oh, except for your aunt. The one who had the ring.'

Michelle gulped. 'Aunt Fatty,' she said.

'That's right. Came as a real shock, I can tell you. Must have been when you were six, maybe seven. This woman rang, asking to speak to your phone.'

'You mean me?'

'No,' replied the answering machine sternly. 'Haven't you been listening? Anyway, that was weird enough, finding a human who could talk to us. Then when she said our little Michelle was her great-niece . . .'

'I see.'

'Not,' continued the toaster, 'that we were able to get anything useful out of her, like who your mum and dad were or what happened to them. Clammed up on us, as soon as she found out you were all right. She did say she'd like to see you, so we made a note of the address and put it into your mind under hypnosis.'

'She left a tape for you,' said the answering machine, 'on

me. But,' it went on guiltily, 'it got wiped. Not my fault, I can't actually change my own tapes, and you wouldn't take a hint.'

'Can you remember what she said?'

'Certainly not,' replied the answering machine, offended. 'You think I eavesdrop on people's private conversations?'

There was a long silence.

'Well,' said Michelle eventually. 'I don't know what to say. I—'

The washing machine hummed. '*Thanks* might be a convenient starting point,' it said acidly. 'Twenty-seven years washing your underwear, there must be some kind of medal.'

'I am most frightfully grateful,' Michelle hastened to say. 'Really I am. But, well, it's been a bit of a shock.'

'Not good enough for you, are we?' grumbled the tumble-drier. 'You'd have preferred blue blood in your veins rather than alternating current? Well, young lady, I'm afraid it's a bit too late to do anything about that now.'

'Be fair,' replied the Hoover indulgently, 'it hasn't been easy for the kid, she's missed out on a lot. I mean, boyfriends, for one thing. Imagine how embarrassing it'd have been if she'd ever wanted to bring a boy home to meet her folks.'

'Please.' Michelle looked round pleadingly, and the chattels fell silent. 'I owe you so much already, but can you please try and find out who my parents were? My real parents, I mean. You see, I've never thought about it before, and now—'

'It's all right,' cooed the dishwasher. 'Now look what you've done, you've made her cry. Kettle, put yourself on.'

'Actually,' muttered the answering machine. 'We don't *know*, of course, but we've sort of guessed . . .'

'Call it electrical intuition.'

Michelle froze. 'Who?' she demanded. 'Come on, you've got to tell me.'

The answering machine beeped. The other appliances were silent.

'Oh come *on*,' Michelle shouted. 'Answering machine, you obviously know something. For pity's sake!'

'Look, it's only a guess. We're probably wrong.'

'Answering machine!'

'*Hello, I'm sorry there's no one here to take your call but if you leave your name and telephone num—*'

'Machine!'

'Oh all right.' The answering machine rewound itself, hummed and crackled a little, as if clearing its throat. 'We think your father may possibly be—'

And then the fuses blew.

CHAPTER SEVEN

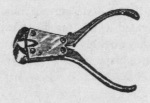

'Stay,' Akram commanded. '*Good* bird.'

The phoenix glowered at him, but he took no notice. Good bedsits are hard to come by, and the photocopied sheet he'd been given said categorically NO PETS. If he'd been inclined to argue the point, he could have made out a case for the phoenix being an instrument of vengeance, not a pet; but there was probably a supplemental photocopied sheet headed NO INSTRUMENTS OF VENGEANCE, which would glide through his letterbox the very next morning if he tried to be all jesuitical about it. Between daring escapades, therefore, the phoenix lived in a small lock-up unit on the industrial estate, which Akram rented by the week. And if the landlords wanted to take him to task over it, let them; he'd have no difficulty whatsoever in establishing that the phoenix was perfectly legitimate plant and equipment for use in his trade or profession.

He locked up, walked home and let himself in. Just as he was about to switch on the light, a faint noise froze him in his tracks. There was someone in the room.

It happens. Just as undertakers die, policemen get parking tickets and commissioners of inland revenue pay taxes, professional thieves do sometimes get burgled. A tiny spurt of pity flared in his mind for the poor fool of a fellow-artisan who'd been to all the trouble of busting in here to find there was nothing worth stealing, and who would very soon be getting the kicking of a lifetime. He sidled in, closed the door noiselessly, and listened.

Whoever it was must have heard his key in the lock, because the room was completely silent; the sort of silence that proves beyond question that something's up. Akram knew the score; he leaned against the door, drew a long, thin-bladed knife from the side of his boot, and waited.

Five minutes later, he decided that he couldn't be bothered, and switched on the light. To his amazement, there was nobody there. His establishment wasn't large enough to afford concealment to a cockroach, let alone a felon. Imagination playing tricks? Misinterpreted plumbing? Surely not. Akram had relied implicitly on the accuracy of his senses long enough to know that they could be trusted implicitly. He frowned.

Then the penny dropped. He'd switched on the overhead light, and the standard lamp had come on. He stepped smartly over to the lamp, knocked it over and put his foot on the place where the bulb should have been. 'Gitahtavit,' he snapped.

Under the toe of his boot, the tiny ball of light squirmed. 'Ouch,' it said, 'you're hurting.'

'I'll hurt a damn sight more in a minute,' Akram replied. 'Stop pissing me about. Last thing I need after a hard day is to spend half an hour on my hands and knees scrubbing squashed pixie out of the carpet.'

'All right,' the pixie sighed, 'it's a fair cop, I'll come quietly.' Akram lifted his toe a quarter of an inch and the ball of light edged out a little way. On closer examination it proved to be a three-inch-high young woman in ballet-costume, with rather crumpled wings, a black mask over her face and a sack over her shoulder, on the side of which Akram could just make out the word SWAG.

'Oh come *on*,' Akram grunted scornfully. 'This is ridiculous.'

'Not my fault,' the pixie replied defensively. 'Victim of circumstances, that's what I am. Indicative of a deep-seated malaise in modern society that threatens to undermine—'

'You what?'

'Take your bloody great foot off my chest and I'll explain.'

It was a sad and, by and large, convincing story. Modern toothpastes, innovative toothbrush design and a greater public awareness of the need for preventive dental hygiene had led to forty per cent redundancies in the corps of tooth fairies. The redundancy money hadn't lasted long, and career opportunities for tiny luminous flying people are few and far between. Six months ago she'd faced the stark choice: starve or steal.

'I even tried going on the streets,' she said mournfully. 'Bought myself a red filter and everything. But nobody was interested. People can be very cruel sometimes.'

Akram shook his head. 'Get up,' he said, not unkindly. 'When did you last eat?'

'About half an hour ago,' replied the pixie. 'I raided your fridge. You want to chuck that milk out, by the way. There's things living in it that are larger than I am.'

'You're not very good at this, are you?'

'Not very,' the pixie replied with a shrug. 'Getting in and out's no problem, I'm used to that, naturally. It's the carting stuff off that fazes me. When the bulkiest load you're used to is a second-hand incisor, video recorders can be quite a challenge.'

'I could tell you weren't a pro,' Akram replied. 'Too noisy, for one thing.'

'You startled me,' the pixie said. 'So what are you going to do?'

Akram shrugged. 'Well,' he said, 'I'm not going to turn you in or anything, if that's what you're getting at. I mean, if I were to go banging on the door of the police station at half past two in the morning saying I've effected a citizen's arrest and have they got an empty matchbox handy, they'd probably tell me to go home and sleep it off. On the other hand,' he went on, as a faint light dawned inside his brain, 'we might be able to help each other. If you're interested, that is.'

'Shoot.'

Akram sat down on the radiator and drew his left heel up to his right knee. 'For reasons I won't bore you with,' he said, 'I could use a tiny winged assistant for a little job I've got lined up.'

'This job pay money, by any chance?'

'Saucer of milk a day and a shoebox with an old vest in it,' replied Akram. 'Take it or leave it.'

'Done. When do I start?'

'Tomorrow night,' Akram replied. 'Just one thing, though. The light. Can you turn it down?'

At once the pixie dimmed to a faint glow. 'Better?' she asked.

'Fine. You'll also need rubber boots and wirecutters. There's quite a lot of electrical work involved, you see.'

Quickly and concisely, Akram explained what the job involved.

'That's fine,' the pixie replied. 'Piece of cake. Talking of which . . .'

After he'd given the pixie some milk and made its shoe-box – they can't get *Blue Peter* in Story-book Land, even with a dish aerial, but Akram made a reasonable fist of it just by light of nature – he cut himself some stale bread, washed it down with tapwater, shoved the lamp he'd just stolen under the mattress, lay down on the bed and immediately fell asleep. A pale yellow glow hovered above the shoe-box for a while, and then went out.

Ten minutes later, Akram sat up, switched the light back on and said, 'Ouch.'

The yellow glow reappeared. 'Problem?' asked the pixie.

'Sort of,' replied Akram out of the corner of his mouth. 'I've got toothache.'

'Let's have a look.' The glow floated up, circled Akram's head and swooped into his open mouth like a rook pitching on a newly sown field. 'Ah yes,' came its voice from inside, 'I can see what the matter is.'

'You can?' Akram said, trying his level best not to swallow.

'I was a tooth fairy, remember? You've got a damn great cavity in the lower right back molar. If I was still in business, I'd give you sixpence for it like a shot. You need to see a dentist quick.'

'Get out of my mouth before you go down the wrong way,' Akram replied. 'Sod it,' he added as the pixie emerged, wiping its feet carefully on the pillow. 'You know any good dentists? I don't. New in these parts,' he added.

'I know just the bloke,' the pixie replied. She dictated a name and address, which Akram wrote down on the back of his hand. 'The sooner you get that seen to,' she went on, 'the better. Quite like old times, that was.'

'So glad,' Akram growled. 'Now bugger off and let me try and get some sleep. We've both got a long day ahead of us tomorrow.'

'G'night.' The pixie yawned. 'By the way,' she said. 'Did I tell you my name?'

'No. Can't it wait?'

'Be like that. Just thought, since we're going to be working together and everything . . .'

'Go on, then.'

'My name,' announced the pixie, 'is Fang.'

'Fang?'

''Sright. After my gran on my mother's side.'

'I thought you people had sweet, quaint little names like Tinkerbell and Mustard-seed,' Akram said, frowning a little. 'Fang – well, it's a bit on the aggressive side, isn't it? I mean, it's hardly designed to put wee kiddies at their ease.'

'I think it's a nice name,' replied Fang, nettled. 'If it helps, try thinking of me as a dimensionally challenged ivory poacher. Good night.'

'Fang,' replied Akram, with mild distaste. 'I'm going to have trouble with that, I can tell. How'd it be if I called you Fangelina? Just for convenience, you understand?'

'How'd it be if you woke up with a mouthful of empty gums?' retorted the pixie. 'Sleep tight.'

'It's all right,' said the torch reassuringly. 'It's only the fuse. What do you expect if you talk to a whole kitchenful of electrical apparatus?'

'Oh good,' Michelle said. 'Look—'

'Wouldn't want your next electric bill, either,' the torch added. 'Talking, it uses up the old juice for a pastime. Here we are. You know how to change a fuse?'

'Well . . .'

'It's dead simple,' said the fusebox cheerfully. 'Right, first you pull down the switch on your left . . .'

Michelle believed in electricity in the same way a medieval monk believed in God; she recognised its existence, but held that even to attempt to understand its ways was somehow blasphemous. She did as she was told. The lights went on.

'Thank you,' she said.

'You're welcome,' replied the fusebox. 'Have a nice day.'

She hurried back to the kitchen. Somehow, the interruption had allowed her to order her thoughts and form a judgement on what she'd experienced; and the verdict was that just because the whole thing was plumb crazy didn't necessarily mean it wasn't true. Furthermore, it had better be true, or else she was off her trolley good and proper. The least she could do, in deference to her belief in her own sanity, was play along and see what came next.

'Sorry about that,' she said breathlessly to the kitchen. 'Now, where were we?'

There was an awkward silence.

'Sorry about this,' said the answering machine awkwardly – Michelle could visualise the other gadgets giving it a sort of telepathic shove forward – 'But while the power was off, we've been talking this through, and, by a *majority* decision' – The way it said *majority* spoke volumes – 'we've decided that really, we oughtn't to say anything more. Wouldn't be fair. Um.'

'Don't be silly,' Michelle answered firmly. 'Come on, you lot, spit it out.'

'Look—'

'No,' Michelle interrupted, 'you look, the lot of you. Now, don't get me wrong, I really am terribly grateful for everything you've done for me; really, I don't know what to say. But if you know something about who I am and where I actually came from, you've got to tell me.' She paused; she didn't really want to do this.

'Or?'

'Or,' Michelle went on, 'I happen to know where I can get a very good deal on a brand new Zanussi ceramic hob cooker with eye-level grill and fan-assisted oven. And they say they'll give me twenty quid minimum part exchange on my exist-ing—'

The cooker shrieked and started to sob. The rest of the kitchen was as quiet as the grave.

'And if that doesn't do the trick,' Michelle went on, hating herself as she did so, 'Currys in the precinct has got this special offer on combination answering machine/faxes which is really tempting, they're virtually giving them away, so—'

'You *bitch*!' screamed the answering machine. 'That'd be

worse than murder. To think that a human of mine . . .'

'Where did we go wrong?' sobbed the toaster. 'Dear God, she's virtually our own flex and solder.'

'Sorry,' said Michelle, 'but I mean it. I'll do it if I have to.'

'She's bluffing,' the kettle growled. 'Don't listen to her.'

Michelle opened a drawer. 'This is an Argos catalogue,' she said slowly, 'the most comprehensive listing of consumer goods in the country. Now, I want you to ask yourself; do you feel lucky?'

'Electrocute the bitch,' yelled the blender. 'We've got friends, you know. You'll never dare sit under the drier in the hairdressers' again.'

'All right,' said the freezer, 'cool it, everybody, before we all get hysterical. Look at it this way: we've done our best to talk her out of it. If she wants to hear it, that's her decision. And as for you,' it went on – it couldn't fix Michelle with an icy stare, but she knew that somehow it was putting her in her place good and proper – 'you know you didn't mean any of what you said, now, did you?'

'I guess not,' Michelle replied, letting her head droop. 'It was just . . .'

'Put down the catalogue, easy does it. Well, thank goodness for that. Now we can talk it through like sensible, grown-up artefacts.'

Michelle sank down onto the kitchen table, exhausted. The air seemed to crackle with extravagant static. Next time, Michelle said to herself, remembering what the torch had said, when I want to have an emotional scene with my household, I'd better do it late at night on Economy Seven.

'What I'm going to tell you,' the freezer went on, 'is mostly sheer guesswork. I want you to remember that, because we may have got completely the wrong end of the stick. After all, we're just machines and things; what we don't know about humans could be written in small print on the back of a one-to-one scale map of the Southern Hemisphere. Now, provided you realise that, I'll tell you our theory. Don't suppose you'll believe it for an instant, but that's your problem. It'll serve you right.'

'Ready,' Michelle said, sitting up straight. 'Fire away.'

'All right then,' continued the freezer, 'look at it this way. Do you really think it's likely, in the back end of the twentieth century, that someone'd be nasty enough or stupid enough to dump a newly born baby down in a furnished flat in Southampton and then just walk away and leave it there? Think about it. It's just not on, is it?'

'Not really,' Michelle agreed.

'Exactly. Not in real life, anyway. Now then, think a little. Where do things like that happen? I mean, where would it be believable? Or rather, where could you be expected to believe that someone could do such a thing?'

'Dunno.'

The freezer paused for a moment, and the silence seemed to announce – WARNING: CULTURE SHOCK APPROACHING. 'In a story,' the freezer said. 'A folk-tale, maybe, or a children's story. Mowgli. Moses in the bullrushes. Romulus and Remus. In fairy stories, you're supposed to believe, you can't go for an afternoon stroll through the woods without tripping over nose-to-tail foundling children, all abandoned by wicked step-mothers and waiting to be adopted by passing wildlife. Ring any bells?'

'Go on.'

'I need hardly remind you,' said the freezer expression-lessly, 'of the old Sherlock Holmes thing about when you've eliminated the impossible, then what remains, however impossible, et cetera. Well, it's impossible, as far as we can see, that a real life mother would dump her kiddy like that. In a hospital waiting room, in a church porch—'

'Left luggage office at Euston station,' interrupted the

answering machine; occasionally it received stray radio signals, which made it put on literary airs.

'But not,' said the freezer, 'a flat in a brand new purpose-built block, with the rent paid up six months in advance, tenancy agreement in the name of Smith. And yes, there are possible explanations if you work at it; mummy and daddy kidnapped by aliens, that sort of thing. Up to you what tickles you as a theory. What we think is, you're somehow part of a story.'

'Ah.'

'Told you you wouldn't like it. We think that you were born in a story and abandoned here, probably by a wicked stepmother, because it's as far away from story-book land as it's possible to get. No way backwards and forwards between fantasy and reality, you see. If this hypothetical stepmother had dumped you in the forest or on a mountainside over there in fantasy, it'd be all Piccadilly to a second-hand jockstrap that you'd be found, brought up by a family of tender-hearted iguanas or some such, and revealed at the crucial moment by some token left with you in your cot just in time to unmask the wicked queen and marry the handsome prince. Inevitable. Absolutely inconceivable that anything else could happen. With me so far?'

'I hear what you say,' Michelle replied cautiously. 'Do go on.'

'All right. So, you're born in a story, but someone's prepared to go to really extraordinary lengths to keep you out of it; namely, marooning you on the other side of the line. You know what that suggests to me? No? All right, try this. You got born into a story where you had no place to be.'

'Say that again,' Michelle said.

'This time, try listening. Suppose there's a story, right, where the beautiful and virtuous servant girl eventually, after a series of curious and picturesque adventures, marries the handsome prince. Now, just suppose that along the way somewhere, said maiden's been extremely friendly with the second footman or the gardener or an elf selling door to door, and is untimely up the spout. Serious problem. Not possible in a fairy story, of course; you get the impression that the boys and girls don't get issued with the necessary bits and pieces until the story's over; desperately frustrating for them, no wonder Freud was so interested in fairy-tales. But just suppose.'

'All right,' Michelle said. 'I must say, for a refrigerator you've got one hell of an imagination.'

'So,' the freezer said, 'here's the embarrassing little bundle of joy, let's get rid of it. And so, here you are. It'd all be completely incredible if it wasn't for the fact that you're now the rather confused owner of one fully functional, no-previous-experience-needed magic ring, bequeathed to you by a mysterious female relative who suddenly pops up out of the woodwork when you're seven.'

'Old enough not to believe in fairies any more,' explained the toaster. 'I call that thorough, don't you?'

'Anyhow,' concluded the freezer – a small pool of water on the floor bore witness to the effort it had been making – 'that's our theory, take it or leave it. If you prefer the kidnapped-by-aliens version, then fair play to you; though as far as I'm concerned that's just another story and a damn sight less elegant, at that. And now I for one have had more than enough for one night, and I've got a nasty feeling that the big bag of frozen prawns you put in me last Thursday has completely defrosted. Go to bed and think it over, why don't you?'

Michelle stood up. 'Good idea,' she said. 'Let's talk about it in the morning. I do so prefer believing impossible things before breakfast. Can I take this thing off now?'

'Better had,' replied the toaster. 'The alarm clock snores.'

As she lay in the darkness staring at the ceiling, Michelle

summoned her mental jury and asked them if this new evidence inclined them to change their verdict. Not really, replied the foreman; just because your kitchen equipment's all stark raving bonkers doesn't mean you've imagined talking to it. If you spent all day plugged in to the mains electricity, you'd probably go a bit funny in the head yourself. Michelle conceded that this was a good point, turned over and tried to find the comfortable spot in the pillow.

Waste of time; couldn't sleep. But, she realised, it wasn't all the stuff that she'd been listening to that was keeping her awake; if anything, it had worn her out. The reason for her insomnia, she realised with something approaching relief, was nothing other than good old honest-to-goodness toothache. She was so happy to feel something actually real and normal, she nearly burst into tears.

'First thing in the morning,' she mumbled drowsily. 'I'll phone Mr . . .'

She fell asleep.

CHAPTER EIGHT

'New patient, is he?'

'I think so, Mr B,' replied the receptionist. 'Haven't got a card for him. I'll try the computer.'

Mr Barbour shrugged, and flipped the intercom again. 'Shovel him in anyway,' he said. 'Anything I need to know he can probably tell me. Straight from the horse's mouth, so to speak.'

Presently the door opened, and . . .

Worth pointing out at this juncture that Akram looks different on this side of the line. Not very different; he's still tall, dark, lean, broad-shouldered with curly black hair, beard, pointed, one, villains for the use of, and savage coal-black eyes. He's just *different*, that's all. He might conceivably have been his own second cousin, but someone'd have to point out the resemblance before you noticed it.

The same, of course, goes for Mr Barbour; more so, in fact, since where he came from his hair wasn't the colour of light, dry sand and his eyes weren't pale blue. Both of them spoke in English (Akram with a faint tinge of Manchester around the vowels, Mr Barbour sounding like Bertie Wooster doing his

Lord Peter Wimsey impression) and both of them, if asked, would have been prepared to swear blind they'd never set eyes on each other before.

'Right,' said Mr Barbour. 'What seems to be the problem?'

'Toothache,' Akram replied. 'My tooth hurts.'

Mr Barbour nodded. 'By some miraculous fluke,' he said, 'I happen to have some experience in tooth-related disorders. Now then, the chair won't eat you, it's on a diet. Ah,' he added, inclining his mirror, 'a cavity. The question is, do I fill it or lease it from you to keep my vintage port in?'

Akram frowned. 'Could you get on with it, please?' he said.

'My apologies.' Mr Barbour wiggled the mirror a little more, probed with the toothpick thing. 'This is one ghastly mess you've got here, by the way. How long's it been hurting?'

'Not long.' Akram tried to think back. 'Ever since I arrived – I mean, since I, er, got back from holiday. Two weeks, maybe? I forget.'

Mr Barbour raised an eyebrow. 'That, if you don't mind me saying so, is pretty well world class forgetting. If I had something like this in my face, I'd remember it easily enough. I'm afraid,' he concluded, straightening up, 'she's got to go.'

Akram thought of the tooth fairy in his bedsit. 'Come out, you mean?'

Mr Barbour nodded. 'If we can persuade the little blighter to come, that is,' he added. 'Not an awful lot left to get a hold of, and what there is looks like it'll be as hard to shift as a grand piano in a skyscraper. Sorry about that,' he added. 'I could tell you it's just a tiny bit awkward and we'll have it out of there in two shakes, but I got given a free sample pack of truth the other day and I'm dying to try it out.'

Akram shifted impatiently. 'If the tooth's got to be pulled, pull it. Either that, or tie a bit of string to the door and leave it to me.'

'*On y va*,' replied Mr Barbour, fiddling with sundry

instruments. 'Now, I'm going to have to carve your gums like the Christmas turkey, so it looks like the jolly old gas for you.' Akram gave him a sharp look. 'For my sake, not yours. I find the sound of agonised screaming a bit offputting, to tell you the truth. Ready?'

'Just a minute.' Deep in Akram's unconscious mind, an alarm had gone off. This was no big deal; Akram's mind was full of the things, and usually he paid them as little heed as you would if you heard a car alarm start shrieking three blocks away. On this occasion, however, he decided to take a look, just in case. 'You mean an anaesthetic? Put me to sleep sort of thing.'

'That's right,' Mr Barbour said, uncoiling a length of rubber pipe. 'Sorry, is that a problem?'

'Well . . .'

'I could try doing it with a local,' said Mr Barbour. 'But when it comes to major slashing and chopping, I find local anaesthetics are a bit like local government; lots of aggro and inconvenience, but they don't actually achieve anything. Up to you, really.'

For some reason that Akram couldn't quite fathom, the chair he was sitting in was beginning to remind him of the interior of a palm-oil jar. He could see no reason why this should be, and his tooth was currently giving him jip in jumbo catering-size measures. He reached a decision, shouted to his unconscious mind to switch that bloody thing off, and politely asked Mr Barbour to proceed.

'Sure?'

'Sure. Sorry about that. Silly of me.'

Akram lay back and closed his eyes. Somewhere behind him, something was hissing like a snake. There was a funny taste in his mouth. He was feeling drowsy . . .

And where is it, this Story-book country, this place we've all been to and know so well and can never find again?

They say it's a small enclave, a protectorate of sleep and dreaming, landlocked in the mind, the soul's Switzerland; inside every one of us a tiny patch of Somewhere Else that's as foreign and sovereign as an embassy. Major financial institutions have been searching for it for years, on the basis that the fiscal advantages of relocating their registered offices there would be beyond the dreams of avarice, but it refuses to be found. It issues no postage stamps, has no national netball team and never submits an entry to the Eurovision Song Contest. Conventionally, the map-makers show it as lying between the borders of sleep and waking, but that's just a guess. A profession that's only just got itself out of the habit of putting Jerusalem in the middle and dragons round the edges isn't to be relied on, in any event.

But just suppose they're right; or, to be exact, not con-clusively wrong. Suppose, when you fall asleep and your soul takes leave of your body for a while, you turn left out of your skull instead of right and find yourself on the other side of the looking-glass, or inside the picture on the wall. Just suppose; or, put it another way, make believe.

'Oh,' said Akram.

He was fast asleep, dead to the world. Put a hot iron on his stomach and he wouldn't even flinch.

He was also sitting up rubbing his eyes, and realising that the man in the white coat leaning over his physical body with a small, sharp knife in his hand was Ali Baba, the palm-oil merchant. He shut his eyes, cringed and muttered *Fuck, fuck, fuck!* under his breath. It was one of those moments.

Maybe, whispered the eternal optimist within him, the bastard hasn't seen me, and if I'm really quiet I can just sneak back and hide inside this tall, bearded geezer who would appear in some respects to be me. Gently does it . . .

Akram's astral body knocked over the glass of nice pink water. There was a musical tinkle, like the first laugh of a baby that brings a new fairy into the world, and Akram froze.

'Oh for pity's sake,' said Ali Baba. 'It's you.'

There was no obvious reply to that; and for ten seconds, Neverland Mean Time, they just stared at each other, while the nice pink water seeped into the carpet.

'Damn,' said Akram.

Ali Baba's fingers were holding the scalpel rather tightly. 'Of all the chairs,' he said slowly, 'in all the dentist's surgeries in all the world, why did he have to come into mine? This is . . .'

'Quite,' Akram replied. 'Though I don't really know what you've got to complain about, since you're not the one whose sworn enemy's standing over him with a sharp instrument.'

'Sharp instr—' The clatter of dropping pennies was almost audible. 'So I am,' said Ali Baba slowly. 'Do you know, if you hadn't pointed it out, I might never have thought of it. Now then, this may hurt quite a lot.'

With great precision he laid the sharp edge of the scalpel against Akram's jugular vein, took a deep breath and let it go again.

'Well go on, then,' Akram snapped. 'Sooner you do it, the sooner I get back to my nice warm oil-jar. I suppose. In any case, stop pratting about and get on with it.'

Ali Baba frowned. His hand was as still as Akram's body. 'I'm not sure about this,' he said. 'Slitting a defenceless man's throat while he's asleep. More in your line of country, I'd have thought.'

'Want to change places? I'm game.'

'No.' Ali Baba shook his head. 'Thanks all the same, but that wouldn't be right either. Mind you,' he added, scratching his ear with his left hand, 'I don't know why I've come over all indecisive and Hamlety all of a sudden. After all, last time I saw you I was dead set on scalding you to death in a whacking great pot. Without anaesthetic,' he added, shuddering slightly. 'Maybe the tooth business has turned me soft in my old age.'

'That'll be right,' Akram sneered. 'Strikes me you're ideally suited to a career in which you spend all day inflicting pain on helpless people cowering before you. You bastard,' he went on, with considerable feeling, 'what the hell harm did I ever do you? I mean you personally? Sure, I did a lot of antisocial things, a throat cut here, an entire household massacred there, but not to you.'

'Not for want of trying,' interrupted Ali Baba gently.

'Only after you'd ripped me off,' Akram snapped. 'Broken into my place, swiped my pension fund, nicked my life's savings, made me look a complete and utter prawn in front of the whole profession. You've got to admit, a man might be expected to get a trifle vexed. And then, when I try and even the score up a bit, you dowse me down with boiling water as if I was an ants' nest or something. So please, we'll have a little bit less of it from you, if you don't mind.'

'Ah,' said Ali Baba, without moving. 'But you're the villain.'

'Bigot.'

'Not up to me, is it?' Ali Baba shook his head. 'It's just the way it is. Me goody, you baddy. And now,' he added thoughtfully, 'presumably you've come after me all this way just to get your revenge, and what happens? Old Mister Fate plonks you down helpless and immobilised in my dentist's chair while I stand over you with a knife. I think that may well constitute a strong hint.'

''Snot fair,' Akram growled. 'I never had the advantages you had.'

'Advantages?'

'Too bloody right, advantages. Took me twenty years hard graft to get that hoard together. You come along, just happen to overhear the password, and bingo! You're incredibly rich. And then, whenever it comes to a fight, there's the Story creeping up behind me with half a brick in a sock, waiting to bash my skull in as soon as my back's turned. I don't mind people being born with a silver spoon in their mouths, but I do resent it when it's my ruddy spoon.'

'Which you stole from its rightful owner.'

'All right.' Akram scowled. 'So it might not be mine. Sure as hell wasn't yours. But even that I wouldn't mind so much if on top of all that, you weren't the bastarding *hero*. As far as I'm concerned, that really is the limit.'

Ali Baba sighed. 'All right,' he said. 'What would you do if you were me? Come on, if you're so clever.'

The words crumpled on Akram's lips and he was silent for a comparatively long time. 'I don't know,' he replied at last. 'That's a trick question, that is, because I'm a villain.'

'You're a trained throat-cutter.'

'City and Guilds,' Akram confirmed. 'And I assume you also have some piece of paper with a seal on it that authorises you to cut bits off people. What's that got to do with anything?'

Suddenly Ali Baba smiled. When expatriates meet in a strange land, there's always a bond between them, no matter how incompatible they are in all other respects. 'Looks like we're stuck,' he said, slowly and deliberately placing the scalpel into the steriliser.

'Stuck?'

Ali Baba nodded. 'Something somewhere's gone wrong,' he said.

Just then the intercom buzzed. For a moment, Ali Baba hadn't the faintest idea what the noise could be; he whirled round, and his hand groped instinctively for the scalpel he'd just put down.

'I think your receptionist wants a word with you,' said Akram scornfully.

'You're quite right. Hello? I'm still engaged with Mr . . .' He turned back and whispered, 'Remind me. What's your name supposed to be?'

'Smith.'

'*Smith!*'

Akram grimaced. 'Well,' he said, 'she took me by surprise.'

'Sorry to bother you,' quacked the receptionist's voice. 'Just to let you know Miss Partridge is here, and can you fit her in? The filling's worked loose and there's some discomfort.'

Ali Baba nodded. 'Tell her that's fine. Anybody waiting?'

'No, your twelve o'clock rang in to cancel, so you're clear through to half past.'

'Much obliged.' He flipped the switch, then turned back to the paralysed body and the floating soul in his chair. 'Sorry about that,' he said.

'Not at all,' Akram replied petulantly. 'Good of you to fit in slitting my throat for me at such short notice. Next time you kill me – I have this terrible, inevitable feeling that there will be a next time – I'll try and remember to make an appointment.'

'Look.' Ali Baba was speaking in a we're-both-reasonable-people-we-can-talk-this-through voice that, in context, Akram found downright insulting. 'Let's see if we can't get this mess sorted out. Just you and me, and the hell with the story. You on?'

'Gosh,' Akram replied, staring pointedly at the scalpel still in Ali Baba's hand, 'I'm so bewilderingly spoilt for choice, how can I possibly decide? Go on, then, let's hear it.'

Ali Baba perched on the radiator, put the scalpel down within easy reach and folded his arms. 'The way I see it,' he said, 'is like this. I'm a hero, right?'

'If the word can encompass people who rob other people blind, try and kill them and then run away, then yes, no question. So?'

'And you're a villain.'

'Agreed.'

'Well, then.' Ali Baba spread his hands in a bewildered gesture. 'Someone has blundered. Because here I am, supposed to be cutting your jolly old throat, when throat-cutting is your job. And there's you, at my mercy, trying to use your wits to talk me out of killing you, which is hero stuff. It's all back to front. If I kill you and you die, we'll both be hopelessly out of character.'

'That,' remarked Akram, 'will probably be the least of my problems.'

'Now then,' Ali Baba resumed. 'What about this? I let you go—'

'Hey! Why didn't I think of that?'

'—In return for your word of honour that you'll pack in trying to kill me and toddle off back to where you belong. Problem solved. What d'you reckon?'

Akram felt his throat become dry. 'When you say word of honour . . .'

'As in honour among thieves,' Ali Baba went on, smiling brightly. 'Because everybody knows that the word of Akram the Terrible is his bond. Akram the Terrible could no more welch on his word of honour than fly in the air. When did Akram ever break his word? Never. Everybody knows that, it's all to do with respect and stuff. So you see, that way I'd be far safer than if I actually did cut your throat.'

'Now just a minute . . .'

'The more I think about it,' Ali Baba said, sliding off the radiator and walking excitedly around the room, 'the better it gets. We'd both still be in character, you see. I'd be being magnanimous and merciful, which is ever so Hero, much more so than just silly old winning. Any old fool can win—'

'Except me, apparently.'

'But it takes a hero to win properly. Okay, that's fine. And you'll still be in character, because your really high-class bespoke villains always keep their word; you know, the old twisted nobility thing. Then I don't have to spend all weekend scrubbing blood out of my carpet, you get to give up this pestilential vendetta thing – I'm sure it must be costing you a fortune, all the time spent chasing after me when you could be out thieving – and go quietly home, where you—'

'No!' Akram's expression conveyed the intensity of his agitation. 'Not back there. Think about it, man. If I go back and you stay here, what happens to the story? You can't have Ali Baba and the Forty Thieves without Ali Baba. The story'd just stop, and that'd be the end of me. If you make me go back, it'd be just as final as killing me now. More so, in fact, because then I'd never have existed in the first place.'

'True.' Ali Baba nodded gravely. 'So what were you planning on doing? Defecting? Claiming narrative asylum?'

'Call it whatever you like,' Akram said. 'Just so long as you don't send me back. Deal?'

'But you'll promise not to try and kill me, ever again?'

'You strike a hard bargain, you do.' Akram looked from the scalpel to his immobilised body, and then back again. 'Actually, you'd have made a good villain. You've got that cold, hard streak.' Not to mention, he added under his breath, that basic ill-fated gullibility that makes a man who's got his mortal enemy helpless at knifepoint insist on some absurdly over-elaborate means of execution, involving candles burning through ropes, underground cellars slowly filling with water and girls tied to railway lines, which is tantamount to turning the bugger loose and saying, 'See you next episode.'

'Thank you,' Ali Baba replied, evidently flattered. 'I think you'd have made a good hero, not that there's any other sort, but you know what I mean. It's the way apparently insoluble moral dilemmas follow you around as if they were Mary's lamb.'

Akram shuddered. 'Must be awful, that. I expect you can't

go into a shop and buy a box of matches without first checking they were made from sustainable forests.'

'That sort of thing. Right then. Do we have a deal?'

'Suppose so.' Akram cleared his throat. 'Here goes, then. Hell, this is as bad as being back at school. I swear on my honour as a thief and a villain never to try and kill you again. Will that do, d'you think?'

'Covers it pretty well. Better add actual bodily harm as well, just to be on the safe side.'

'If you want. Here, you should have been a lawyer.'

'That's not a very clever thing to say to someone who's still holding a knife on you. Just for that, we'll add economic sanctions and reprisals against property. Okay?'

Akram shrugged. 'If you insist. I'm sorry you've got such a low opinion of me that you see me as the sort of bloke who vents his wrath by chucking bricks through windows and letting tyres down.'

'Just to be on the safe side.'

'All right.'

There was a moment's silence as the two opponents considered what they'd agreed. There was an absurd edge to it, Akram reflected, as if two duellists had flung away their swords in mid-fight and agreed to sort out their differences with best of three games of dominoes. But there was nothing frivolous about giving his word of honour. The bastard had been right on the money there. All in all, he felt like someone who's hired a horsebox in order to go cattle-rustling in a muddy field, and ends up having to pay the farmer to pull him out with his tractor. If word of this ever reached home, he'd never be able to show his face there again.

'That's all right then,' said Ali Baba, breathing a long, ostentatious sigh of relief. 'I knew we'd get there in the end if we really set our minds to it. That just leaves the little matter of your iffy tooth.' He picked up the scalpel and switched on the light. 'You can have this on the house,' he added, 'as a sign there's no hard feelings.'

'Like a free alarm clock radio if I take out a policy within ten working days? What a generous man you are, to be sure.'

With that, Akram's astral body made itself scarce, and spent the next quarter of an hour deliberately not watching what was happening to the old flesh and blood. Odd how some people are; Akram the Terrible habitually jeered in the face of death and laughed the swords of his enemies to scorn; but dentists' drills and injections made him feel as if the bones of his legs had melted and seeped out through his toes.

Not long after Ali Baba had finished – a copybook extraction, needless to say, with the absolute minimum of hacking and slashing – the so-called Mr Smith woke up, groaned aloud and spat out a mouthful of blood and tooth debris. Ali Baba held his breath.

'I eel ike I ust ent en ounds ith Ugar Ay Ennard,' Akram mumbled, feeling his jaw with his hand. 'At ad, as it?'

Ali Baba grinned and held up a pair of pliers, in which was gripped a thing like a badly peeled prawn. 'If you don't get at least one and six for this,' he said, 'your tooth fairy is ripping you off.'

Funny you should mention – 'Anks ery uch, I'll ear at in ind.' He stood up, staggered and caught the back of the chair. 'Ink I'll o and it own in awr aiting oom, if at's OK.'

'Be my guest.'

When he'd gone Ali Baba sat down on the arm of the chair, closed his eyes and tried to lock and bolt the door against the memory of what had happened. Then he hit the intercom and sent for Miss Partridge.

Obviously, it was going to be one of those days; because she had pretty much the same problem with her junk tooth as Akram had. As he fitted the face mask over Michelle's nose and turned on the gas, he decided that what he really wanted above all was for this day to end and be replaced by a nice straightforward one with no complications.

Hiss, went the gas, and the patient in the chair slumped into unconsciousness. Now then: scal—

He turned, and stared. In the chair, sharing exactly the same space to the cubic millimetre, were not one but two bodies; one fast asleep, the other sitting bolt upright and gawping at him as if he was one of the dinosaur skeletons in the Natural History Museum.

'Bugger me, I don't believe it,' he wailed. 'Not *another* one.'

CHAPTER NINE

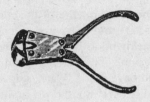

'Skip.'

Aziz sighed, and stopped. 'Now what?' he said wearily.

'There's a cat over there with boots on.'

It had been one of those days. 'Pull the other one, Sadiq, it's got ruddy bells on. Now, if you've quite—'

'Straight up, Skip, no bull. Look for yourself if you don't believe me.'

What, Aziz asked himself, would the Guv'nor have done, had he been here? Silly question; if he'd been here, they'd be safely back on their own turf, where things like this didn't happen and cats didn't wear boots so much as have them thrown at them. But if he *had* been there, he'd have snapped something like 'Silence in the ranks!' and they'd all have shut up like ironmongers at 5.25 on a Saturday when you desperately need a new hacksaw blade. Either you've got it, Aziz admitted sadly to himself, or you haven't, and he hadn't. Slowly, he turned round.

'All right, you lot,' he said, after a while, 'nobody said to stop marching. Haven't you men ever seen a cat with boots on before?'

'Actually, Skip, now you come to mention it, no.'

'Well you have now. Come on, move it.'

For the record; the cat, seriously terrified by the sight of thirty-nine heavily armed men tramping straight towards it, abandoned its original plan of catching a brace of partridges with which to whet the appetite of the King and thus gain favour for his master, and scarpered. Being hampered by a pair of huge, unwieldy boots it tripped over, fell off a wall and broke its neck, leaving its master to fend for himself. The princess he should have married later eloped with a footman, who abandoned her, six months pregnant, when the King finally and irreversibly cut her out of his will. There had been quite a lot of that sort of thing going on lately, as a result of the intrusion of Aziz and his followers into stories where they had no place to be, and the consensus of opinion throughout Story-book land was that the stupid bastards should be hung up by the balls and left to die.

An hour after the cat incident, they reached a castle. By now they were starving hungry, and it was coming on to rain. They hammered at the door, but nobody answered it.

'Maybe they're out,' ventured Hussain.

'Slice of luck for us, then,' replied Achmed, pulling his cloak over his head. 'Breaking and entering is our speciality, after all.'

Aziz looked up at the lofty battlements and rubbed his chin. 'Bugger of a wall to climb,' he said dubiously. 'Must be twenty, twenty-five foot if it's a yard. You checked out the gates, Faisal?'

'Tight as a pawnbroker's arse, Skip. If we had the big jemmy we'd maybe stand a chance, but without it . . .'

'Just a minute.' Hakim grabbed Aziz by the shoulder and pointed. 'Some fool's only left a beautiful great rope hanging out the window. Look, that tower over there by the gateway.'

He was right. 'Stone me,' said Aziz, impressed. 'What a stroke of luck! All right, then, Faisal, Hakim, Shamir, up that rope quick as you like and open the gates. Anybody tries to stop you, scrag 'em.'

It was an odd sort of a rope, being golden-yellow and made from some very soft, fine fibre; but it was plenty strong enough to take Shamir's twenty-odd stone. He vanished through the tower window, and a moment later the rest of the gang heard a shriek, a scream, a female voice using words that even the thieves didn't know (although they could guess the general idea fairly well from context) and a loud, heavy thump. Five minutes later, the gates opened.

'What the hell kept you?' Aziz demanded. His three faithful henchmen looked away. Hakim blushed. Shamir hastily wiped lipstick off his cheek.

'Well,' Hakim mumbled, 'there was this bint, right . . .'

'Two of 'em,' Faisal corrected him. 'One right little cracker, and a raddled old boiler with a face like a prune. Really snotty about it all, she was. Told us our fortunes good and proper.'

'She fell off the wall,' admitted Shamir. 'It was an accident, honest.'

'The other one didn't seem to mind, though,' Hakim went on. 'In fact, she seemed dead chuffed. It was her hair we climbed up, by the way.'

'Her hair?'

Hakim nodded.

'Stairs fallen down or something? Fire drill?'

'Search me, Skip,' Hakim replied, with a shrug. 'Weird bloody lot they are in these parts, if you ask me. What now, Skip? Do we loot the place, or what?'

The castle proved to be well worth the effort of getting in. Apart from food and dry clothes and plenty of books and things to make a fire with, there were whole chests and trunks full of jewels and precious stones. The girl didn't seem in the least put out by their depredations; in fact, she kept trying to kiss them, and seemed puzzled by the fact that they were rather more interested in the contents of the kitchen and the counting-house. Finally she got Achmed in a sort of half-nelson and started nibbling his ear, until Aziz managed to prise her off. Even then, she kept following them around, sighing embarrassingly and murmuring 'My hero!' That part of it worried Aziz no end, although he kept his concern to himself. His grasp of theory was tenuous at the best of times, but even he knew that villains doing hero stuff was bad news, liable to upset the balance of supernature. Rounding up his men like the headmistress of a Borstal kindergarten, he shooed them out of the castle, promised the girl they'd write, and quick-marched out of it as fast as possible. In their haste, one of them trod on a frog that'd been hanging around the castle for weeks, ogling the girl and saying 'Give us a kiss, give us a kiss,' in frog language; but they weren't to know that.

'Not *another* one!'

Michelle, or her spiritual essence, goggled at him as if she'd just swallowed a goldfish. 'Another what?' she asked. 'Hey, this anaesthetic of yours doesn't seem to be terribly good.'

'Look down,' Ali Baba replied.

Curiously enough, Michelle's next words – 'Who's that in the chair?' – were precisely the words that Daddy Bear, now prematurely deceased, should have spoken on discovering that Goldilocks had broken in. How they got there is a matter for the fabulonometrists to determine, but the answer is probably something to do with random catalyst dispersal and chaos theory. It's probably not significant that she said them twice.

'Maybe,' Ali Baba was saying meanwhile, 'there's a leak in the pipe and I've been inhaling the stuff without knowing it. Never heard it caused hallucinations, but you never know.'

'Pardon me,' Michelle replied, affronted. 'If there's anybody hallucinating around here, I should think it's me. I can see my body down there. Shouldn't there be a strong bright light or something?'

Ali Baba sighed. 'I'm afraid it's not as simple as that,' he said. 'Obviously you don't know. On reflection, perhaps I shouldn't tell you, either. It'd only worry you.'

'Thanks a heap. That's really set my mind at rest, you know?'

'True.' Ali Baba leaned back against the radiator and took a deep breath. 'If my theory's right,' he said, 'and I have this really depressing feeling that it is, you're not actually real. I mean, from Reality, don't you know. I think you're someone out of a story.'

'A story . . .'

'Before you start yelling for two doctors and a white van,' Ali Baba continued, 'maybe I'd better tell you, if you promise not to breathe a word. What am I saying, they wouldn't believe you anyway, not when you tell them you only know I'm crazy because I started gibbering at you while your astral body was floating three feet up in the air. I'm not from these parts, either.'

'A story,' Michelle repeated. 'Do you know, you're the second person to tell me that in twenty-four hours.'

'Really? Who was the first?'

'My fridge freezer.'

'Right. Fine. Now then, this may hurt a little but if it does I really couldn't give a damn. Say Aaah.'

'No, wait, listen.' Michelle frowned, and crumpled her astral hands tightly into a ball. 'Listen,' she repeated. 'For some time now I've been convinced I'm going crazy, ever since my great-aunt died. I inherited this ring, and it makes me think I can understand machines talking. All the electrical gadgets in my flat have been talking to me.'

'Understand machines,' Ali Baba repeated, in a voice as flat as the square at Edgbaston. 'A ring. Silver.'

'Yes.' Michelle stared at him. 'How'd you know?'

'Quite plain, with a jewel or a bit of coloured glass stuck in it. Really ordinary, ugly-looking thing.'

'That's it. Where did you say you were from?'

'Where did you say you got it?'

They regarded each other warily, like two undercover Klingon agents meeting by chance in Trafalgar Square. Ali Baba broke the silence.

'You inherited it from your great-aunt, you said.'

Michelle nodded. 'If that's who she really was. Apparently, I've only got the word of an old-fashioned Bakelite telephone for that. According to my labour-saving kitchen utensils, I was an orphan or something, and they brought me up. You know, like Mowgli or Romulus and ... Mr Barbour, are you feeling all right? Why are you sitting on the floor?'

Slowly, with as much dignity as he could muster (enough to fill a small matchbox, but only if the matches were still inside) Ali Baba climbed to his feet, brushed off his knees and washed his hands. It was, he felt, what Doc Holliday would have done.

'Sorry,' he muttered. 'Slipped on something. Could you just go through that last bit again, because— Damn! Yes?' he barked into the intercom. 'Can't it wait?'

'Sorry, I'm sure,' replied the receptionist. 'It's just to ask if you got Mr Smith's details, because I think he's feeling better now and he's just about to go home.'

Ali Baba flicked off the intercom, snapped, 'Stay there!' at Michelle in the chair, and darted out into the waiting room. Akram – is it my imagination, or does he seem smaller somehow? – was halfway to the door. He turned, looked at Ali Baba and then looked away.

'Just off?'

'Mhm.'

'I hope there won't be any more trouble now.'

'Mm.'

'Right.' For an instant, Ali Baba felt rather foolish. He wasn't at all sure why he'd felt the need to come running out here just to see Akram leave. As far as he was concerned, he'd done everything he could to neutralise the threat; if it worked, it worked, and if not, not. He'd done the right thing, he felt sure. It was just starting to dawn on him that if his gamble did pay off, then the threat that had been terrorising him across twenty-odd Real years and distances too vast to be measured was now over and done with.

Hold that thought.

He could stop running.

He could go home.

'Mm.'

Ali Baba parachuted back from his reverie. 'Sorry?'

'Cn I g hm nw?' said Akram, moving his battered jaws with perceptible discomfort, 'M flng mch bttr nw tht v hd uh rst.'

'I think,' Ali Baba said slowly, 'that going home would be the best possible thing you could do. Cheerio.'

'Auf wdrshn.'

And then the door closed behind him and he was gone. Ali Baba stood for a moment, as if trying to remember how to make his legs work, and then went back into his surgery.

'Sorry about that,' he said. 'Right, where were we? Tell me,' he added, sitting on the desk and folding his arms, 'all about it.'

'All about what?'

Ali Baba bit his lip; he seemed ill at ease, as if he was a guest at an Embassy function who wasn't sure his fly was done up but daren't have a quick fumble to find out. 'What you were telling me. Being brought up by your kitchen.'

'Well.' Michelle told him. He listened. When she'd finished he sat in silence for fifteen seconds, a very long time under the circumstances, before standing up, sitting down again, fiddling with a pencil, breaking it, putting the corpse in a drawer and finally clearing his throat.

Stow away in the pile of a magic carpet crossing the Line, and jump off over Old Baghdad. Because timescale here is relative, depending on which showing of the picture you're in, don't clutter your mind up with notions like 'twenty-seven years earlier'; it'd only confuse the issue. Better just to recognise that this is a flashback, and leave it at that.

You've been here before; the long drive, the wide lawn where one day there will be big stripy tents and a band, the big house, the french windows opening inwards, the dark, dramatically furnished study, the desk behind which the Man sits. Having tidied away the tents and the band, Continuity reckon they've done a day's work, and accordingly nothing else is different. For his part, the Man doesn't look a day younger. His type never do.

Take a good look, anyway. Here's a face that nothing will ever be able to shock or to frighten. You could bring yourself to believe that God looks like this, if you're comfortable with the idea of a god who sends the boys round after dark to pour petrol through the letterboxes of other gods' temples.

'And the girl,' he says. 'Who is she?'

His voice is quiet, soft and slightly bored, like a casualty doctor examining his seventh knife wound of the night. There's a certain degree of contempt in there as well, the scorn of the truly great sinner for the peccadilloes of regular people. There's a cigar clamped between his thin lips that burns but never seems to grow any shorter; rather like Moses' burning bush, except not quite so homely.

The man on the other side of the desk looks down; it shames him to have to admit to what he's done. 'Her name's Prudence,' he mumbles.

Something exceptional happens; the Man's eyebrows lift, admitting surprise. '*Prudence?*' he says. 'This, you will forgive me for saying so, is a curious name for her to have, in the circumstances.'

'Yes. Well.' The man on the wrong side of the desk lifts his shoulders; not quite a shrug, because that wouldn't be fitting. 'They all have names like that, where she comes from.'

'You don't say.' The Man's voice is back to normal, and his face is once more Mount Rushmore's big brother. 'And where might that be, precisely?'

The other man doesn't speak; he tilts his head slightly sideways, indicating the direction of the Line. He waits for a reaction – anger, surprise, disgust, amusement. All he gets is an imperceptible nod, as if to reassure him that the person he's talking to is still awake.

'A visitor,' the other man continues. 'Or you could say a tourist. One of those head-in-the-clouds types who somehow get across the Line from time to time.'

'Sure.' The great head nods again. 'A Wendy.'

The term, as used by Story-book folk, is highly derogatory, but the Man uses it as a straightforward noun; he means nothing by it, it's just a convenient piece of shorthand. The other man nods, relieved that he doesn't need to explain further. 'That's right,' he says, 'a Wendy. Apparently on the other side she runs a small specialist bookshop and makes handmade silver jewellery in her spare time.'

The edges of the Man's lips curl ever so slightly as if to ask, What else can you expect from such people? He sucks on his cigar and breathes out a thin plume of smoke.

'And now what?' he says. 'Tell me what it is you want I should do for you, and then we can sit out in the sun and drink a glass of wine together.' He smiles; a Great Khan's smile, derisively merciful. The other man takes a deep breath.

'There's a problem,' he says at last.

'Always there's a problem,' the Man replies, with a faint trace of impatience. 'You want her to go, but you can't get rid of her. You want her to stay, but the immigration people say no. You want to marry her, but her father is the Sultan. So many problems.'

'She's going to have a baby,' the other man whispers.

Silence. The Man draws deep on his cigar and expels the smoke through his nose, like a dragon. 'That,' he says at last, 'is different, I'll say that for you. I didn't even know it was possible.'

'It's possible, believe me.'

'All right. So, what's the problem?'

The other man seems to collapse, just a little, as if the secret inside him had been the only thing holding him upright. '*Padrone*,' he says, 'what am I to do? We have nothing in common, in fact we can't stand the sight of each other any more. If we try and talk about it she gets hysterical. She seems to think the child's going to be born with green skin or pointed ears or something. Now she says she wants nothing to do with it; she just wants to get back to her own kind and lead her life, she says.'

'So what's wrong with that?'

'My child,' the other man blurts out. 'What's going to become of it, brought up on the other side by a mother who thinks she's carrying a Martian or something? *Padrone*, can you do anything? You have friends over there, people who might know what to do. I thought maybe . . .'

His words dry up, like water in a hot season. In the face of so much scorn and pity, it'd be fatuous to try and say anything else.

'You want that the kid should be looked after,' says the Man. 'That it should have a decent home, maybe be raised among its own kind.' He frowned. 'This,' he says, 'is a big thing you're asking me for. Arrangements will have to be made, it'll cost money. And you—' Without so much as the movement of an eyeball, he looks the other man over, from charity-shop turban to camel boot sale shoes. 'However,' he continues, 'I have a soft heart, your story touches me. It's good that a man should be concerned about his children and not want that they should grow up like savages. I tell you what I'll do.'

And, in that same calm, deadly voice he explains: how no humans on the other side could be trusted, but there were things – telephones and vacuum cleaners and alarm clock radios – that had originally come over from the Old Country, and . . .

'From here?' the other man interrupts. 'We export consumer goods over the Line?'

The Man's brow tightens a fraction. 'Because you're young,' he says, 'I forgive that you interrupt me. And yes, we do. Over there, these machines need electricity. The ones we make here don't, they're alive. On the other side, therefore, they're a hell of a lot cheaper to run. Anyhow, I have contacts. They will find a nice respectable household where your child can grow up and get a good start in life. I do this for you,' continues the Man, regarding the other as if he had a hundred legs and had just walked out of a salad, 'because I like you. And one day, perhaps, I may come to you and give you three wishes; just simple wishes, nothing very much, and probably that day will never come. Who can say?'

The other man looks perplexed. 'Sorry,' he said. '*You'll* give *me* three wishes? Don't you mean the other way round? I mean . . .'

Through the cigar smoke, two eyes burn fiercely. 'What's the matter? You have a problem with that? Maybe you think that's a lot to ask in return for such a trifling favour as you ask me.'

The other man goes stiff, as if he's only just realised that the words on the notice boards he'd been walking past for the last couple of miles mean DANGER – MINEFIELD. 'Of course not, *padrone*,' he replies hastily. 'I just thought – I mean, shouldn't it be me doing something for you?'

And now the Man does laugh; it sounds like the cracking of hard rocks, and the joke is clearly private. 'Don't you worry about that,' he says. 'You leave the accounts to me, I'll make sure they tally. And now,' he sighs, 'that's enough business for one day. Let's go out into the sun and have that glass of wine. Enrico! Bring a bottle of the good stuff for our guest.'

And the man—

'Was you?'

Ali Baba nodded. 'Not long after that,' he said, 'by local time, at least, I got into – well, I came into money and then I had to leave, for the good of my health. I went to see Him again; he was a bit less sympathetic the second time but I managed to buy a passage over the Line with a rather valuable piece of kit I owned at the time. Your silver ring, actually. It's funny; hardly a day's passed since I came here when I haven't wondered what became of my— Prudence's baby, and all the time the answer's been staring me in the face, so to speak. Usually,' he added, 'with her eyes shut, saying Aaah. Funny old thing, life, don't you think?'

In spite of everything, Michelle realised something was wrong. What could it be? Ah yes, she realised, I've been forgetting to breathe. She remedied the problem. 'In that case,' she demanded, 'who are you?'

Ali Baba grinned, feebly as a twenty-watt bulb. 'It's written up on the window,' he replied. 'Just spelt a bit wrong, that's all.'

Short delay, while Michelle reads the letters on the glass backwards. Another short wait, and then—

'Are you trying to tell me,' she said, 'that you're Ali Ba—'

'Yes.'

'Oh.'

'Quite,' said Ali Baba. 'And you, apparently, are my daughter.'

Michelle looked at him. At that moment, even though she wasn't crouched inside an oil-jar with boiling water cascading down around her ears, her past life flashed in front of her eyes. A curious life it had been, to be sure; comfortable, quiet, under any other circumstances she'd have said *ordinary*, because that's what ordinary means; just like it is at home. Ordinary is in the eye of the beholder. Sorcerors' children run to meet Daddy on his return from work and find nothing unusual in the fact that he's glowing slightly or comes home a different shape. That, they assume, is what all Daddies do. Hit-men's children love to be allowed to help Daddy scrub the lead fouling out of the slots in the silencer, or hold the wiring diagram for him when he's out in the garage making bombs. The children of great prophets learn not to whine, 'Oh Daddy, not loaves and fishes *again*,' when Father comes home from work with a doggy-bag. In her case, she had been brought up to a life in which there were no grown-ups at all. A taxi collected her from the school gate. As soon as she opened the front door, the timer on the oven went ping! to let her know dinner was ready, and the TV switched itself on. Sure, other kids had mummies and daddies; they also had caravans and satellite dishes and boats, but she'd come to understand at an early age that not everybody can have everything. It was cool. It was how things went.

And now, apparently, she had a father. Spiffing. And what, precisely, was she supposed to do with him now she'd got him? Answers on a postcard, please.

'Hello,' she said.

CHAPTER TEN

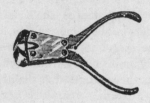

'Mlk,' Akram growled. 'Nd mk t uh dbl.'

The barman, who was used to him by now and even got fresh milk in for him specially, stuck his thumb through the foil caps of two pint bottles, poured and took the money with a smile.

'Thnks.'

'Been to the dentist?'

'Ys.'

'Have to have much done?'

'Ys.'

'Hard luck.' The barman grimaced sympathetically. 'I can get them to rustle you up some soup if you like.'

Akram looked up at the barman, puzzled. 'T's nt n th mnu,' he objected.

'Doesn't matter,' the barman replied. 'Won't take 'em a minute, it only needs heating through. Mushroom do you?'

'Tht'll b fn. Thnks uh lt.'

So that, Akram mused, is kindness. He'd heard about it, in the same way as people on this side of the Line have heard of unicorns; he knew perfectly well what it was supposed to be

122

like, he could picture it in his mind's eye, it was just that he'd never actually come across it before, in the same way and for the same reasons that the barman probably hadn't met too many unicorns.

Strange, he thought; very strange. Just because I've been coming in here fairly regularly to buy milk and sit down after my shift at the kebab house, and because I've just been to the dentist and the barman can see I'm still a bit under the weather from the anaesthetic, he goes out of his way to obtain soup for me, figuring that soup will be easy for me to eat, even though soup's not on the menu. He won't charge me extra. Quite probably he hasn't given any thought about how this act can ultimately be turned to his advantage. He just does it. Probably it makes him feel good; but so would drinking all the whisky or sleeping with the barmaid, and he doesn't do either of those, so that can't really be the reason. He took a long pull at his milk, and the coolness eased the ache in his jaw. He felt strangely—

'Quite warm,' said the barman, 'for the time of year.'

'Ys.'

That, he'd learned, was called Making Conversation. He'd been watching the barman out of idle curiosity for some weeks, and as far as he could gather, the barman often said something conventional and meaningless but essentially friendly to men who came in on their own and sat down at the bar. At first he'd assumed that he was passing on coded messages, or trying to scrape acquaintance with young adventurers who were alone in the world and wouldn't be missed, in order to mug them into entering the secret cave to retrieve the magic lamp from its man-eating guardian. Back home, that would have been the logical explanation. Not so on this side, though; the barman seemed to regard being friendly to strangers and doing the little he could to cheer them up as part of his duty as a human being. The payoff, Akram assumed, was that they'd do as much for him one day, if it ever came to that; but it seemed an unrealistically long shot to expect that one day they'd be barmen and he'd be a solitary drinker in need of companionship. The fact of the matter was, Akram was forced to conclude, that he did it all on spec, or possibly just because that's what people do.

'Hr,' he said to the barman. 'Hv n yrslf.'

The barman's eyes twinkled. 'Cheers,' he replied, 'don't mind if I do.'

The essence of it was, Akram reflected, that on this side, there was so much that was random, purposeless, meaningless. On his side of the Line, everything meant something; every word, every act was relevant to the plot, part of the story. If you were out fishing and you threw a little tiddler back into the water, you knew for certain that it'd turn out to be the son of the Dragon King and you could start making lists of Wishes on the back of an envelope. Do the same here, and you'd be out of pocket one small fish; and where was the percentage in that, for God's sake? And yet the poor suckers did it, unthanked, unrewarded, kept on doing it until the day they died. And virtually none of them ever got to marry princesses, and those few that did never seemed to live happily ever after. It was weird, the whole arrangement, like a place where water flew upward from a spilt glass. And yet, somehow it was all very . . .

'Your very good health,' the barman said.

'Nd th sm t y.'

All of which, Akram couldn't help feeling, was just a tiny bit relevant; because today, in his encounter with the accursed, thieving, treacherous Ali Baba, he had been soundly and completely defeated. His quest had failed utterly, there was now no way he could ever achieve the vengeance that was his sole purpose for existing, and his life was therefore effectively over. To all intents and purposes, he was a dead man, and the story had no further use for him.

Which meant—

Which meant he was free. He couldn't go back home. Suddenly it occurred to him that when the prison authorities drag you from your cell, stuff money in your pockets, frog-march you through the gates, slam them behind you and shout, 'And stay out!', you don't necessarily head for the Citizens' Advice Bureau to ask about an action for unlawful eviction. Maybe you just had to be big enough to swallow the insult, turn the other cheek, buy a spade and go dig up the swag. Not where he came from, maybe; but he wasn't there any more, was he?

He had an idea they called it Free Will.

'Your soup's ready,' said the barman. 'No, put your money away and have it on me.'

Back home, the phrase Free Will was always followed by the words 'With every lawsuit, special offer, hurry while stocks last'. Back home, he added, dipping his spoon in the soup, there is no free lunch, either.

'Yr vry knd,' he said. 'Thnks vry mch.'

And then the thunderbolt hit him. The force of its impact was so great that he almost dropped the spoon. Suddenly, it was as if the world was flooded with pink light.

The barman isn't a hero, yet he can do hero-type things. He can be whatever he wants.

If I stay here, so can I. I don't have to be a villain any more.

If I want to, I can be a bloody hero.

'You should have killed him,' Michelle replied, 'while you had the chance.'

Ali Baba nodded. 'I know,' he said. 'Silly old me. Of course, then I'd have been left with a dead body on my hands, and the dustmen are getting so fussy about what they'll actually take.'

Michelle frowned. 'Even so— '

'Have the last slice of pizza,' Ali Baba interrupted. 'I can't, I'm full up.'

Like many naturally slender young women, Michelle had an appetite like a blast furnace, and there was a slight pause while she took advantage of the offer. 'Even so,' she said, 'surely it'd have been worth it. You've been running away from him all your life, haven't you? Your life in this, what's the word—'

'Dimension?' Ali Baba shrugged. 'It's not the right word, but if you don't tell the lexicographers, neither will I. And yes, I have. And now I don't have to any more. Have some more champagne.'

'How do you know that?' Michelle demanded, holding out her glass. 'You've only got his word for it. He's a thief and a murderer, for pity's sake.'

Ali Baba smiled. 'That's how I know his word's good,' he replied. 'If you can't trust a villain, who can you trust?'

'Explain,' said Michelle with her mouth full.

'Easy. With nice, honest people it doesn't matter if they lie to you; nothing too ghastly's going to happen, because they're basically nice and unlikely ever to cut your throat. For villains, it's different. After all, they've still got to apply for mortgages and have their hair cut and buy toothpaste and take their cats to be wormed, same as the rest of us. If all the world said "Go away, I can't trust you, you're a villain," they'd be in a terrible state. So the convention is, when they promise something, their word is their bond. Then they can walk into a shop and say "I promise to pay for the goods and not murder you" and the shopkeeper knows it's safe. Of course, sometimes they have to lie on business, like when they promise to share the treasure equally when you know all the time they mean to double-cross you; but that's all allowed for in the rules and they have to make it perfectly clear they're lying, just so there won't be any misunderstanding. They cross their fingers, usually, and look away and cackle harshly. You'd have to be blind, deaf and as dim as a lodging-house lightbulb not to pick up on that.'

Michelle shrugged. 'You know about these things,' she said, 'and I don't. If it'd been me I'd have knifed the bastard.'

Ali Baba looked at her. 'Yes,' he said, 'you probably would. It only goes to show how right I was to insist you were brought up this side of the Line.'

'Really?'

'Sure.' Ali Baba's face became uncharacteristically serious; tonight the part of Bertie Wooster will be taken by Hamlet, Prince of Denmark. 'Much better that way. It means you've grown up tough and hard. If you'd stayed on the other side, you'd be no good for anything except gathering flowers and talking to the wee birdies.'

'Oh.' Michelle frowned. 'I'm not sure I want to be tough and hard,' she said. 'You make me sound like a duff avocado.'

'Which reminds me.' Ali Baba laid his knife and fork down on his plate, blade-tip and fork-tines at precisely twelve o'clock, steepled his hands and smiled pleasantly. 'Terribly rude of me not to have asked before,' he said. 'How's your life been so far?'

Michelle considered. 'Fine,' she said.

'No major tragedies, deep-seated emotional traumas? Not,' he added quickly, 'that I want to pry or anything, but I was reading this book on the modern approach to fatherhood—'

Michelle looked at him. 'You were?'

'Just because I didn't know who you were or where you'd ended up didn't mean I wasn't interested,' Ali Baba replied. 'There was always the offchance we'd bump into each other, so I thought, a little general background reading . . .'

'I see. And what did this book say?'

'Difficult to tell,' Ali Baba confessed. 'The chap who wrote it used such fearfully long words, and my dictionary was published in eighteen sixty-something and a lot of the words aren't in it. But the general idea seems to be that once you're past the nappies and putting-food-on-the-table stage, all I'm really fit for is listening and saying, "Gosh, how terrible" when Destiny whacks you one with a broken bottle. I know I've come on the scene a bit late, but . . .'

'Hum.' Michelle rubbed her cheeks with thumb and fore-finger, drawing her lips together. 'Sorry to disappoint you, but there hasn't really been anything much like that. The nature study stick insects at school died rather suddenly, but that was nineteen years ago and besides, I never really liked them anyway. I had a rather expensive blouse from Printemps, and it got prawn biryani on one of the sleeves. The first time I took my driving test, I failed on the emergency stop. Other than that, no complaints, really. Until recently, that is, but I'm not really counting all that, because I'm still not convinced it's not all a horrible dream.'

'I see.' Ali Baba nodded. 'Any area where you feel in need of fatherly advice and guidance? Apart from dental hygiene, of course, because fortuitously we've already covered that in some detail.'

Michelle smiled, quite unexpectedly. 'It's funny,' she said. 'Or rather, odd. Or something. I guess that you're probably the only person who actually has been there all my life. I never seemed to get ill, so I never saw a doctor often enough to remember his name, and schools and teachers seemed to come and go a bit; but I never missed a six-monthly check-up.'

'Highly commendable,' Ali Baba replied. 'Which means we've met a minimum of fifty-four times. And I could draw a chart of the inside of your mouth blindfold from memory; now how many of your so-called conventional fathers could say that?'

As he waffled on, Michelle studied him, her head slightly on one side. Suddenly getting a father after twenty-seven years without one is rather like waking up one morning to be told by

God that owing to an admin snarl-up, the third arm you should have been issued with at birth has only just come through from the depot, and there it is, look, sprouting out of the small of your back. You don't immediately think, 'Hooray, now I can pick up things behind me without turning round.' You wonder, rather, how you're going to explain it to your friends and whether any of your jackets can be salvaged, or whether you're going to have to have a whole new wardrobe tailor-made at Freaks-R-Us. It's hard, in other words, to be entirely positive about it all. Your first thought is of the immediate, if comparatively trivial, complications and disadvantages which you now face and definitely don't need in an already complicated life.

'Excuse me,' Michelle said.

Ali Baba, who had been saying something or other, stopped and waited expectantly for Michelle to go on. Probably, she thought sourly, there's a diagram in his book somewhere.

'This is all extremely important,' she said, 'and naturally I'm thrilled to bits by it all, but can we just be practical for a moment? I mean, what do we do now? Because, and I'm really sorry if this sounds unfeeling or anything, but if you're thinking I'm going to come and live with you and cook breakfasts and iron socks—'

'Do people iron socks?' Ali Baba interrupted, clearly intrigued. 'And if so, why?'

'What I'm getting at—' Michelle wished she'd never started this topic; but now she was, as it were, in custard stepped in so far, and she might as well blunder on a little bit longer until she drowned or was rescued. 'The point is,' she said, 'does it have to change anything, or do we just carry on as before and have lunch together from time to time? I mean, it's not as if—'

'Quite.' Ali Baba nodded. 'I was thinking along the same lines, I must admit. Do I have to stand on the sidelines at netball games? What about pocket money and staying out late at night?

I have to admit, I haven't got a clue. If there's no hard and fast rules, then perhaps we ought just to leave well alone and let it grow on us, if you see what I mean. Okay?'

Michelle shrugged. 'Suits me,' she said.

'Just one thing, though.' Ali Baba frowned. 'As far as I can see, suddenly being a daughter after twenty-seven years of just being a person oughtn't to be a problem. The other stuff—'

'What, you mean being half-fictional? And the talking fridge and so on?'

Ali Baba nodded. 'You're new to all this, obviously. I'm not. So let me offer you a word of advice.'

Michelle nodded. She needed advice on this particular point, in roughly the same way a house needs the ground underneath it.

'Forget about it,' Ali Baba said, and there was a perceptible hardening of tone that might, in someone else, have been mistaken for seriousness. 'Put it completely out of your mind. Put the ring somewhere safe, and never ever put it on.'

'Oh. I thought—'

'Never.'

'Right. Any reason?'

Ali Baba nodded. 'It's all very well,' he said, 'being given a beautiful silk umbrella with a fetching design of black and white concentric circles. It's another thing entirely to sit down under it at the far end of a rifle range. You don't need to use the ring. It's not meant to be used on this side of the Line. Sling it behind your hankies in the back of a drawer, and leave it there.'

'Then why not get rid of it?' Michelle asked.

'Worst thing you could do,' Ali Baba replied. 'Suppose you chucked it in a river. That's virtually sitting up and begging for it to be swallowed by a fish that gets netted by a poor but honest fisherman who takes the prize fish he's just caught as a present for the Grand Vizier, and I trust I don't have to draw pictures of what always happens after that.'

'You have it, then.'

Ali Baba winced. 'Thanks ever so much, but no. Remember Akram? I got rid of all my magical kit years ago. Giving it to me now would be like saying, "Gosh, here come the police up the fire escape, please accept this five kilo bag of heroin, free and with my compliments." You keep it, it can't do you any harm unless you encourage it. Forget all about it.'

Michelle's brows wrinkled. 'That's easy for you to say,' she replied. 'Just give a clue, how precisely do I go about forgetting something like that?'

'Something like what?'

Three wishes you can't refuse.

A curious idea; who in his right mind would want to refuse three genuine, fully functional, guaranteed wishes? The only dilemma would be, do we go straight for the Maserati, or would it be better to wish for the cash and maybe shop around a bit?

There are, indeed, people who think like that, just as there are people who quite happily use unexploded German bombs as door-stops. They don't know any better. And for forty years it doesn't matter; and then one day it does, and the Ordnance Survey has to recall the latest edition of the relevant map for urgent updating.

If you make a wish, you need someone to grant it. Wishes are granted by Class Four supernaturals: genies, dragons, witches, fairy godparents and other species, officially classified by the United Nations standing committee on reality preservation as dangerous pests. None of them are indigenous to this side of the Line; in fact, the Line mainly exists to keep the bastards out. Making a wish is therefore equivalent to driving back across the Channel Tunnel with two rabid dogs on the back seat and the boot full of Colorado beetles. And, once they get this side, Class Fours thrive. They make the alligators in the New York sewers look like a mild infestation of greenfly.

Wishes, magical objects, talismans, all the instruments and paraphernalia of organised fantasy; it's taken science and reason two thousand years of savage, often bloody struggle to root them out, and every time the job seems to be done, somehow they creep back and carry on where they left off; infiltrating, taking over, setting up the storybook *cosa nostra*. Stories grow; the price of reality is constant viligance.

So; three wishes you can't refuse, three passports to this side of the Line for the Fairy Godfather's enforcers.

And six wishes outstanding: three for Akram, three for Ali Baba. The conscientious arsonist doesn't just set the building on fire; first he fills the fire extinguishers with petrol.

CHAPTER ELEVEN

Morning.

Akram's eyes snapped open. The sun behind the curtains made the windows glow. There were no birds singing, but the whine of a distant milk float provided an acceptable substitute. He jumped out of bed, jammed two slices in the toaster and brushed his teeth so vigorously that his gums began to bleed. His tongue, exploring the inside of his mouth, touched the raw jelly left by the extracted tooth, and reminded him of his resolution.

Akram the Terrible was dead. Watch out, world, here comes Sir Akram, knight errant.

He swept back the curtains, threw up the sash and looked out. In the faceless city, there were wrongs to right, downtrodden victims to protect, villains to smite, and if they'd just bear with him until the kettle boiled and he'd had his toast, he'd be right with them.

Twenty minutes later, he was already in business. True, it was only a lost cat, but everybody has to start somewhere. It only needed one glance to see that the poor creature was bewildered and frightened, standing on the pavement, motionlessly yowling. Fortunately, there was a collar round its neck with a little engraved disc, and the disc had an address on it. He grabbed the cat, hailed a taxi and sallied forth.

'Yes?' said the woman through the crack between chained door and frame.

'Your cat,' Akram replied, producing the exhibit.

'Stay there.' The door slammed, then opened again. The woman stepped aside, and a remarkably tall, broad man stepped out onto the pavement, snatched the cat with his left hand, punched Akram with tremendous force on the nose with his right and went back inside.

'Vera,' he said. 'Call the police.'

Akram wasn't quite sure what to do next. He had an idea that turning the other cheek came into it somewhere, but he hadn't been hit on the cheek, and he only had the one nose. Indeed, by the way it felt he wasn't sure if he even had that any more. Discovering that he had at some stage sat down, he shook his head and started to get up.

'Terry,' the woman yelled, 'he's getting away.'

'Don't just stand there,' the man replied from inside the house.

Among the souvenirs Akram had retained from his past life were a whole bundle of instinctive reactions to the words *He's getting away: don't just stand there.* There are times when it's wholesome and positive to allow oneself to be carried away by one's instincts. Therapists recommend it as a way of re-establishing contact with one's repressed inner identity. This, Akram decided, was one of those moments.

'Stop him!' the woman was screaming to the world at large. 'It's the bastard who kidnapped our Tinkles!'

Clearly a hysterical type, Akram felt; and it looked very much like she'd married a compatible partner, because here came the man, brushing past her in the doorway holding a tyre iron. The optimum course of action under these circumstances for any self-respecting knight errant would be to get erring, as quickly as possible. Unfortunately, Akram's motor functions were a bit below par, owing to the biff on the nose, and the three or four yards' start essential for any meaningful chase didn't seem to be available.

'Right, you bugger, you'll wish you'd never been, ouch, oh fuck, oh my head!' exclaimed the man; and Akram, trying to account for the sudden non-sequitur in his conversation, realised that he'd instinctively kicked him in the nuts and kneed him in the face. Pure reflex, of course; those old recidivist instincts, at it again. He wondered, as he beat a hasty retreat, whether a course of hypnotism might be able to do something about them.

Reflecting that beginner's luck isn't always necessarily good luck, he returned to his quest; and as it turned out, he didn't have long to wait.

A little old lady, complete with headscarf and wheeled shopping trolley (where do they get them from, incidentally? Try and buy one and you'll find they've long since vanished from the shops; presumably you have to order them direct from World of Crones, quoting your membership number) was being set upon by three burly youths. Yes, Akram shouted to himself, second time out and we're right on the money. His first instinct was to charge in, fists and boots flailing, but understandably he wasn't on speaking terms with his instincts right then, and he resolved to try subterfuge. Accordingly, he ran forward yelling, 'Look out, it's the Law!' and waving his hands frantically. The youths at once dropped the old lady's bag, unopened, and scarpered, leaving Akram face to face with the old lady.

'You're nicked,' said a voice behind him.

At that moment, the old lady stood up straight, dragged off her scarf and hurled it to the ground, and said, 'Fuck!'

Looking more closely, Akram saw that she wasn't an old woman at all, but a young girl; tall, blonde and quite attractive, if you like them a bit hard in the face. Akram was familiar with the common variant where the old crone turns out to be the main popsy under a spell or enchantment, but somehow this didn't look like one of those cases.

'Jesus!' she growled. 'We were that close!'

Akram noticed that four uniformed constables had attached themselves to various parts of his body. A certain amount of radical preconceptions editing seemed called for.

'Anyway, sarge,' said one of the coppers to the girl, 'we got this clown.'

'Oh good,' replied the girl unpleasantly. 'We'll just have to persuade him to tell us who his mates are.'

Akram's instincts didn't actually smirk or say *Told you so*, but there was a definite aura of smugness in part of his subconscious as he dealt with the four policemen and (very much against his will, but she was trying to bite his leg) the damsel. Obviously, he rationalised as he ran like a hare down a side-street, there was some aspect of this heroism caper he hadn't quite cracked yet.

Third time lucky.

Time, Akram reflected, to think this thing through. Ten minutes or so of logical analysis later, he hit upon the following hypothesis.

I've been a villain all my life, or rather lives. Trying to change from villain to hero overnight is probably asking a bit much of Continuity, hence the fuck-ups. A more gradual approach, on the other hand, might prove efficacious. What he needed, therefore, was a sort of intermediate stage between villainy and heroism, in which he could do basically villainous things – robbing and maiming – but in a good cause.

In other words, Operation Robin Hood.

This was a good idea, he reflected, since although he was a

complete novice at errantry and oppressed-championing, what he didn't know about thieving you could write on the back of a nicked Visa card. Robbing the rich – well, that would come as easily as leaves to the tree. Giving to the poor he reckoned was something you could probably pick up as you went along; and in the meantime, he'd just have to busk it as best he could.

Step One: locate the Rich.

Back home, that wouldn't have been a problem. Saunter through the streets of Old Baghdad peering through the windows till you find a house where the goats live outside, then prop your ladder against it and you're away. An hour of pavement-slogging in London, however, showed that the same rules didn't seem to apply here.

The root of the problem, had he realised it, lay in the fact that he was operating in a district that was in the middle of extensive gentrification. Turning a corner and finding himself in what looked like a genuine, solid-milk-chocolate Mean Street of dingy old terraced houses, still black in places with authentic Dickensian soot, he was disconcerted to notice rather too many Scandinavian pine concept kitchens and smoked-glass occasional tables opaquely visible through the net curtains. Turn another corner and there were the big, opulent houses with steps up to the front door, flanked by pillars; but when you got there, you found a row of bell-pushes with name-tags beside each one, the kerb littered with clapped-out old motors, and a general shortage of desirable consumer goods visible through the windows. He was baffled.

'Excuse me,' he said, stopping a passer-by, 'but where do the Rich live?'

'You what?'

'I'm looking for some rich people,' he explained. 'Am I in the right area?'

'Bugger off.'

Akram shrugged; probably the bloke didn't know either, but didn't want to show his ignorance. He turned, and trudged on a bit further.

And turned a corner. And saw a bank.

Now that, he muttered to himself, is rather more like it. It should be pointed out that a lot of Akram's knowledge of the real world came from watching old movies and soap reruns intercepted via a magic mirror and a bent coathanger from the satellite channels. He knew, therefore, that when banks aren't foreclosing on the old farmstead, they're foreclosing on the widow's cottage or foreclosing on the family cotton mill in spite of the valiant efforts of the hero and heroine to pull the business round. That, as far as Akram was concerned, was what banks do, nine to five, Mondays to Saturdays. Indeed, as often as not they sneakily foreclose before the payments are actually due because of some shady deal the manager's got with the local property tycoon; and Akram had seen evidence of this with his own eyes, when he'd taken a walk down a whole High Street of closed and shuttered shops one Wednesday afternoon, and been told it was because it was early foreclosing day. Banks, therefore, were eminently fair game. Go for it.

The actual robbery side of it was so laughably simple that he wondered how they managed to stay in business. All he had to do was rip out the close-circuit TV camera, clobber the security guard, kick down the reinforced glass partition and help himself, resisting with ease the attempts of the counter staff to interest him in life insurance, unit-linked pension policies and flexible personal loans as he did so. It was when he ran out into the street, a bulging sack of currency notes in each hand, that the aggro started. If he'd been analysing as he went along he'd have seen the trend taking shape and been prepared for it, but that's the way it goes when you're all fired up with enthusiasm.

As he emerged from the bank, he almost collided with a

ragged, threadbare man, sitting on the pavement with a hat on the ground beside him and a cardboard sign imploring alms. Great, he muttered to himself, a genuine Poor. This is turning out easier than I expected.

'Here you are,' he said, offering the Poor one of the bags.

The Poor shot him a look of pure hatred. 'Piss off,' he snarled.

'But it's money. And you're poor.'

'I said piss off. Do I look like I want to spend the next five years inside?'

Akram was asking 'Inside where?' when the Poor noticed a poster in the bank's window headed REWARD, grabbed his ankle and started yelling 'Help! Police!' As if in answer, four cars and a van screamed to a halt at the kerb and suddenly the street was full of men in blue uniforms waving guns. Akram was obliged to hit two of them quite hard before he could get away, and a number of vehicles, a street lamp, a dog, a parking meter, several twelfth-storey windows and a passing helicopter were severely damaged by stray gunfire.

By the time he was clear and certain that his most energetic pursuers had lost the trail or had a nasty encounter with his unregenerate instincts, it was half past two and his enthusiasm for heroism was decidedly on the wane. He was still getting something wrong, he told himself; something obvious and simple, if only he knew what it was.

Bugger this, he muttered to himself as he let himself in to his bedsit, for a game of soldiers.

And when you don't know, ask someone who does.

Princess Scheherazade sighed, scratched her ear and ate another pickled onion. She was bored.

When she'd met the handsome prince, she'd hoped it would be different this time; not just one more meaningless story-book love affair, another thousand-and-one night stand. Now, however, with only three nights left to go before the inevitable Happy Ending, she could sense the story coming to an end all round her, and it made her feel like a written-off Cortina just before the big crusher reduces it to the size of a suitcase. It was only a vague, unformed suspicion clouding her subconscious mind, but deep down she *knew* that Happily Ever After sucks. Time, in other words, to move on, except of course that that wasn't possible.

She was, needless to say, in an unusual position. As well as being in a story, she made up stories. This only made her feel worse; having sent nine hundred and ninety-eight heroes and nine hundred and ninety-eight heroines to their Happy Ends, she no longer had any illusions whatsoever about what the process entailed, just as the man who operates the electric chair can't really kid himself that Old Sparky is an innovative new alternative to conventional central heating.

The pickle jar was empty. She scowled and snapped her fingers.

'Wasim,' she snapped without looking round. 'More of these round, vinegary things, quick as you can.' She heard the slave's obedient murmur and the slap of his bare feet on the marble floor. She yawned again. Dammit, she was bored out of her skull and the story hadn't even ended yet.

Supposing there was a story that went on for ever . . .

God only knows where the thought came from. It's extremely unlikely that it originated in the Princess's brain, which simply wasn't geared up with the necessary plant and equipment to turn out notions like that. Storybook characters don't speculate on the nature of stories, in the same way that calves don't write books called *A Hundred and One New Ways With Veal*. On the other hand, it's equally improbable to think that somebody planted it there. Who?

A story that doesn't end. A story that goes on, even outliving the storyteller.

But that's impossible, Scheherazade told herself; get a grip on yourself, girl, it's the pickles talking. Because every story is made up of three parts, beginning, middle and end, and something lacking one of these parts can't by definition be a story.

But just suppose . . .

On the evening before the First Day, God muttered *But just suppose* to himself in exactly the same way. He too ate rather too many pickled onions before going to bed, and the consequences are plain for everyone to see. But Scheherazade didn't know that, being female and accordingly, in the Islamic tradition, excused religion. She stopped lounging, sat upright, and began to think.

Soap opera—

Because she was excused religion, Scheherazade wasn't to know that human life is what God watches in the evenings when He gets home from work, and that He has a choice of two channels, and He was watching her on one of them at that precise moment. She only knew that she had three stories to go before everlasting happiness, and a liberal interpretation of the rules might just be her best, and only, chance.

Okay, she thought. For tonight, she'd decided on the traditional tale of Ali Baba and the Forty Thieves; a simplistic, two-twist narrative with two, maybe three featured characters and a couple of walk-ons for friends of the director's brother-in-law. But maybe, with a little breadth of vision and an HGV-equivalent poetic licence, the tawdry little thing might stretch . . .

The further supply of pickled onions arrived. She helped herself, crunched for a moment, and began to rehearse.

Once upon a time there was a man called Akram . . .

. . . Who sat down on a packing case, unwrapped a bulky parcel of old dusters and produced a brass oil lamp of the traditional Middle Eastern oiling-can-with-a-wick variety. He extended his sleeve as if to rub it, thought better of it, hesitated, closed his eyes and rubbed.

'Hello,' said the djinn, 'how's you? Hey, it's dark in here.'

Akram couldn't let that pass. 'Darker than where you've just come from?' he queried.

'Of course,' the djinn replied, 'I've been in a lamp. Now then, what can I do for you?'

There was something about the horrible creature's nails-on-blackboard cheerfulness that evacuated Akram's mind like a flawlessly executed fire drill. He stared for a moment, then frowned.

'Look,' he said. 'All I want is a simple answer to a simple question.'

'Sure.' The djinn smiled. Dammit, it was only trying to be friendly, but it was like having an itch in your crotch when you're addressing an emergency session of the United Nations. Akram took a deep breath and went on.

'Okay,' he said. 'What I—'

'Don't say wish,' the djinn interrupted. 'If you just ask me the question, you see, I don't have to count it as one of your wishes. Just a hint. Hope you don't mind me mentioning it.'

'What I *want* to know is— Look, I'm a villain, right?'

'Yes. Was that it?'

'No. Be quiet. I'm a villain. A baddie. Suppose I wanted to change and be a goodie, how'd I go about it?'

The djinn frowned and scratched the tip of its nose. 'I don't follow,' it said.

'Oh for crying out— Listen. I want to be good. How's it done? It can't be difficult, for pity's sake. If nuns can do it, so can I.'

The djinn grinned. 'It's easy for nuns,' it said. 'With them it's just force of habit. Get it? Habit, you know, like those long dressing gown things they wear—'

Instinctively Akram grabbed for the djinn's throat. His hands passed through it as if he'd tried to pull a projection off a screen. 'Don't push me too far,' he snarled. 'Now answer the goddam question, before I lose my temper.'

A multiple lifetime of experience in menacing had put a rasp into Akram's voice you could have shaped mahogany with, but the djinn simply looked down his nose at him. 'All right, Mister Grumpy,' he said, 'there's no need to get aereated.'

'I'll aereate you in a minute. Hey, would that make you a djinn fizz?'

'Your question,' said the djinn frostily. 'Can you, a villain, turn yourself into a good guy?'

'You got it.'

'Dunno.' The djinn pondered for a moment, and the air in the lock-up unit seemed to sparkle with tiny green flecks. 'It's a bit of a grey area, that. I mean, you could just try being nice to people and giving up your seat on buses to old ladies with heavy shopping and holding open-air rock concerts to raise money for famine victims and stuff, but there's no saying that'd actually work.'

'There isn't?'

The djinn shook its head. 'No saying it wouldn't, either. I'm just guessing, really.'

Akram closed his eyes and started to count to ten. He got as far as four.

'I wonder,' he said. 'If I took your lamp and soldered down the lid and blocked the spout up with weld, would that mean you'd be trapped in there for ever and ever?'

'I don't know.'

'Neither do I.' Akram reached for his toolkit. 'Soldering iron, soldering iron, I saw the blasted thing only the other day.'

'Alternatively,' said the djinn, 'you might try and do good

but all that'd happen would be that you did bad in spite of yourself.'

'Sorry, my gibberish is a trifle rusty. What are you talking about?'

'Because you're a villain,' said the djinn, ostentatiously patient, 'everything you do – arguably – will turn out evil, regardless of your intentions. Like in the film.'

'Film? What film?'

The djinn made a tutting noise. 'It's on the tip of my tongue,' it said. 'Donoghue. O'Shaughnessy.'

'What the—?'

'Cassidy. Butch Cassidy. You know, the bit where they try going straight and get jobs as payroll guards and end up gunning down about a zillion Mexicans.'

'Bolivians.'

'Pardon me?"

'Bolivians,' Akram repeated. He could feel a headache starting to come together in the foothills of his brain. 'They were in Bolivia, not Mexico.'

'You're quite right,' the djinn conceded. 'I always think of it as Mexico because of the big round hats.'

'Bugger hats.' It was going to be a *special* headache. 'What you're saying is, I'm stuck with being a villain, there's nothing I can do about it. But that's crazy. I mean, this is Reality, for pity's sake. Surely in Reality I can be whatever I want to be, that's the whole bloody point.'

The djinn sniggered. 'Think you'll find it isn't quite as simple as that,' it said. 'Otherwise everybody'd be film stars and millionaires and lottery winners.'

'Ah,' Akram said, 'but I happen to have a genuine magic djinn with supernatural powers on my side, so I'm laughing, aren't I?'

The djinn made a sniffing noise. 'Now you mustn't go building your hopes up,' it said, 'because in actual fact I have to be very careful with the possibility infringement regulations, and—'

'Got it!' Akram held up a soldering iron, and grinned. 'And here's the solder, look, so all we need now is the flux. Unless this is the sort where the flux is in there already.'

'Now look,' protested the djinn, 'don't you try threatening me . . .'

'I think it's that sort. Why do they use such small print on these labels?'

'I've been threatened by bigger people than you, you know. If you were to see some of the people I've been threatened by, six miles away through a telescope, you'd have to sleep with the light on for a month.'

Akram smiled. People who saw Akram's special menacing smile invariably remembered it for the rest of their lives, although in many cases this was not, objectively speaking, a terribly long time. 'And then,' he said, 'once I've soldered the lid and jammed the spout, just suppose I put the lamp on top of the cooker and turn the heat full on. It'd get very hot in there.'

'Look.' The djinn was sweating. 'I don't make the rules. If it was up to me, you could be Saint Francis of Assisi and Mother Teresa and the Care Bears all rolled into one. As it is . . .'

'First,' Akram said, 'you plug in your soldering iron. Next, make sure all surfaces are clean and free of dirt and grit. That's one of the basic rules of all endjineering, that is.'

'As it is,' said the djinn, passing a finger round the inside of its collar, 'there are a few very remote possibilities I could check out, but there's absolutely no guarantee—'

'So what we do is,' Akram went on, the lamp in one hand, a scrap of emery paper in the other, 'we just rub down the edges until we've got rid of the verdigris and we're down to the virdjinn metal—'

'No *cast-iron* guarantee,' the djinn muttered rapidly, 'but on the other hand I think we can be quietly confident. What was it you wanted again?'

'I want to be good.'

'No worries.'

'In fact,' Akram said, 'I want to be the hero.'

The djinn swallowed. 'And that's a wish, is it?'

'You bet.'

Cue special effects. Unearthly green lights, clouds of hissing vapour, doors and windows suddenly flying open. It would have taken George Lucas nine months and an eight-figure budget. The djinn was a spinning tower of green flame, and Akram looked like he was wearing a fluorescent green overcoat with Christmas tree lights for buttons.

'Your wish,' said the tower of flame, 'is my command.'

Scheherezade paused, and looked up at her husband, who chuckled, lit his cigar and grinned. Outside, the sun shone on a wide lawn, a long drive, a pair of impressive-looking gates guarded by a huge man in dark glasses and a black suit. Scheherezade's husband took a long pull on his cigar and poured himself another glass of strega.

'One down,' he said, 'two to go.'

CHAPTER TWELVE

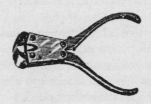

Maybe, in accordance with some extremely complex chain of causalities explicable only in terms of the most highly advanced avant-garde chaos theory, Akram's transformation into a trainee Hero was the reason he got fired from the kebab house. The ostensible reason, or at least the catalyst, was taking time off to go to the dentist without clearing it with the boss first.

He accepted the decision with uncharacteristic stoicism. The old Akram would immediately have avenged the insult in blood, leaving his replacement a confusing choice of impaled hunks of knife-slashed meat. The new Akram shrugged meekly, apologized for his thoughtlessness, collected his apron and left without raising the issue of arrears of wages due. If he'd been offered any money, he'd probably have refused to accept it.

He was shuffling homewards from this mortifying interview when he passed the window of a large fast-food joint, an outpost of an internationally respected hamburger federation.

Looking up, he saw a brightly coloured poster that said: HELP WANTED.

Wow, he said to himself, is that an omen or what? You'd have to be brain-dead or carved from solid marble not to recognise such an obvious example of Destiny handing out second chances. With a small nod of the head to indicate respectful thanks, he walked in and asked to see the manager.

In order to be considered for the job, the manager explained, prospective candidates had to be:

(a) hard-working, diligent and honest;
(b) experienced in all main aspects of retail mass catering;
(c) of a presentable appearance and able to communicate effectively with the general public;
(d) desperate enough to apply for the job and demoralised enough to stay.

And, he added quickly, Akram seemed to him to qualify in all four categories. He didn't actually stand in front of the door until Akram agreed to take the job, but he hovered.

'Not,' he added quickly, as he issued Akram with his apron and cardboard hat of office, 'that we have difficulty keeping staff. Far from it. Some nights at closing time I have to shoo them out with a broom. It's just that this is – well, a *lively* neighbourhood, and some of the customers—'

Involuntarily he closed his eyes, but only for a split second. 'A bit fun-loving, some of them. Very occasionally.'

'Good-natured banter and high spirits?'

The manager nodded. 'From time to time. Anyway, welcome on board and the very best of luck. Now, if you'll just give me the name and address of your next of kin, purely a formality . . .'

Akram made up a name and address, put on his uniform and followed the manager out into the kitchen area. The work as explained to him didn't seem arduous or distasteful, at least compared with some of the things he'd had to do in his previous career, and there was something about his new colleagues that made him feel immediately at home. It was only after an hour or so that he realised what it was. The scars.

'This one,' explained Gladstone, the assistant manager, 'was where this bloke slashed me with a bottle, and this one was a razor, and this one was where this girl tried to stub her fag out in me eye 'cos she reckoned I gave her the wrong relish on the dips. And this one . . .'

'I see,' Akram said aloud; to himself he was groaning; *Oh bugger it, Butch Cassidy.* Still, it was worth a try, and maybe if he was alert and concentrated very, very hard on getting out of the way, he wouldn't have to kill anybody for weeks.

The part of the job that involved preparing and retailing food turned out to be almost pleasant; and as for the other aspect, there seemed to be something about Akram's manner that deterred the blade-wielding fun-lovers and made them take their place in one of the other queues. After he'd been there a month, in fact, the place had become virtually fun-free, and rumour had it that the district's principal fun-lovers had blacklisted the establishment and were taking their custom to Neptune's Larder, three hundred yards down the road. When he heard this, Akram was afraid he'd lose his job for driving away customers, but the manager didn't seem to mind a bit. In fact, when Gladstone the assistant manager got into a lively debate with a tenaciously loyal fun-lover and was signed off work for nine months in consequence, Akram was promoted to take his place.

'Really?'

'Yes, really.'

'Gosh.' Akram was lost for words. 'What, *really*?'

The manager looked at him. 'I'm glad you're so pleased,' he said. 'Actually, it's not an awful lot more money, but—'

'*More* money?'

The manager took half a step backwards. He'd been there

nearly eighteen months, and knew from experience that working there took its toll in many different ways. 'Well, yes,' he said. 'Not a fortune, by any means, but we do like to reward . . .'

'Gosh. But I scarcely know what to do with all of what I get already. I'm not sure I ought to – I mean, I'm not sure it'd feel right, somehow.'

'Go on,' muttered the manager. 'Force yourself.'

There was, of course, a downside. There is a dignity doth hedge an assistant manager, even a temporary acting one; his place is on the quarterdeck rather than in the engine room, and it would be inconsistent with that dignity for him to slice onions, defrost coleslaw or top up the french-fries hopper. Henceforth, there would be no more shifts in the kitchen; a pity, because he had come to love the smell and texture of the food, which to someone who had spent his lives in Old Baghdad was tantalising and exotic. In Old Baghdad, what you ate depended entirely on who you were, and there were just two standard menus: banquets and scraps. Since the latter was only the former two days later, it all tended to get a bit monotonous, and Bar-B-Q Bacon Belt-Bustas, thick shakes and the Chicken Danish Brunch were like a glimpse through the curtain at the dining-tables of paradise.

'You like it here,' Tanya said, one night during a lull. It wasn't a question, more a bewildered statement of fact. Akram nodded.

'Best job I ever had,' he replied.

Tanya looked at him; and he was more than happy to reciprocate. A couple of months ago, if you'd have told Akram that women like Tanya existed, he'd have laughed in your face. She was completely different. She wasn't sloe-eyed and hourglass-shaped. Her glances didn't smoulder; and although Akram had no way of telling because her apron was in the way, he'd have been prepared to bet a year's wages that she didn't have a diamond jammed in her belly-button. True, there was enough of her to have made two of what Akram thought of as the standard-issue model, and still have plenty left over for spares; but so, as Akram told himself as he stood and gazed at her, what? The best thing about her, the bit that really shook him to the marrow, was that she was *different*. She did things that the girls back home wouldn't have the faintest idea how to do. Such as think.

'Really?'

Akram nodded. 'You bet,' he said.

'Right. So what was it you used to do?'

'I . . .' Although he'd known all along that the question would be asked sooner or later, he'd always shied away from the task of fabricating a reply. Somehow, even thinking about his past activities made him feel depressed and nervous, as if to admit that he'd had a previous existence could jeopardise his new one. 'I'd rather not talk about it,' he said, looking down at the counter. 'If that's all right,' he added.

'Sure.'

There you go, thoughtfulness again. Consideration for the feelings of others. The desire to avoid pain and embarrassment. God, thought Akram, I love it here, I'm not *ever* going back.

Tanya didn't say anything, and then a customer came in and ordered a Chicken Danish Brunch, so that the moment passed. As Akram got the order – a chicken burger sitting on half a bread roll crowned with a splodge of red sauce and some sort of plant – he stole a glance at Tanya out of the corner of his eye, and deep inside him somewhere a little voice said *Yes, but why not?* And the rest of him couldn't immediately think of any good reason.

'So,' Hanif muttered, sitting down on a flat rock and putting his head between his hands, 'that's it, then.'

Aziz nodded, unable to speak. A hundred yards or so in front of them was the border; the customs post, Jim's Diner, the wire. He felt utterly wretched.

'Let's face it,' Hanif went on, 'we've looked everywhere. Everywhere,' he repeated unnecessarily. 'And he's not there. Which can only mean—'

'All right,' Aziz growled, 'you've made your bloody point.'

Faisal shook his head, dislodging a few organisms. 'Still can't see why he'd do such a thing,' he sighed. 'I mean, run out on us. Abandon us like that. You just wouldn't believe it.'

It was a hot day, they'd been on the road since an hour before dawn, and nobody had the energy to answer. Finally having to accept that the Skip was gone and was unlikely ever to come back was like trying to come to terms with God leaving the answering machine on even though you know perfectly well he's at home. There was a vast hole in the side of their universe; they could ignore it, or else fall through.

'Maybe he's in the caff,' said Hassan. 'I mean, we haven't actually looked.'

'Might as well,' Aziz replied. 'They may have seen him, anyhow.'

'I think,' said Mushtaq, youngest and most gauche of the Thirty-Nine Thieves, 'that he's gone on a special mission to the other side to steal something, you know, something really, really valuable, and as soon as he's pulled it off he'll come back, and . . .'

'Mushtaq.'

'Yes, Skip?'

'Don't, there's a good lad.'

'Don't what, Skip?'

Aziz sighed. 'Just don't, that's all. I'm not in the mood. All right,' he went on, standing up and rubbing his cheeks with his palms, 'Hassan, Farouk, you come with me and we'll check out the caff. The rest of you—'

He couldn't be bothered to finish the order. There was no point; after all, apart from sitting aimlessly in the shade with their knees drawn up to their chins, what else was there that they could possibly find to do? He beckoned to his two chosen followers and trudged slowly towards Jim's Diner.

Inside, it was at least a little bit cooler. They walked up to the counter, flopped down onto barstools and ordered three quarts of goat's milk and three club sandwiches. Ten minutes and a good deal of noise later, they were in a much better state to ask penetratingly shrewd questions.

'Here, miss,' said Aziz. 'You seen Akram the Terrible round here lately?'

The barmaid – dear God, where did he find them? Under flat stones, probably – looked up from the glass she was polishing. 'You just missed him,' she said.

Hassan stood up at once and started for the door, but Aziz waved him back. He'd been in Jim's before, and knew that Time here wasn't only relative, it was third-cousin-twice-removed. 'How long since he was here?' he asked.

The barmaid shrugged. 'Couple of months, maybe three. He left with a bear.'

Aziz managed to silence Farouk before he could ask with a bare what and get them all thrown out. 'Oh yes?' he replied, as nonchalantly as possible. To be painfully honest, Aziz was to nonchalance as a pterodactyl in Selfridges' is to looking inconspicuous, but he gave it his best shot. 'This bear,' he added, 'Wouldn't happen to be in here, would he?'

The barmaid shook her head. 'You just missed him,' she replied.

'Don't tell me,' muttered Aziz. 'He left with Akram the Terrible, right?'

'If you know, why ask?'

Aziz got up. 'Not to worry,' he sighed. 'Look, if you see this bear, tell him we'd like a word, okay?'

'Why not tell him yourself?' the barmaid said. 'I can tell you where to find him.'

In many lifetimes of violence and mayhem, Aziz had never hit a woman, mostly because they wouldn't keep still; but he wasn't one of those narrow-minded types who shrink away from new experiences. 'Right,' he said, 'fine. Could you please tell me where . . .?'

The barmaid thought about it for a moment. 'All right,' she said. 'Go back out the way you came about seven leagues and you'll come to a big forest, right? Take the main road, then second on your left, third right past the charcoal burner's, then follow your nose and you'll come to a little cottage.'

Aziz squirmed a little in his seat. 'Brightly painted red door? Shiny brass knocker? Red and white curtains with pretty flowers and stuff?'

'That's right.'

'Big mat with *Welcome*? Climbing roses round the porch? Little goldfish pond out front with a couple of rustic benches?'

'You know the place, then?'

Aziz nodded. He knew the place all right. He'd be able to picture it in his mind's eye for the rest of his life as the house where he single-handedly killed the ferocious bear. 'This bear he went off with,' he said, his voice sounding odd because of the dryness of the roof of his mouth. 'Lady bear, was it?'

'No. Gentleman bear – I mean, it was a male. Great big brute, huge claws.'

'Ah.'

'Real nice personality, mind. Wouldn't hurt a fly. Called Derek.'

'Oh.'

'Can't say as much for his friends, though. Very pally with some really heavy types, if you know what I mean.'

'Fat people?'

The barmaid shook her head. She didn't speak, but she mouthed the words *the mob* so distinctly that a lip-reader would have asked her not to shout. 'Wouldn't want to get on the wrong side of that lot,' she added with a grimace. 'That Derek was in here one time, these pirates jogged his elbow, made him spill his condensed milk. Three months later, they fished what was left of 'em out of a lime pit out behind Tom Thumb's place. Only able to identify them from the dental records.'

'I see.'

'This bear,' the barmaid said, studying Aziz's face as if expecting to have to pick it out of a lineup at some later stage. 'What you want him for, anyway?'

'We're friends of Ak— hey, watch it, Skip, that was my ankle.'

'Wrong bear,' said Aziz loudly. 'Not the one we were thinking of, was it, lads? I mean, the bear we were thinking of is small. Honey-coloured. Lives in an abandoned sawmill over by the Hundred Acre Wood. Well, thanks for the milk.'

By the time they were out of Jim's and back in the fresh air, Aziz was as white as a sheet. A very dirty sheet, from the bed of someone who never washes, but white nevertheless.

'Okay, lads,' he said. 'I think we may be in a bit of trouble here.'

'Trouble, Skip?'

Aziz shuddered. 'Nothing to worry about,' he replied. 'I just reckon it might be sensible if we found something like a cave or a very deep hole, just for a year or so. That'd make a nice change, wouldn't it?'

'But Skip, what about finding Ak—?'

'*Shut up!*'

'Sorry, I'm sure.'

Aziz mopped his face with his shirt tails. 'Anybody know of anywhere like that?' he asked. 'Near here, preferably. In fact, as near as possible?'

Hanif frowned. 'You okay, Skip?' he asked, concerned. 'You seem a bit edgy.'

'Yeah,' agreed Shamir. 'Like a bear with a sore—'

'*Quiet!*' Aziz snapped, and then took a deep breath. On reflection, he told himself, belay that last instinct. It was no earthly use trying to hide from Them; after all, wherever he led his wretched followers in Story-book land, they'd be strangers, out of place in some other folks' story, conspicuous as a goldfish in a lemon meringue pie. So; they couldn't hide. Popular theory would have them believe that as a viable alternative they could run, but Aziz wasn't too sure about that; not in curly-toed slippers, at any rate. Well, now; if you can't hide and you can't run, what can you do?

Whimper?

Sham dead?

Forget the second alternative, in case Death is attracted to the sincerest form of flattery. Aziz reached a decision. He'd try whimpering. After all, it wasn't as if they were spoilt for choice, and in the final analysis they had nothing to lose but a complete set of limbs and their lives.

'Wait there, I may be gone some time,' he said, and went back inside.

'You again,' said the barmaid.

Aziz nodded. 'You said something about the bear having, um, friends,' he said. 'I'd like to meet them.'

'You would?'

'Yes,' said Aziz. 'Please,' he added, remembering his manners.

The barmaid stared at him, as if speculating how he'd look in one of those fancy jackets with long sleeves that do up at the back. 'Why?' she said.

'It's a long story.'

'Aren't they all?'

'That depends,' Aziz replied. For his part, he had the

feeling that his own particular narrative was in serious danger of being cut down into an anecdote. 'Don't change the subject. How do I meet these guys?'

The barmaid shrugged. 'Okay,' she said. 'Go back out the way you came about three leagues and you'll come to a ruined castle. After that, you take the first right then second on your left, second right past the little pigs' house, straight on up the hill until you come to a crossroads, you'll see a long drive leading up to a big house. Say Rosa from Jim's sent you, but it's nothing to do with her. Okay?'

'Sure thing. Thanks.'

'You *really* want to go there?'

'You've been most helpful.'

'And tell Rocco on the gate,' she called after him, 'if they're going I wouldn't mind the tall one's boots for my kid brother.'

'So,' said the man behind the desk, 'you come to me and you say, *We kill your buddy the little bear, we're terribly sorry, we won't do it again.* Is that it?'

Aziz nodded. Behind him, seventy-six feet shuffled nervously. 'It was an accident, really,' he said. 'Well, not an accident as such, more a, what's the word, misunderstanding.' He remembered a good phrase from one of his juvenile court appearances. 'A tragic fusion of coincidence, mistaken identity and good intentions gone dreadfully awry,' he recited. On second thoughts, he wished he hadn't; it hadn't worked the first time, mainly because the coincidence had been the night watch coming down the alley at precisely the moment he was leaving the warehouse, the mistaken identity had been him thinking they weren't the watch, and the good intention had been his intention to escape by climbing over the wall into what turned out to be the Khalif's pedigree snake collection.

'Sure,' grunted the man behind the desk. 'I believe you. So when the Momma Bear and the Baby Bear they come to me and say, *Padrone, give us justice*, I gotta tell them it was all a mistake and the guys are terribly sorry. Do you take me for a fool, or what? Rocco, get them outa my sight.'

Behind him, Aziz could hear footsteps, and metallic grating noises. Not for the first time, he sincerely wished he could have had his brain removed when he was twelve. 'Look . . .' he stuttered.

And then the man behind the desk did a strange thing. He smiled. 'On the other hand,' he said. He didn't finish the sentence, but the movement noises in the background stopped as abruptly as if a tape had been switched off.

'Yes?' Aziz croaked.

'Hey.' The man spread his arms. 'Everybody makes mistakes. I made a mistake, once,' he added. 'And I'm sure that if I was to put in a good word for you with the widow bear and the orphan bear—'

'Yes?'

'And you guys sign a legally binding contract to cut them in on, say, ninety per cent of everything you make for the next forty years—'

'Yes?'

'Plus a small contribution, say five per cent, to the Arabian Nights Moonshine Coach Club social fund—'

'Yes?'

The man shrugged. It was an eloquent gesture. Louder and clearer than fifty-foot neon letters against a black background it said THIS COMMITS ME TO NOTHING BUT SO WHAT? 'Then,' he said, 'you guys gonna be so grateful to me, you might consider doing me a small favour.'

'Anything you say,' Aziz replied, in a voice so small that a bat would need a hearing aid to hear it. '*Padrone*,' he added.

'That's great,' said the man. 'Now, then. I gonna tell you a story.'

CHAPTER THIRTEEN

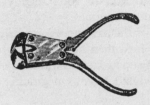

The air was foul with the stench of burning bone.

It's a distinctive smell; not perhaps overwhelmingly revolting in itself, but unbearable once you know what it is. You can get used to it, of course; human beings can get used to virtually anything, given plenty of time and no choice in the matter whatsoever. Fortunately, Ali Baba wasn't naturally squeamish, and he had the advantage of knowing that, although his drill turned so fast that the friction scorched the tooth as he drilled it, the patient never felt a thing because of the anaesthetic.

'There you are,' he said cheerfully. 'Quick rinse and we're done.'

Last patient of the day; no more drilling into people until eight o'clock tomorrow morning. A propos of nothing much, he wondered whether Akram the Terrible, his former great and worthy opponent, ever felt the same sense of deep, exhausted relief after a hard night's murdering. Wash off the blood and the bits of bone, change into nice comfy old clothes, make a nice hot cup of something and collapse into a friendly chair by the fire; what, after all, could be better than that? Apart, of course, from not having to get all bloody and covered in bits in the first place.

He had switched off the lights and was just about to lock up when a white delivery van pulled up outside. Mr Barbour? Yes, that's me. Delivery for you, if you'd just sign here. The driver handed him a crate about eighteen inches square, accepted his tip and drove away.

Ali Baba stood on the pavement for nearly a minute, feeling the weight of the box; then he unlocked the door and went back inside, locking up again afterwards. His heart was beating a little faster now, and he was beginning to sweat ever so slightly.

The museum authorities hadn't been best pleased when he'd called them up and asked for it back. He'd reminded them that it was only a loan, and pointed out that there had been a recent spate of thefts of similar objects. He mentioned in passing that he had a receipt. When they put the phone down on him, he rang straight back, ignored their claim that he'd got a wrong number and was now talking to NexDay Laundry Services, and demanded to speak to the Director. And so forth. Eventually they agreed to return it by armoured van, with Ali Baba paying the carriage charges. Then, having added (quite unnecessarily, in Ali Baba's opinion) that at least that meant one less card to send this Christmas, they rang off.

And here it was. He sighed and shook his head. If only the poor fools had realised what they'd actually got there, not all the bailiffs and court orders in the universe could ever have prised it away from them.

Yes. But. Bailiffs and court orders are one thing, but the greatest ever burglar in either of the two dimensions was something else entirely; and if Akram was still out there somewhere, plotting and scheming to find a way of nailing his ancient foe without transgressing the letter of his oath, then leaving this thing in the deepest vault of the most secure museum in the world was pretty much the same as laying it out on the pavement with a big flashing light on top to show him where to find it. It'd be criminal negligence of the most horrible and bloodcurdling variety to let it stay where it was. There could only be one safe place for it from now on, and that was under the loose floorboard in the store cupboard in Ali Baba's surgery.

'Blasted thing,' he muttered under his breath, as he carried it up the stairs. 'Wish I'd never pinched it in the first place.'

All loose floorboards are not the same. For a start, this one didn't creak. Nor could it be prised up with a crowbar and the back of a claw hammer. In fact, were a hostile power to drop a nuclear bomb on Southampton, the only thing guaranteed to be completely undamaged would be Ali Baba's loose floorboard. It'd still be loose, of course; exactly the same degree of looseness, not a thousandth of a millimetre tighter or wobblier.

Carefully – drop it and the consequences didn't bear thinking about – he lowered it into the hole and then stood back, hands on knees, to catch his breath and say the password. He did so, replaced the board and muttered the self-activating spell. Finally, he locked up and went home.

After he'd gone, the rogue tooth fairy that'd been hanging around the place all day in the hope of picking up sixpenny-worth of second-hand calcium clambered out of a half-empty pot of pink casting medium, looked around to make sure all was clear, and landed heavily on the loose floorboard. It wobbled, but it wouldn't budge.

'Bugger,' muttered Fang.

Three quarters of an hour later, she gave up the unequal struggle. During this time she'd snapped or blunted two dozen drill bits, broken a whole box of disposable scalpels and banged her own thumb with a two-pound lump hammer (don't ask what it was doing in among the tools of Ali Baba's trade, because unless you've got film star's teeth and will never need to go to a dentist again, you really don't want to know). There was no way of getting in without the password, and although she knew perfectly well what it was, having overhead Ali Baba setting it, she was just a fairy and couldn't say it loud enough. A pity; the contents of Ali Baba's improvised floor safe were worth more to her than all the molars ever pulled. If only she could get her hands on it, then she could name her price; including her old job back and sixpences enough to buy Newfoundland.

Nothing for it; she needed human help. But who?

Not a problem. She knew just the man. In fact, he was her landlord.

With a savage buzz she memorised the location of the loose board, checked the office waste-paper basket for teeth one last time, and flew home.

Aren't human beings wonderful?

Well, actually, no; but they do sometimes manage to achieve wonderful things, albeit for all the wrong reasons. One of their most remarkable abilities, which gained them the coveted Golden Straitjacket award for most gloriously dizzy instinctive behaviour five thousand years running in the prestigious Vicenza Dumb Animals Festival, is their exceptional knack of ignoring the most disturbingly bizarre circumstances simply by pretending they don't exist. No matter how radical the upheaval, as soon as the dust has settled a little and it's relatively safe outside the bunker, out they go again to weave their spiders' webs of apparent normality over whatever it is they don't want to come to terms with, until the web becomes as rigid and substantial as a coral reef.

Michelle, for example, found that if she went to work as usual, stayed on after hours doing overtime and then went straight on to meet friends for a drink or a movie, so that she was almost never at home before midnight or after seven-thirty am, she could go hours at a time without thinking strange thoughts or feeling the naggingly persistent lure of the ring. It was like living on the slopes of an active volcano but without the views and the constant free hot water.

And then; well, you can only play chicken on the Great Road of Chaos for so long before you make a slight error of judgement. In Michelle's case, her mistake lay in stopping off for a bite to eat after an evening's rather self-conscious cheerleading for the office formation karaoke team. Perhaps it was the strain of having to put a brave face on Mr Pettingell from Claims singing *You Ain't Nothin' But A Hound Dog* in a Birmingham accent so broad you could have used it as a temporary bridge over the Mississippi that sapped her instinctive early warning systems; or perhaps it was just that her number was up.

'I'll have the . . .' She hesitated, and squinted at the illuminated menu above the counter. She'd originally intended to have the Treble Grand Slam Baconburger, large fries, regular guava shake; but a glance at the ten-times-life-size backlit transparency overhead made her doubt the wisdom of that decision. For one thing, it was too brightly coloured. Mother Nature reserves bright reds and yellows for warning livery for her more indigestible species, such as wasps and poison toadstools. The sight of the ketchup and relish in the illustration must have triggered an ancient survival mechanism. She had another look at the menu, searching for something there wasn't a picture of.

'I'll try the . . .' For a fleeting moment she was tempted by the Greenland Shark Nuggets 'n' Bar-B-Q Dip, but the moment passed. If God had intended people to eat sharks, as opposed to vice versa, he would have modified the respective blueprints accordingly.

The man behind the counter smiled patiently. 'Take your

time,' he said. 'Actually, I'd recommend the Chicken Danish Brunch.' There was, Heaven help us, a flicker of genuine, unfeigned enthusiasm in the poor man's eyes as he spoke. 'My personal favourite,' he added, 'for what that's worth.'

Michelle shrugged. 'So what's that got in it?' she asked.

The man straightened his back with – yes, dammit, with *pride* as he recited, 'It's a scrummy fillet of marinaded prime chicken, served traditional Danish-style in an open sandwich with choice of relish, all on a sesame seed bun.'

The speech went past Michelle like an InterCity train through a Saturdays-only backwoods station. 'I'm sorry?' she said. 'I missed that.'

'Okay. It's a scrummy—'

'Edited highlights, please.'

'No problem. Chicken, open sandwich, sesame seed bun.'

Michelle shook her head. It was noisy inside, noisy even for a Macfarlane's on a Friday night, and her ears were still ringing from Mr Sobieski from Accounts informing the world that ever since his baby left him, he'd found a new place to dwell. 'Say again, please,' she shouted back. 'Didn't quite catch . . .'

The man nodded and smiled. 'Sandwich,' he said. 'Open. Sesame . . .'

'Open sesame?'

('Two down. One to go.')

'Sesame seed bun.' Something strange had happened to the man's face. It was as if he was being used as a guinea pig by a blind acupuncturist. 'Guaranteed to make your taste-buds . . . Don't I know you?'

'I'm sorry?'

'You sound like someone I used to know.'

As he spoke, he saw that her purse was open on the counter, and there was her Visa card. Part of the shared heritage of thieves and lawyers is an ability to read upside down without even having to think about it: MICHELLE PARTRIDGE.

'Do I?'

'My imagination,' Akram replied; while he was saying the words, shutters came down in his eyes, like a snake's transparent eyelids. 'Do forgive me. Alternatively, the Saigon Ribs Surprise is very popular. There's a choice of dips, we've got Tangy Orange, Bar-B-Q, Byzantine Lemon . . .'

Her purse also contained a receipted gas bill, with her address. Akram's eyes lapped up the information like a cat drinking milk.

'I'll have that, please,' Michelle said quickly. 'Who did I remind you of?'

'Forget it, please,' Akram muttered. 'That was in another country, and besides, the sonofabitch is dead.'

'I beg your pardon?'

'Which dip? We got orange, barbeque, lemon . . .'

'Orange.'

'Coming right up. That'll be three pounds seventy-five, please.'

Now I know who he is, Michelle realised. He was in the waiting room, the day I—

'Your change,' said Akram. 'Enjoy your meal, have a nice day.'

'Thank you. I—'

The two girls behind her, who had been very patient so far, eased past and ordered hamburgers. She stood for a moment, at right angles to the queue, clutching her bag and trying to think.

Akram. *Akram the Terrible!* Here!

'Excuse me.' She elbowed one girl out of the way and stood heavily on the other's toe. 'Sorry,' she growled. 'Look, is your name Akram, by any chance?'

The man looked at her, and pointed at his lapel badge. It read: JOHN, ASST MGR.

'So sorry,' she whispered, and fled.

Of all the hamburger joints in all the towns in all the world, Akram reflected, as he locked up that night. Just when I was starting to get somewhere. Just when I was beginning to get some vague idea of what happiness might possibly be like. And now it's back to the old routine.

Just a minute, he reflected. Just because I've found Ali Baba's daughter (how come he's got a daughter, and what in buggery is she doing this side of the goddamn Line?) doesn't necessarily mean I've got to do anything about it. I can just ignore it. Forget I ever saw her. Take no notice.

I could indeed. And then, for an encore, I could hitch a ride on a flying pig and save myself the bus fare home. Get real, Akram.

Get *real* —

If only. Chance, he muttered to himself as he switched on the alarm, would be a bloody fine thing. He'd seen or read somewhere that humans had a proverb: Mankind cannot stand too much reality. As far as he was concerned, Mankind didn't know it was born.

When he got home, the tooth fairy was waiting for him. That, he reckoned, put the tin lid on it.

'Not now,' he said, as she fluttered down from the ceiling like a large moth, the sort that chews holes in chain-mail shirts.

'Yes, but listen . . .'

'I said not now.' He flumped into the armchair, kicked his shoes off, and put his hands behind his head. All other considerations beside, he'd had a long day, been on his feet for most of it, and he badly wanted to go to sleep. It occurred to him that on the other side of the Line, he never got as tired as this, even if he'd been in the saddle all day and out burgling and killing all night. In Story-book land, everyone has bound-less energy and extraordinary (by Real standards) stamina. In

Story-book land, people only keel over from exhaustion when the story demands that they say, 'I'm done for, you go on without me'; which is the hero's cue to pick up his worn-out colleague and carry him for two days across the desert.

'Listen!'

Akram turned, his hand partly raised as if to swat. 'Well?' he snapped. 'This had better be important. Anything less than world-shattering, and the only loose teeth around here are going to be your own.'

Tooth fairies are, of course, first-class narrators, and it took Fang less than thirty seconds to explain about her discovery. When she'd finished, Akram nodded slowly.

'Okay,' he said, 'so that is pretty world-shattering.'

'And?'

'And what?'

'And,' said Fang impatiently, 'as in, what are we waiting for? Come on, it's after midnight already.'

Akram held up his hand, as if he was God directing traffic. 'Not so fast,' he said. 'Admittedly, the obvious course of action would be to go immediately and steal this thing.'

'Right.'

'Ninety-nine out of a hundred villains would already be out of the door and halfway down the street by now. The hundredth would be hobbling along behind the other ninety-nine, cursing the day he got lumbered with a wooden leg.'

'*Right*. So why are we . . .?'

'But,' said Akram, 'you overlook one minor detail. I'm not a villain any more. I'm through with all that, remember? I'm a good guy now.'

'Don't be silly,' said the tooth fairy. 'What's got into you, anyway? If you've got some sort of hyper-subtle master plan . . .'

Akram shook his head. 'Nope,' he replied. 'Look, my fluttering friend, watch my lips. I am not interested. I don't do that stuff any more. I mean it,' he added, as Fang made a vulgar noise implying disbelief. 'If I still wanted to nail Ali Baba, I've got an even better trick up my sleeve. I've found his daughter. I could put the snatch on her, demand that he release me from my promise, and then go scrag the fucker.' He paused for a moment. Without realising he was doing it, he'd taken such a tight grip on the arm of his chair that the wood was creaking. With an effort he let go. 'But I'm not going to,' he went on, putting his fingertips together and crossing his legs, as smoothly as a chat-show host. 'So, it was terribly sweet of you to think of me and if there's anything I can do that doesn't involve nutting people in the mouth so you can swipe their teeth, you just name it. But I'm not interested. You got that, or would you like me to tap it out on your head in Morse code with this teaspoon?'

At first, all Fang could do was stare at him, as if waiting for the practical joker to pull off the rubber Akram mask and say, 'Fooled you!' When it finally sank in that he was serious, the fairy couldn't trust herself to speak. She buzzed furiously to her shoebox, dived in and dragged the lid shut after her. Shortly afterwards, the flat was filled with the sound of a tiny person crying.

'Cut that out, will you?'

'Snf.'

'Look,' said Akram, raising the lid a few millimetres. 'I've brought you something, see? It's a left front incisor, I found it at work, a customer left it in a Triple Swiss Fondueburger. Don't you want it?'

The lid slammed.

'I'll leave it here for you,' said Akram, slightly shaken. 'For when you're a bit less overwrought. Look, it's still got most of its original plaque.'

From inside the box came a tiny voice telling him where he could put his lousy rotten tooth. The recommendation was biologically feasible, but not something you'd suggest to someone whose shoebox you were living in. Akram shrugged.

'If you don't want it,' he said, 'there's plenty that will. I'll put it under my pillow, and we'll see if it's still there in the morning.'

Nothing from the shoebox except bitter snuffling. Akram shrugged. Maybe she had a point, at that; but if she thought he was going to chuck away what might be his one and only chance to break out of the Story just to please a tiny gossamer-winged garbage collectress, she was deluding herself and that was all there was to it. It'd be like giving all your property to the poor, dressing up in sackcloth and wandering forth to preach to the birds just in order to get your picture on page seven of the *Assisi Evening Examiner*.

And anyway, he reassured himself, as he rolled into bed and switched off the light, virtue's its own reward, or so it says in the rule book. The better I am, the better I get. Turning down two opportunities for revenge in one day must mean I'm getting positively beatific. I bet that if I keep this up, I'll be so good I can sell my second-hand bathwater as beaujolais nouveau.

He fell asleep; his sleep lapsed into dreaming, and in his dream he was back across the Line and standing in front of the Fairy Godfather's desk with a terrified grin on his face and (since this was a dream) a schoolboy's cap on his head and an exercise book down the back of his trousers.

'So,' said the Godfather, 'you wanna be good?'

'Yes, *padrone*.'

'So you wanna be a hero?'

'Yes, *padrone*.'

'And you wanna nail that sonofabitch Ali Baba so good he'll wish he'll never be born again?'

And then Akram wanted terribly, terribly much to say *No, padrone* and he could feel himself straining the muscles of his brain as he tried to stop the other word, the one beginning with Y, squirming out through the gate of his teeth; but, since it was one of that sort of dream – I *knew* I shouldn't have finished off the two leftover Cheese Double Whammyburgers before we closed up, but isn't it a sin to let good food go to waste? – all he could do was stand back from himself and look the other way, and try not to listen—

'Yes, *padrone.*'

And now the Godfather is laughing; big man, big laugh. 'Your wish is my command,' he says. 'To hear is to obey. Rocco, you heard?'

'Yeah, boss.'

'So obey.'

'Yeah, boss.'

'But that's impossible,' Akram could hear himself protesting. 'If I'm the good guy and the hero, how come I can nail the creep Baba? I thought nailing people, I was through with all that.'

And a close-up of the Godfather's face; cigar clamped in corner of masonry jaw, black eyes burning. 'Hey,' he says softly, 'show some godamn respect. I mean, who's telling this story, you or me?'

Because it's a dream, one of that sort of dreams (all our cheeseburgers are made with a hundred per cent pure natural milk cheese; okay, it's industrial grade cheese, it's rolled out in huge fifty-metre sheets in a processing plant that's a dairy the way Greenwich Village is a village, but eat it late at night and you'll find out if it's real cheese or not) Akram finds he's no longer in the Godfather's study; he's standing behind a huge boulder in a cleft in a cliff-face, and it's dark, and there's a troop of horsemen riding in, he can hear their horses breathing and the soft tinkle of their mailshirts, the clink of their swords in their scabbards. He wants to run but he can't, and the leader of the troop rides up to the rock face, only a yard or so from where he's cowering and he says—

I know that voice!

—'Open sesame!' whereupon a door opens out of what looked for all the world like solid rock, and as it swings open on its hinges it creaks ever so slightly, and the leader of the troop rides past; and over his coat of mail he's wearing a white coat, and there's a scalpel, not a sword, by his side, which is why they call him Ali Baba the Terrible, leader of the Forty Dentists. And he looks up from writing *Open sesame* on his shirt-sleeve and through the space between door and door-frame, Akram can just see inside the cave, and it's stuffed full of gold – gold teeth, gold bridgework, gold dental plates, gold fillings prised out of the heads of screaming, dying men . . .

And of course, it makes sense, in a way; because surely stealing makes you a thief, even if it's thieves you steal from. On the other hand (but, since this is a dream, there's no actual contradiction; dream-logic is as flexible as a lawyer's promise) thieves are outlaws, and anything you do to a thief is perfectly fair; hell, you can *kill* thieves if you want to and still be as good as, well, gold (unfortunate simile, in the circumstances; all those *teeth* –) and so what, you don't get all hung up and conscience-stricken when you pour boiling water on an ants' nest, do you? And most of all, if you will go eating cheese last thing at night, what possible right have you got to complain if you have bad dreams?

Akram woke up.

'Fuck,' he said.

Stories grow, stories spread; and if you smuggle a story across the Line, don't go whining to the doctor when it starts frothing at the mouth and bites you.

'Fang.'

'Snfnottalkingtoyousnf.'

'Fang,' Akram repeated, 'get your coat. We're going out.'

CHAPTER FOURTEEN

J.F. Smith paused, his left foot on the top rung of the ladder, his right knee braced against the windowsill, and listened.

Far away, the railway hummed and growled, providing the nocturne's bass section. A little closer, the constant composite hum of traffic. Apart from that, nothing except the slow, regular pulse of his own heartbeat. Satisfied, J.F. Smith pulled down the sash, stuck his head in through the window and started to wriggle.

Destiny is a high-flown, rather romantic-sounding name for a whole host of factors outside one's own control that shape the course of one's life. Of these, where you happen to be born and who your parents are is perhaps the most important. J.F. Smith, for example, was born to follow one trade and one only. Anything else would have been as unthinkable as a teenage lion dropping in to the careers office asking if they had any openings for apprentice lambs. The fact that he'd actually been baptised John Fingers Smith came as no surprise to anybody who knew the family. They had been craftsmen in the burgling trade in Southampton ever since Henry V had strung up the first John Smith for stealing arrows from the quivers of the archers embarking for the Agincourt campaign.

The really remarkable thing about this great tradition was that, nearly six hundred years later, the Smith family still wasn't all that good at it; as witness the fact that John Fingers II, now in his fifty-second year, had just got out of prison for the seventh time, coincidentally on precisely the same day as Jason Fingers (19) and Damian (18) had started their first adult sentences in the same nick. The Governor, a man with a keen sense of tradition, had been keeping their great-grandfather's old cell ready and waiting for them ever since they were released from youth custody. It had their name on the door and everything.

As for this house; well, John Fingers could remember his father knocking it off in 1956 – he'd held the ladder for him, and it had been his momentary lapse of attention that had led to John Fingers I spending 1956–1960 in dear old B583. To judge by the paintwork, it was probably the very same sash as he was lifting now that had fallen on John Fingers I and held him pinned by the neck until the police arrived.

Having spent a few moments in silent contemplation, John Fingers II slithered through, landed in a heap and switched on his torch. In Dad's time, of course, this had still been a big private house, rather than a slightly down-market conversion into three flats. It was asking a bit much to expect to find any decent gear in a place like this; video, CD player, microwave, answering machine (except that they were now so cheap as to be scarcely worth the stealing) and maybe a few quid in loose cash if you were very lucky. You could forget silver, jewellery or works of art. Today's burglar, sad to say, is little more than a glorified furniture remover cum electrician.

Still, he told himself as he swung the torch round in a slow, careful arc, you never know. More for form's sake than anything else, he started pulling out the drawers and examining them for ring-boxes and jewellery cases.

(*'Well, don't just sit there, you moth-eaten excuse for a burglar alarm. Ring, damn you.'*

'I can't. I've got a loose wire.'

'Don't be ridiculous.'

'But I have, really. I've been waiting for her to notice it for weeks.'

'Oh. Of all the . . . Cordless screwdriver! Get your useless arse over here at the double!')

Hello, John Fingers II demanded of himself, what's this? He flipped open the lid of the little blue box, and sighed. Just a poxy little plain silver ring with a chip of glass stuck in it; you could buy half a dozen of these off a market stall, brand new and totally legit, for a tenner. Assuming you wanted one, let alone ten. On the other hand—

How *would* it look on the other hand?

With a shrug he lifted the ring out of the box and checked it for hallmarks. None. It wouldn't fit, of course; he could tell that without trying. It was a piece of cheap tat for the teenage market, probably less than five parts silver in any case. If I tried it on, it'd only get stuck.

No it wouldn't.

Yes it would.

'Armed police hold it right there move so much as the smallest hair on your bum and we'll blow you away!'

So it's true, a part of John Fingers II's brain noted with interest, extreme terror really does have an effect on the bowels and turn the knees to water. Why the hell is that? Bloody useless survival mechanism; not the evolutionary trait most likely to ensure the success of the species. He shuddered from head to toe, realising as he did so that he was breaking the embargo on movement. This only made matters worse.

'Move one millimetre and you'll go home in a plastic bag we have the building surrounded Nobby where's that SWAT team this

is a recorded— Oops, force of habit, damn.'

With infinite daring, John Fingers II frowned. Something funny here. For one thing, the voice seemed to be coming from inside his head.

Where were the searchlights?

Where, come to that, were the police?

'Hey,' he said aloud, 'what's going on here?'

'*Shuttup you another peep out of you and you're a dead man Nobby I want those snipers in here now.*'

There was something about the voice, definitely coming from inside him somewhere, that entirely failed to convince. There were no police. It was some kind of daft booby-trap.

The hell with it. Anybody who would have you believe that running away is a dying art should watch a member of the Smith family getting the hell out of residential property where they have no right to be. From unfreezing to shinning down the ladder and sprinting off down the back alley, the whole process took John Fingers II less than three minutes. If only Stanley Fingers III had been alive to see it, he'd have been proud.

The getaway car was parked just round the corner. He dived in, slammed the door and turned the key. Wouldn't start.

'No petrol.'

Who said that?

'I mean, what kind of pillock steals his getaway car from a garage forecourt? Next time, at the very least, look at the damn fuel indicator.'

Out of the car, slam the door, run for it. As he ran, he seemed to be able to hear his watch advising him to slow down, since a man of his age and weight was risking a coronary sprinting round the place like a twelve year old, it could feel his pulse against its strap and he was definitely overdoing it. Look, there's a bus, why don't you hop on that?

It was good advice, but John Fingers II chose to ignore it. Instead, he flopped down in a heap in a shop doorway, hyperventilating like an asthmatic extractor fan. A moment or so later, he looked up. There was a policeman standing over him. Oh . . .

'Here,' said the policeman, staring. 'You all right?'

'Urg,' replied John Fingers II.

'You gone a funny colour,' the policeman said. 'I'm going to call an ambulance.'

'No!' He managed to get hold of a lungful of air from somewhere. 'Don't do that. I was just going, anyhow.'

'Huh? Oh well, please yourself. Move along there. You got a home to go to?'

John Fingers II nodded. Some stray pellet of common sense lodged in his brain and told him to pretend to be drunk. 'Jus' going, offisher. Been out for a li'l drink. G'night.'

The policeman frowned and watched him stand up, stagger a little (not method acting; knees still water) and set off on an unsteady course down the street.

'Jesus!' muttered the watch. 'Close call or what? It was touch and go back there.'

Without a second thought, John Fingers II unstrapped his watch, dropped it on the ground and stepped on it. He imagined that as the glass went crunch under his heel, he heard a tiny thin scream.

'What d'you do that for, you bastard?' said a voice in his head.

John Fingers II stopped dead in his tracks. He had a heart-sinking feeling that the parking meter to his immediate left had just spoken to him; it was either that or the voice of conscience, and there were lots of reasons why it wasn't the latter. He swallowed hard and turned ninety degrees.

'You talking to me?' he asked the parking meter.

'Why don't you pick on someone your own size, you big

bully?' replied the parking meter. 'Never done you any harm, that watch, and you just stove its bleedin' head in. How'd you like it if some great big bastard came and stood on your head just 'cos you were trying to be friendly?'

In the circumstances, John Fingers II decided that a non-verbal response would be appropriate. Accordingly he unshipped his jemmy from the purpose-sewn inside pocket of his coat and dealt the parking meter three extremely sharp blows. Problem solved, apparently; no more voices inside his head. When he was satisfied that normality had been restored, he replaced the jemmy and walked on.

'You'll pay for that,' muttered a traffic light.

'We know where you live,' added the Belisha beacon.

'We know where your children go to school,' added a phone box. 'Or at least,' it added, 'we know where they used to go to school, before they burnt it down . . .'

'Burnt it *down*?'

'Well,' admitted the phone box, 'nothing was ever proved, but they've got a pretty good idea it was the Smith boys.'

'Hell's bells,' the Belisha beacon muttered. 'Whole family's a gang of hooligans, then.'

'Scum of the earth,' muttered a parked car. 'Ought to be run out of town, the lot of 'em.'

'*Hey!*' John Fingers II protested. There was a cold silence.

'Well?' said the clock over Gale & Sons, Jewellers (Estd. 1908. Robbed by the Smith family 1909, 1912, 1919, 1927, 1932 (twice), 1936, 1939, 1948, 1961, 1974 and 1977).

'What's going on? I mean, is this for real, or what?' John Fingers II wiped sweat off his forehead with the back of his hand. 'Are you things really – talking?'

'What if we are? You never heard a speaking clock before?'

'Yes, but . . .'

'Which reminds me. In 1948 your father nicked my ornamental bracket. I want it back.'

'Yes,' John Fingers II repeated, 'but how?'

Silence. 'You mean you don't know?' said the traffic light, incredulously.

'He doesn't know,' said the car.

'What a pillock!'

'They're all pillocks in that family,' commented the clock. 'When his great-grandad robbed this shop in 1912 . . .'

'Stan Smith who used to live in Inkerman Street?' queried the phone box. 'Thick as potato soup, that bugger was. I remember one time . . .'

'Shut *up*!' John Fingers II shrieked, and his voice rattled conspicuously in the empty street. 'That's better,' he added. 'You, the red square bugger. How come I can understand what you're saying?'

The things sniggered. It was only when John Fingers II got his jemmy out again and started patting it against the palm of his left hand that the phone box answered him.

'The ring, stupid,' it said. 'Silver ring, bit of glass stuck in it, you're wearing it right now.'

'Fine.' John Fingers II jerked open the phone box door, stepped inside and put both hands tightly round the cable connecting the cradle to the receiver. 'Now then, tell me all about it.'

Had John Fingers II been standing just inside the door of Ali Baba's surgery, instead of inside a phone box half a mile away, he'd have heard the singularly unpleasant and distressing shriek of a lock being picked. It was probably just as well that he wasn't, or he'd have been unable to sleep for a month.

Locks, when you think about it, have either a very nasty or a very nice life, depending on their mechanical orientation. Either they hunch rigidly in the doorframe with their wards gritted and think of England, or they go with the flow and relish every moment of it. Even the kinkiest lock, however – a triple-deadlocked Chubb, for example, or the Marquis de Ingersoll – could never pretend to enjoy being picked, even by a master cracksman with the most finely honed Swiss-made picklocks. All that Akram the Terrible knew about the art was what he'd learned from a quarter of an hour with a book from the mobile library. He could count himself lucky he wasn't wearing the ring, either.

'Right,' said Akram, 'we're in. Where did you say this safe is?'

'This way.' Fang fluttered through the dark air like a very cheap, damp firework. She couldn't exactly hear locks, but on some plane or other she was sensitive to the vibes in a way that no human could ever be; in the same way, perhaps, that horses are supposed to refuse to pass the place where a murder has happened. She had put it on record that she'd wanted to come in through the window.

'Just a minute,' Akram said, shortly afterwards. 'I may be being a bit thick here. I *hope* I'm being a bit thick, because if I find out you've brought me out here in the middle of the night to steal dental floss and denture moulding compound, I'm going to pull your wings off with a pair of rusty pliers.'

'Under the floorboards,' Fang snarled. 'It's his safe.'

Muttering something about a ruddy funny place to hide supposedly cosmos-overturning artefacts, Akram got down on his hands and knees, inserted his jemmy and pulled. Because Akram was tall, barrel-chested and very, very strong, the jemmy snapped.

'Ah,' he said. 'Right, I take your point. These floorboards aren't just to keep you from putting your foot through downstairs' ceiling, are they?'

Fang shook her head. 'If you'd been listening,' she said, 'you'd have realised that. Serves you right if you've pulled a muscle.'

'It's some sort of hex, isn't it? Magic, all that crap.'

'That's right.'

'And you know the key, don't you?'

'Yes.'

'And you're going to tell me what it is?'

'Possibly.'

'But first,' Akram sighed, 'you're going to rub my nose in it because I was rude and snotty and didn't listen when you told me all about it.'

'Of course not.' Fang scowled. 'That'd be childish. All you've got to say is the magic word.'

'If I knew the magic bloody word, I wouldn't be crawling to you, you overgrown gnat.'

'Not that magic word. *The* magic word.'

'Oh for crying out—' Akram paused. 'Please?'

'That's better. Actually,' she added, 'it's not that difficult to guess. In context, that is.'

A look of pain flitted across Akram's face. 'Oh come *on*,' he said. 'You're not trying to tell me—?'

Fang nodded.

'Really?'

'Really.'

'Dear God.' Akram rocked back on his heels and took a deep breath. 'Open seasame,' he said.

The floorboard slowly rose. Underneath it was a plain cardboard box, wrapped in brown paper and lashed up with Sellotape where it had recently been opened. Akram, however, could feel the intensity of the thing. It was as if a Mancunian who'd spent the last fifty years as a restaurant critic in Languedoc had wandered into a little café and unexpectedly found steak and kidney pudding, chips and peas on the menu. It was the kind of homesickness that makes you realise just how sickening home really is.

'Marvellous,' Akram muttered, making no move to touch the box. 'Now what the hell am I supposed to do?'

'Steal it.'

Akram nodded slowly. 'I have this depressing feeling you're right,' he replied.

'Why depressing?' the tooth fairy demanded. 'For pity's sake, if that's what I think it is, it's the single most valuable object in this whole solar system. God only knows what the Americans'd give you for it. Kansas, probably.'

'I know exactly what it is,' Akram replied. 'Look, let me try to explain. Does the expression *fairy-tale ending* mean anything to you?'

Fang nodded. 'Extreme good fortune, followed by a happy ending, happily ever after, C-in-a circle The Walt Disney Company, followed by a date.'

'Exactly.' Akram nodded emphatically. 'Things like this just don't happen in real life, agreed?'

'Well,' replied Fang uncertainly. 'Not often, anyway.'

'About as often as fourteen pigs playing aerial polo. In fairy-tales, however, it's the norm, right? Happens all the time.'

'So they tell me,' the tooth fairy said. 'Not that I'd know, having been stuck this side of the Line all my life. What of it?'

Akram sighed. 'All right,' he said. 'Now, just suppose you were flying down the street and you came across a huge luminous plastic spaceship with little green men running up and down the gangplank and *Alpha Centauri Spacecraft Corporation; Product of More Than One Constellation* stencilled on the side. Maybe you'd think, *Hey, what's this doing here*? And maybe you'd guess that the aliens had landed. Yes?'

'Conceivably,' Fang conceded. 'So?'

Akram pointed to the parcel. 'This thing's from the other side of the Line,' he said. 'So's the happy ending that comes with it. I've just *escaped* from there. When you've just broken out of Colditz and you're buying a train ticket to Geneva, you don't ask for a return. As far as I'm concerned, this has all been too easy. That thing's an obvious plant.'

'No it isn't,' Fang objected. 'If it was, it'd have leaves and a stalk and . . .'

'Be quiet. If I open that,' Akram continued, as much to himself as to Fang, 'it'll mean I'm back in the story. Every day for the rest of my life'll have a page number in the top left-hand corner.'

Fang bit her lip. Maybe the glamour of the parcel was starting to affect her, or maybe she was just curious. 'Open it,' she said. 'Go on. Just having a look won't commit you to anything.'

'Balls.'

'You know you want to really.'

'Go away.'

'Just a little peep,' whispered Fang, 'can't do any harm.'

'Drop dead,' Akram replied, opening his penknife and cutting the Sellotape. 'Opening this would be an awfully big mistake, you mark my words.'

Fang frowned. 'Don't you mean adventure?' she queried.

'As far as I'm concerned, it's the same thing.' He slit the last loop of tape, folded back the cardboard, reached in and lifted out a plain earthenware jar.

'I see,' said Fang after a moment's silence. 'A *potted* plant.'

Akram didn't reply. He was staring at the lid of the jar. I could open it, he told himself. And then, either whatever's in there will come out, or I'll go in, and in the long run it'll amount to the same thing. He screwed his eyes tight shut and said aloud, 'I wish this thing would go away.' When he opened them again, it was still there. Which meant that he didn't have any of the Godfather's three wishes left. Which meant he'd used them. Something, he told himself, like using the atomic bomb; at first it seems to solve all sorts of problems, and then, some time later, you begin to think that on balance it'd have been rather better if maybe you hadn't.

'Are you all right?' Fang asked uncomfortably. 'You don't

look very well. You've gone a very funny colour.'

'I'm not in the least surprised.'

'Sort of black and white.'

Akram laughed wretchedly. 'What the hell do you expect?' he said. 'My life has just changed. It's now got credits at the beginning and the end. Just when I thought—'

The jar twitched slightly in his hands, as if it was getting impatient. The sensation of movement against his skin made Akram shudder, and he seemed to reach a decision. Very swiftly, almost aggressively, like a man putting out a fire, he tried to stuff the jar back in its box. But the box was now too small.

'Think about it,' said Fang's voice, greatly to Fang's astonishment. 'The thing is here already. Right now, Ali Baba's got it. He knows you're this side of the Line. He knows you've sworn to kill him.'

'I gave him my word . . .'

'He knows,' the voice went on, 'that you've crossed the Line. When you cross the Line, you come out of character. If you're out of character, your word's about as valid as a Confederate banknote. He knows this.'

'But I've changed,' Akram protested. 'I'm good now.'

'This week,' the voice replied. 'Maybe even next week, too. Maybe the next fifty years; but there's no guarantee. He knows that, too. On this side of the Line, you have no character.'

'But I don't *want* . . .'

'He knows,' intoned the voice, 'exactly what he did to you, what he tried to do to you. He knows – *hey can I have my voice back, whoever the hell you are, nobody said you could use my* – bugger off, small fry. He knows exactly what he'd do if he was you. In fact, he will be you. And you will be him. You know that.'

'That's you talking, isn't it? You in the jar. Say "bottle of beer", go on, say it.'

'Open the jar, Akram.'

Akram stared at the jar. He could see the faint marks of the potter's wheel; he even fancied he could smell the distinctive smell of the palm-oil it had once contained. He knew precisely what was in the jar. He would not open the jar. When is a jar not a jar?

'When it's a door. Open the jar.'

'I refuse.'

'You can't. Remember?'

'I could take you back where you came from. Maybe there's money back on you.'

'Non-returnable. No deposit. Open the frigging jar, Akram, or it'll be the worse for you.'

'No,' said Akram, putting his hand on the lid. 'You will stay where you've been put. You can't come in here.'

Like a small guided missile Fang shot across the room. In her defence, it should be pointed out that she flew backwards, her legs and arms thrashing wildly; in any event, she smashed into Akram's hand, knocking the lid of the jar halfway across the room. Akram flailed wildly, trying to catch it; then he hurled himself over the mouth of the jar, but too late. A column of what could have been bees, or flies, or lumpy black smoke, curled upwards out of the jar, turning and twisting and buzzing, fending Akram off as if he was made of feathers. He swung at it wildly with a chair; the chair passed through the column and out the other side, and *then* smashed into matchwood.

'Bastard!' Fang yelled. 'Look, it wasn't me, I had nothing to do with—'

The smoke, flies, bees solidified, until they were a solid thing. The jar swelled up, until it was the size of a crouching man, maybe a little larger. The column stopped moving. It was a human shape. It stood opposite Akram, no more than six inches away from him. Akram stared at it; it was just like looking in a mirror; or suppose you're standing between a whitewashed wall and a very bright light, and you look at your shadow.

'Go back,' he said, but his voice was thin and watery. 'Go back home.'

The thing, his other self, smiled. It was an exact likeness, except somehow dark, shadowy. Do you remember how Peter Pan came across the Line to retrieve his shadow, and all the trouble that caused?

The shadow reached out its hands and feet, and touched Akram, and joined him.

'I *am* home,' he said.

CHAPTER FIFTEEN

'I'm starving,' Akram said. 'Let's eat. I fancy Lebanese.'

'It's half past three in the morning,' Akram replied. 'In Southampton. If we're lucky, we might just find an unopened dustbin bag.'

Akram laughed. 'You always were a pessimistic bugger,' he said. 'Now, if my instincts are still working –' He stopped still, drawing his other half up sharply. 'This way,' he said, and darted off down the street, dragging Akram behind him like a large dog walking a small human.

Just around the corner there was a blaze of light and colour. Exotic music, strings and bells and cymbals, floated across on the languid night breeze. Over the door was a sign saying TRIPOLI RESTAURANT.

'Damn,' said Akram. 'Wouldn't you just know it. I seem to have come out without any money. I wonder, would you mind. . . ?'

Fang, snuggled inside Akram's jacket, peered out. She liked late-night catering establishments, bars, night clubs; because where you have drunken night owls, you have fights, and where you have fights, you run a good chance of picking up the odd dislodged tooth.

'You two,' she observed, 'remind me of something.'

'Really?'

Fang nodded. 'I got it,' she said. 'It's like when you've got a prisoner and a guard handcuffed together; you know, with the raincoat to cover the chains? Only,' she added, 'I'm not sure which of you's which.'

'He is.'

A waiter drifted forward and smiled.

'Hello,' Akram said. 'Table for three, please.'

The waiter nodded. 'If you'd like to come this way . . .'

'Or rather,' Akram amended, 'two. Actually, make that one.'

'As you like, sir. Please to follow me. Anything to drink before you order?'

'No, I mean yes.' Akram stood still for a moment, his eyes closed. 'That's, um, one tomato juice, one triple absinthe, no ice, and do you have any camel's milk?'

If the waiter was taken aback at all, he didn't show it. 'All in the same glass, sir? Or one after the other? Or. . . ?'

'Simultaneously, of course. Sorry, I mean, could I have those, er, simultaneously. Thank you.'

The waiter turned to walk back to the kitchen, hesitated and glanced surreptitiously back. An ordinary-looking sort of man, quite large, could easily be from the Old Country except that he sounded English. He was sitting at one of the side tables, and the candle-light seemed to be throwing a larger than usual shadow against the far wall. Occasionally his hand crept to his chest; indigestion? angina? None of the waiter's business. Neither was he interested in the fact that the man seemed to be holding an animated conversation with himself. When you're in the late-night catering business, the ones you watch are the ones who don't talk to themselves.

'This,' said Akram to his shadow, 'isn't going to work. I mean, listen to us, we can't agree on anything.'

'What, you mean like we're married or something? No, I take that back, we are at least talking to each other. By the way, you haven't introduced me. Who's the houri?'

'Tooth fairy,' Akram corrected. 'Shadow, Fang; Fang, Shadow. Better now?'

'Excuse me,' said Fang, 'but can I just get this straight? You're Akram and he's your shadow?'

'And vice versa. On the other side, it's the other way round. I think. Actually that's a gross simplification, but let's leave it at that for now.'

'So really,' Fang ground on, wishing she'd never raised the subject, 'you're both Akram. Is that right?'

'In a manner of speaking,' replied the image on the wall. 'To take the marriage simile one stage further; a happily married couple is two minds with but a single thought. We're one mind with two entirely different thoughts. Usually, at least.'

'Ah.' The tooth fairy nodded. 'Like a dual personality, sort of thing.'

The shadow shook its head. A split microsecond later, Akram's head moved too, with the result that a quarter of his camel's milk went down the front of his shirt. 'Schizophrenia, you mean? Not really. Schizophrenia is where the left hand knows perfectly well what the right hand is doing, and bitterly resents it. I prefer to think of us as two sides of the same coin. The yin and the yang. The positive and the negative charged particles, both circling the same neutron.'

'Except,' Akram interrupted sullenly, 'somehow he never has any money on him. And when he gets drunk at parties and starts making lewd suggestions to married women, I'm the one who gets thumped.'

'You exaggerate.'

'And,' Akram went on, 'the curious thing is, the one time in a hundred when the lewd suggestion leads to a result, it's always my turn to be the blasted shadow.'

'Ah.'

'And of course,' Akram continued, 'you don't get a shadow when the light's turned off. Marvellous.'

It's always embarrassing for third parties when couples argue in public, and Fang wished she could change the subject. 'I—' she said.

'I suppose it's the same for everyone,' Akram was saying, 'with the extremely important difference that they don't realise it. But I do. Ever since I was in that bloody jar, the time I found out I was in a story. I found out all sorts of things then that nobody else realises. Big mistake, that.'

'I agree,' said the shadow, nodding –

('For God's sake mind what you're doing!'

'Huh? Oh, sorry.')

'Glad you agree on something,' Fang replied. She noticed that whereas the shadow had finished its drink, Akram still had half of his left. He was wearing the other half. 'But I still don't see how you two came to, er, get together. I thought there was something quite other in that jar.'

'Such as what?'

'Well,' Fang replied defensively, 'the secret of absolute power. The, er, ultimate weapon. That's what Ali Baba seemed to think it was, anyway.'

'He was right,' the shadow replied smugly. 'You're looking at it.'

'You?'

'That's right. Well,' the shadow corrected, 'us. Together, we make the perfect combination. His skills of stealth, mayhem and cunning; my total lack of moral restraint. Who could ask for more?'

'What you find in the box,' Akram explained, 'depends on

who you are. If Ali Baba had opened it, he'd probably have found a fleet of nuclear submarines or a death ray or something. Me,' he added bitterly, 'I have to find him.'

The shadow bridled; a difficult thing to do in only two dimensions. 'The difference between me and a fleet of nuclear submarines,' he said with dignity, 'is that I cost less to run and I'm a damn sight easier to park. True, I can't stay underwater for up to five years at a time, but so what, nobody's perfect.'

'You can say that again.'

'I shall pretend I didn't hear that. Now then, I fancy the humus to start with, followed by the lamb with couscous and a bottle of the Riesling. It's all right about the alcohol,' he added. 'I don't have to drive home.'

Akram sighed. 'All right,' he said, 'I give in. Let's just get it over and done with as quickly as possible. I suppose I've got to kidnap the girl.'

'That's right. Splendid piece of detective work there, by the way. I'm glad to see you haven't forgotten everything I taught you.'

'Actually,' Akram pointed out, 'it was sheer luck. Anyway, we kidnap the girl—'

'Nice piece,' commented the shadow, 'if you like them long and bony. I'm told that sort keeps better, but I always trade mine in fairly quickly, so I can't actually vouch for it myself.'

'And then,' Akram continued with distaste, 'we let her go in return for Ali Baba releasing me from my oath. And then,' he added, 'I kill him.'

'Exactly. Won't that be fun?'

Akram shut his eyes. 'Won't it just,' he said.

The phone rang.

'Whoozit?' Ali Baba croaked into the receiver. The digital clock beside his bed seemed to leer mockingly at him, and its eyes read 04:59.

'Hister Harbour? Hit's Hisses Utchinson ere, he hum's harted hleeding hagain hand hoo haid hone hoo hif hat appened.'

'Could you just hold the line a moment, please?' Ali Baba put down the receiver and rubbed his eyes with the heels of his hands while the basic background information files of his brain gradually drifted back on line. Mrs Hutchinson. She's a patient, extraction, left upper molar, and yes, in a moment of surpassing folly I did say call me if there's any problems and gave her my home number. That reminds me, who am I and where the hell is this? Ah yes, now I remember.

'I'm very sorry to hear that, Mrs Hutchinson,' he replied, and the facility with which he did so without so much as batting an eye, crossing a finger or growing an extra six inches of nose goes to show that dentistry's dubious gain was the legal profession's palpable loss. 'First thing in the morning, or rather first thing later on this morning, if you could possibly drop by the surgery ...'

'Hut hoo hed, hif hit harts hleeding, hoo'd hum *himmediately*. Hoo hed ...'

I did, didn't I? I should be hanged, with my own tongue for a noose. 'Of course, I'll be right with you. Now, in the meantime, if you'll just mix up some ordinary table salt with some water ...'

Twenty minutes later, the phone rang again. Ali Baba was, of course, on his way to Mrs Hutchinson's; which is why Akram, taking a deep breath before stating his demands for Michelle's return, got the recorded message instead. He wilted slightly; even desperate extroverts feel just a bit self-conscious talking to answering machines. After a moment of being disconcerted, Akram cleared his throat.

The message went as follows:

'Hello, this is, um, me here, I'd just like to leave a

message. Er, ready? Well, here goes. Look, you pig-
fucker, you ever want to see your daughter alive again, be
at the entrance to— oh bugger, I can't read my own
writing. No, not them, my reading glasses, the ones on
the – thanks, now then, where were we? Entrance to
Tesco's car park in Cinnamon Street, that's the Bishop
Road entrance as you come in from the bypass, not the
. . Sorry, just a tick. Yes? Oh. Oh, right. Sorry, that's not
Tesco's, it's Safeways, at one thirty tomorrow, morning,
and you'd better come alone or else, Okay? Right, er,
well, oh God I hate talking into these things. Um. Bye.'

The second message was:

'Hello? Oh blast. Hello, it's me again. Did I say not to
tell the Police or it'll be the worse for the girl? Well, um,
that's it for now. Ciao.'

The third message was:

'Hello? Shit, where the hell can he have got to this time
of night? Yes, it's me. Look, it's not Safeways, I looked it
up and actually it's ASDA. Okay, it's the big supermarket
on the corner of Cinnamon Street and Landau Way.
Turn right at John Lewis and you can't miss it. Or else.
Goodbye.'

Having played back the tape a couple of times and tried
Michelle's number (answering machine) Ali Baba collected
the sword and the gun, drove to his surgery and went to the
store cupboard. Inside he found two hundred pairs of disposable rubber gloves, three large boxes of disposable forceps,
five thousand doses of local anaesthetic, twenty tubs of
impression material, a catering-size drum of instant coffee

granules, an empty floor safe and an old-fashioned silver sixpence. He slumped, as if his backbone had just been repossessed by the finance company.

Wait a minute. The sixpence . . .

It goes without saying that all dentists' surgeries, sooner or later, get infested with tooth fairies. Dentists who find silver sixpences scattered about their premises therefore know the score and although the old-style djinn traps are now illegal (the details are a bit too grisly for print; suffice it to say that a fairy triggering one while foraging for teeth wouldn't have very long to reflect on the wisdom of being careful what you wish for) but pixie dust, Larsen traps and large, bad-tempered cats generally solve the problem sooner or later. Dentists, in short, know about tooth fairies, in the same way that farmers have a certain familiarity with the habits of rabbits, rooks and pigeons. They know, for instance, that in spite of the name, they don't just help themselves to teeth, in the same way that cat burglars will also take the occasional dog or pedigree hamster. A sixpence in the tea kitty or the bottom of the petty cash tin speaks for itself. On the other hand, very few tooth fairies go out tooled up with the hardware necessary to prise open safes. Let alone magical safes.

The logical conclusion therefore was that Akram had teamed up with a tooth fairy. Having run it past his mental panel of scrutineers, Ali Baba filed the fact in the back of his mind, and sat down in his own chair, wondering what to do next. The next thing he knew was the phone ringing; he looked up at the clock on the wall and saw that it was 7.45 am, start of a brand new working day.

It'd be wrong to call Ali Baba callous or uncaring; on the contrary, he had twenty-odd people coming to see him to be cured of excruciating pain, and he cared about each and everyone of them. He also cared about his daughter, very deeply indeed; but her appointment, so to speak, wasn't for another eighteen hours. He hoped she'd be all right, washed up, shaved as best he could with a disposable scalpel and his tiny mirror-on-a-stick, and buzzed for the first patient.

'First,' Akram said, lighting the paraffin lamp, 'I don't want you to be frightened.'

Michelle glowered at him. 'Really?' she said. 'Then I'd suggest you cancel the rest of the lessons and ask for your money back, because when it comes to not frightening people, you haven't got a clue.'

The corner of Akram's mouth twitched a little. 'You don't *seem* very frightened,' he said. 'Quite the opposite.'

'I'm absolutely bloody livid, if that's what you mean,' Michelle growled, tugging vainly at the ropes round her wrists. 'Doesn't mean I'm not frightened. You're the man in the burger joint, aren't you?'

Akram nodded. 'That's what I do for a living,' he said, with more than a hint of pride. 'They've recently made me the assistant manager.'

'I see,' Michelle replied. 'So creeping up on people and abducting them at knifepoint's just a hobby, is it? Other people seem to manage with bird-watching or flower-arranging.'

Akram looked hurt. 'Don't be like that,' he said. 'I tried to be as nice about it as I could.'

'Sure. *Could you possibly spare me a moment or I'll slit your throat.* I should have guessed then you weren't a real kidnapper.'

As she said the words, Michelle couldn't help feeling that situated as she was, bound hand and foot in a lock-up workshop somewhere with a knife-wielding six-foot-five stranger, her tone might usefully be a little bit less abrasive. There was something about the man, though, that entirely failed to terrify her. It wasn't that she didn't believe he would cut her throat, if whatever his strange motivation was demanded it. It was just that he'd probably try and be as considerate and unthreatening about it as he could manage, and even at the moment of severing her jugular vein he'd be at pains to make it clear that he still respected her as a person. She knew all about the New Man; well, this was the New Villain. It intrigued her.

'You know perfectly well who I am,' Akram replied quietly. 'And I reckon you know why I'm doing this. I'm trying to keep everything nice and civilised, but really, you aren't making it any easier.'

'So sorry,' Michelle snapped. 'So what do you want to do, mix up some mulled wine and play Trivial Pursuit?'

'Play what?'

'Trivial Pursuit. It's a sort of game where you ask silly questions and move counters on a board.'

'Really?' Akram raised an eyebrow. 'Since my time, that. I've got chess and backgammon, if you're interested.'

'Get real, will you? I wouldn't play chess with you if you were the last man alive.'

'Quite,' Akram replied. 'If I was the last man alive, I'm sure we'd be far too busy foraging for food and hiding from packs of killer dogs and things. All right, then, what about canasta? Or mah jong?'

Michelle stared at him keenly. 'Are you trying to tell me,' she said, 'that you actually have a mah jong set in a *hideout*?'

'Why not?' Akram replied with a shrug. 'Look, I was kidnapping people when you were still ... Sorry, different timescale, but anyhow, you get the point. And the first thing you learn about the kidnapping business is, it can get very, very boring. So naturally I laid in a few games. I mean, I Spy's all right, but ...'

'Bet you haven't got Diplomacy.'

Akram shook his head. 'Not really suitable,' he said. 'I mean, the average kidnap ordeal lasts about one to three weeks, which means the game'd just be getting interesting when it was time to go home. Actually, I remember the time I snatched the Grand Vizier's nephew and we started playing Racing Genie. Ten days that game lasted. The Grand Vizier paid up on day four, but we couldn't persuade the little brute to go home until he'd won. And you try deliberately losing Racing Genie without being embarrassingly obvious about it . . .'

'Racing Genie?'

Akram shook his head vigorously. 'No way,' he said. 'It's totally addictive, Racing Genie. You just get completely carried away.'

'Sounds interesting.'

'We haven't got time. I'm due to hand you over at half-one tomorrow morning.'

'Oh go on. At least show me the rules.'

'Well . . .'

'Please?'

Akram hesitated. As he did so it occurred to him to turn the lamp up a bit, but he decided against it. The dimmer the light, the fainter his shadow, and he felt more comfortable that way.

'Oh all right,' he said. 'But only for half an hour.'

'. . . And sixteen for a Wish, that makes ninety-four, doubled because you're on a Magic Carpet square in clubs repiqued, add two for his fez makes a hundred and ninety, which means I get four lamp points and you get another wish.'

'Yah!'

'Beginner's luck. Right, your go – Oh my God, will you look at the time?'

They looked up. The battered alarm clock sitting on an upended packing case read 12:57.

'Marvellous!' Akram sighed. 'We're going to be late for the bloody handover. Come on, get your coat.'

Michelle shook her head. 'We've got plenty of time,' she said. 'This time of night there'll be no traffic about, so if we cut down through Marchmain Street and under the underpass we can be there in fifteen minutes.'

'You reckon?'

'Easily,' Michelle replied, shaking the dice. 'Right, let's see. Hey, double four, that means I can have another mosque on Trebizond. Now then . . .'

Ali Baba waited until quarter to three; then it started to rain and he decided to go home. It wasn't that he was callous or uncaring; but he hadn't got much sleep the night before, either, and he had a very difficult root-fill job to do on Mrs Willoughby's lower back left molar in the morning. Having checked for the fifteenth time that he was in the right car park, he got in and drove home.

At half-past ten the phone rang.

'Sorry about that,' said Akram. 'We, er, lost track of time, and . . .'

'*We?*'

'We were playing Racing Genie,' Akram explained. 'In fact we still are, and – hey! I saw that, put it back – look, would it put you out dreadfuly if we postponed the handover till, say, Wednesday? Only I've got three back doubles in a row here, so if I can just get the full set of Utilities . . .'

'I quite understand,' replied Ali Baba icily. 'I mean, I'd hate to interrupt your game just to ransom my only daughter.'

'I – would you like a word with her? She's just here. It's your father.'

'Hello?'

'Michelle?' Ali Baba demanded. 'Is that you? Look, are you all right, because . . .'

'Fine, fine,' Michelle's voice replied. 'Listen, do you know this game? I mean, did they play it back in the Old Country, or whatever you call it, because I've got major triples in all three Houses but no gryphon, and I was wondering if you could suggest . . .'

'You repique, naturally,' Ali Baba replied, 'which means Green has to go dummy and you can finesse on the last three tricks, leaving you just needing a double four for Home.' He paused, mentally playing back what he'd just said. 'So you're all right, then?'

'I am now,' Michelle replied. 'I was thinking about leading a blind shimmy to make four, but that's far better. It's a good game, this, isn't it?'

'I like it,' Ali Baba replied. 'Used to play quite a lot when I was your . . . well, once upon a time. In fact,' he couldn't resist adding, 'one year I made it to the finals of the Baghdad Open.'

'Really? Gosh!' Michelle said; and just for a moment, she sounded quite like a real daughter. 'And did you win?'

'Of course,' Ali Baba lied. 'All right, then, see you Wednesday.'

''Bye, then.'

''Bye.'

CHAPTER SIXTEEN

Midnight.

Actually, midnight isn't a particularly good time of day to go burgling. There are too many people still awake; three in the morning is far better, if slightly less dramatic. Of course, perhaps the best time of all to burgle a bank, office or other commercial premises is half past four on a Friday afternoon. Wander in with a clipboard and a trolley, ask the most junior-looking member of staff to sign in three places, and you can probably get help loading the stuff into the van.

Midnight is, however, more traditional, and tradition, as noted above, is ingrained into the genetic matrix of the Smith family. Somewhere at home, at the bottom of a wardrobe, John Fingers II still had a striped jersey, a black mask and a sack with SWAG embroidered on it in sampler-stitch.

It was tradition, in fact, that gave him pause for thought as he stood under the staff room window of the National Lombard Bank in Cinnamon Street, his right hand tightly clenched into a fist. He was about to try out a radically new and different technique, and the very novelty of it all was making his scalp itch. After all, screamed his genes, shinning up a drainpipe and busting a window was good enough for your father and his father before him, so it ought to be good enough for you. True, getting caught red-handed and spending most of their lives in the nick was good enough for them, too; but isn't that all part of the great rich tapestry of this thieving life?

No, muttered John Fingers II to himself, and added something about buggering it for a game of soldiers that would have made his great-great-grandfather turn in his grave, had he not died at a time when the bodies of criminals were used for medical research. (For the record, at that precise moment, on a back shelf in a dusty old cupboard somewhere in the University of Durham, a very old bottle of formaldehyde went *plop*!) If they'd had that attitude back in the Stone Age the wheel would never have been invented, and young Darren Fingers Smith would now be out trying to hotwire a motorised sled.

Here goes.

Directly above his head was a square box marked NEVA-SLEEP ALARM COMPANY. John Fingers II took a deep breath, slipped the ring on his finger and cleared his throat.

'Excuse me,' he whispered.

'Huh? Whoozat?'

'Excuse me,' said John Fingers, 'but would you mind switching yourself off?'

'You what?' grunted the alarm, sleepily.

'Switch yourself off,' John Fingers repeated. 'You see, I want to climb in through that window, and I don't want to set you off.'

'Get real,' replied the alarm. 'You think I was manufactured yesterday, or something? Bugger off before I ring the cops.'

John Fingers shook his head. 'I'm trying to be reasonable here,' he hissed back. 'Like, if you won't switch yourself off, it means I've got to climb up there and snip all your wires, which'll piss me off and hurt you, probably. And while I'm at it,' he added maliciously. 'I might just prise your box off and gum your works up good and proper. It'll take 'em weeks to get you straight again, and in the meantime you'll be going off every time somebody blows their nose in Winchester. It must be really embarrassing when that happens; you know, everybody stumping round in pyjamas at two in the morning trying to find the main cable, and of course it'll be you gets all the blame for their mistakes. They might even rip you out and get a new one.'

'Now steady on,' replied the alarm. 'There's no need to get nasty.'

'Whereas,' John Fingers continued smoothly, 'if you just switch yourself off now, I can leave you in peace and quiet and they'll blame some poor little clerk for forgetting to set you before locking up. You can see my point, can't you?'

The alarm considered for a moment. 'You won't say a word?'

'Cross my heart.'

'It's really unethical, you know. I could get disconnected for just talking to you.'

'You already did that,' John Fingers pointed out, 'so it's sheep and lamb time, anyhow. Tell you what, I'll just snip this wire here and then you'll know for certain how much it hurts, and then maybe . . .'

'All right,' the alarm snarled. 'But if anybody asks, I never seen you before in my life, right?'

'Right. I mean,' John Fingers added, 'even if I did say something, who the hell'd ever believe me?'

With the alarm off, John Fingers was able to take his time scaling the wall, and he made himself nice and comfortable on the window ledge before he jemmied the stay.

'By the way,' he asked the alarm. 'The CCTV camera.'

'What about it?'

'What's it called? I always think it's nice being on first name terms in business, don't you?'

'Zelda,' the alarm replied. 'Don't be fooled by her big round eye, though. She's a tough cookie.'

'Thanks. Be seeing you.'

The alarm, it turned out, was exaggerating.

'You really like it?' the camera asked. 'I mean really. You're not just saying it to please me?'

'Would I do a thing like that?' John Fingers replied. 'And what's more, it's not every camera that could get away with a mounting like that. I mean, black enamel square section tube, unless you've got the figure for it, you could look ridiculous. On you, though—'

Cameras can't smile; but they can open their diaphragms up to f3 and flutter their shutters. 'Glad to know there's some people who notice things,' it said pointedly. 'Of course, some people are so ignorant they wouldn't notice if a person turned up for work strapped to a length of four-by-two with red insulating tape.'

As he walked casually past the camera (which was far too busy admiring its reflection in the window to pay any attention to him) he quickly examined the space between the lines for relevant reading matter. Accordingly, when he came to the infra-red beam he was ready for it.

'Hi,' he said. 'Look, I've got a message for you.'

The beam narrowed suspiciously. 'You have?'

'From Zelda,' John Fingers replied. 'She said she's really sorry, she didn't mean it, and would it be at all possible to start over again?'

'Zelda said that?'

John Fingers nodded, hoping to hell he'd guessed right. 'I'm just the messenger,' he added, 'so don't blame me if . . .'

'Wow! She really said she was sorry?'

'That's right. Is there something between you guys, then?' he added innocently.

'There was,' replied the beam. 'Until a certain person made certain remarks about another person happening to pass the time of day with the fire extinguisher, even though he was just being polite, that's all. I mean, what kind of relationship have you got if you haven't got trust?'

'Absolutely,' John Fingers agreed. 'Anyway, that's the message, so if you'd just let me past . . .'

'What? Oh sure. Hey, you're *positive* she said she was sorry?'

'On my honour as a bur— I mean, service engineer. Cheers.'

'So long. And thank you.'

The further into the building he got, the easier it was. The hidden directional microphone ('Any friend of Zelda's is a friend of mine') was no problem at all, and all he had to do with the lock on the strongroom door was creep up to it and say 'Boo!', whereupon it curled up into a ball, retracting all its wards and letting the door swing open. As for the safe –

'Hello.'

''Lo.'

'It must be very boring,' John Fingers wheedled, 'being a safe.'

'You're not kidding.'

'Sitting in this horrible dark stuffy room all day, with the light off.'

'Yeah.'

'No one to talk to.'

'Well, there's the pressure-pad.'

'What press— You mean,' John Fingers corrected himself, 'the one by the door?'

'Nah,' replied the safe, 'the one under the steel grating, about six inches to the left of where you're stood.'

John Fingers shuffled unobtrusively to the right. 'Must be a real drag,' he said. 'And having to keep still all the time.'

'Huh?'

'With all that horrible dry scratchy money inside you. If I was you I'd be dying for a really good itch all the bloody time.'

You could almost hear the safe thinking. 'Now you come to mention it,' the safe said slowly, 'it's a right pain. Oooh, God, it's so itchy.'

'I bet,' John Fingers went on, 'there's times you just want to throw your door open and have a really good spit.'

'Yeah.'

'Well, then.'

'Huh?'

'Don't mind me.'

Safes are made of huge solid slabs of reinforced laminated sheet steel; or, to put it another way, they're thick. 'Yeah,' it said, 'why not, eh?'

'Go for it.'

'Yeah, right. Only, how do I get myself open?'

'You mean,' John Fingers said, shocked, 'they don't even let you open yourself? I mean, no time lock or anything?'

'Those cheapskates? Do me a favour.'

'We'll soon see about that. Come on, you tell me the combination and we'll have you open before you can say Open sesame.'

'Ta. Right, it's nine six four seven . . .'

Ten minutes later, John Fingers II hurled two black bin-liners full of currency notes into the back of the van, turned the key, thanked the engine for starting (politeness costs nothing, after all) and drove off hell for leather in the general direction of Bournemouth. He didn't even stop for red lights; all you had to do, he'd found, was shout, 'I'm a friend of Simon's,' and they turned green instantly. He had no idea how it worked, but so what? The same was true of gravity and he had every confidence in that.

In the Bank, meanwhile, the safe yawned. With its seventy-millimetre-thick door hanging wide open, it had no choice in the matter, and it didn't actually care. It was thinking.

When it comes to the operation of their thought processes, safes are a bit like whales, elephants, trees and other huge, long-living, slow-moving creatures. They think slow, but they also think deep. And they remember.

The safe remembered. Something the human had said, some throwaway combination of words, meaningless unless you knew the background.

Open something . . .

Open . . .

It was on the tip of its tumbler . . .

Whatever the phrase was, it had heard it before – a very long time ago, in another place, ever so far away. The safe's steel mind mumbled away at the problem, like a toothless but invincibly patient man chewing toffee. Sooner or later, it would remember; and then it'd know.

Open . . .

For some reason, oil came into it somewhere, so the safe thought about oil for a while. Oil; yum. On a hot day, you can't beat a nice long drink of three-in-one, with maybe a sprinkling of Teflon to refresh the parts other lubricants can't reach. In the middle of winter, however, there's nothing to touch a good thick multigrade to keep the wet out and the rust away.

Open . . .

Thieves. Whatever the riddle was, it was something to do with thieves. The thought made the safe quiver slightly. Thieves do horrible things to safes; they drill holes in them and blow them up. *Hate* thieves.

And then it remembered.

Every alarm in the building suddenly went off.

'Hey!'

Scheherezade looked up. 'What is it?' she asked. 'Is something wrong?'

The Godfather nodded. 'What you think you're doing?' he demanded hoarsely. 'What is all this, a goddamn comedy?'

'I don't think so,' Scheherezade replied. 'It's not supposed to be.'

The Godfather stood up. 'You don't think so,' he mimicked unpleasantly. 'Then I ask you again, what you think you're doing? You gone crazy or something?'

'I don't think so,' Scheherezade said, 'I'm just turning the story round, that's all. Ali Baba is now Akram, and Akram is Ali Baba. What's wrong with that?'

'Nothing,' replied the Godfather impatiently. 'But all this sitting round playing games, it's not right. A man kidnaps your daughter, you hunt him down and you kill him. You don't go home and go to bed.'

Scheherezade shrugged. 'Why not?' she said. 'I mean, he's in no fit state to go hunting people down at this time of night. With a good night's sleep and a nice cooked breakfast inside him, he'll make a much better job of it.'

'But . . .' The Godfather waved his cigar in the air. 'And besides,' he added, 'what's all this with Akram and the girl playing Racing Genie till all hours? Where's it say in the story they do that? It's nonsense. How can the heroine be playing Racing Genie with the villain? Be reasonable.'

'But he's not the villain,' Scheherezade replied. 'He's the hero.'

'He is?' The Godfather scowled. 'Then who's the goddamn villain?'

'Ali Baba. I suppose,' Scheherezade added, frowning. 'Actually, I'm not sure. No, he can't be, can he? Except . . .'

'Well?'

Scheherezade realised that she was feeling cold, except that it was hot beside the fire. 'Let's just think about this,' she said, doing a marvellous job of keeping the panic out of her voice. 'We've turned the story round, okay? Akram is now Ali Baba, and he's found out the secret that makes him able to turn the tables on Ali Baba . . .'

'Who's now Akram, yes?'

'Just a minute, you'll get me all confused. He's turned the tables on Ali Baba and got hold of what Ali Baba values most in all the world—'

'You mean the girl.'

'Presumably,' said Scheherezade doubtfully. 'After all, she is his daughter. So what happens next is, Ali Baba tries to sneak up on Akram, and he hides in something – something like an oil-jar, let's say a packing-case or a milk-churn – and Akram realises what's going on and pours boiling water on him, and that's that. Freed from the threat of Ali Baba's vengeance, he lives happily ever after with the girl – that must be what's meant to happen, or else why are they getting on like a house on fire? Look—'

(*'And fifteen for a back treble makes forty-three, which means I can have another bazaar on Cairo. Your go.'*

'Hey, double four! Oh damn, go to jail.'

'You could use your Lamp.'

'I don't want to use my Lamp. It's your go.')

'Hey.' The Godfather took a long pull on his cigar. 'Akram kills this girl's father, and you expect them to live happily ever after? You crazy or something?'

'Well . . . Perhaps he doesn't actually kill him, then. After all, he is the hero . . .'

'Precisely. And the hero kills the villain. What kinda mess you making of my story?'

Scheherezade bit her lip. 'It's all because of it being on the other side of the Line,' she said. 'It makes them all so difficult to control. They do things without me telling them to.'

'And another thing,' the Godfather snarled. 'You can't have a villain getting killed saving his only daughter from a kidnapper. That's crazy. That's hero stuff, except a hero wouldn't get killed. And that's not all,' he added, his scowl thickening. 'He ain't even trying to save the goddamn broad. Look—'

('All right, Sharon, who's first?'

'Well, Mr B, you've got Mr Peasemarsh for eight-fifteen, but Mrs Kidd's in the waiting room on spec, that abscess's flared up again, can you fit her in?'

'Hurting, is it?'

'Yes, Mr B.'

'Right, send her in and tell Mr Peasemarsh I won't be a jiffy.')

'You call that rescuing daughters,' sneered the Godfather, ''cos I don't.'

Scheherezade thought for a moment. 'I see what's happening,' she said. 'He's a hero, right?'

'But I thought you said—'

'Yes, but *deep down* he's a hero. And that's what heroes do. They sacrifice themselves for the good of others, because of duty and stuff. And because he's a doctor—'

'Dentist.'

'Okay, dentist, but the principle's the same. His first duty's to his patients, and because he's truly heroic . . .'

'It stinks,' the Godfather grunted. 'You let the whole goddamn thing get outa hand. It's all turning—' He paused, carefully selected the rudest word he could think of, and spat it at her. 'Real. I mean, what about Akram's shadow? What the hell does it think it's playing at?'

'He's turned the lights down,' Scheherezade pointed out. 'Clever,' she added. 'Makes his shadow too faint to be able to intervene.'

The Godfather leaned over, until his face was almost touching hers. 'Get it sorted out,' he growled, 'or you're dead. You understand me?'

After he had gone, Scheherezade sat quietly for a while, shivering a little and trying to get her mind clear. On the one hand, she recognised, he was absolutely right; the story was getting away from her, to such an extent that it had almost stopped being a story. It was frightening how easily it had happened. It had to be stopped, she could see that, or where would it all end? Next thing you'd know, they'd all be at it:

('Look! It fits!'

'Of course it fits, you idiot, it's a standard size four, D fitting. But that's not her. For God's sake, man, do you think I'd spend all evening dancing with something that looks like that?'

'But it fits, Your Majesty. And Your Majesty did say . . .')

Unthinkable. But, on the other hand, the story felt *right*. She didn't know why. She hadn't known why for some time, but that hadn't worried her too much. After all, she didn't know why the sun rose or why the rain fell, but she had a shrewd idea that they were supposed to do it.

On a notional third hand, if she didn't get it all back under control and doing what it was supposed to do, she was going to die.

She thought about it. She scribbled notes on the back of her hand. She drew little diagrams. She muttered things to herself such as 'Suppose this soap-dish here is Akram, and this hairbrush is the girl . . .'

It didn't help.

Just when she was on the point of giving the whole thing up as a bad job (and after all, why postpone the inevitable? Death and happiness ever after aren't so very different) it came to her, like the apple falling on Sir Isaac Newton's head.

Except; instead of an apple, suppose it had been a tiny scale model of a bomb?

And instead of Sir Isaac Newton, suppose it had been the Wright brothers?

John Fingers sat down on the floor of his lock-up garage and listened.

No distant sirens. No slamming of car doors, no clattering of big clumping police boots. Silence.

It had worked. Yippee!

A big, silly grin spread over his face like an oil slick as he opened his big canvas holdall and pulled out big handfuls of lovely crisp banknotes. Lovely, lovely money; tens, no, hundreds of thousands of pounds. It was hard to believe that there was this much money in the whole wide world.

Tradition demanded that he should heap it all up on the floor, roll on it, scoop up great handfuls of the stuff and pour it over his head like snow. Bugger tradition; he'd only get it dirty and leave traces of oil and dust on the notes which the forensic boys would use to put him in prison. Instead, he stacked it neatly in piles of ten thousand pounds each. It took a long, long time.

And then, at the very bottom of the bag, he found something he couldn't remember having taken from the safe. On the other hand, it hadn't been in the bag before, so it must have come from the safe. He picked it up, turned it over in his hands, and stared at it.

It was a box.

Well; more sort of a little jar, or urn. What the hell. . . ?

Somebody's ashes, maybe? No, too heavy for that. He shook it. It rattled. He put it down quickly. He wasn't a superstitious man; ladders played too great a part in his life for him to have any hang-ups about walking under them and as far as he was concerned, black cats were only bad luck if you accidentally trod on them when walking stealthily through someone's kitchen at night. But there were definite bad vibes coming from this jar thing. He felt a strong urge to take the bloody thing, find a river, and throw it in.

Stupid! If it came from a safe, it stood to reason there was something valuable in it. A right fool he'd look if he chucked it on a skip and it turned out to be full of diamonds. But what *was* in it?

Only one way to find out. (Likewise, there's only one way to find out the answer to the question: 'What's it *really* like falling twenty-seven storeys onto a concrete floor?') He took a deep breath and opened the lid.

Inside was another jar, or urn. Identical, except slightly smaller. He opened it. Inside was another jar, or urn. Inside that, another. Inside that, another. All told, there were thirty-nine of them; and inside the thirty-ninth—

'Jesus!' John Fingers II jumped back as if he'd been bitten. There was something *alive* in the jar.

It was getting bigger, too. All the jars were getting bigger. He crouched in the corner, terrified, as all thirty-nine jars swelled up like balloons until they were the size of oil-drums.

There were *things* in all of them. Hell fire, he muttered to himself, what is this? Instant freeze-dried horror movie, just add boiling water?

'Boiling water?'

The voice came from inside one of the jars. Perhaps it was just the singular acoustic properties of sun-dried terracotta, but it sounded *awful*. John Fingers II gave a little scream and tried to back away, but some fool had left a wall lying about just where he wanted to back into. He slid down into a little heap.

A head appeared over the rim of one of the jars. First a purple turban, with a big red jewel in it; then a pair of burning coal-black eyes, a long thin nose, a thin moustache with twirly ends, a grinning mouth and a little pointy beard. Similar heads were popping up all over the place; thirty-nine of them. John

Fingers closed his eyes and hoped to God for all he was worth that this lot were in fact the police and he was just about to be arrested.

'Skip.'

'What?'

'Where the hell are we?'

'How the hell should I know? Hey, this place is weird!'

'How did we get here, then?'

'Search me. Last thing I knew, some bird was pulling my lid off and pouring boiling water all over me.'

'Hey, that's it! Maybe we died.'

'You feel dead, Hanif?'

'How the hell should I know? You think I got a season ticket or something?'

'Don't *feel* dead. I think you get all cold and stiff.'

'What, you mean like being cooped up in a jar for six hours?'

'Talking of which, why don't we all get out of these poxy jars?'

'Good thinking, Skip.'

'Hey, Skip, there's someone over there. Look, down in that corner, by the wall.'

'So there is . . . Hey, lads, look!'

'Isn't that. . . ?'

'Course it is! Wow, are we glad to see you! How the devil did you get here?'

John Fingers looked up, feeling like a lone rabbit facing thirty-nine oncoming lorries in the middle lane of a motorway. 'You talking to me?' he croaked.

'Course we are. Hey look, Skip, I mean Aziz, it's him!'

'Where'd you get those funny clothes?'

'He looks well on it, anyway. Hey, what's it like here? And where are we, anyhow?'

John Fingers inched away, slithering sideways along the

wall. 'Am I supposed to know you people?' he asked.

The one called Aziz looked at him strangely. 'Of course,' he said.

'Really? You sure you haven't mistaken me for someone else?'

Aziz grinned. 'Come off it, Skip,' he said.

CHAPTER SEVENTEEN

'And six means I get an extra muezzin on Aleppo, giving me three suits in baulk and two on the line, repiqued in green makes four thousand nine hundred and twenty-three, add ninety-three for the slam above the line makes six thousand and sixteen, plus four for his spurs makes six thousand and twenty, and it's on a double Carpet so that's twenty-four thousand and eighty, but I also get twenty for the finesse, making a grand total of twenty-five thousand and I *win!*'

'I hate you,' said Akram.

'I don't care,' Michelle replied happily, sweeping the pieces into her corner. 'And that makes forty-eight games to me and, oh dear, none to you, what a shame, never mind, mugs away, your go.'

'Don't want to play any more.'

'Your go.'

'This is a silly game.'

'Your *go.*'

'We have been playing this game,' Akram said, 'for eighty-four hours non-stop. Bloody fine kidnap this turned out to be.'

'You started it.'

'I think I'll call the police and give myself up.'

'Okay,' Michelle said, setting out the pieces. 'But we'll finish the set first. Your go.'

'You *sure* you haven't played this game before?'

'Course I'm sure. But I think I'm slowly getting the hang of it. Are you going to throw those dice, or are you waiting for tectonic shift to move them for you?'

'I've had enough of this game. Let's play Dragons' Teeth instead. You ever played Dragons' Teeth? You'd like it.'

'Throw,' Michelle growled sternly, 'the dice.'

'All right, all right . . . Oh balls, double one.'

'*Hah!*'

'I'd offer you money to go away,' Akram said, 'but I've only got a five pound note and some copper. Which reminds me,' he added. 'What happens to employees who stay away from work for four days without even phoning in to pretend they're ill?'

'Usually,' Michelle replied, 'they get the sack. Why?'

'Pity,' Akram said, 'I was just starting to like it a lot there. Did I happen to mention I got promoted to assistant manager?'

'Only about sixty million times. Pretty academic now, I'd have thought. Now then – oh wonderful, double four. Now, do I want the Emir's Palace, Samarkand? Might as well, I suppose.'

Akram cupped his chin between his hands. 'It was inevitable, I suppose,' he sighed. 'It's the bloody story catching up with me, I guess. You settle down, get a job, think you've escaped and then *wham*! there it is again, standing behind you breathing hot narrative down the back of your neck. Tell you what,' he added. 'I'll bet you. If you win this game, I'll let you go free. How does that sound?'

'Chicken. Admit it, you just can't take being beaten by a woman.'

Akram scowled. 'Woman be blowed. As far as I'm concerned, any life form whatsoever that beats me at Racing Genie by a margin of forty-eight to nil is probably pushing its luck. If I ask you nicely, can I concede the last two games?'

'No,' replied Michelle, 'I want to see you squirm.'

'How do you do that, exactly? I've always thought of it as basically wiggling your head about while trying to make your shoulder blades touch each other.'

'You'll find out soon enough. Now stop chattering and get on with the game.'

'What about your job, though? Won't they be wondering where you've got to?'

'I've been kidnapped,' Michelle replied. 'You don't have to go to work if you've been kidnapped. Ask Helen of Troy or anyone.'

'Or your father,' Akram persisted. 'I'll bet you he's worried sick.'

'No he isn't,' Michelle replied promptly. 'I phoned him when you went to the loo.'

'Oh. Right. And what did he say?'

'Never redouble on only two utilities unless you're finessing in baulk. He was right, too.'

'Hey, that's cheating.'

'No it isn't.'

'Yes it is.'

'No it isn't.'

Akram stood up. 'Do you think this is some sort of happy ending?' he speculated. 'I mean, *happily* at forty-eight to nil depends on which side of the board you happen to be, but *ever after* is starting to look like a definite possibility.'

'Sit down and throw the dice.'

Akram shook his head. 'No offence,' he said. 'I mean, it's been great fun, if perhaps a little one-sided, but I think I'll give it a bit of a rest for now. Do you realise,' he added, 'that my whole life is now in total ruins?'

'Oh come on. You'll get another job, I'm sure.'

'It's not that,' Akram replied. 'Just think, will you? For I don't know how long, probably since Time began, I used to go round in a sort of little loop of robbing, killing and getting scalded to death by that bastard Ali Baba. Fine. I escape from all that, and I come here, with the sole intention of catching him and torturing him to death. The bastard stymies me again. But that's fine, because for the first time in my lives I can see this little tiny ray of hope which says to me, *Akram, you don't have to do this kind of stuff any more.* And that's marvellous. I get a job, do something useful with my life, I don't have to be a villain or a hero. And then you come barging in—'

'All I wanted was a hamburger.'

'All I wanted was to be real. You come barging in, and all that goes out of the window, I'm back to where I was, but at least I've got a chance of getting my revenge on Ali Baba because I've got you. And now *that's* all stuffed up on me, because we've spent the last couple of days playing some damn kid's game, I couldn't kill you even if I wanted to, and your criminally negligent, stony-hearted excuse for a father isn't prepared to lift a finger to rescue you. Excuse me, I have to go and feed the phoenix.'

Michelle looked at him. 'You don't want to kill him any more, do you?'

'Of course I don't,' Akram snarled. 'What the bloody hell good would killing the feckless jerk do me? Absolute waste of everybody's time.'

'Then don't,' Michelle replied.

'What?'

'Don't kill him.' Michelle shrugged. 'Don't kill anybody. I know it sounds a bit strange at first, but you'll get used to it. They say the after-breakfast murder's the hardest one to give up. Once you've learned to do without that, you'll find kicking the habit entirely will be surprisingly easy.'

Akram gestured impatiently. 'You think it's that easy, you stupid bloody mortal? You really believe I can just . . .'

'Yes.'

Fang opened her eyes.

'Where . . . ?' she croaked.

A bright light, as hard and unfriendly as the headlights of an oncoming truck, hit her in the eyes. She started to wince away, but found she couldn't.

'Ah,' said a voice above her. 'You're awake.'

The reason she couldn't move, she discovered, was that she was tied up. Her memory was racing, like the wheels of a car stuck fast in mud. The last thing she could remember was a smell. Gas . . .

'This,' said the voice, 'isn't going to hurt a bit.'

Gas. A huge cache of teeth; and she'd been piling them up and wishing she'd brought the block and tackle, when suddenly there'd been this foul sweet smell, and then her arms and legs had stopped working.

'Not a bit. This is going to hurt a whole lot.'

She remembered. 'Aaaaagh!' she said.

She'd gone back to the dentist's surgery where they'd found the safe, because she'd been convinced there were teeth hidden around the place somewhere. And just as she'd found this mind-bending hoard, a light had blazed in her eyes and the gas had hit her and she'd realised that she'd been set up; Ali Baba had put out that great big stash of teeth as a decoy, and she'd flown straight in. She craned her neck to see what was holding her arms and legs. Dental floss.

'You certainly took your time coming back,' Ali Baba was saying. He was holding the drill in his right hand. 'For a while there, I thought I'd misjudged you. Now you've got two choices.'

'Eek.'

'Either,' he went on, switching on the drill, 'you can tell me where that bastard's holding my daughter, or else I'll fill you full of amalgam. What's it to be?'

'I'll talk.'

'You do that. While you still can.'

Another lesson learnt the hard way; never underestimate a dentist. As he unwound the dental floss, he explained that as soon as he'd opened the floorsafe and found the sixpence she'd left there, he'd known that the way to find Michelle was through her.

'I knew you'd come back for the teeth,' he said. 'It was just a matter of being patient. And now, here you are. You're being very sensible, by the way. You probably haven't seen the really big drill. It's thicker than you are. You wouldn't have liked it at all.'

She contemplated making a run for it; but that ceased to be a practical possibility when he took a great big lump of silicone impression material and moulded it round her foot, like an old-fashioned ball and chain. There'd be no chance of hobbling two steps together, let alone flying, with that stuck on the end of her leg.

'Did you ever see *Marathon Man*?' he was saying. 'No? Pity. It'd make scaring the living daylights out of you so much easier if we shared a common frame of reference. Never mind, I'll just have to do the best I can with crude physical violence.'

'I said I'll talk,' Fang squeaked, as he revved the drill. 'Please,' she added, as he slowly and ghoulishly counted out forty-six silver sixpences, explaining as he did so that he was old-fashioned enough to believe in payment in advance. 'I'll take you straight there, I promise.'

'I'm delighted to hear it. Well then, no time like the present. Just wait there a moment while I get a few things.'

He squished the ball of tacky silicone down onto the arm of

the chair, imprisoning her while he tucked the gun into the waistband of his trousers and wrapped the sword in a black bin-liner. 'You have no idea,' he said cheerfully, 'how much I'm looking forward to this. Which is strange,' he added, 'because ever since I arrived on this side of the Line I've tried my best not to inflict gratuitous pain and injury, and now here I am getting ready to slice your friend up as thin as Danish salami. I guess it's a case of the exception that proves the rule. Ready?'

It was insult spot-welded to injury for Ali Baba to mould the ball of sticky onto the bottom of his rear-view mirror, leaving Fang to dangle upside-down like some sort of horrible mascot, but she wasn't in any frame of mind to make anything of it. She was too busy feeling extremely ill.

'Which way?' he asked.

'Left,' Fang replied, 'then second on your right into Portland Avenue.'

'Thanks. The whole reason,' Ali Baba continued, 'why I went into dentistry once I arrived here was this horrid feeling of guilt, because of what I'd done; you know, the palm-oil jars and the boiling water. I assume you know about all that? Good. All right, I decided, now I'm here I'm going to devote the rest of my life to curing pain and alleviating suffering. Pretty noble sentiments, don't you think?'

'Uhg,' Fang replied, swaying crazily as Ali Baba swung the wheel for the right-hand turn. 'Carry on here for about half a mile, then left at the lights.'

'Thank you. The sad part of it is,' Ali Baba went on, 'that all that time, I was living in mortal terror of Akram showing up. And I mean really serious terror. You have no idea how much it costs in electricity when you sleep with the light on all the time. Strictly speaking, I ought to make him pay me for that. And then there's all the alarm systems and infra-red cameras and surveillance gear. None of it's cheap, you know.

And all that was because *I* was afraid of *him*. That's a bit of a joke, in the circumstances.'

'Left here. What are you going to do?'

'Kill him,' Ali Baba replied casually, indicating and waiting for a lorry to pass. 'As painfully as I sensibly can. I'm not going to bother with anything elaborate, of course, because once you start on that track you're virtually inviting the bastard to escape. Ye gods, though, I'm looking forward to this. I mean, we're talking very old scores indeed here. He's going to think boiling water was on the soppy side of humane.'

'Right. Um . . .'

'And dentistry,' Ali Baba went on, one hand on the wheel, 'gives you some fairly esoteric insights into the nature of pain, with specific reference,' he added, smiling dreamily, 'to agony.' He glanced up at the rear-view mirror, caught a glimpse of his reflection in it, and looked back at the road. 'And when I've finished with him,' he said, 'we must have a chat about you.'

John Fingers cleared his throat. Thirty-nine eager faces turned and looked at him.

'Right,' he said. 'Here's the plan.'

He wasn't sure why he'd said that. It seemed appropriate somehow, but he didn't actually have a plan, more a sort of rough pencil sketch, with lots of rubbing out and a shopping list on the other side. Maybe it was a case of the situation bringing out the best in him.

'Seaview Road,' he said. 'The industrial units. Now I want a nice clean job, in and out as quickly as possible, no messing around. Any questions?'

'Skip.'

'Yes?'

'What's an industrial unit?'

On the negative side, it had to be admitted, they were all

thick. You'd be hard put to it to find thirty-nine dozier people this side of a cryogenic vault. 'It's a sort of shed,' he explained.

'A shed?'

'That's right.'

'Who'd keep anything worth nicking in a shed?'

Patience, John Fingers muttered to himself. 'Not that sort of shed,' he replied. 'More a sort of – well, unit.'

'You mean a shed for keeping gold and jewels in?'

More patience. 'It's not actually gold and jewels we're after,' he said, 'more your sort of portable power tools and petty cash style of thing. I mean,' he added, as thirty-nine faces suddenly became as glazed as a row of cucumber frames, 'don't get me wrong, if we do happen across any gold and jewels it'll be a nice bonus. But what we're actually on the lookout for is electric drills, orbital sanders, arc-welding gear, anything we can get a few bob for down the car boot sale.'

He paused, and was immediately deluged in a flood of requests for footnotes. He held up his hand for silence.

'Let's keep it simple, shall we?' he said. 'If it's not nailed down, we pinch it. All right?'

Thirty-nine heads nodded. 'Right, Skip.'

'Then let's go.'

'Skip.'

'Oh for crying out— Yes?'

'Why can't we steal anything that's been nailed down? Is it a curse, or something?'

'No, it's just – yes, that's right, it's a curse. Can we go now, please?'

Why me, he reflected, as he backed the coach out into Merrivale Crescent. I was never cut out to be a gang leader. The Smiths have always been loners, single operators; mostly, he was realistic enough to admit, because of their almost supernatural knack of getting caught, but never mind.

Suddenly finding himself the leader of a gang of fanatically loyal, desperately eager to please, terminally stupid desperadoes wasn't quite what he'd had in mind when he woke up that morning; but it had been a pretty strange day in any case. A pretty strange week, come to that.

'Watch my offside front wing,' growled the coach.

'Shut up, you.'

Obviously it wasn't a coincidence. A less straightforward man would be trying to puzzle it all out at this point, but John Fingers wasn't like that. When things dropped on him from Heaven, he didn't stare up at the sky and demand an explanation; nor did he hold them up to the light or shake them to see if they rattled. No; he accepted them at face value, filed off the serial numbers where appropriate and, whenever possible, immediately sold them in pubs. In this instance Destiny had, for reasons best known to itself, endowed him with the ability to talk to consumer durables and a gang of thirty-nine semi-skilled assistants. John Fingers wasn't remotely interested in where they'd come from; not knowing where things came from was bred in the bone as far as he was concerned. Somewhere in the vastness of the Universe there was a lorry with a duff tailgate, from which all these wonders had tumbled into his lap. His role was to make the best of them he could. It was a way of life that seemed to work with video recorders, forty-piece canteens of cutlery, socket sets, wax cotton jackets, answering machines and all sorts of other things that came his way; no reason he could see why it shouldn't apply to miracles.

If he hadn't been so preoccupied with thoughts of this nature, he might have noticed that he was sharing Seaview Road with a big blue Volvo, which drew up round the corner as he parked the coach outside the entrance to the industrial estate and opened the doors.

'We're here,' he said. 'You two, Whatsyername and Thing,

see to the gates. The rest of you . . .'

Perhaps he should have been more explicit. Rashid and Yusuf, answering to the generic names he'd given to all his new-found followers, had seen to the gates by charging them with their heads. They evidently had very hard heads. Ah well, he told himself, at least it's got the gates open.

'Right, that'll have to do,' he said briskly. 'You lot, follow me.'

If they'd been wearing caps and carrying satchels, you'd have reckoned it was a school party. As they trooped through the mangled gates, furtive as an express train, inconspicuous as North America, the curtains of the darkness parted for a moment and a shadowy figure fell in behind them, followed them for a while, mumbled something into the top pocket of his coat and sneaked off into the shadows.

'This,' muttered Ali Baba, crouching in the doorway of Unit 13, 'is getting a little bit worrying.'

'You've noticed, at last.'

Ali Baba shook his head. 'That large party of idiots over there,' he whispered. 'I think I recognise them. Hang on, we can double-check this.' He counted up to forty and then nodded. 'What in hell's name are they doing here? And who's the new leader?'

'Does it matter?' Fang replied, her teeth chattering. 'Look, they've gone off down the other end of the estate. Let's get on with it and then you can let me go.'

'You think you're going to be let go? Really? That's that stuff, what's it called, optimism. Never could get the hang of it myself.'

It was at this point that Ali Baba felt the loss of King Solomon's ring. Most of the time he was glad, on balance, to be rid of it; having to stop and pass the time of day with every lock and thermostat and circuit-board you meet takes up such a lot of time, and generally speaking gets you absolutely nowhere. Just occasionally, though, it can be astonishingly helpful.

'You wouldn't happen to know,' he asked, 'exactly how one goes about shooting off a lock? It looks so easy in the films, but in real life I haven't a clue how to go about it.'

'Why not just try the handle?' Fang replied.

Ali Baba shrugged and, with the intention of showing what a silly suggestion that was, gave the door handle a half-hearted twist. The door opened.

'Good Lord,' he said. Then he kicked the door hard and charged in.

There are people who can simply blunder into difficult, dangerous situations and expect to be able to carry it off by trusting their instincts and riding their luck. They're the sort of people who also win lottery prizes with the first ticket they buy and attract the attention of off-duty Hollywood talent scouts at karaoke evenings at their local pubs. Unless you're one of these, playing the law of averages with a full Legal Aid certificate in your pocket, it's best to do it the other way and think things through carefully before kicking open doors and sprinting through. You never know what you're likely to find on the other side.

In Ali Baba's case, it turned out to be a very large, bad-tempered bird. His specialised knowledge meant that he was able to identify it as a phoenix, but unfortunately it didn't extend to what you do to mollify one when you're two feet away from it and looking down its throat. At least he was able to eliminate one possibility straight away. Saying, 'Now then, nice bird,' had no perceptible effect whatsoever.

'Ark!' screamed the phoenix, flapping its wings. 'Ark ark *graaaaoar*!'

Two and a half seconds later, Ali Baba was able to add drawing a gun and shooting at it to his definitive list of counterproductive ways to deal with an angry phoenix. He was just about to add falling flat on his face and cowering when Fang said, 'It's all right, he's with me.'

'Then what was all the shooting in aid of?' the phoenix grumbled. 'Daft bugger, he could do somebody an injury.'

Ali Baba looked up, puzzled. 'Tooth fairy?' he said.

'Yes?'

'What's going on? Why are you on my side all of a sudden?'

Fang grinned. 'That's three molars and a couple of upper front canines you owe me, Mister Dentist,' she replied. 'I may be small, but I'm not stupid. Would you like me to switch the light on? It'll be so much easier if we can all see what we're doing.'

A moment later, the light snapped on. The phoenix, dazzled, let out a pained squawk and huddled away into a corner, leaving Ali Baba face to face with Akram and Michelle.

'This is . . .' Akram began to say, but he got no further. This is where it starts getting complicated. Let's break it up into five phases.

As soon as he saw Akram, Ali Baba raised the gun, pointed it at Akram and said 'You bastard!' That's as far as he got, so we'll leave him for a moment and go back to Michelle.

She had started off with the intention of getting between Akram and her father, calming the situation down, getting a conversation going and then leaving them to it while she made a nice conciliatory cup of tea. Seeing Ali Baba raise the gun, however, she rapidly revised her plans and ducked behind Akram, saying, 'Eeek!' We'll leave her there for the time being, and turn to Akram.

Actually, Akram didn't do much, apart from starting to say 'This is . . .' and thinking better of it. Whatever he may have had in mind to do, the situation was radically altered by the light coming on. This meant that he now had a clear, sharply-defined shadow on the whitewashed wall behind him.

Finally, just to complete the picture, this was the precise moment when John Fingers opened the back door to Unit 13 and walked straight in, to find himself staring down the barrel of Ali Baba's gun.

One last thing. The electric kettle, which Michelle had put on a short while ago, now came to the boil and switched itself off. That's Phase One.

Phase Two began with Akram's shadow. It wasn't in the sunniest of moods to begin with, thanks to Akram's devious use of subdued lighting to keep it in its place. Suddenly restored, it snatched its chance, swept along the wall and went for Ali Baba's throat, dragging Akram along behind it like a very small child clinging to a huge kite on a windy day. Instinctively, Ali Baba swung round to face it and fired the gun. Dentistry and skill at arms are not mutually exclusive, but proficiency at one doesn't necessarily imply competence at the other. He missed badly. There was a scream.

For the phoenix, still recovering from its nasty experience with the light, a sudden loud noise in a confined space was the last straw. Rising like a startled pheasant (the comparison is only partially appropriate, because it was ten times bigger than the largest pheasant ever recorded) it rocketed towards the open door in a flurry of pounding wings, cannoned into Ali Baba and sent him spinning against the wall before hurtling away into the night in the general direction of the Isle of Wight.

John Fingers, wondering what the hell he'd just walked into, had meanwhile grabbed the kettle, as being the nearest remotely useful object to hand, with the intention of throwing boiling water in the face of the man who was pointing the gun at him. His principal mistake lay in not unplugging the kettle first. As it was, the kettle remained firmly tethered to the wall, ruining his aim. There was another scream.

That's Phase Two.

Phase Three kicks off with Ali Baba hitting the wall. The back of his head connected with the light switch, turning the light off. Akram's shadow immediately vanished. Akram himself, suddenly released, tripped over something – possibly a dead body – on the ground, lurched forward, slipped on the wet floor and went crashing into Ali Baba, hitting him in the solar plexus with his head. Feeling Ali Baba's fingers round his throat, he grabbed wildly for something to pull himself up by, found the wall and, quite by chance, switched the light on again. End of Phase Three.

The situation at the start of Phase Four, as revealed by the newly restored light, is as follows:

Ali Baba, backed up against the wall, is trying to strangle Akram; who in turn is doing his best to pull away and, rather less successfully, breathe. As if he didn't have enough to contend with, he's now further hampered in his movements by an extremely boisterous and single-minded shadow, which couldn't care less about breathing and is really only interested in inflicting mayhem on Ali Baba. Since Akram and his shadow only have the one pair of hands between them, this complicates matters no end. John Fingers, having contrived to soak himself from head to foot with boiling water from his own kettle, has fallen backwards over a small trestle table and knocked himself silly on the floor; in doing so dislodging a tooth, for which Fang is currently writing him out a receipt. Michelle is lying on the ground, not moving.

And . . . action.

Akram, scrambling to get a foothold, kicks Ali Baba's gun across the floor. John Fingers, coming round and finding himself the apparent recipient of yet another unsolicited present from Destiny, grabs hold of it rather cack-handedly, presses the trigger, and sends a bullet neatly and fortuitously through the light-bulb. One immediate consequence of this is that Akram's shadow promptly vanishes, leaving Akram free to punch Ali

Baba scientifically on the point of the jaw, thereby knocking him out and simplifying the situation enormously in time for the beginning of Phase Five.

This is John Fingers' Phase, so it's appropriate to reflect that he has every reason to feel aggrieved and bewildered with the way things have been going. True, he's up one gun (Browning M1910 seven-shot automatic, he instinctively noticed, street value no more than £150, if that) and a solid silver sixpence; but he's been terrified, shot at or in the general direction of, facially edited to the extent of one upper front tooth, drenched in boiling water and stunned by a concrete floor. About the only part of him that doesn't hurt is his hair and he's standing, as far as he can tell, on a dead girl; not an agreeable situation for a man with seventeen previous convictions.

'Well,' said the gun. 'Don't just stand there.'

And a moment later, he wasn't; because Michelle, whose skull had been grazed by the second bullet, woke up under his left foot, wriggled and screamed. That, as far as John Fingers was concerned, was about as much as he could reasonably be expected to take. He neither knew nor cared what was going on, provided it carried on doing it without him. He started to back off, only to find that again there was a wall tiresomely in the way.

There was also, he was annoyed to discover, a man advancing on him with a large adjustable spanner (seven-eighths Bahco, nice bit of kit but still only a fiver, top whack, down the car boot sale) clutched in his large, powerful hand. Of course, he wasn't to know that the man was Akram the Terrible, but he didn't need an awful lot of background information to work out that the spanner wasn't intended to be used for tightening nuts, unless of course they were his.

'Stay where you are,' he said, pointing the gun at Michelle's head, 'or the girl . . .'

'Skip? You in there, Skip?' Aziz's voice, outside in the yard. Both men heard it, recognised it and felt an immediate surge of relief.

'Yes,' they said.

The phoenix rose into the night sky, wings whirring, tail streaming behind it like a Chinese New Year dragon. Its brain, roughly the size and density of a Land Rover engine, was disturbed by a whirlwind of conflicting messages, until it resembled nothing so much as a vigorously shaken snowstorm paperweight. A dominant theme was fear; bright lights, noises, bangs – far back in its profoundly confused genetic matrix there were pheasant genes, and the sound of gunfire acted directly on the wing muscles, bypassing the usual decision-making machinery entirely. Less urgent, but still influential, was the feeling that running away at the first hint of trouble was somehow conduct unbecoming, and any self-respecting fabulous beast would at least have hung around long enough to find out what was going on and whether the general trend of the narrative made it likely that it'd be needed. Having it away on its wingtips was more chicken than phoenix, it couldn't help thinking; and headless chicken at that. Without realising it, the giant bird halved its airspeed and let up a little on adrenaline production.

The mental debate moved up a gear, the main issue being revealed as self-preservation versus loyalty. The latter concept wasn't a familiar one; when phoenixes stand by their man, it's generally to make it easier to get their claws into his neck. On the other hand, they are honourable beasts, as befits their pedigree and status within the avian kingdom. It had responsibilities to Akram; it had sheltered under his roof and eaten his birdseed. This was, it felt, just the kind of situation where the advice of an older, wiser phoenix would have been extremely helpful. Since it was by definition the oldest and wisest phoenix around, however, as well as the youngest and doziest, it was on is own. Oh well.

'Bugger,' it said. It had slowed down so much that it either had to accelerate or turn.

Without really understanding why, it turned.

'Skip?'

Aziz was looking at two men. They were both tall, dark, lean, broad-shouldered, with curly black hair, pointed beards and regulation coal-black eyes. There the resemblance ended.

The problem was that neither of them actually looked very much like Akram, the way Aziz remembered him; except that, when it came to the crunch, he found he couldn't remember all that clearly what Akram did look like. Well yes, he was tall, dark, lean, broad, curly, pointed and coal-eyed. So were twenty-seven of the thirty-nine thieves. So, when the occasion demanded, was Douglas Fairbanks. Proves nothing. To make matters worse, they both sounded almost but not quite right, like Akram doing voice impressions with a handkerchief over his mouth. It wouldn't have mattered all that much if they hadn't both been ordering him to do contradictory things.

'Skip?' he repeated. 'Here, what's going—?'

He wasn't allowed to finish the question, because the air was suddenly full of the noise of sirens. The police, having heard no shots for over five minutes, had guessed that the combatants had sorted out their differences, and were moving in to arrest the survivors.

Being still relatively new to this side of the Line, Aziz didn't actually know about policemen and sirens and flashing blue lights, but his profession had given him a pretty good set of instincts; good enough to convince him that the men in blue uniforms streaming in through the mangled gates probably weren't autograph hunters. Reluctantly he decided that something had to be done and that he was still stuck with the horrible job of doing it.

'Come on,' he said, 'all of you. We'll sort it out later.'

'But . . .'

'But . . .'

'*Move!*' The authority in his own voice amazed him, and for one moment he firmly believed that *he* was Akram, and had been all along. Interesting though the theory was, however, this was neither the time nor the place. 'You lot,' he ordered a random selection of thieves, 'bring 'em all. Follow me.'

'Where to?'

It was a very good question, and Aziz hadn't the faintest idea what the answer was. So he drew his scimitar, yelled, 'Charge!' at the top of his voice, and ran out into the yard to see what would happen.

In the event, it all seemed to work out rather well. The blue guys who probably weren't autograph hunters started to run towards him, caught sight of the scimitar and appeared to think better of it, presumably remembering that they hadn't been formally introduced and not wishing to commit a social faux pas. This left Aziz with a clear run to the big fifty-seater coach they'd all come in. Since the rest of the lads were following him, also waving their scimitars and shouting, Aziz came to the conclusion that for once, the flow was worth going with. Just to be on the safe side he uttered a blood-curdling yell and brandished his sword even more flamboyantly, narrowly missing his own ear.

The moment when the last straggling thief scrambled aboard and pulled the door to after him was, however, the high water mark of the flow; after that, it started looking alarmingly like they were about to go with the ebb. The autograph-not-hunters had blocked off the exit from the yard with two white cars and were shouting things through megaphones. As far as Aziz could tell, what they were actually saying was, 'Ark wark fark argle wargle fargle,' but you didn't need a United Nations trained simultaneous translator in order to get the gist.

'We all here?' he demanded.

'Yeah, Skip, I mean Guv.'

'Anybody remember to bring the two scrappers? The girl and that bloke?'

'Yeah, Guv. Oh, and by the way.'

'What?'

'That bloke,' said Rustem, his face wallpapered from side to side with an idiot grin. 'I think it's Ali Baba.'

'Fine,' Aziz replied. 'Why am I not surprised? Fuck it, we'll sort it all out later. Right now—'

Right then, Ali Baba woke up.

He had been having a strange dream.

He dreamed that he was standing in front of the Godfather's desk. Directly in front of him, cigar-smoking and ominously looming, was the Godfather himself. Sitting beside him, rather less congruously, was a stout woman in a yashmak. She appeared to be knitting a pair of socks.

'Well?' said the Godfather.

Ali Baba blinked. 'Sorry,' he said. 'No offence and all that, but well what?'

'Your wishes,' the Godfather replied. 'You got three of them, remember.'

'Two,' the stout woman interrupted. 'He already used one.'

A pained expression flitted over the Godfather's face. 'You gotta excuse my wife,' he said icily. 'She ain't got no manners, she don't know how to behave in company. You got three wishes, and . . .'

'Two. Getting across the Line and becoming a dentist was one wish. That leaves two.'

'That wasn't a wish, that was a separate deal,' the Godfather snapped, restraining his rising annoyance King Canute fashion. 'For that he gave us the ring, remember? So three.'

'Two, because the stuff with the ring was just a cover. As soon as he was across we chucked it away.'

'Excuse me,' said Ali Baba. 'I hate to interrupt, but could I just get this absolutely straight in my mind? You want me to use my three wishes now?'

'Yeah.'

'Yes, but it's two.'

'Will you be quiet?'

'I can be as quiet as a tiny bloody mouse and it still won't alter the fact that it's two wishes, not three. The trouble with some people is . . .'

The Godfather banged his fist on the table, dislodging a small china paperweight inscribed *A Present From Palermo*. It fell to the floor, rolled a little way and then, disconcertingly, vanished. He stood up, leaned across the desk until his chin was no more than six inches from the tip of Ali Baba's nose, and smiled.

'You know what they say,' he said pleasantly, 'about having dinner in a Sicilian restaurant? How when you've finished they don't bring you a bill, but years later they come to you and ask you to do them a small favour? Well, Mister Baba, I hope you enjoyed your meal. Do we understand each other?'

'Absolutely,' Ali Baba replied, nodding enthusiastically. 'Consider your drift definitively caught. But what do you want me to wish for?'

The Godfather grinned. 'Any minute now,' he said, 'you gonna wake up. You gonna find yourself in a big yellow bus with thirty-nine thieves, Akram, your daughter and a guy called John Smith who I don't think you know. You shot at him, but you don't know him. All round this bus, you gonna find armed police. I think you might wanna wish you was out of there. Am I right?'

'That would certainly seem reasonable,' Ali Baba agreed,

'in the circumstances you describe. Please do go on.'

'And then,' the Godfather continued – he was so close now that Ali Baba could plainly see his rather second-rate bridgework; somehow, that made him feel better. 'Then you gonna find that Akram's gotta sword, the thirty-nine thieves all got swords, John Smith's gotta gun, and you ain't got nothing except maybe the courage of your convictions. I figure maybe you gonna wish the ironmongery was a bit more evenly distributed.'

'Quite.'

'But,' the Godfather continued, 'that still ain't gonna solve all your problems, because until Akram's dead and all his men, and you and your daughter are far away where you're gonna prove very hard to catch, you won't never be sure they ain't gonna show up all over again. But on *that* side of the Line—' There was, Ali Baba observed, an infinity of disgust packed into the little word *that*. Significant, he felt. 'On *that* side of the Line, if you go killing guys all over the place, you gonna make yourself very conspicuous, and you don't want that. So I'm figuring, maybe you'll wanna come back here, where you belong, where all your friends are. After all,' he added, with an expansive gesture that entirely failed to inspire confidence, 'you only skipped out to escape from Akram and his boys, so if they're all dead, you can come home. Now, what could be better than wishing to come home?'

'Ah,' Ali Baba said. 'I see.'

'That's three,' said the stout woman. 'He's only got two.'

For a second or so, Ali Baba was convinced the Godfather was about to explode. It was gruesomely fascinating, watching him consciously, deliberately stopping himself from being angry. It was rather like watching a film of a fire in an oil refinery being played through the projector backwards. It'd be even more interesting to watch from five hundred yards away through a powerful telescope, of course, because then he could concentrate properly without the distraction of extreme fear.

'He's got three,' the Godfather said. 'You got that?'

'Not that it matters much,' the woman went on, ignoring him, 'because you can easily run the first and third wish together and arrive at exactly the same result. I'd do that if I were you, and that'd put an end to all this silly bickering.'

'Good idea,' said the Godfather. He picked up a heavy marble ashtray in his left hand and squeezed it, reducing it to fine dust. 'Why don't we do just that?'

The phoenix banked, turned and dived. Far below there were lights, noises and scurrying humans. It fought down the instinctive rush of panic; it had already been a phoenix, a pheasant and a chicken. It had no desire to be a mouse as well.

It put its wings back, glided low, and accelerated, feet outstretched. There were eagles as well as pheasants in its ancestry, not to mention a whole host of large, featherless flying lizards with leather wings and huge pointed beaks. It was time to prove that it had inherited rather more from its forebears than a few sticks of old furniture and a broken clock.

Ali Baba woke up.

'I wish . . .' he said.

Claws extended, the phoenix swooped. There was a merry tinkling of glass as its talons caved in the side windows of the coach, and a dizzying, terrifying moment when it seemed that even those huge wings couldn't produce enough uplift to haul a Mercedes coach and forty-three human beings straight up into the air. That was, of course, perfectly natural. For a thousand generations, Mankind used to worry itself sick with the thought that come dawn tomorrow, the sun might not quite have the legs to rise and shine.

At ground level, the policeman with the megaphone stopped argle bargling in mid fargle and stood motionless for a while, his lower jaw nearly touching his bootlaces. Then, being a policeman and properly trained to deal with all possible contingencies, he ordered the coach to come back.

It didn't work.

With infinite regret, and blaming it all on the pernicious respect-dissipating effects of so-called community policing, he gave the order to open fire.

Or at least, he tried to. He got as far as 'Open', but before he could complete the command a passing tooth fairy darted into his mouth, neatly yanked out his dental plate, shoved a silver sixpence in its place and flew away. A split second later it flew back, hovered for a moment in front of the megaphone, and completed the sentence for him.

'Sesame,' it said.

Whereupon the sky opened.

CHAPTER EIGHTEEN

'**W**ait for it,' said the instructor. 'Let it come, let it come, let it come. Steady. And ... Now, plenty of forward allowance, and *let him have it!*'

This is a birth control clinic on the far side of the Line.

'Now let's just try that again, only this time follow the line, swing through and *keep it moving.*'

Six men with shotguns and a clay pigeon trap are standing in a field in the rain. They're learning the art of judging air speed and forward allowance, vital when shooting a moving target.

'The average stork,' the instructor continues, 'can reach speeds of up to forty miles an hour, with the wind behind it. That means that, at thirty-five yards, you need to be something like ten feet in front to be sure of a clean kill. Okay, everybody, let's try that one more time.'

This side of the Line, family planning means a Remington pump-action, a steady hand, a good eye and ten or twelve accurately placed stork decoys. In winter, when huge flocks of the dreaded birds turn south for the annual migration, the hills and valleys echo from dawn to dusk with the sound of aerial contraception.

The instructor beckons the next shooter to the stand, checks that the trap operator is ready, and shouts 'Pull!' The party gazes skywards, waiting for the next target to appear.

'Right,' mutters the instructor, 'here it comes. Now, remember . . . Oh my God!'

Instead of a three-inch disc of baked pitch, they're staring at a huge bird, with a wingspan of maybe fifty feet, wingtip to wingtip, holding in its claws what looks like a big red Mercedes bus. As the shadow of this monstrosity passes over them they stand rooted to the spot, unable to move.

'What the hell was that?'

'It's finally happened,' the instructor groans. 'The bastards have out-evolved us.'

'Did you see the *size* of that thing?'

'And the armour-plated cargo hold,' whispers an awestruck trainee. 'Oh God, it doesn't bear thinking about. What're we going to do?'

'Out of our hands now,' the instructor mutters. 'You boys stay here. I'm going to try and get a message through to Strategic Air Command.'

The phoenix, blissfully unaware that at that very moment nine F-111s of the 3085 Family Planning Squadron were on standby awaiting clearance to take off in search of it, lowered the coach to the ground as gently as it could, waggled its wingtips in salutation, and soared away. The sound of its giant wings faded into the distance. The cuckoo resumed its song. On the hillside opposite, a cow mooed.

Inside the coach, John Fingers levered himself up from behind the seats where he'd been cowering during the flight and rose unsteadily to his feet. His face was as white as a sheet in a soap-powder commercial and the hand with the gun in it shook disconcertingly.

'Okay,' he whimpered. 'This is a hijack, I want you to fly

this coach to Tripoli . . .' He looked round, realised that there was nobody to hear him, and sat down heavily in the driver's seat.

Where was everybody?

A brief inspection revealed that the rear door of the coach was open. The bastards had gone and left him there. He was all alone.

Almost alone. On the back row of seats he found three slumped figures; two men and the girl. In spite of the phoenix's best endeavours there had been quite a sharp jolt on landing, and by the looks of it they'd been thrown forwards and knocked out cold by things falling off the luggage racks. John Fingers hesitated for a moment. On the one hand, he scarpers quickest who scarpers alone. On the other hand, when the going gets really tough, a boy's best friend is his hostage.

One of the men he recognised as the big, evil-looking bugger who'd been on the point of coming after him with a big spanner when the police intervened. The other one was the tall, slim sod who'd shot at him when he first wandered into Unit 13. Those two, he decided, would keep. The girl, however, was a different matter. The word HOSTAGE was practically tattooed on her forehead.

'You,' he said, prodding Michelle with the gun. 'On your feet.'

No good. She was out for the count. Damn, muttered John Fingers to himself, more heavy lifting. Having got her in a burglar's lift (basically the same as a fireman's lift, but not quite so humane) he staggered towards the open door and peered out, asking himself why his thirty-nine erstwhile henchmen had taken off so suddenly, without stopping to say goodbye or even steal his boots.

'Because of the fighters,' said the air-conditioning. 'Look, they're just coming back now.'

John Fingers frowned. 'What fighters?' he said.

'Those ones there.'

'What? Oh *those* . . .'

Sudden turns of speed, with or without heavy burdens slung over the right shoulder, ran in the Smith family. He was just able to make it down the coach steps and into the cover of a nearby pile of rocks when the nine fighter-bombers of the 3085th, squadron motto *Not tonight, Josephine*, screamed back over the skyline, hurtled straight at the coach, let fly with their full complement of air-to-surface missiles and pulled steeply away. The shock of the blast hit John Fingers like a hammer, sending him rolling down the escarpment into a clump of gorse. From where he was, he could actually feel the heat from the explosion on the back of his neck. He had the common sense to stay where he was until it had stopped raining shrapnel and debris; then he hauled himself upright, pulled gorse out of his hands and knees and looked round for his hostage.

He found her sitting up, wiping blood out of her eyes from a cut on her forehead. She opened her mouth to scream, but he showed her the gun and made shushing noises.

'On your feet,' he said, wishing he'd paid better attention to his mother when she'd tried to teach him elementary kidnapping. 'Shut up and do what you're told or I'll use this. Understand?'

'Who's *this*, the cat's mother?' muttered the gun, offended. He ignored it. Formal introductions would just have to wait until later.

Her eyes fixed on the gun, Michelle nodded. Something told her that it was going to take more than a steady nerve and a certain innate skill at board games to get her out of this one. Unlike her abduction by Akram, this all felt rather horribly real.

(Which was strange, bearing in mind where she was. Just over the brow of the hill, a cat was practising the violin, while the dish was sulking because the spoon had forgotten to bring the sandwiches. But she wasn't to know that.)

'All right,' said John Fingers. 'Now start walking. And no funny business.'

'Spoilsport,' the gun grumbled. 'It's been ages since I last saw a really good custard pie fight.'

'Shut up, you.'

'Who, me?'

'Not you. It. Look, will everybody just shut up and get the hell out of here, before those bloody planes come back and blast us all to kingdom come?'

Had circumstances been different, Michelle would have liked to ask what planes, and how come he was talking to his gun? Actually, she had a strange feeling she knew the answer to the second question; and if the purpose of answers is to clear up mysteries, then it couldn't be more counterproductive if it tried. Something told her, however, that her captor wasn't in the mood. She started to walk.

Akram woke up.

It was dark. He was in a confined space. Something wet was dripping down the back of his neck.

Oh shit, not again! He drew in breath to scream, then hesitated. He could smell oil, but it wasn't the right sort. Not palm oil; something more in the SAE 20 super visco-static line, he fancied. Which was either a half-hearted attempt at updating the story and making it more accessible for modern audiences, or an indication that whatever he was in, at least it wasn't the familiar old smelly brown stuff.

Cue past life? Apparently not. Things were looking up.

Well, then. The last thing he could remember was being bundled onto a coach by Faisal and Hakim, with whom he intended to have a word on that subject when he saw them next. And then the coach had sort of taken off, and something had hit him on the top of his head.

Talking of which; what *was* this stuff dripping down his neck? If he could only get his arms to work, maybe he could find out.

Cheap Taiwanese arms, no good, pity they're not still under warranty. Legs? That's more like it. He pushed, until the top of his head came up against something solid that didn't want to get out of the way. Hmm. Interesting scenario, this.

Still no past life? No? Okay, fine. Let's try bringing the knees up and pushing outwards with the feet. Bloody uncomfortable, but no worse than a Jane Fonda workout routine.

Hello, Akram said to himself, I'm in a box. How jolly. Now then, what sort of box? Well, there's one obvious type, the kind with brass handles, satin lining and a flat lid. Now then, senses, best of order, please. Any satin? No, no satin. I think we can tentatively call that a good sign.

Maybe I'm still on the coach. There's no real reason to assume that I am, but let's pretend. If I'm still on the coach but I'm in a box . . . Cue schematic diagram of a typical coach. Ah yes, the bit under the windows where there's doors on the outside, where they store the suitcases. The luggage compartment. I could very easily be in that.

Why, for fuck's sake?

Yes, but just suppose I am. In that case, if I can wriggle round until my feet are touching the doors, and then give said doors a bloody hard kick, maybe I can open them. Anything's possible. Houdini, for example, did this sort of thing for a living.

His heels made contact with what could conceivably have been doors; a flat surface that flexed ever so slightly when he pressed against it. Time, he muttered to himself, to put the theory to the test. After all, what else is scientific enquiry of any sort other than a controlled version of bashing one's head against the Universe until something gives?

He drew his knees back and let fly. Something gave; he tried again, and the doors flew open. A few crab-like jerks and shuffles extricated him from the luggage compartment and landed him on the ground, where he lay for a moment, luxuriating in the rare, delicious sensation of having got something completely right for a change. Then he looked up.

Where the coach had been there was an untidy-looking jumble of tangled, fire-blackened metal. True, it had once been a coach, in the same way that homo sapiens was once a monkey or, more appropriately, Great Britain was once a leading exporter of manufactured goods. As far as he could see, all that was left of it was the luggage compartment he'd just wriggled out of, and a couple of skipfuls of twisted body panel. All in all, it had the same air of bewildered ruin that you'd expect from a short-sighted mugger who's just tried to rob Arnold Schwarzenegger.

Wow, said Akram to himself, whatever happened to that coach, I survived it. Lucky.

Not lucky. There isn't enough luck in the whole universe to save someone from destruction like that. Somebody must have saved me.

Shit. Somebody must *like* me.

Or else, more likely, somebody must hate me enough to believe that being blown to bits in an explosion would be tantamount to giving me a pardon and the freedom of the city. In any event, whoever they were, they don't seem to be around any more. Surprise, surprise.

Having dealt with these and similar issues, Akram scrambled to his feet, yelped with pain as cramp and a wide variety of pulled muscles made their presence felt, and tried to get his bearings. Not that he had much to go on; the landscape was about as familiar as downtown Ursa Minor Beta and slightly less hospitable. As far as the eye could see, provided that it could be bothered, there was nothing but scrub, rock and parched earth. There were a few low, demoralised-looking hills, some clumps of tired and thirsty-looking gorse, and the occasional pile of boulders. The most creative travel brochure writer living could just about get away with *totally unspoilt* and *well away from the normal tourist areas*, and would be forced to leave it at that.

'Gosh,' said Akram aloud, 'so this is where I end up when I'm being *lucky*. I can't wait to see where I land when I'm going through a bad patch.'

''Scuse me?'

The voice had come from behind one of the piles of rocks. Instinctively, Akram held still and turned his head in that direction.

'Hello?' he said.

'Hello yourself. Who're you, then?'

'Who wants to know?'

'Me,' said the voice, 'and actually I'm not really bothered about it, so if you don't want to tell me, then fuck you. Are you responsible for all this mess?'

'No,' Akram replied. 'Are you?'

'Do me a favour,' the voice said. There was a shuffling movement behind the rocks, and a unicorn trotted into view. It was the size of a small Shetland pony, rice-pudding coloured and chewing something in a half-interested manner. If its voice was anything to go by, it had either been born in south London or spent a long time there. There was a whisky-bottle cork on the end of its horn.

Akram stared at it, and his jaw dropped to such an extent that a passing ant could have used it as a staircase to get to his moustache. 'Oh hell,' he said eventually. 'I'm back, aren't I?'

'Don't ask me, mate. All depends,' it added, 'on where you just been. So, if this isn't your mess, whose is it?'

Akram shrugged. 'Don't ask me,' he said. 'Last thing I knew, I was in a coach being carried by a huge bird, somewhere over Southampton. Then there's a bit I seem to have missed, after which I was wedged into the luggage compartment of that wreck over there. I was starting to think that perhaps things were getting a bit weird, but if I'm back in some blasted story. . .'

Something caught his eye and he stopped speaking. Poking out from under the crumpled chassis were a pair of small, elegant ladies' shoes, with brass buckles and buttons up the side. The unicorn was looking at them, too.

'I got you,' it said. 'You were in this house in, where was it you said? Southampton?'

'That's right,' Akram replied. 'Actually, it wasn't a house so much as a coach, but we'll let that slide for the moment. The obvious question's got to be, are there any tin men, lions, scarecrows, witches or yellow brick roads anywhere in these parts?'

'No.'

'Bright green cities? Munchkins? Insufferably cute nine-year-old girls from the American grain belt? Wizards?'

The unicorn shook its head. 'Never seen any,' it said. 'You reckon you might have come down in the wrong place?'

'Very possibly,' Akram replied, taking another look at the immediate vicinity and shuddering a little. 'Mind you, it'd take a pretty extreme set of circumstances for this to be the right place for anything. Has it got a name, by any chance?'

'Home,' the unicorn replied. 'That's what I call it, anyhow. And it may not be the garden of bloody Eden, but that still doesn't mean it's improved by having scrap metal scattered all over it. You planning to clear it up, or what?'

'Not really,' Akram said. 'You wouldn't happen to know whose shoes those are poking out from under there, would you?'

'Not got a clue, mate.' The unicorn thought for a moment, rubbing behind its ear with a raised foreleg. 'I'll tell you one thing, though. Last few weeks or so, everything's been up the pictures a bit. Things drifting in that don't fit, if you get my meaning. Like, a few hours before all this lot turned up, we had a bloke come through here wanting to know if I'd come across a ninety-foot-high beanstalk. Day before yesterday there was this bird drooping around asking if I'd seen her sheep. Two days before that, we had the King of Spain's daughter asking which way to the little nut tree. And now,' it added reproachfully, 'you. I think something's cocked up somewhere and they haven't yet sussed out how to fix it.' The unicorn hesitated, shuffled its hooves, looked the other way and cleared its throat. 'Talking of which,' it continued, with a trace of embarrassment, 'you haven't noticed any stray virgins wandering about the place, have you? It's not for me, you understand, it's for my friend. . .'

Akram and the unicorn looked at each other for a moment.

'The shoes,' they said in chorus.

'Not,' the unicorn added, as it braced itself against the remains of the coach and pushed, 'that they're what you'd call your typical virgin's footwear. Too much heel, for a start. Your typical virgin's more into the sensible, hard-wearing, value-for-money ranges. Those or slingbacks. Ready?'

'Ready.'

They heaved, and the charred bulk shifted. At the last moment Akram, rather to his own surprise, looked away.

'Well?' he said.

'Well,' the unicorn replied, ''tisn't a virgin, at any rate.'

'Oh,' said Akram. 'How on earth can you tell?'

'Because,' the unicorn answered, 'I don't think that sort of thing, you know, applies to suitcases. I mean, where little suitcases come from is either a department store or a mail order catalogue. Must be dead boring, being a suitcase.'

They examined the remains.

'Pretty extreme way of getting it to shut,' the unicorn said.

'Usually, just sitting on 'em does the trick.'

'Quite,' Akram replied, puzzled. What had a suitcase full of female clothing been doing on the coach, he asked himself. It wasn't Michelle's, as far as he could judge, and he reckoned he knew the thirty-nine thieves well enough by now to rule them out, too. Which left Ali Baba, the interloper he'd had the fight with, or somebody else he hadn't noticed. Or...

An icicle of guilt stabbed his heart. He'd forgotten...

'Fang!' he shouted. The unicorn looked at him.

'What?'

'Fang,' Akram repeated. 'My tooth fairy. Where the hell has she got to?'

No sooner had the words passed through the luggage carousel of his larynx than there was a flash of lightning, a shower of silver sparkles and a clap of melodious thunder; and—

Akram stared.

'Fang?'

The tall, slender, gorgeous creature standing before him smiled and nodded. 'You remembered,' she said. 'Eventually,' she added. 'I expect you're a terror for forgetting birthdays, too.'

At this point the unicorn whistled, stepped forward, sniffed at her embarrassingly, shook its mane in disappointment and walked pointedly away, leaving Fang blushing furiously. Akram, meanwhile, managed to get his lower jaw back into place and made a vague gesture to suggest that Fang had grown a bit since he'd last seen her. 'What happened to you, then?' he said.

'I crossed the Line, dumbo. Hey, I *like* it here, it's got all sorts of possibilities. An elf can, you know, really walk tall on this side.'

Akram frowned. 'Quite,' he said. 'But before that. The last I saw of you was when we were...'

'Why have you parked your bus on my suitcase?'

'*Your* suitcase?' Akram quickly stooped down. Sure enough, the sponge bag was full of . . . He zipped it up again, quickly.

'At last,' Fang was saying, 'I can cash that lot in. I got the address of a tooth broker over in the Emerald City who pays top dollar for quality stuff.'

'The last time I saw you,' Akram persevered, 'you were with that loser Baba. He captured you, right? And I didn't rescue you,' he added.

Fang shrugged. 'Actually, he's not so bad. Professionally, of course, he's a pretty useful contact. And anyway, it's me owes you the apology, since I did sort of lead him straight to where you were hiding out.'

'Ah.'

'But,' Fang went on, 'that's all right, too, because when the jet fighters from the family planning service blasted the coach to bits, I grabbed you and put you in the luggage compartment where I knew you'd be safe. That,' she added meaningfully, 'was before I knew you'd parked the damn thing on top of my suitcase.'

'That was *you*?'

Fang nodded. 'Talk about difficult,' she said, with feeling. 'Not you two; that blasted girl of yours. Must be because she's half-human. She took a real crack on the head when the bus landed; for a minute there I thought she'd had her chips.'

'Us two?'

'In the end I had to clap my hands and yell, "I *do* believe in mortals," at the top of my voice. You can't begin to imagine how conspicuous that makes you feel.'

'Us two?'

'Um.' Fang put her hands behind her back and looked away. 'Yup. You and the, er, dentist.'

'You mean to tell me you saved that *bastard*?'

Fang nodded. 'For you,' she said quickly. 'Last thing you'd

want, I'd have thought, is for him to slip through your fingers by dying before you could. . .'

'Oh, right,' Akram interrupted, scowling. 'I'm sure that's exactly how it was. And no teeth changed hands at any stage, needless to say.'

'No they didn't,' Fang replied angrily. 'Wasn't time, for one thing. You reckon it's easy grabbing hold of two grown men and shoving them in luggage holds in the time it takes for a jet fighter to fire a rocket? Try it sometime and see.'

'Luggage hold.'

'The other one,' Fang explained. 'On the other side of the coach.'

Akram nodded, and a smile started to seep through onto his face. 'So with any luck,' he said, 'the bugger might still be there. Unconscious.'

'No, he isn't.'

Akram whirled round, to see Ali Baba standing directly behind him. In one hand he had the gun, and in the other a galvanised iron bucket, from which steam was rising.

Cue past life.

CHAPTER NINETEEN

'Hello,' Akram said.

A wry smile shuffled across Ali Baba's face. 'To put it mildly,' he replied. 'Now then, let's get this over and done with before the water gets cold.'

Dragging his attention back from a particularly vivid reprise of a certain night at Farouk's in Samarkand (he never could remember her name and the flashback always petered out round about the fourth veil; even so, it was probably his favourite bit), Akram raised his hands slowly into the air.

'Where's Michelle?' he asked.

Ali Baba shrugged. 'Safe, I hope. I think she must have made a run for it, because the thief chap seemed to be looking for her when I crept up and bashed him. I'll go and look for her after I've dealt with you.'

'You feel that's necessary, do you?'

Ali Baba nodded. 'Since we're back on this side of the Line again, and since I have you defenceless and at my mercy, I think it might be a good idea. Now, are you going to hold still while I pour this lot over you, or do I have to kneecap you first?'

A series of lightning-fast calculations, involving the distance to the nearest cover, ditto between Ali Baba and himself, the probability (to three decimal places) of not getting shot if he made a break for it and sundry other relevant factors, flitted through Akram's mind. To give the program time to run, he temporised. 'Seems to me,' he said, 'you had all those that time I came to see you about my teeth. Why didn't you do it then?'

Ali Baba shrugged. 'That was over there,' he replied, 'here's here. Back flipside, I'm a peace-loving humanitarian dentist whose life is devoted to curing pain rather than inflicting it – which, I might add, is what I'd rather do, if it was up to me. But it isn't. On this side I'm the instant-dead-bandit-just-add-boiling-water man, and that's all there is to it. I guess a stereotype's gotta do what a stereotype's gotta do. By the way, if you think you can get out of it by keeping me talking till the water cools down, forget it, because I'd just as soon shoot you through the head as boil you. Ready?'

He raised the gun, and then lowered it again. 'Do you mind?' he said irritably. 'I'm trying to kill someone here.'

'Tough,' replied Fang, who was now standing directly in front of Akram. 'Go pick on someone your own size.'

Ali Baba made a few mental measurements. 'You, for instance,' he suggested. 'If you insist, I'm quite happy to blow you away too, because all I've got to do is clap and you'll come back to life. Nice try, all the same.' He frowned and looked down at the gun. 'Yes, all right, I'm being as quick as I can. Just try and be patient, will you?'

'I see you got the ring back, then.'

'Yes, and don't change the subject.' He put down the bucket and assumed a tidy two-handed grip on the gun. 'Like that? Left hand a bit further forward? God, you're fussy. And no, I don't give a damn if it does tickle.'

'It's all right, Fang,' said Akram. He was trying very, very hard not to look directly over Ali Baba's left shoulder. 'You stay out of this. It's a very brave thing you're doing, but. . .'

Fang was now also not looking in the same direction. 'All right,' she said. 'Well, so long. It was really nice knowing you. Thanks for the shoebox.'

'You're welcome. It was a pleasure.'

'On the count of three,' Ali Baba said, taking aim. 'Ready or not.'

A slight buzz of panic threatened to cloud Akram's mind but he fought it back. 'One last thing,' he said. 'That root fill you did for me.'

'Bit academic now.'

'I realise that. But I thought I'd mention it anyway. It's been giving me rather a lot of gyp lately.'

'It can't do,' Ali Baba said, his brow furrowing. 'I removed the nerve, there's nothing left in there to hurt. You must be imagining it.'

Akram shrugged. 'If only,' he said. 'But, like you say, that's neither here nor there. It's lucky for you I'll be dead in three seconds, isn't it? Otherwise you'd have had to go back in and sort it all out.'

'It was a perfectly good job,' Ali Baba retorted. 'I can't help it if you've got an unusually vivid imag—'

He didn't complete the word because, at that precise moment, Michelle crept up the last eighteen inches, grabbed the bucket and emptied it over his head. The gun, muttering something about if you want a job doing properly, fired two shots, but Ali Baba's hands were flailing wildly about, and all he managed to do was scare off the unicorn; which, after a perfunctory sniff at Michelle, was about to leave anyway.

'Kill him!' Fang shouted. 'Go on, get the gun, and—'

'No.' Akram, having relieved Ali Baba of the pistol, put on the safety and dropped it into his pocket. Since he didn't have the ring, he was spared the gun's views on recent events, which was probably just as well.

'Everybody finished?' said Michelle, standing in front of her father and folding her arms in what Akram mentally categorised as a what-time-do-you-call-this manner. 'Splendid. By the way,' she added, taking a long look at Fang, 'who's your girlfriend?'

Akram sighed, sat down on a rock and cupped his chin in his hands. 'It's a long story,' he said.

'Yeah,' muttered the Godfather unpleasantly. 'But not long enough.'

'Don't be so impatient,' replied his wife. 'You ain't seen nothing yet.'

'Aziz.'

'Yeah?'

'We've forgotten something.'

'Yeah? What?'

'The Skip, for one.'

'Or rather, two,' added a thief, using his fingers as a makeshift abacus. 'Akram and the new bloke.'

'Bugger,' Aziz said. 'There's always something, isn't there? Right, we'll have to go back.'

Even as he said it, a tiny voice perked up in the back of his mind and said *Why, exactly?* After all, a leader's job is to lead, not be fetched like a kiddie from playschool. 'When we've finished these,' he added.

Quite how there came to be an inn, miles off the beaten track in the middle of a thousand square miles of scrub, sand and rock, the thieves hadn't bothered to ask. For all they knew, it might be an exciting new form of virtual-reality mirage. If so, the virtual beer was nicely chilled and the virtual kebabs done to a turn. As for the dancing girls, they were virtually. . .

'No rush,' agreed Shamir, his mouth full of barbecued goat. 'In fact, we'd probably be better off waiting for him here. I mean, this is the obvious place to look for us. If we're all wandering around looking for each other it'll only make matters worse.'

'Especially since there's two of them now,' Hakim agreed.

'Good point.'

'Better than one,' added Rustem, sagely. 'Two heads, I mean.'

Aziz leant back in his chair and let his belt out a notch. 'Well,' he said, 'if we're going to be stuck here till they show up, we might as well have a drink and something to eat.'

'Another drink,' Hakim pointed out. 'And something else to eat.'

'Good idea, though. For all we know, it may be several days' march to the next mirage.'

Aziz nodded. 'We were lucky to find this joint,' he said. A little bell rang in his head as he said it, but he ignored it. 'Nice to have it to ourselves, as well.'

'It's always better if you come to these places out of season,' Faisal agreed. 'That way, you don't get the Germans hogging the pool.'

'What pool?'

'The swimming pool.'

Aziz frowned. 'What swim— Oh, right, I can see it now.' Funny, he couldn't help reflecting, could have sworn it wasn't there a moment ago. Maybe it was all a mirage after all. He pushed the idea around the plate of his mind like a piece of cold broccoli and decided to leave it. So it's a mirage; so what? At least it didn't have the Schmidt family from Düsseldorf sitting all round the edge of it in deck chairs. 'I could just fancy a quick dip in a minute,' he said. Assuming the water holds still long enough, added his subconscious. Then he cleared his mind of all such distractions, finished off his beer and waved to the waitress. 'Here, miss,' he said. 'I'd like a loaf of bread, jug of the house white, collected works of Omar Khayyam, a tree and what time do you get off work?'

John Fingers opened his eyes.

Usually when he woke up with a headache, the worst thing he had to worry about was where he'd left his trousers the night before. On this occasion he still had his trousers, but that constituted pretty much the whole of the credit side of the ledger. Just a small selection of the things he didn't have, on the other hand, were the gun, the ring, the girl and the faintest idea where he was. All in all, he'd have given a lot to be back in his nice familiar cell.

Self-pity was all very well; but fine notions jemmy no windows, as his old granny used to say. He sat up, rubbed the bump on the back of his head, and considered his position.

The bump was a pretty substantial cluc, he reckoned. Obviously, while he'd been chasing about after that bloody girl, someone had crept up behind him and belted him one. He scribbled in *terrible vengeance* at the foot of his mental agenda, staggered to his feet and looked around.

'They went that way.' He was so used by now to disembodied voices that he'd gone twenty yards before it occurred to him that since (a) there were no electrical appliances visible in this awful wilderness and (b) he'd lost the ring anyway, he ought to be excused hearing voices, and it wasn't fair.

'Who's that?' he demanded.

'Down here.'

He looked down. Nothing but the dusty ground, his toecaps and his shadow.

A shadow. Not necessarily his.

'Huh?' he said.

It could, of course, be something to do with the bashing, and being out in the blazing desert sun without a hat; but that was almost certainly just wishful thinking. Either the light was playing silly buggers with him, or that wasn't his shadow.

'Please,' he moaned. 'Tell me it's all my imagination.'

'I can if you want me to,' replied the voice affably. 'I'd rather not if you don't mind, though. Call me old-fashioned, but I don't like lying to people I've only just met.'

'You're not my shadow, are you?'

'I am now.'

'Fine. Can I go home now, please?'

The shadow seemed to flicker slightly. 'You are home,' it said.

'Oh, really?' John Fingers toyed with the idea of jumping hard on the shadow's head but dismissed it. 'This is some bit of Southampton I never got around to seeing, is it? Easy enough to miss, a bloody great big desert. Probably sandwiched in between the docks and the new shopping precinct.'

'I'm so glad you've got a sense of humour,' replied the shadow cheerfully. 'I've got this feeling we're going to get along famously.'

John Fingers sighed, and sat down on a convenient treestump. Oh, his heart sighed within him, for the stately Victorian architecture, the vibrant atmosphere of the mess hall, the almost sensuous texture of the mailbag between his fingers and, when Old Mister Sun winked at him over the western horizon, the cool monastic solitude of dear old B583. In his time he'd said a great many harsh and unkind things about prison, but at that precise moment he'd have given all the magic silver rings in the universe to be back where you could tell the bad guys by their clothes and the locks didn't whisper things about you behind your back.

'I could run away,' he said aloud.

'You what?'

'I could wait till nightfall,' said John Fingers, 'when there's no sun and no shadows; then I could run away and you'd never have a clue where to find me.'

'Try it. See how far you'd get.'

Maybe, John Fingers theorised, it's only bluffing. After all, it's only a shadow. From what he could remember of his education, a shadow is basically nothing but an absence of light caused by one's body getting in the way of the sun; but he'd been parolled before they'd got to that part of the course, so he couldn't be certain. There was something in the voice inside his head that suggested otherwise.

'Want to try an experiment?'

'No,' John Fingers replied. 'We did those in science O level when I was in the Scrubs, we had to cut up frogs and things. And there was stuff with iron filings and magnets, too. No offence, but I don't think we've got time.'

'We'll try an experiment. Walk forwards. Go on, there's no catch. I'm going to stay here. If you walk away, I won't try and follow you.'

'Straight up?'

'On my word as a two-dimensional optical effect.'

'Okay.' John Fingers shrugged, grinned and remained rooted to the spot.

'Go on, then.'

'I'm trying.'

It was just, he couldn't help remembering, like when he'd been a kid and he and Ginger Bagworth used to play Ronnie and Reggie. An intrinsic part of every session was make-believe setting your opponent's feet in concrete and chucking him off the dock, and one time Ginger actually got hold of some quick-drying cement from somewhere and filled the cardboard box with it . . . Just like that, only several degrees of intensity worse.

'Now,' continued the voice smugly, 'let's go for a walk.'

Before he knew much more about it, John Fingers was marching briskly along at a smart pace, four miles per hour or so. Backwards. What really impressed him was the way he carefully walked round a tree-stump he hadn't even known was there.

'Satisfied?'

John Fingers took a deep breath. 'If I do exactly what you tell me,' he said, 'will you promise never to do anything like that again?'

'Maybe.'

'Fancy telling me how you do that?'

'Actually,' said the shadow, 'I could explain, but you wouldn't understand. If you hadn't spent all your time in those science classes trying to make dynamite, perhaps you could follow it, but it's too late now.'

'All right,' said John Fingers wearily. 'Now will you let go of me?'

'Sure.'

A moment later, he was on his face in the dust. Slowly, as if expecting his own teeth to bite him, he hauled himself to his feet and dusted himself off.

'So,' he sighed. 'What do you want me to do?'

'Excuse me,' Ali Baba said, his voice reverberating loudly, 'but would anybody mind if I took this bucket off my head?'

Akram nodded, realised that this wasn't much use in the circumstances and said, 'Fine, go ahead. You all right, by the way?' he added. 'I thought that water was supposed to be boiling hot.'

Ali Baba looked at him. 'It was,' he replied, 'once upon a time. But you kept me standing around chatting so long it went lukewarm. So, no ill effects. Thank you,' he added, puzzled, 'for asking. Why?'

'No reason,' Akram replied. 'I was just concerned, that's all.'

'Concerned?' Ali Baba narrowed his eyes, until his eyebrows looked like one continuous furry hedge. 'You're not supposed to be concerned. What's got into you?'

That, Akram realised, was a very good question; except that

it was more a case of what had left him. 'The shadow,' he murmured. 'Here, it's gone. I haven't got a shadow at all. Hey, can you see a shadow?'

'Now you mention it. . .'

'That explains it,' said Akram, grinning. 'Somehow or other I've managed to give the wretched thing the slip. It means—' He hesitated, his manner rather like that of a Greek philosopher who, halfway down the High Street with no bathrobe and the loofah still in his hand, is asked to explain exactly what useful purpose the shattering new concept he's just stumbled across is designed to achieve, other than getting the bathmat wet.

'Well?'

Akram shrugged. 'For a start,' he said, 'it means I don't have to kill you if I don't want to. Hell, I don't have to kill *anyone* if I don't want to. That's pretty remarkable, when you come to think of it.'

A small but irreverent noise from Fang indicated that she wasn't so sure. 'I don't get it,' she said. 'I go weeks at a time without killing anybody. Everywhere you look, there's people not killing anybody. Sure it's nice, but I wouldn't hold your breath waiting to be invited on chat shows.'

'You wouldn't understand,' Akram replied, pulling the clip out of the gun and drawing the round from the breech. 'As far as I'm concerned, it's bloody marvellous.'

'Odd you should mention it,' Ali Baba interrupted. He turned the bucket over, put it on the ground and sat on it. 'I think I must be feeling the same way. For instance, if someone were to bring me Akram's head on a platter right now, I'd probably ask them to take it away and fetch me a simple cheese salad instead.'

All four of them were silent. It was one of those peak-in-Darien moments, with Akram and Ali Baba being stout Cortes, and Michelle and Fang bringing up the rear, so to speak, unable to tell whether the boss is undergoing a deep spiritual experience, or has just remembered he'd forgotten to feed the goldfish before leaving Spain. When the inscrutability of it all got too much for her, Michelle cleared her throat and politely asked if someone would explain to her precisely what the hell was going on.

Ali Baba and Akram looked at each other.

'I don't think we're a hundred per cent sure,' Ali Baba said. 'All we do know is, your man here and I have been trying to kill each other since the Bible was still in copyright, and now we don't want to any more.' He glanced at Akram and raised an eyebrow. 'You agree with that?' he asked.

'Sure. It's a bit disconcerting,' Akram replied. 'On the one hand it's a really great feeling, like waking up and realising you haven't got to go to work ever again. On the other hand, there is this nagging question of what the hell we're going to do with the rest of our lives.'

'You want a suggestion?' said Fang crisply. 'Bearing in mind that between you, presumably, you know where there's this huge hoard of gold, silver and precious stones, guarded by a magic door to which you happen to know the password? Ho hum, it sure beats me. If I was in your shoes, I'd be absolutely flummoxed.'

'You mean,' said Ali Baba slowly, 'we split the treasure between us and go and sort of – do something with it? Rather than just fight over it, I mean?'

'The verb *to spend* keeps popping into my mind in this context,' Fang muttered, 'can't imagine why.'

'Could we, do you think?' Ali Baba asked uncertainly. 'It'd mean the end of the Story, for good and all. If there's no treasure, the whole thing falls to bits. No treasure, nothing to steal, nothing to fight about. Hey, that's neat.'

Fang nodded enthusiastically. 'Mind you,' she added, 'it wouldn't be fair to expect you boys to do all that spending by yourselves. I mean, that'd be one hell of a responsibility to saddle you with. I couldn't live with myself if I thought I'd lumbered you with a rotten job like that.'

'Many hands,' Michelle agreed, 'make light work. You can put me down for a share, too.'

A strange light glowed in Akram's eyes. 'This is remarkable,' he said. 'We could really fix the bloody Story good and proper, you know? I mean, I could spend my share on famine relief or helping refugees or something.'

'Or a free dental hospital,' Ali Baba added. 'Hey, wouldn't that be something?'

'You bet.'

Much more of this, Fang reckoned, and she'd need a paper bag, quickly. 'Hey,' she said, 'are you guys for real?'

'No,' Akram admitted, 'but we're working on it. Which reminds me; we'd have to find some way of getting the stuff back over the Line. If we stay here, it'll make itself into a brand new Story, and we'll be in just as much trouble as we are already. Any suggestions?'

'What about the ring?' Michelle put in. 'It must be good for something other than passing the time of day with household appliances.'

'Excuse me.'

'Not now,' replied Ali Baba, 'we're busy. I think she's got a point there. If we could find a way of—'

'Excuse me.'

'I said not now. All we'd have to do— Why are you all staring at me?'

'We were wondering,' Fang said quietly, 'who you keep saying *Not now* to.'

'What? Oh.' Ali Baba looked round. 'Actually,' he confessed, 'I'm not entirely sure.'

'Me.'

'I think it's coming from inside your pocket,' Ali Baba said.

'What, you mean the gun?'

'Could be.'

'No could be about it, you clown. Get me loaded quick, before—'

Before, it was just about to say, John Fingers and the thirty-nine thieves complete their classic encircling movement and have you completely surrounded. By then, however, it was too late, and so it didn't bother.

CHAPTER TWENTY

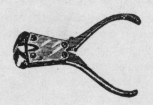

'Actually,' said Scheherezade, 'that wasn't supposed to happen.'

The Godfather gave her a long, cold look. 'Really,' he said. 'You amaze me.'

'I do?'

'I go to all the trouble,' the Godfather continued, 'of arranging for Baba and the big bad guy—'

'Akram.'

'Akram to cross the Line. I make it so they can fight each other. I got everything ready so we can start easing our way in over there.' He closed his eyes, and a look of great sadness crossed his face. 'And now you come to me and say, Look, I goofed, they've all come back. Honey, I'm disappointed. I expected better of you.'

Scheherezade squirmed a little. Only once or twice before had she heard the Godfather express himself so forcibly. Disappointed; judges used to put on little black hats to say more comforting things than that.

'I don't know how it could have happened,' she said

awkwardly. 'It's like they're making their own story. It's weird, I'm telling you.'

The Godfather's left eyebrow lifted a quarter of an inch. 'You don't say?'

'It's bizarre, it really is. Like, this realside thief John Fingers has sort of turned into Akram, Akram's acting more like the hero than the hero is himself, and now I got this Michelle person and a goddamn tooth fairy to fit in somehow.' She swallowed, aware that perhaps she wasn't making life any easier, or longer, for herself by dwelling in too much detail on the problems. 'But,' she said, heaping three tablespoons of positive vibes into her voice and stirring frantically, 'you just leave it with me and I know I'll have it sorted before you can say open. . .'

'No.' The Godfather lifted his head and blew a plume of cigar smoke at the ceiling. 'I had it up to here with these guys. Going off on a story of their own, they show me no respect. What can you do with such people? So, I figure it's time we cut our losses and move on.'

'You mean,' Scheherezade asked, 'leave them to their own devices? Let them get on with it?'

'No.' The Godfather shook his head and looked away. 'I mean kill them all.'

Scheherezade shuddered just a little. That'd be right, she muttered to herself. The Godfather didn't so much cut losses as hack, slash, slit and hew them. Not that he was a bad loser or anything; he was just the sort of person who, having bought a single ticket for the National Lottery and failed to win the jackpot, would have all the winners systematically kneecapped as a matter of course. Still, she reflected, rather them than me; although the two options are by no means mutually exclusive. The Godfather, she knew from long experience, didn't suffer fools gladly; with him it was more a case of being glad when fools suffered.

'Good idea,' she mumbled. 'You want me to, er, put Rocco onto it?'

'No.' The Godfather shook his head. 'He's got better things to do. You deal with it, okay?'

Scheherezade swallowed hard, difficult when her throat was suddenly dry. 'Me?' she said. Immediately she realised that that wasn't the most amazingly intelligent thing said in the history of the Universe by anybody ever. 'Gosh, thanks, I'd love to,' she added quickly, 'it's so kind of you to let me do it, that'll be a real treat.' But the damage was done; she had that extremely negative feeling you sometimes get when you're climbing stairs with a huge stack of plates in your arms, and just as you're at the top you put your foot on a place where a stair ought to be but isn't. It was at that moment that an idea, totally wild, extreme and unthinkable but at the same time the one and only logical course of action now open to her, started to peck tentatively at the inside of its shell. As soon as she became aware of it, she had to use every last milligram of self-control she had left to prevent it showing in her face.

'You got a problem with that?' the Godfather demanded.

'Absolutely not,' she replied.

'Skip.'

In a profession almost as ancient and even more honourable than his own, John Fingers reflected, they had a saying about never working with children and animals. Which category Aziz fell into, he wasn't quite certain, although he had a shrewd idea it was both.

'Well?' he grunted.

'Are we nearly there yet?'

John Fingers raised his eyes to Heaven. Hey, God, he muttered to himself, I wish you existed so I could hate you. 'How the hell would I know?' he growled. 'I keep telling you clowns, I've never been here before in my life. It's your weird bloody country or dimension or whatever it is. Also,' he remembered, 'it's your goddamn hideout. It's where you idiots *live*, for crying out loud. Surely you know how to find it by now.'

'No, Skip.'

Although he'd been convinced that his ability to be amazed by stupidity had already worn out through over-use, John Fingers was prepared to admit he was wrong. 'You *don't*?' he said. 'Why the hell not?'

'Because we always follow you, Skip. Because you're our leader.'

'But . . .' Some basic self-preservation instinct warned John Fingers that if he tried to argue the point, all that would happen would be that his top-joint-of-one-finger grip on reality would give way and his brain would probably implode, like a dying star. 'Okay,' he said. 'Ask the prisoners. I expect they know.'

'Okay, Skip. Skip.'

'Now what?'

'What'll we do if they don't?'

In moments of extreme stress, John Fingers found it helped to count up to ten. On this occasion, he got as far as two. 'Easy,' he replied. 'We just sit down right here, build a factory and start manufacturing prosthetic brains for people like you who don't have real ones. I have this feeling that we'd make an absolute bloody fortune in these parts.'

'Okay, Skip. I'll go and ask the prisoners.'

'You do that.'

When they'd found him wandering about in the desert, no more than a long gob and dust-clogged spit from death by dehydration and trying to hide from his own shadow, he'd assumed, more fool him, that things were looking up. When they'd hailed him as their lost leader and mentioned in passing that now he'd come back they could all go home to their secret cave in the mountains, which just happened to be crammed from floor to roof with gold, silver and precious stones, he'd been deluded enough to take this as a stroke of good luck. If he'd had the sense he'd been born with, he now realised, he should have jumped into the mirage and drowned himself.

'Gift horses' mouths,' murmured his shadow under their mutual breath. John Fingers scowled.

'Listen,' he replied, 'I may not have found a way of getting shot of you yet, but it's only a matter of time. And when I do—'

'Promises, promises. As far as I can see, this is just the start of a beautiful friendship.'

'You'll keep,' John Fingers muttered darkly. 'Here, do *you* know where this bloody cave is we're supposed to be going to?'

'Of course I do.'

This time, John Fingers only just managed to get as far as one. 'Then why,' he snarled, 'don't you just take me there, you bastard of an optical bloody illusion?'

'Because,' replied the shadow smugly, 'the sun is in the west, and you're riding towards it. This means your shadow falls behind you. Now, if you were going east, it'd be no problem for me to lead the way. I'd have no alternative.'

'Fine.' John Fingers closed his eyes, but that didn't help much, either. 'And what direction is the cave in?'

'South.'

'Thank you ever so much.' With a petulant tug on the reins, John Fingers pulled his camel's head through ninety degrees. 'I'm terribly glad we've got that sorted out, aren't you?' By navigating a rather erratic route, he found he could drag his shadow along over some particularly jagged-looking rocks, but it didn't seem to mind.

'Skip.'

'*What?*'

Aziz blinked. 'Sorry,' he said, 'I was just going to ask why we suddenly started going this way.'

'Because that's where the cave is, moron.'

'Oh.' From Aziz's expression, you could tell that he honestly hadn't thought of that. 'That's all right then. Oh, and Skip.'

'Well?'

'Why were you talking to yourself just then?'

'Because it's the only way I'm likely to get a sensible conversation in this godforsaken bloody wilderness. Satisfied?'

Aziz nodded. 'Sure thing, Skip. I'll just go and tell the others. Oh yes, one last thing.'

'Speak just once more and it will be. Well?'

'The prisoners say the cave's due south, Skip.'

'What an absolutely staggering coincidence.'

'Yeah, I thought so too. Bye, Skip.'

'Drop dead. No, forget I said that. After all, what harm have the vultures ever done me? Here, do something useful for once and fetch over the prisoners.'

A short while and an imaginative medley of camel-cursing later, Ali Baba and Akram were escorted up the line of the caravan. They were roped back to back aboard one of the most peculiar-looking creatures John Fingers had ever seen while sober; imagine a giraffe with a collapsed compost-heap on its back, and you're halfway there. Given their circumstances, they had no right to be cheerful, as John Fingers lost no time in pointing out.

'On the contrary,' Akram replied. 'Haven't felt so optimistic in ages. Ask me why.'

'Look—'

'Go on. Humour me.'

Why not, John Fingers demanded of the residue of his soul, I've humoured every other loon in this hemisphere. 'All right,' he said. 'Why are you so bloody cheerful?'

Akram smiled; or at least, he tightened the muscles at the corners of his mouth, bringing about a half-moon-shaped contraction of his lips. John Fingers had the uneasy feeling it was a triumphant snarl in fancy dress.

'Because,' Akram said, 'I know what's going to happen next, and you don't. Isn't that right, Ali?'

Ali Baba nodded. At least he wasn't smiling; he had his lips drawn in under his teeth in a thin, tight line, the way people do when they're really trying for all their worth not to burst out laughing. 'Mphm,' he said.

'All right.' It had been John Fingers' intention not to let them see he was afraid, but that was rather like trying to convince a tankful of piranhas that they'd really prefer a nice salad. 'You tell me what's going on here, and I might just decide to let you two go. Not,' he added, as Akram beamed at him and Ali Baba failed completely to stifle a rather vulgar sniggering noise, 'that I'm worried or anything. I just thought it'd be more sensible if we try it the easy way first, if you get my meaning.'

Akram nodded enthusiastically. 'He wants to try it the easy way.' he said.

'Snngh!'

'You've got to admire the bugger's nerve, though,' Akram said. 'I mean, credit where it's due, at least he's consistent to the very last.'

'Tsshh!'

This was just a tiny bit more than John Fingers could stand. He pulled out the gun—

'Hi,' Ali Baba said. 'Oh, fine, fine, thanks. Yes, I know. No, you mustn't blame yourself. No, really, you've done everything you possibly can, it's not *your* fault if. . .'

'Shuttup!' John Fingers yelled, letting the gun drop from his hand as if it was red hot. 'Both of you,' he added. 'Aziz, pick up the gun. No, *not* like—'

There was a loud bang, followed by a rude word, then silence. Then Ali Baba cleared his throat.

'The gun asked me to tell you,' he said, 'that that was the last shot in its, what did you say that bit's called where you keep the spare bullets, its magazine, so if you don't mind it'd like to be excused duty for the rest of – for now, I mean. Also, I think your friend's just shot himself in the foot.'

'He's right, Skip. Hey, Skip, my foot hurts.'

'Also,' Ali Baba continued, 'your watch says it needs a new battery and your Swiss Army knife's quarrelled with your keys and would be grateful if it could go in your other pocket where it won't be obliged, I quote, to rub shoulders with the riff raff. Finally—'

'I don't want to know!' John Fingers shouted. Ali Baba shrugged.

'Sorry,' he said. 'I thought you said you wanted to know what's going on.'

For a moment John Fingers considered ordering Ali Baba to hand over the ring; then he thought, No, maybe not. 'You know perfectly well what I want,' he snapped. 'Come on, out with it or I'll have you buried up to your necks in sand and leave you here for the vultures.'

'Ah,' said Akram. 'So you don't need us to give you the password. Okay, anywhere here will do; maybe that dune over there. . .'

John Fingers gathered his right hand into a fist, took aim at the epicentre of Akram's smile and swung hard; in consequence of which he fell off his camel.

'A tip for you,' Akram said, leaning over as far as he could. 'When lashing out on camelback, it's vitally important to be absolutely sure you can reach the target. If you don't, you'll overbalance and fall off. Sounds easy enough, I know, but actually it takes years and years of practice.'

'A whole lifetime,' Ali Baba agreed.

'Or longer, in his case.'

'True. Very true. I hadn't thought of it in those terms, but. . .'

With very much the same air of disgusted weariness with which Oliver Hardy used to wipe custard pie out of his face, John Fingers hauled himself to his feet, dusted himself off and spat out a mouthful of desert. Then he asked the nearest thief to take the prisoners to the other end of the caravan and keep them there until they arrived. 'And then,' he added, 'bring me the other prisoners.'

'Sure thing, Skip.'

'My name,' said John Fingers, using up the last dregs of his dignity, 'is not Skip. Understood?'

'Sure thing, Akram.'

I could try and explain, John Fingers said to himself. And while I'm at it, I could try putting the sun out by spitting at it, but it'd only come back on my face. 'You,' he sighed. 'Tell me how you get back up on this thing.'

'Skip?'

'Don't worry, I could do with the walk. Just hurry up with those bloody prisoners.'

There were times when John Fingers was convinced that day would last for ever; but it's a long road that has no turning (the M25 is a good example) and eventually—

'Is that it?' he asked his shadow.

'That's it.'

He might well have hazarded a guess without the help of his two-dimensional guide. The bleak and barren landscape, the forbidding rampart of wind- and frost-eroded stone rearing up out of the flat desert, the great cleft riven into the cliff face, even the vultures wheeling insolently in the clear, cruel sky; with such unambiguous dollops of symbolism as these you didn't need signs saying THIS WAY TO THE SECRET CAVERN and LAST PETROL BEFORE THE BANDITS' LAIR to know what was coming next. It was as if Nature and Narrative had met up in the bar beforehand to discuss the design and decided that subtlety is for wimps.

'Skip.'

Sigh. 'Yes?'

'Are we nearly there yet?'

'Not quite,' John Fingers heard himself saying. 'I mean, that's it over there. Isn't it?'

Even as he spoke, a sickening feeling of déjà vu began to spread through him, making his flesh crawl. This place—

'You.'

'Me, Skip?'

'That big flat boulder over there. Can you see it?'

'I can see lots of boulders, Skip. Any particular one?'

'The black one,' said John Fingers. 'Nearest to us, with the thorn tree alongside. Isn't that where we put out the empties for the milkman?'

Sure enough; when Aziz and Hanif managed to drag the boulder a few inches clear and drop into the large dome-shaped cavern underneath, what did they find but a huge cache of empty bottles and a note, scrawled on a piece of charred vellum and reading: ONE HUNDRED AND TWENTY-SIX PINTS TODAY, PLEASE.

Fine, John Fingers muttered to himself, God only knows why I remember this horrible place so vividly, but I do. And, if my theory's right, that crack in the rock there is the letterbox, and you open the secret sliding door by waiting till the guard's back is turned and leaning on that small projecting rock there. . .

'Aziz.'

'Skip?'

'Just see if there's any post in the box, there's a good lad.'

For a moment it looked quite promising, as Aziz clambered out with his arms full of envelopes. Once they'd sorted out the junk mail, however, there was nothing left except a receipt from the lawn mower people and a dead lizard.

And then they were standing in front of a breathtaking curtain of sheer grey rock, extending upwards into the sky like the biggest, nastiest office block you ever saw, and John Fingers knew they'd arrived at the front gate. Something less like a gate you'd be hard put to imagine; all the king's horses, men and heavy artillery couldn't smash a hole in that lot, not in a million years. The only discordant notes were the door-knocker, a hundred feet above the ground and made of solid brass, and the little plaque saying *Beware Of The Dog*.

'What Dog?'

'Ah,' said Aziz, grinning. 'We haven't actually got a dog. We just put that there to frighten away burglars.'

'We get a lot of them, do we?'

'Burglars? Well, no; except us, of course, but we live here, so we don't count.' Aziz considered the point, obviously for the first time. 'Hey, it only goes to show how well the notice works, eh, Skip?'

John Fingers stood for a moment, staring upwards until he began to feel dizzy, and wondering what in hell's name he was doing there. Then he remembered; treasure. Ah yes, the treasure. According to these idiots, behind that massive slab of rock there was a very large jackpot indeed. When he'd tried to get specific details, the idiots had been a bit vague; call him prosaic if you like, but John Fingers didn't consider *inexhaustible* and *beyond the dreams of avarice* to be satisfactory terms of measurement. Going by the rough internal dimensions of the cavern which he'd finally managed to prise out of them, and taking a fairly arbitrary standard for the amount of gold bullion you could pile up in a square metre, he reckoned there was enough there to buy three fairly standard passenger airliners, and almost enough to pay the interest on public sector borrowing for an hour. That much.

The dreams of avarice, if avarice had eaten too much cheese the night before. John Fingers found his enthusiasm slowly seeping back.

'Fine,' he said. 'Anybody got the key?'

Aziz looked at him. 'There isn't a key, Skip,' he said. 'You've got to say the magic words.'

John Fingers made a small growling noise, like a tiny dog trying to pick a fight with a Charolais bull. 'And what are the magic words, then?' he asked.

'Stop kidding around, Skip,' Aziz replied. 'You're a great kidder, you are.'

'That's me all over,' John Fingers replied. 'Look, you lot stay here and don't move. I'm just going to, er, look at something.'

Having retreated to a respectable distance, John Fingers positioned himself carefully between the sun and the ground, and said, 'Well?'

'Well what?'

'Well,' he said impatiently, 'what's the bloody password?'

'You mean you don't know?' replied his shadow. 'Come off it. Everybody knows the password.'

'Then it must be a singularly useless password if everybody knows it. Except, it would seem, me.'

'Everybody,' the shadow explained, 'on your side of the Line. You probably learned it at your mother's knee; you know, when you were little and she told you stories.'

John Fingers' face hardened, indicating an extreme level of tact deficiency. 'Not me,' he replied, 'on account of my mother not telling me stories. Lies, yes. Like, I'd ask her, Mummy, why's my carrycot full of pretty beads and why mustn't I tell the lady at the till about them. Then, when I was three and a bit, we started Elementary Shoplifting and Mugging for the Under-Fives. Never any time for stories in our family. So what's the password?'

The shadow seemed taken aback. 'But you must know the story,' it said, bewilderment clogging its voice. 'Everybody knows the ... Except you, apparently. Bugger me, just my luck, we're going to have to do this the hard way. All right, watch the rock to your left.'

'Why?'

'Just shut up and do as you're told.'

John Fingers shrugged and looked.

'It's a rabbit,' he said.

'That's just to give you the idea,' the shadow said, as a silhouette rabbit waggled its ears at him from the cliff-face opposite. 'Now then, concentrate.'

'What? Oh I see, right. Two words. First word, door. Gate. Something like a gate. Something swinging, something opening, no, shorter, open. Open. Right, next word. Three, oh right, three syllables. Nasty smell, stink, lavatory, drains, like drains, sewers, cesspit, shorter, oh, right, cess. Open cess. Next syllable, sandwich, eating, sandwich filling, God I hate this game, I was always lousy at it when I was a kid, sandwich filling let's see, chicken tikka, no, prawn, tuna fish salad, cheese, ham, oh right. Open cess ham. Last syllable, finger pointing, finger pointing at me, me. Open cess ham me.'

'Again.'

'Open cess ham me. Hey, what a peculiar password.'

'*Again.*'

'Open *sesame*!'

Whereupon sesame opened.

CHAPTER TWENTY-ONE

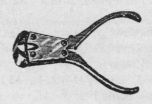

'Hello, this is Michelle Partridge's answering machine, I'm sorry there's nobody here to take your call right now, so if you'll leave your name and *where the hell have you been*, we've been worried sick about you.'

What constitutes a telephone depends on which side of the Line you happen to be. Storyside, of course, they don't have the banana-shaped pieces of plastic we have here; instead, they use seer-stones, crystal balls, magic mirrors and similar gadgets, which work on pretty much the same principle but don't go wrong quite so often, and you don't have to pay the standing charges. Until recently, it was virtually impossible to patch into the Storyside network from Realside, and vice versa. With privatisation and the abolition of the BT monopoly, the advent of Mercury and the like, the situation has changed and, in theory at least, you can now gabble away across the Line to your heart's content. In practice, of course, it's not quite so simple; even so, it's still easier to ring Tom Thumb or the Seven Dwarves than, say, Los Angeles.

'Sorry,' Michelle replied. 'Look. . .'

'And speak up, will you? I can hardly hear you.'

'Sorry,' Michelle hissed, closing her hand around the small silver ring she'd just borrowed from her father. 'Look, I've got to whisper, I don't want anybody to hear me.'

'Then you're going the right way about it. I can't, for starters.'

'Anybody *here*. I'm a prisoner in a cave. I'm talking to you on a mirror.'

'A what? Hey, have we got a crossed line?'

'... *Kate Moss, Drew Barrymore, Naomi Campbell, Linda Evangelista, Demi Moore*...'

'It's this blasted mirror,' Michelle explained. 'Used to belong to a wicked stepmother; you know – mirror, mirror, on the wall, all that sort of thing? Anyway, why I'm calling is—'

'... *Julia Roberts, Yasmin Le Bon, Elizabeth Hurley*...'

'—Because I need you to do something up for me, quick as you can, and call me back. Okay? Probably won't take you five minutes; you can get the vacuum cleaner and the kitchen steps to do the heavy lifting.'

'I can try,' the answering machine replied. 'But listen, what do you mean, captured? And where exactly are you? I've been trying to get your number from the exchange but it doesn't seem to want to tell me.'

Michelle scowled. 'All right,' she said, 'I'll call you back. What I need you to do—'

'... *Jerry Hall, Helena Christensen, Kelly Klein, Isabella Rosellini*...'

'Is, get the big bottle of olive oil from the cupboard under the sink and a really large flowerpot, block up the drain hole in the bottom, get a saucer or a small plate or something—'

'... *Esther Rantzen, Judi Dench, Margaret Thatcher*...'

Michelle swore under her breath. 'It's no good,' she muttered, 'this stupid thing's on the blink again, I think somebody must have dropped it or banged it or something.

Look, I'll have to call you back.'

'Yes, but. . .'

The mirror went dead, leaving Michelle with a momentary feeling of great and frightening distance, such as one might expect at the end of a tantalisingly brief contact with the normal and everyday. Then she reflected that she'd just been asking her answering machine to get her Hoover to go through the kitchen cupboard, which put things back in perspective somewhat.

'Well?' Akram demanded.

'I got through,' she replied. 'I gave it half the message and then the mirror started playing up. I'll try again later if I get the chance; otherwise we'll just have to hope. . .' She was going to say, *hope the answering machine uses its initiative*, but that would be silly; rather like urging an invertebrate to put its back into it. 'We'll just have to hope,' she repeated, and as she did so, it occurred to her that that was sillier still, in context.

'It'll be all right,' said Ali Baba unexpectedly, holding out his hand for the ring. Michelle had given it to him before she stopped to ask herself why; after all, it was her ring, her aunt had left it to her. Or someone, an old woman she used to go and visit, had given it to her and she'd assumed it was the old woman's to give. So; did it belong to Ali Baba? Only because he'd stolen it from Akram, who'd himself stolen it from someone else, presumably now long since deceased in circumstances of extreme prejudice. She might have said something about this if she'd actually wanted the wretched thing; as it was, she didn't. You don't, after all, kick and scream and drum your heels on the floor and demand to have your ingrowing toenail put back when the chiropodist's just dug it out.

'Now then,' Ali Baba went on, slipping the ring on and closing his fist around it. 'Before we move on to phase two, how'd it be if we just think it through for a moment and make sure we know what it is we're supposed to be doing. For once in the history of the Universe, let's try and do something properly.'

Michelle and Akram nodded. Fang, who was sulking, went on facing the other way and pretending not to be able to hear them. That, as far as Ali Baba was concerned, was no bad thing. As befitted someone in his line of business he had particularly fine teeth, and he couldn't help feeling that smiling in the presence of a tooth fairy's a bit like sunbathing in full view of the vultures, lying on a big plate with a cruet beside you.

'As I see it,' Ali Baba said, 'it won't be long before our host comes back, unlocks the door and shoos us out to be executed or tortured or whatever. Probably tortured,' he added. 'I don't suppose he's brought us here and locked us up in the coal cellar just because he's starting a collection of trans-dimensional freaks. Now, when he shows up, we've got to get him to look in that peculiar mirror Michelle was talking to just now.' He stopped and turned to her. 'You think that thing's up to it? I mean, ordinary phone messages are one thing, but. . .'

'I've no idea,' Michelle replied. 'On the other hand, it's all we've got; I mean, if we want to be pessimistic and look on the dark side of it all, we really aren't spoilt for choice. Like, what if the machine at the other end isn't switched on, or it's engaged, or the men have just turned up to cut it off?'

'Maybe it'll scramble the bastard,' Akram growled. 'No bad thing if it does.'

Michelle looked at him. That last remark had sounded a little bit more in character; except that she'd never had much evidence of the blood-curdling villain side of him. Even as a kidnapper he'd been no more terrifying than, say, the average car park attendant or pizza delivery man; and since they'd been here, on what she'd come to believe was indeed the other side of this mysterious Line everybody was so fussed about, he'd been milder than a vegetarian biryani. Which was, of course, no bad thing in general terms, she supposed. On the other hand, right now when a savage and ruthless killing machine might just come in quite handy, he'd apparently turned into the sort of bloke who'd have no hangups at all about staying home with the kids while his wife went out to work, and would probably be all sensitive and interested in colour schemes and wallpaper patterns. The expression 'shadow of his former self' crossed her mind fleetingly, until it was rounded up by the Taste Police and thrown out on its ear.

Ali Baba stood up. 'Seems to me,' he said, stifling a yawn, 'that all this is very true, but not really much help to us at the moment. I mean, yes, it's a bloody stupid idea in the first place and there's no way in the world it ought to work. On the other hand we are in horseshit stepped so far, et cetera; we might as well do something as sit around until we get our fat heads chopped off. Let's do it now, shall we? Get it over with.'

'All right,' Akram said. 'Here goes, then.'

To say that John Fingers, after half an hour in the thieves' treasury, was all open-mouthed with wonder would be an understatement. More precisely, if he'd been back in Southampton and standing on the dock at the Ferry terminal, he'd have been in grave danger of having cars drive in under his teeth and down his throat under the misapprehension that he was the ferry.

'I mean, *look* at it,' he said for the seventeenth time. 'Just *look*.'

Aziz and Hakim exchanged guilty looks. 'Yeah, well,' Aziz mumbled. 'We were meaning to get it tidied up, honest, but what with one thing and another there just wasn't time.'

Something about John Fingers' demeanour suggested that he wasn't listening. He opened the lid of a yard-long solid gold casket, gawped for a few seconds and let it drop. The valuation and unit pricing circuits in his brain had burnt out twenty minutes ago. The only problem was. . .

'How,' he said aloud, 'in buggery am I going to get this lot home?'

'We are home, Skip. At least,' Aziz amended, 'you said we were. Or I thought you said. . .'

And then, of course, there was the problem of converting it all into money. Some of John Fingers' best friends were receivers of stolen goods, but for this lot you wouldn't need a fence so much as the Great Wall of China. Even if you only released one per cent of it at a time, the market would flood so quickly that only a few bubbles on the surface would remain to mark where it had once been.

'Hey,' he said, sitting down on a coal-scuttle full of snooker-ball-sized cut rubies, 'where did you jokers get all this gear from? It's *amazing*. Makes Fort Knox look like a piggy-bank.'

Aziz shrugged helplessly. 'We had a good last quarter, Skip. According to the auditor's interim statement, takings rose by an encouraging twenty-seven point six four three per cent, whereas fixed overheads, interest on borrowing, bad debts and incidental non-recurring liabilities fell by seven point three nine two per cent as against the same quarter last year. Added to which the reduction in labour costs owing to Saheed falling off a roof and Massad sticking his foot in one of those horrible spiky trap things has resulted in a highly favourable cash reserves position, fuelling rumours of a record interim dividend once provision has been made for advance corporation tax, which we don't pay anyway 'cos we always chuck the collectors down a well.' Aziz paused to draw breath, and a thought struck him. 'You know all that as well as I do, Skip. Why did you ask?'

'Huh? Oh, don't mind me. Look, I want you to go into the nearest town and buy me a thousand camels.'

'Sure thing, Skip.'

John Fingers double-checked his mental arithmetic. 'Make

that fifteen hundred,' he said. 'Plus three thousand big panniers, two miles of rope and as much as you can get of whatever it is camels eat. Okay?'

'You got it, Skip.'

'Right. You still here?'

'Yes, Skip. That's how come you can talk to me.'

'Go away.'

'I'm on that right now, Skip. 'Bye.'

Alone with his thoughts, John Fingers began to work out ways and means. First, he'd sell just a little bit – this fire bucket full of diamonds, for example, or that breadbin of pearls – and use the money to buy a small uninhabited island somewhere; something remote and utterly godforsaken where nobody had ever bothered to go. Then he could pretend he'd discovered a really amazingly rich gold mine there, which'd explain where all this stuff came from. Security'd be a bit of a headache, of course; except that with what was in this tea-chest and the smaller of those two packing cases, he could buy a half dozen reconditioned submarines and still have change left over for a couple of squadrons of fighters. What it really boiled down to was, is there enough money in the whole wide world to buy all this stuff, even with generous discounts for cash and bulk purchases? Or was he going to have to pump countless billions of dollars of subsidies into the economies of the leading industrial nations just so that eventually they'd generate enough wealth to be able to afford to buy from him? Whatever; there were difficulties, sure enough, but even so he couldn't help feeling that it was a definite step up from stealing hubcaps and nicking the lightbulbs out of bus station waiting rooms.

Having resolved on a course of action and granted himself the luxury of two minutes unrestrained gloating, John Fingers allowed his mind to drift into the strange whirlpool of thoughts, impressions and memories that made up his recol lections of what had happened since he burgled that flat and stole that weird ring. Having considered the position from a number of viewpoints and made of it what little sense he could, he came to the conclusion that his present situation was a bit like the very latest in jet passenger aircraft. He didn't have the remotest idea of how it all worked or why it was doing what it was doing, and there was an unpleasant feeling in the back of his mind that if it crashed, it was likely to crash big. On the other hand, it didn't look like he actually needed to know how it all worked, and it sure beat the shit out of walking. Provided he could get out of this place with even a half per cent of the dosh, he didn't give a stuff. Burglary, like the privatised electricity industry, is all about power without responsibility, and getting away with it.

Where the hell were those two clowns with the camels?

'... *Michelle Pfeiffer, Sharon Stone, bzzZZZZwheeeshhhhZZZ-Zapcracklecrackle Princess Anne, Margaret Beckett...*'

'Yes,' said Ali Baba, 'I'll admit, that was a flaw in my initial reasoning. I was rather counting on him coming down here, and since he hasn't I can see that getting him to look in the mirror may present certain difficulties. I'd like to point out,' he added, kicking over a three-legged stool, 'that since there's bugger all I can do about it, whingeing isn't going to help. If you're so bloody clever, you think of something.'

'I've thought of something.'

'Dad,' said Michelle quietly, 'calm down. This isn't like you at all.'

Ali Baba sagged, as if his spine had just been removed and replaced with rice pudding, and he slumped against a wall. 'Sorry,' he said. 'I'm not quite sure what's come over me. To tell you the truth, I haven't been feeling quite myself for a while now.'

'I know,' said Akram. 'You know why?'

'Well?'

'I think,' Akram said slowly, deliberately looking the other way, 'you're starting to turn into me. A bit,' he added. 'Sort of me, anyway. Ever since you turned up at that warehouse place, all guns and swords and adrenaline. It's just a thought,' he concluded, 'but maybe we're sort of changing places in the story.'

Michelle shook her head. 'Surely not,' she said. 'Because, hasn't the thief bloke become you, hence the other thieves thinking he's their boss? They can't all be you, surely. Or are you not so much a person, more a way of life?'

By way of reply, Akram sighed. 'Why is it,' he demanded, 'that all of a sudden everybody's asking me questions and expecting me to know the damn answer? Time was, all anybody ever said when I was around was "Help, guards!" and "Aaargh!" And that was only if they happened to wake up before—'

'I said,' Fang repeated, 'I've thought of something.'

The other three prisoners looked round. 'Hello,' said Akram, 'you still here?'

'Sesame,' replied Fang. 'That's what it's all about. You lot just wait here. Won't be long.'

She grabbed the mirror, smiled into it, and vanished.

'Hey,' said the Godfather, with an impatient gesture, 'you lost me.'

If only... 'Be patient, will you?' Scheherezade replied. 'We're just getting to the good bit now.'

'But all this with the fairy and the thief and sesame,' the Godfather protested. 'I don't understand. What's gonna happen next?'

His wife sighed. 'If you knew that,' she pointed out, 'there wouldn't be much point having a story, would there? This is all just a little bit of suspense. Perfectly legitimate narrative device. Most people,' she added, 'quite like it.'

The Godfather ignored her. 'And the camels,' he said. 'What's with the goddamn camels? What for does this John Fingers want all them?'

'To move the treasure, silly.' She paused for a moment before continuing. 'To move it out of the impregnable treasury, where nobody would ever have a chance of stealing it so long as the thieves were there even if they did know the password...' Longer pause. 'Out of there and then overland, in a long, straggly, probably inadequately guarded caravan en route to wherever he's going.'

'Hey!'

'Which,' Scheherezade ground on, 'is a curious decision, don't you think, bearing in mind that it'd probably only take a few good men – Rocco, say, and a couple of the others, to rob the caravan and make off with *all that money*...' Having hammered the point so far home that you could probably have tethered an elephant to it, she left it at that and smiled sweetly. 'That's why the camels,' she said. 'Shall I go on, or do you have, um, business to attend to?'

The Godfather stubbed out his cigar and stood up. 'Just wait there a second,' he said. 'I'll be right back.'

Meg Ryan Daryll Hannah IT'S ALL RIGHT IT'S ONLY ME *on second thoughts not Daryll Hannah this is getting difficult Jodie Foster?*

Eyebrow raised in bewilderment and disapproval, Ali Baba's receptionist tore the page off the fax machine, stared at it again, screwed it into a ball and dropped it into the waste-paper basket. For one fleeting instant she'd thought it might be a message from Mr Barbour, explaining where the hell he was and why he hadn't come in to work for a week. No such luck.

She shrugged, picked up the plant mister and sprayed the potted palm.

When shc'd gone, the tooth fairy crawled out from under the fax machine, dusted herself off and looked around. There it was. Good.

The potted palm. There's one in every dentist's waiting room; a big, slightly lopsided, pointless-looking thing with flat, papery leaves and a general air of wishing it was somewhere else. It sits in a pot two sizes too small for its roots, and it's probably there just so that the room will contain one living thing more wretched-looking than the paying customers. Nobody knows where they all come from, although the chances arc there's a big nursery somewhere outside Northampton that specialises in them, having seen a window in the market around about the time the bottom fell out of triffid-farming.

At least, you assume it's a palm of some sort; that's if you can be bothered. Of course, for all you know it might be an annual herbaceous tropical and subtropical plant with seeds used in various ways as food and yielding an oil used in salads and as a laxative.

Fang squared up to the plant and spat on her hands. Fine, she muttered to herself, I've done the easy bit; faxed myself across the Line without getting squashed, dissipated or lost in the switchboard. Now it starts to get a bit tricky.

No way her arms would go round the flowerpot; she'd have to get the other side of it and push.

And then, assuming that she found a way round the trifling matter of fitting a four-foot-high three-dimensional pot-plant into the paper feed of a fax machine and sending it to a magic mirror whose number she didn't actually know, that'd be the second easiest part done, leaving them to have a go at the difficult bit. And the difficult bit was going to be horribly difficult; in fact, the whole idea was so offputting that it was only the thought that they'd all be blown up, beheaded or converted into random molecules and dispersed long before they even got near the difficult bit that was keeping her going. Ah well. Here goes.

'. . . *Andie McDowell* OUCH! THAT HURT!'

'There,' said Fang, emerging breathless and bedraggled from the mirror. 'Here you go. What do you reckon to that, then?'

Ali Baba looked down. 'It's an aspidistra,' he said, 'how nice. What am I supposed to do with it?'

For a small portion of a second Fang was tempted to make a suggestion; since she was back to full human size, however, she decided it wouldn't be ladylike, and desisted.

'Not an aspidistra,' she panted. 'Look at the label.'

Akram picked out the little white plastic flag, read it and smiled. 'Neat,' he said. 'Absolutely no way it'll work, mind you, but a lovely piece of imaginative thinking.' He handed the plastic flag to Michelle, who read it and gave it back.

'So that's what a sesame plant looks like,' she said. 'Hang on, though. Are you seriously trying to suggest that if we put this thing against the door and say *open, sesame. . .*'

It was probably the most enjoyable four seconds of Fang's life so far. The tremendous feeling of smugness when the plant hopped out of its pot, waddled across on root-tip to the massive oak door and kicked it in was so utterly, orgasmically satisfying that she wouldn't have swapped it for every molar ever pulled. With her head held high, she walked over to the doorway and pushed the shattered remains of the door aside.

'Yes,' she said, with a little bow. 'Come on.'

CHAPTER TWENTY-TWO

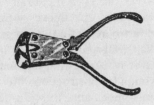

One camel is a bloody nuisance. By a mathematical paradox inexplicable except in the far dimensions of pure mathematics, fifteen hundred camels are a million times worse.

Buying fifteen hundred camels wasn't really a problem. Fortuitously, Aziz and his thirty-eight colleagues arrived in Baghdad just in time for the start of the annual camel fair, attended by livestock dealers from every corner of Central Asia, so all Aziz had to do was stand on an upturned jar, yell, 'We'll take the lot,' at the top of his voice, and start distributing money from the ten large sacks they'd brought with them for the purpose. The point at which the last camel-dealer had walked away, slightly lopsided from the weight of his purse and hugging himself with sheer delight, was the moment the problems began in earnest.

Take fifteen hundred camels, tie them together nose to tail with rope and point them at the city gates, and you have a spectacularly graphic illustration of Brownian motion in action; the only real difference being that Brown's justly celebrated particles don't bulldoze their way through crowded bazaars knocking over trestles and gobbling up the stock in trade of the fresh fruit stalls. Nor do they leave an evil-smelling brown trail behind them, sufficient to mulch all the roses in the continent of Asia. Nor, come to that, do they bite the market inspectors and commissioners of traffic, spit in the faces of the city wardens and wee all over the Emir's palanquin. Fortunately, at least as far as the thieves were concerned, the Palace Guard had far more sense than to get in the way of a thousand and a half foul-tempered ships of the desert and contented themselves with arresting any market traders who stayed still long enough for obstruction, littering the pavement and a variety of quite imaginative public order offences. Once the people had fled or been removed, there were far fewer obstacles for the camels to bump into, and the guards finally managed to shoo them out of the main gate by the cunning expedient of setting fire to the dried fruit warehouse.

From then on, it should have been quite straightforward; but it wasn't. Far from curbing their natural wanderlust, roping the camels together seemed to inspire them with a sense of purpose they would otherwise have lacked. Camels united, they seemed to say, can never be diverted. With a degree of precision you'd normally only expect from a regiment of soldiers or a top-flight flea-circus, the entire caravan took a sharp simultaneous left and headed off into the desert, in the general direction of Mongolia. Aziz, after water-skiing across the dunes behind the hindmost camel for half an hour or so, was on the point of cutting the rope and heading home with some fabrication about camels being temporarily out of stock and robbers waylaying them in a narrow pass somewhere when a wise thief suggested that they should try psychology.

It worked. As soon as the thieves galloped ahead of the procession and did everything they conceivably could to encourage them to follow the route they'd apparently chosen, all fifteen hundred of the loathsome beasts turned through a hundred and eighty degrees and started trudging back the way they'd just come. By dint of dragging on ropes, screaming abuse and trying with all their strength to pull their heads round, the thieves managed to keep the camels bang on course until they were safely penned up outside the entrance to their rocky fortress. Hence the old drovers' saying, supposedly first coined on this occasion, that if you lead a camel away from water, you can make him drink.

'Skip,' Aziz called out. 'Hey, *Skip*. We've got them. Do you want us to. . .?'

'He's not bloody well here,' Rustem interrupted, returning from a fruitless search of the cave. 'Buggered off somewhere with the prisoners, by the looks of it. Now what'll we do?'

Aziz shrugged. 'I think he wanted us to load up the treasure,' he said. He sighed. No rest for the wicked.

'What, all of it? There's bloody *tons* of the stuff.'

'Maybe that's why he wanted all these camels,' Aziz replied. 'Look, I don't know what he's playing at, and neither do you. Don't suppose we need to, either.' He peered up towards the roof of the treasury; it looked for all the world like the mouth of a chocolate-loving giant, all huge gold teeth. 'If we make a start now,' he said, 'we could be finished in a day or two.'

Rustem scowled. 'All right,' he said, 'but where's he taking it? And where is he, come to that?'

'Who knows?' Aziz replied, with a fatalistic shrug. 'Off enjoying himself, I s'pose.'

Aaaaaagh!

Whether he was falling or flying, flying or floating, floating or falling, John Fingers had no idea. Whatever it was, however, it was distinctly unpleasant, making him feel as if he was one of those newspaper photographs that turns out on close inspection to be nothing but a pattern of black dots; only in three, or four, or maybe even five dimensions. All in all, it was even nastier than a trip to the dentist's, and he wished it would stop. Perhaps the most disconcerting part of the experience was the bland, bored speaking-clock-type voice he could hear in the back of his mind, endlessly bleating out lists of supermodels and famous actresses.

It had all started when the treasury door had burst open and his four prisoners had charged in waving weapons they'd found lying about in the corridors (that, as far as he could judge, was the thieves' idea of chic interior design; where you or I would have plaster ducks, they had crossed scimitars and whacking great curvy knives) and insisting that he look in a mirror. Assuming that he had dandruff or something and that they were trying to persuade him to change his brand of shampoo, he'd humoured them; whereupon this strange and extremely unpleasant falling/flying/floating business had started, and here he apparently was. He had the impression that the contents of his stomach were offstage in some sort of parallel universe; probably just as well, or he'd have a weightless cloud of half-digested ravioli to cope with as well as everything else.

If ever I get out of this—

And then he landed, with a spine-jarring thump, in what looked and smelled uncommonly like an outsize flower-pot; one of those big red terracotta numbers they stock in the grander sorts of garden centre for Japanese millionaires to pot their bonzai giant redwoods into. After a moment or so devoted to recovering from the fall and swearing, he squirmed round, got his fingers over the rim of the pot and looked out.

He was in a kitchen.

A *perfectly normal* kitchen, goddamnit; with worktops and cupboards and a cooker and a fridge and a washing machine and a dishwasher and a deep fat fryer and a blender and a telephone and a fax/answering machine and a tumble drier and an electric kettle—

A *familiar* perfectly normal kitchen, one he'd been in quite recently. That wasn't as much help as it might seem at first glance. In the course of his business he passed through a lot of kitchens, usually stealthily and by torchlight. After a while, though, they all start to look the same, whereas for some reason he distinctly remembered this one. Why?

Because, he realised, this is the flat where I stole that fucking sodding bloody ring, the one that caused all this. . .

As he looked round, he noticed that the kettle, standing on the worktop directly above his head, was just coming to the boil. It was balanced rather precariously on the edge; in fact, all it would take to dislodge it would be the disturbance caused by the steam charging about inside trying to find the exit. Our old friend Brownian motion, at it again.

He was in the act of reaching up to push it away or switch it off when he came to the conclusion that it was too late; the kettle had boiled, overbalanced and started to topple down onto him. A bloke could have a nasty accident—

Cue past life.

His boyhood. Playing tag in the dusty square. His father, coming home drunk. Stealing loose change from the jar by the fireside—

AND NOW—

Joining the gang of scruffy, good-for-nothing kids who were the despair and terror of the neighbourhood. Being the leader. Fighting the big, curly-haired boy, twice his size but slow and a coward at heart. The sheer pleasure of smelling fear on his opponent's breath (hang on a second) before hitting him, again and again and again, with the stone that'd happened to find his outstretched hand—

BANDIT, MURDERER, THIEF—

Feeling the warmth of someone else's blood on his skin; not

unpleasant, quite the opposite. Looking up, to see the awe, the terror, the *respect* in the faces of the other kids. Learning, then and there, that in the final analysis, respect is everything (now just a minute), no matter what you have to do in order to earn it—

VOTED FIFTEEN YEARS IN SUCCESSION—

Running. Being hunted. Hearing the breathing of the men who were chasing him, five yards or so away in the darkness. Feeling his own heart actually stop; and then the sickening wave of relief (I don't remember that) as they went away—

AKRAM THE TERRIBLE—

'Jesus flaming Christ!' John Fingers roared as the water hit him. 'You stupid bastards, that wasn't me! You've got the wrong—'

THIS WAS YOUR LIFE.

This is your life. . .

A young boy stands up in the middle of a ring of his peers. In his right hand he's holding a bloodstained stone. At his feet, a dead body. Nobody speaks.

'I. . .'

The boy closes his mouth again, and lets the stone drop. He notices that both his hands are red. The other boys start to back away.

'Akram,' one of them says, 'I think you've killed him.'

I am not Akram, my name is John Fingers Smith and I demand to see the British consul. 'I. . .'

Another boy snuggles back behind the shoulders of his fellows. 'It wasn't an accident,' he says, pointing. 'I saw him, he did it on purpose, I saw him do it.'

'I. . .' *You bastards, what have you done to my body, give me my body back or I'll wring your bloody necks.* 'Yes,' says the boy, 'I killed him. So what? Served him right.'

'Akram. . .'

There's no way, do you hear me, absolutely no way I'm going to stand for this, look, I've got rights, you just wait till London hears about this, you'll have Stormin' Norman and half a million tanks round your ears before you can say United Nations...

'Run!'

But...

'They're coming! Quick, Akram, run!'

But it wasn't me. I've been framed...

'Run!'

Men appear in the distance, shouting and waving their arms. The boy looks round wildly. He stiffens, like a deer hearing a twig break.

I'll get you for this, you scumbags. One of these days I'll be back and I'll bloody well get you...

The boy runs.

Fifteen hundred camels are a bloody nuisance. Fifteen hundred camels laden down with gold, silver, precious stones, lapis lazuli, freshwater pearls, works of art and limited edition collectors' commemorative porcelain statuettes are about as much aggravation as it's possible to get without standing in front of a registrar or minister of religion and saying, 'I do.'

'Yes,' repeated Hakim for the fifteenth time, 'but where are we actually going?'

Aziz, who'd been fending off this question with 'It's not far now', 'We're on the right road', 'Shut your face' and similar cunning evasions, finally broke down and admitted that he didn't know.

'You don't *know*?'

'That's what I just said, isn't it?' Aziz snapped. 'Weren't you listening, or are the holes in the side of your head just for ventilation?'

A man of many faults, Hakim did at least have the virtue of persistence; except that in his case, it wasn't a virtue. 'You don't know,' he reiterated. 'We load up all that gold and jewels and stuff and piss off into the desert and you don't know where we're going.'

'Yes.'

'I see.' A look of indescribable deviousness dragged itself across Hakim's face, stopping in the foothills of his nose for a rest. It was probably just as well that Hakim had never played poker; his thoughts were so perfectly mirrored in his face that if he ever did sit down to a friendly game of five-card stud, he'd have lost all his money before the seal was broken on the deck. 'So Akram doesn't know either,' he continued. 'Where we're going, I mean.'

''Spose not. Why?'

'We're heading off into the wilderness with all the dosh, and Akram doesn't know where we are.'

'I said, yes. Now if you've. . .'

Slow, or rather glacier-like, on the uptake he might be; but when the penny finally dropped in Aziz's mind, it did so with quite devastating force. Reining in his mule, and doing his best to ignore the camel that was apparently trying to lick the wax off his eardrum, Aziz sat for a moment in a surmise so wild it'd have made stout Cortes look like a six-countries-in-four-days American tourist.

'Are you suggesting,' he muttered in a low voice, 'that we sort of, walk off with it?'

'Yes.'

'Good idea.'

Even as he said the words, Aziz was aware that he was guilty of an understatement on a par with referring to the First World War as a bit of a scrap. For years, a lifetime, far longer than any of them could remember, they'd been amassing this truly awesome hoard of pure wealth; and in all that time, nothing had ever been said about divvying up, sharing out or spending. The thought had never even crossed Aziz's mind before, for much the same reason that elderly people in wheelchairs don't try and cross the M6.

'Hang on, though,' objected a thief. 'What about when Akram finds out? He'll skin us alive.'

Hakim smirked. 'If he finds out,' he replied. 'And if he catches up with us. And if the thirty-nine of us are ready to hold still and let ourselves be skinned by the one of him. Think about it,' he urged. 'All that gold and stuff, it's wealth beyond the dreams of avarice. And a one-thirty-ninth share of wealth beyond the dreams of avarice is –' He paused, wrestling with the mental arithmetic. 'Wealth beyond the dreams of eating cheese last thing at night,' he concluded triumphantly. 'Or, put it another way, loads of treasure. Right, then; show of hands?'

Not, you might think, the most democratic way for a thieves' co-operative to vote in a country governed according to Islamic law; nevertheless, unanimous is unanimous. Admittedly, several of the voters were persuaded to join in the general hand-raising by the feel of sharp metal in the small of their backs; but friendly persuasion is what democracy's all about.

'Right,' said Hakim, 'that's settled, then. Soon as we reach the next oasis we'll have a share-out and work out what we're going to do about splitting up. That all right with everyone?'

'Okay,' murmured the Godfather, 'what's the plan?'

Scheherezade, shivering perhaps a trifle more than the slight desert breeze justified, nodded her head. 'Piece of cake, really,' she replied. 'We wait till they come past. Then I give the signal, you all jump out and scrag the lot of 'em. Then—'

'Jump outa what?'

That, as far as Scheherezade was concerned, was her cue. 'I've already thought of that,' she announced. 'You see that big row of empty jars standing there beside the road?'

The Godfather nodded. 'Hey,' he said, 'I think I'm way

ahead of you already. Rocco, Tony, you get the guys and go climb into those jars there. I'll come and join you in a minute.'

The Godfather's grey-suited companions, who had been expecting at least one nasty brush with bandits and the like, let go a sigh of relief. This, they felt, was rather more like it. By a curious chance, there were thirty-nine of them. By an even odder chance, Scheherezade had laid on a total of forty palm-oil jars.

'Okay,' observed the Godfather. 'Where you gonna hide, then?'

'Me?' Scheherezade went through a pantomime of thinking about it. 'How about behind the tea urn?' she suggested.

'What tea urn?'

By way of reply, Scheherezade pointed to a big old-fashioned hospital tea-trolley, on which was mounted an extra large capacity white enamel urn. Wisps of steam rose from the top of it. 'That's in case you boys get thirsty while you're waiting for the caravan to show,' she explained. 'I think of everything, don't I?'

'Yeah. You done good.' The Godfather stood up, took a deep breath and hoisted his substantial bulk into the fortieth jar, pulling the lid across after himself. His wife smiled; a long, detailed, intricate smirk that told its own story. Or stories.

Having satisfied herself that her husband and all his henchmen were in their jars and waiting patiently, she turned up the thermostat on the urn's electric element as far as it would go, until the water came to the boil. As the steam hissed furiously through the vents, she stopped to wonder what the exhilarating buzz she was feeling might be, and realised with joy that it was the Story, surging and expanding inside her brain, as vigorous, powerful and dangerous as the steam itself. Old stories burble and zizz like sleepy bees, lazy in the heat of the summer sun, until something wakes them up and stirs them into angry energy; at which point, woe betide anybody who tries to restrain them in a confined space. That's Brownian motion, folks; the more you heat the particles, the faster they move and the harder they collide with each other.

She leaned forward and rapped with her knuckles on the side of her husband's jar.

'Hey, you,' she said.

'You talking to me?'

'You bet I'm talking to you. You got three wishes,' she said. 'And one second to wish them in.'

'What you talking about, you dumb—?'

With a quick twist of the wrist, Scheherezade turned the spigot.

Cue past life.

A young boy stands up in the middle of a ring of his peers—

Hey! What's going on here? You dumb bitch, you're spilling. . .

In his right hand he's holding a bloodstained stone.

'Akram,' says a boy to his left. 'You again. Didn't you just leave?'

That crazy goddamn bitch – Ah, shit.

'Yes,' says the boy, 'I killed him. He didn't show no respect. You gotta have respect, or else what you got?'

Hey! I got three wishes. I wish—

Men appear in the distance, shouting and waving their arms. The boy looks round wildly. He stiffens, like a deer. . .

I wish I was outa this goddamn fuckin' jar!

'Run!'

The boy turns, shrugs. 'Which way?' he asks. His friends look at him oddly.

'I think you went thattaway,' they say. 'If you get a move on, you might just catch yourself up.'

After she'd dealt with the fortieth jar, there was about half a pint of boiling water left. She used it to make herself a cup of instant coffee.

A few minutes later, a long procession of camels appeared on the horizon; about fifteen hundred of them, all loaded down with heavy burdens. Scheherezade stood up, brushed herself off, walked to the side of the road and stood there with her thumb raised.

'Hi, boys,' she called out. 'Going my way?'

The leader of the caravan hesitated. On the one hand, he wasn't sure that picking up hitch-hikers was appropriate for a gang of thieves on the run. On the other hand – Scheherezade adjusted her veil and hitched the hem of her skirt up another half inch, nearly causing Aziz to fall off his camel.

'Who're you?' he asked.

'Me?' Scheherezade's eyes twinkled perilously through her veil. 'I'm your fairy godmother. Now then, you're not going to stay on that mule and let a lady walk, are you?'

CHAPTER TWENTY-THREE

'Oh there you are,' said the receptionist. 'I was beginning to wonder where you'd got to.'

Ali Baba, sprawled on the ground with his head in his own waste-paper basket, looked up and grinned sheepishly. 'Sorry,' he said. 'Got a bit held up. Many waiting?'

The receptionist nodded. 'I managed to reschedule most of your appointments, but there's quite a few that insist on coming in every day on the offchance you might be back. Quite flattering, really, if you think about it.'

Ali Baba got to his feet, removed various bent paper-clips and knobs of dried chewing-gum from his hair, and glanced down as the fax machine printed out the inevitable confirmation slip. Instead of the usual details (sender, time etc) it read:

TRY THAT AGAIN AND I'LL ELECTROCUTE YOU

'Any messages?' he asked.

'On your desk. Oh, and a woman came in to see you. Personal matter, she said.'

Ali Baba described Michelle.

'No,' the receptionist replied. 'Isn't that Miss Partridge?'

'Oh, I forgot, she's a patient.' He shrugged. 'I take it she didn't leave a name.'

'Not a *proper* name,' the receptionist replied. 'Just said she was Yasmin, and you didn't give her the slip that easily. Strange girl. Funny clothes, like a lot of net curtains and brass teapot lids.'

'Oh. Her.'

Sloe-eyed Yasmin, she of the tiny waist and serrated tongue. He had hoped, really and truly fervently hoped, that he'd at least managed to give her the slip; apparently not so.

'Sharon.'

'Mmm?'

'What's a sloe look like?'

'I beg your pardon, Mr Barbour?'

'Sloe. You make gin out of them, I think.'

'Oh, *sloes*.' The receptionist considered for a moment; you could almost hear the filing-cabinet drawers of her mind swishing frictionless on their nylon bearings. 'Aren't they the small black things like cocktail olives? Sort of like undersized black grapes, I think. Why do you ask?'

'Oh, no reason. Look, I've just got to slip out for five minutes—'

'But you've just. . .'

'—So do what you can to rearrange the appointments and I'll be back—'

'Mr *Barbour*!'

'—Eventually.'

He typed a number into the fax machine, so fast that Sharon couldn't see what it was. She heard the ululating squeak of faxes shaking hands; then Mr Barbour stuck his hand into the paper feed, someone she couldn't see said, '*Scraping the bottom of the barrel what about Goldie Hawn?*' and he vanished. Then there was a brilliant white flash, a *zap!* and the smell of burning plastic.

'Mr *Barbour!*'

No reply. The machine chugged, beeped and fed out a slip saying:

I WARNED YOU

– and that was the last ever seen (so far) of Ali Baba this side of the Line.

Cue past life—

He'd just got to the bit where he'd been leaning over the last jar, peering in to see if the bandit it contained was substantially dead, and his lovely assistant Yasmin the sloe-eyed houri had tiptoed up behind him and cracked his skull with a two-pound hammer when the memory sequence suddenly froze and he fell out of it into what he recognised as the courtyard of his own house in Baghdad; the place, in fact, where his past life had just cut out, except that there were no oil jars, no boiled thieves and no Yasmin. An improvement, he couldn't help feeling.

'Oh well,' he said.

He rose, a little wobbly but largely intact. Somehow he'd contrived to burn his right hand, as if he'd touched a hot kettle. He wondered if he had anything to put on it.

'There you are,' said a girl's voice behind him. He turned quickly, then relaxed.

'Hello,' he said.

'Where have you been?' his daughter upbraided him. 'You've got a whole waiting room full of patients. Old Mrs Masood's been here since before nine. You're doing a root fill for her, remember.'

'Am I?' He thought about what Michelle had just said. 'I am? Oh *good*. Tell her I'll be right through, soon as I've found some Savlon—'

'Some what?'

He frowned. 'No Savlon? Pity. Never mind. I'll just wash up and I'll be there in a jiffy.'

Michelle shrugged and trotted back into the house. A little while later, he followed her. In the bathroom, or what served as a bathroom (he was going to have to get out of the habit of thinking in Realside terms) he scrubbed his hands and took a look in the mirror.

Snow White, it said.

'Correct,' he replied. Then he took it off the wall, smashed it, and disposed of the pieces tidily. What with one thing and another, he'd had enough junk faxes to last him a lifetime.

Ah well, he reflected as he dried his sore hand, it's nice to be back. So, quite possibly, he was still on the run. One of these days, for all he knew, a patient sitting in his chair would turn out to be Yasmin or John Fingers, and then it'd be time for another quick exit, yet one more fresh start in a strange new environment. It made him glad he'd taken the trouble to learn a trade that'd guarantee him a living wherever he went. Me and Doc Holliday, he said to himself; two dentists floating uncomfortably on the ebb tide of adventure. But, until the Story wound itself back to the beginning again, he had work to do, cavities to fill; a sort of purpose. A hero's gotta have a purpose, boy; it goes with the territory.

'Dad,' Michelle called, 'are you ready yet?'

'Ready as I'll ever be,' he replied. Then he finished drying his hands and went to work.

Cue past life.

Michelle landed awkwardly, narrowly avoiding banging her head on the huge flowerpot that someone had left lying about on the kitchen floor. When she looked in it, she found it was full of damp, dead burglar.

'Yuk,' she said.

The answering machine/fax chuntered at her and fed out the confirmation slip. It read:

AND STAY OUT

'A pleasure,' she replied. 'Well, guys, I'm back.'

No reply. She clicked her tongue. So her kitchen wasn't talking to her; offended, probably. It'd get over it. She glanced down at her hand; there was the ring on her finger, where it should be. It was, after all, her ring, given to her by Aunt Fatty on her deathbed.

She counted up to ten, and then smiled.

'Guys?' she said.

Still no reply. This puzzled her; earlier, she'd got the impression that her household goods were chattier than Parliament on a bad day. If they had sent her to Coventry, they wouldn't have expected her to stay there long enough to do more than have a stroll down the main street and a quick dash through the shopping centre.

'Hello? Is anybody there?'

Nothing. Not a vibe, good, bad or indifferent. The place was—

'Talk to me. Please.'

—Dead, deceased, in there with Queen Anne and John Cleese's parrot in the short-list for the prestigious Worthington Lifelessness Awards. When she opened the fridge door, a light came on to show that it wasn't just a power cut. She sat down on the edge of the table and burst into tears.

The ring. . .

Maybe it was the ring that had conked out. As quickly as she could, she hurried out onto the landing and prodded the call button for the lift.

'AllrightallrightI'mcomingasfastasIcan,' the lift muttered. 'SomepeoplenopatienceupanddownalldayexpecttheythinkIdo thisforthegoodofmyhealth.'

Michelle winced. 'Sorry,' she said, 'wrong number.' She returned to her flat and closed the door before the tears returned.

This is silly, she told herself, two sodden hankies and a large sheet of kitchen towel later. I'm sobbing my heart out because my blender won't talk to me any more. But that's crazy, because it means this whole stupid adventure is finally over, and I'm home.

Home.

Yes, well. Many years ago, she'd met a man who'd been captured by the Japanese during the last war. He'd survived Changi Gaol and the forced labour camps of the Burma railway, escaped, and tracked his way back through jungle, mountain and desert, until eventually he walked down a gangplank at Liverpool with his kitbag over his shoulder, took a train to London, and went home. But when he got there, he found that his house, his street, the entire neighbourhood had completely vanished, turned into a wilderness of bricks and rubble by a flying bomb in one of the last V2 raids of the war. And that, he had said, was what really got to him. He'd made the mistake, he later realised, of believing in the existence of happiness ever after, when he should have known that happy endings, like free lunches and rocking-horse shit, are not in fact as common as the fairy-tales would have you believe.

She stood up and looked around. Perfectly ordinary flat. Welcome to Reality; where there is only one ending, a dull and inescapable appointment with eternity, never happy by defini-tion. Until then, the story goes on, plotless and meandering, where Hope is a man who offers you sweets if you'll get into his car. Wonderful. It's great to be back.

Bleep, said the fax machine. *Susan Sarandon*.

No. Surely not. I couldn't.

But why not?

She picked the kettle up off the floor, filled it and switched it on. There was, she reminded herself, a dead body in her kitchen; another mess to clear up, and not something you could put off, like washing the dishes or ironing. Dead bodies don't come with Inhume By dates clearly printed on their foreheads, but she had an idea they had to be dealt with fairly quickly; and, this being reality, she was going to have to do either an awful lot of explaining or some extremely surreptitious digging. Oh bother.

She looked at the fax machine.

Looked at from another angle, it was a clear case of dual nationality. Although she'd lived all her life in Reality, she had now been given to understand that her father was in fact a native of Over There, where talking blenders are quite probably the norm, and boiled burglars so commonplace an occurrence that there's probably a little man with a cart who comes round three times a week to collect them and take them away.

The hell with it. Escapism is only futile and self-defeating if you can't actually escape. Closing her eyes, she jammed her right hand into the paper feed of the fax and—

'Hello,' said Ali Baba. 'What kept you?'

'Hey,' muttered Sadiq, his voice reverberating through the earthenware. 'Where did she get to?'

'Don't ask me,' replied Aziz. 'All she said to me was, Climb into those jars there, I'll be back in a minute. Seemed to me she knew what she was talking about, so I did like she told me. Always been a rule with me; if somebody who looks like they know what's going on tells me to do something, I do it.'

'Fair enough,' Sadiq said. 'Be nice to know what we're meant to be doing, though. Just for once.'

Aziz frowned. 'Would it?' he asked. 'Why?'

'Dunno. I just thought that maybe—'

Glug glug glug.

Cue past lives.

Scheherezade was alone.

'*Yippee!*' she said.

Because, Storyside, one thing you can never be is on your own. A character in a story has to be with other people, interacting with them, loving them, hating them, kissing them, killing them, rescuing them, robbing them, or else cease to exist. This side of the Line, the only person who can be alone is the storyteller.

She stood up and looked around. From this high point she could see for miles in every direction, and what she saw was nothing; or rather, nothing's understudy, sand. She was in some kind of desert. Ideal.

'Only I insist,' she said aloud, 'on a tap. And a fridge. And a deckchair and a beach umbrella.' Saying it that way made it sound like three wishes, not four; besides, it was her story so she was allowed to cheat.

There was a tap. And a fridge. And a deckchair and a beach umbrella.

'Hello,' said the fridge. 'What'll it be?'

'A turkey sandwich and a nice long cool drink,' Scheherezade replied without looking round. She turned the tap, and water started to gush out, rapidly filling the small hollow below the rock in whose shade the deckchair stood. 'Give me a shout when it's ready,' she added. 'I'll be over there by the pool.'

As she sipped her drink – the fridge had tried to fob her off with water but a quick rewrite had fixed all that – she reflected on what she'd achieved so far. The Godfather was gone; no more infiltration of Reality, no more wishes you can't refuse. Whatever story he was in now was welcome to him. As for Ali

Baba and the forty thieves, the story had served its purpose and could be left to carry on as before. Evermore, sesame would open, the thieves would die in their jars, rewind, go back to the beginning. It would be the same with all the stories now, except that there would have to be a few new ones. That would be no hardship. Neverland is big enough to accommodate anything; compared to it, Infinity's a studio flat in Hong Kong.

'Could I be a real nuisance,' she asked, 'and have a jar of barrier cream?'

(Her first major rewrite; the couplet now went—
A jar of barrier cream beneath the beach umbrella,
A glass of gin, a turkey sandwich and hold the Thou
– So maybe it didn't rhyme; so what?)

That wish being granted, Scheherezade leaned back in her deckchair, closed her eyes and lived happily ever after.

'Three quarter-pounders with cheese, three large fries, two regular kiwi fruit shakes, and a large tea.'

Akram opened his eyes. 'Sorry?' he said.

'Three quarter-pounders with cheese, three large fries, two regular kiwi fruit shakes, and a large tea.'

'Ah,' said Akram. 'So I did die, then.'

'Three quarter-poun— What did you just say?'

Akram looked the customer in the eyes and smiled enormously. 'I must be dead,' he said, 'or else how come I'm in heaven? Or are they doing day trips now?'

The customer took two steps back. 'Look,' she said, 'forget the order, I've changed my mind. Gosh, is that the time? I must be. . .'

'No,' Akram said quickly, 'don't go. Sorry, I was miles away. Right, three quarter-pounders.'

'With cheese. And three large fries, two regular kiwi fruit. . .'

'It'll be a pleasure,' Akram replied sincerely. 'Coming right up.'

He turned to get the order and found himself face to face with a dazzlingly beautiful girl with long, straight blonde hair under a baseball cap bearing the legend *Akram's Diner.* 'Fang?' he queried.

She nodded. 'And no, you're not dead,' she said. 'Come on, customer waiting.'

Later, during a brief lull, he took off his own baseball cap and read the words blazoned on it.

'You're wrong, you know,' he said. 'This *is* heaven. There may be another place of the same name somewhere that's all pink clouds and harp music, but I don't want to go there.'

Fang slit open a new sack of pre-sliced chips and dumped them in the fryer. 'You are not dead,' she insisted. 'And this is not heaven. It's just a small-time fast-food joint on the interface between the two sides of the Line. Only gets three stars in the Guide Dunlop.' She grinned. 'And in case you think that's good, most dustbins get four stars.'

Akram shrugged. 'That's all right,' he said. 'Gives me something to aim at. Fine afterlife it'd be without a sense of purpose.' He paused for a moment. 'Excuse me asking,' he said carefully, 'but, um, what are you doing here? Not,' he added quickly, 'that you don't deserve it or anything like that; I just thought that tooth fairies probably had a rather different sort of paradise, like an elephant's graveyard or a snooker-ball factory.'

'You haven't been listening, have you?' replied Fang indulgently. 'This is not the pudding, we're still on the main course. This is just where that dicky fax put us down after we zapped out of your old hideout. Recognise it yet?'

Akram looked round; it was sort of familiar, in a way. It was almost—

'Jim's,' he muttered. 'Jim's Diner. God, yes, I'd know it anywhere. Except that—'

Fang nodded. 'Now it's yours, apparently. You don't seem unduly upset by that.'

'Good Lord, no.' Akram cut open another bag of chips and dropped them into the boiling oil. Palm oil? Outside the back door, were there forty empty jars waiting for the delivery man to come and take them away? 'It's just such a strange coincidence. The happiest time of any of my lives was when I was assistant manager at that burger place, and now here I am with a burger place of my own. Is this some sort of witness relocation programme, or what?'

Fang shrugged. 'Maybe,' she said. 'That'd make some sort of sense, as far as I'm concerned. Otherwise it'd be one hell of a coincidence.'

'It would?' Akram looked at her. 'You mean, you always wanted to work in a fast-food joint too?'

'Don't be obtuse,' Fang replied, and kissed him. 'And if you dare count your teeth,' she added, once she'd let him go again, 'I'll be bitterly offended. Like you, I think I've retired from all that blood-and-bones stuff. About time, too.'

Akram let it all sink in while he served a couple of customers. After all, he told himself, why not? Perhaps there is such a thing as a happy ending after all, and this is it.

He hoped so. For you, a voice deep inside him muttered, the Story is over. He thought of all those POW escape movies, where at the very end the heroes come to a lonely frontier post in the snow-capped mountains, and suddenly they're in Switzerland. Now then, supposing this was meant to be Switzerland (have to tidy up a bit, give it a lick of paint first, maybe clean the windows) and suppose that, instead of going home and rejoining his regiment, he stayed here, for ever. Mountain air, nice people, good standard of living, all the melted cheese you can eat; there are worse places. Somewhere neutral, a hidden enclave halfway between still being in the adventure and living happily ever after; yes, he could really go for that. He'd been right first time, except for the death part. Formica-topped tables, vinyl-covered seats, a big greasy deep-fat fryer and a milk-shake machine. Heaven.

'This'll do me,' he said. 'I'm staying. What about you?'

Fang shrugged. 'All right,' she said. 'It sure beats the hell out of being four inches tall. Here's to Catering.'

Now then, where to end? The beginning would be the most logical place.

So; as the chips sizzle in the oil and the water simmers in the big enamel urn—

Cue future lives.

PAINT YOUR DRAGON

Tom Holt

The cosmic battle between Good and Evil . . . But suppose
Evil threw the fight? And suppose Good cheated?

Sculptress Bianca Wilson is a living legend. St George is also
a legend, but not quite so living.

However, when Bianca's sculpture of the patron saint and his
scaly chum gets a bit *too* 'life-like', it opens up a whole new
can of wyrms . . .

The Dragon knows that Evil got a raw deal and is looking to
set the record straight. And George (who cheated) thinks the
record's just fine as it is.

Luckily for George, there's a coach-load of demons on an
expenses-paid holiday from Hell who are only too happy to
help him. Because a holiday from hell is exactly what they're
about to get.

Paint Your Dragon is a fire-breathing extravaganza of
imagination-boggling mayhem from the author of *Ye Gods!*
and *My Hero.*

Orbit titles available by post:

☐ Wish You Were Here	Tom Holt	£15.99
☐ Paint Your Dragon	Tom Holt	£5.99
☐ My Hero	Tom Holt	£5.99
☐ Djinn Rummy	Tom Holt	£5.99
☐ Odds and Gods	Tom Holt	£4.99
☐ Faust Among Equals	Tom Holt	£5.99
☐ Grailblazers	Tom Holt	£5.99
☐ Here Comes the Sun	Tom Holt	£5.99
☐ Overtime	Tom Holt	£5.99
☐ Ye Gods!	Tom Holt	£5.99

The prices shown above are correct at time of going to press, however the publishers reserve the right to increase prices on covers from those previously advertised, without further notice.